Praise for *The End of Drum-Time*

Finalist for the 2023 National Book Award
Named a Best Book of 2023 by NPR,
Time, the *Christian Science Monitor*, *Vox*, and *Kirkus Reviews*
Named a Most Anticipated Book of 2023 by *Elle*

"In prose that is both luxuriant and precise, Hanna Pylväinen vividly transports the reader to the remote Scandinavian tundra of the 1850s, introducing complicated characters who reveal their deepest joys, sorrows, fears, and hopes. This stunning novel manages to explore major themes of identity, race, politics, and faith, all while putting the focus firmly on the human stories at hand. *The End of Drum-Time* masterfully takes us to a place, people, and time unfamiliar to most readers but one that becomes completely alive—and closely mirrors the most divisive and potent aspects of our contemporary lives."
—2023 National Book Award Citation

"The writing is so beautiful and so ent
harsh realities of herding and hunt
the doctrines dictated by a culture ce

"A monumental feat of melodic prose and astute observation, Hanna Pylväinen's historical fiction novel *The End of Drum-Time* transports readers to the otherworldly tundra of Scandinavia, circa 1851, where minister Lars Levi is 'always after' the 'heart' of the native Sámi reindeer herders, whom he seeks to convert. When one of these Sámi falls for Lars's own daughter, the resulting adventure is one as powerful and profound as the book's awe-inspiring setting."
—*Elle*

"The best type of historical fiction—electrifying, edifying, and set in an utterly enthralling time and place."
—*Star Tribune*

"Pylväinen's tale offers not only exquisite prose and insightful observations, but also fresh perspectives on family bonds, cultural traditions, and religious colonialism."
—*The Christian Science Monitor*

"Pylväinen's breathless, exquisite prose rushes fast as meltwater through a story of reckless lovers and desperate religious passions to an ending that feels like a flood in its inevitability and destructive force. This is a book as beautiful and unforgiving as the land it describes."

—Constance Grady, *Vox*

"A deeply researched story about obedience, defiance, and what happens when the tectonic plates of two different cultures collide."

—*Time*

"Ambitious and resonant, a vivid, fascinating, and moving novel . . . Beautifully written and masterfully researched, the book's greatest triumph is the characters, full of human foibles, passions, and tenderness, jealousy, courage, doubts, and moments of transcendence."

—*Kirkus Reviews* (starred review)

"Transcendent."

—*Publishers Weekly* (starred review)

"With engrossing details of reindeer herding, a beautifully rendered setting and powerful echoes of America's own dark history of settlers forcing their religion on Indigenous peoples, *The End of Drum-Time* will leave a lasting impression on all readers of historical fiction."

—*BookPage* (starred review)

"Brilliant. Infinitely moving. I am transfixed, inspired, and awestruck."

—**Jacqueline Woodson**, *New York Times* bestselling author of *Red at the Bone*

"*The End of Drum-Time* explores some of the most complex themes in literature in some of the most gorgeous prose imaginable. Hanna Pylväinen's novel of cultural collision in the far north is an extraordinary feat of research and imagination by an author who reminds you with every page what fiction can accomplish."

—**Anthony Marra**, *New York Times* bestselling author of *Mercury Pictures Presents*

ALSO BY HANNA PYLVÄINEN

We Sinners

THE END OF
DRUM-TIME

THE END OF DRUM-TIME

A Novel

Hanna Pylväinen

A Holt Paperback
Henry Holt and Company
New York

Holt Paperbacks
Henry Holt and Company
Publishers since 1866
120 Broadway
New York, New York 10271
www.henryholt.com

A Holt Paperback® and ❿® are registered trademarks of
Macmillan Publishing Group, LLC.

The Library of Congress has cataloged the hardcover edition as follows:

Names: Pylväinen, Hanna, author.
Title: The end of drum-time : a novel / Hanna Pylväinen.
Description: First edition. | New York : Henry Holt and Company, 2023.
Identifiers: LCCN 2022035965 (print) | LCCN 2022035966 (ebook) |
    ISBN 9781250822901 (hardcover) | ISBN 9781250822918 (ebook)
Subjects: LCGFT: Novels.
Classification: LCC PS3616.Y55 E53 2023 (print) | LCC PS3616.Y55 (ebook) |
    DDC 813/.6—dc23/eng/20220728
LC record available at https://lccn.loc.gov/2022035965
LC ebook record available at https://lccn.loc.gov/2022035966

ISBN 9781250871817 (trade paperback)

Our books may be purchased in bulk for promotional, educational, or
business use. Please contact your local bookseller or the Macmillan Corporate and
Premium Sales Department at (800) 221-7945, extension 5442, or by e-mail at
MacmillanSpecialMarkets@macmillan.com.

Originally published in hardcover in 2023 by Henry Holt and Company

First Holt Paperbacks Edition 2024

Designed by Meryl Sussman Levavi

Printed in the United States of America

1 3 5 7 9 10 8 6 4 2

This is a work of fiction. All of the characters, organizations, and events portrayed in this
novel either are products of the author's imagination or are used fictitiously.

To Anne-Maret Labba

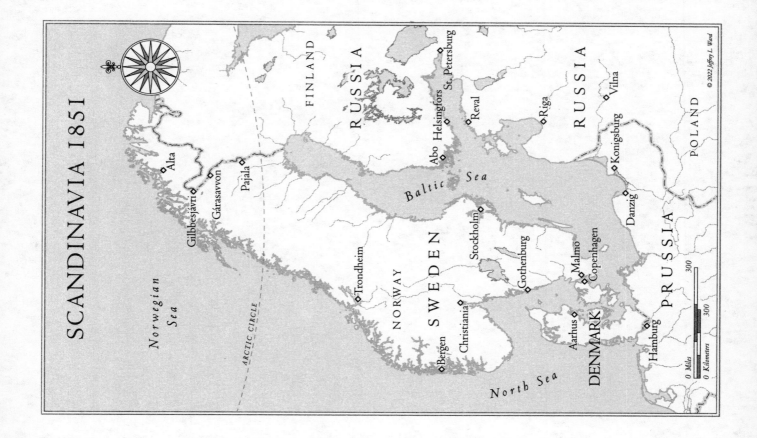

SCANDINAVIA 1851

© 2022 Jeffrey L. Ward

Norwegian Sea

Baltic Sea

North Sea

ARCTIC CIRCLE

FINLAND

RUSSIA

RUSSIA

RUSSIA

POLAND

PRUSSIA

DENMARK

NORWAY

SWEDEN

Alta
Gilbbesjávri
Garasavvon
Pajala
Trondheim
Bergen
Christiania
Gothenburg
Stockholm
Abo
Helsingfors
St. Petersburg
Reval
Riga
Vilna
Konigsburg
Danzig
Malmö
Copenhagen
Aarhus
Hamburg

0 Miles   300
0 Kilometers   300

The Laestadius Family

Lars Levi & Brita

Nora

Willa

Carl

Levi (*deceased*)

Lorens

Four daughters, unnamed

One son, unnamed

The Tomma Siida

Nilsa & Anna

Risten (Kristina)

Elle (*deceased*)

Nilsa's brother and wife

Their children

The Rasti Siida

Biettar & Biret (*deceased*)

Ivvár

Two of Biettar's brothers, unnamed

Ánde & Niko, Biettar's nephews

The Lindström Family

Henrik

Frans, Henrik's uncle

Let the reindeer decide.

Sámi proverb

PART ONE

I

THE DAY OF THE EARTHQUAKE WAS THE DARKEST DAY OF THE YEAR. THIS far north what counted as day was just twilight stretched thin, so that no shadows fell, and the steeple of the church made no impression on the snow, and the river and forest and hills were all suspended in the same half-finished light. The effect of this was a shared, if unexpressed, uneasiness, but most people were used to it—if given the choice they would have said, let there be darkness, and gone back to their work. That was the sentiment anyway around people who had grown up here, Lars Levi among them—he found the cold and the dark invigorating, he was a man of extremes and so he was drawn to extremes, they suited him, they spurred him on.

But even he had to admit the morning was off-kilter somehow. He had dreamed the night before of something of importance, what, he couldn't say, and it troubled him, that he might have missed its message. He was a man who put credence in these things, in the importance of what was felt, in part because his mother had been that way and in part because the land made everyone here that way—no one could live beneath the northern lights and the midnight sun and not come out of it sure there was something besides rationality at work, least of all Lars Levi, the pastor of this most northern parish for the past twenty-two years, a man of some hubris but not a man who could be accused of insincerity. He was here to preach, he believed in what he spoke, but today he was especially sure of his purpose, and the weight of that purpose made him anxious. He paced up and down the side aisle, inventing little tasks to check on—had Henrik rung the bell? Had Willa made the fire in the stove?

The church was filling up, it really was, the Finns in their usual places toward the front, while behind them were the Laplanders, the Lapps, the Sámi, whatever you called them—he used Lapp when he spoke to the Swedes, and Sámi when he spoke to the Sámi—and it occurred to Lars Levi that he was doing it, he had eight hundred and twenty-nine parishioners stretched over a hundred miles and a good quarter of them were here. The Finns had skied for hours along the frozen river, and the Lapps had harnessed their reindeer to the sledges and they had driven twenty, forty miles through the snow to get here, to a tiny church-village in Sweden where ten of the forty inhabitants were his own family; to hear him speak, him, Lars Levi Laestadius—but had Henrik rung the bell?

Henrik had rung the bell, and then he had promptly gone back to his store, which was also his home, which people called the dark house because you could get alcohol there, technically illegally, but in the first place the law was impossible to enforce because too many people broke it, and in the second place Henrik was not one to stand on principle, he was one to stand on getting himself out of debt, and moreover, he was of the opinion that the darkness was going to drive them all mad so they might as well go down drinking. He wasn't from here, and he hadn't grown up to be cold and call it happiness—my God, if he'd had the money he would have left the day he'd arrived! He would have left and he would not have come back. But since he couldn't leave this very end of the earth he would, at the very least, leave all the talk about sinning to those who cared to sorrow endlessly over their sin. He, for one, was worn out by such talk, and all the lecturing about drinking, sometimes from the very same people who came to him later to buy something to drink. But more practically, there was a very good chance someone would sneak down during the service, wanting to buy a bottle of something or other, and he couldn't lose the sale. And, anyway, how could Lars Levi even notice if he wasn't there? Now that so many came?

No one did notice that Henrik hadn't returned. The church was so full it was starting to get warm in there for once, and everyone had taken off their hats, and when they shook the snow off their coats bits of loose fur drifted to the floor, as if it were snowing indoors as well as out. The same sense of flurry came from sound, from one conversation atop another, alternately polite or hearty tones, hello, hello, it's nice to see you again, hello, what a coat, hello, hello, before anyone moved into any real business. Probably people should have waited until after the sermon to talk about it but no one could help it, it got inserted in anyway, did you hear, people said, in tones that conveyed worry but really suggested horror, about the Heikkillä boy who'd been born with two thumbs on his right hand?

That was the news among the Finns, anyway. The Sámi didn't tend to know much about the Finns, and had their own interests to exchange—they wanted to know how everyone else's herds had done over the summer, though no one wanted to reveal how their own had done, and no one was really going to ask or answer this directly, but still, it could be inferred, by whether someone had a new coat on, or how they talked about the migration, how long it had taken them to come up from the sea, and even if someone wouldn't say anything straight out about their own herd they might talk about someone else's—how many white calves the Tommas hadn't slaughtered, for instance, just leaving them in the herd to show off. The Tommas were easy to talk about, because everyone resented them slightly—they were reindeer-rich. They didn't brag, per se, but they didn't need to—every year it seemed the Tommas were hiring someone else to help with the herd, and that did its own talking. Plus it was even easier to talk about them today since they weren't actually there—and, there was the very interesting news that Risten Tomma was engaged to the Piltto boy. Not really what anyone would have expected, but if you were already that wealthy, then maybe it didn't really matter who you married. No one said that, of course, but they all understood they were saying it. He'll need good luck with Nilsa Tomma for a father-in-law, people said, as if they pitied the Piltto boy instead of envied him.

What no one said was what they were all really doing there. Lars Levi was right, that the effort it took to get to church was so great most went only when required, on the four high holy days, to pay taxes and be confirmed and pick up supplies from Henrik's store, but none of them dared admit to each other that they'd all come this time for the same reason: over the summer it had been said that Lars Levi's sermons had become particularly wild, and that people who went to hear him were stricken with some sickness and threw themselves around, and so they were all there, mostly, out of the curiosity to see someone else go crazy. Though if they thought about it Lars Levi had already been getting a bit strange the year before . . . or had it started a few summers earlier, when his son had died?

In the aisles the dogs snapped at each other and the children wandered about, staring at strangers. In the front Lars Levi, newly nicknamed Mad Lasse, eyed them all, estimating when it would make sense to begin, since more people were certain to arrive late. It was how everything was here, there were no clean lines, there was no even break to any bit of wood, and the only way to manage was to accept that if services were generally begun in the morning around first light, ten in the morning or so, that really they might begin around ten-thirty or even eleven, and he had to cling to the success of holding the service at all.

Not that Lars Levi blamed any of them for this. He had some interest in his Finnish parishioners, who made up a quarter of his congregation, and he felt a responsibility toward them, especially their poverty, but it was the heart of the Sámi he was always after. He couldn't have said why that was—was it, simply, how poorly they'd been treated for so long by other pastors? Was it his own Sámi blood and sympathies, his feeling that they were unfairly maligned? Was it—did he—simply like them better as people, admire and even envy their vitality, how hard they worked, never a day off? Or maybe it was defensiveness, plain and simple, from his own days in the south at seminary school, where he was mocked for being so poor, for dressing so shabbily? It had got so that he was happy enough for anyone to call him a Lapp, though, usually, no one did. But wasn't he just like them? Wasn't he too full of feeling, didn't he also understand what it was to know without knowing, to have his feeling know first? Of course just then he saw one of them, drunk in the back pew, asleep on his back, and he was annoyed, he took it too personally, though he supposed he should just be glad the man had come at all. No, he wouldn't let it bother him, he decided, he would preach with such strength, such vigor, even the drunks would sit up and hang their heads with shame.

By now, without realizing it, he had made his way to the back of the church, where he'd opened the door, looking outside to see how many were still tying up their reindeer to the posts, but a new snow had begun to fall, getting in the way of his view, and he became too distracted to count. He shut the door.

Henrik had rung the bell, Willa told him.

She was kneeling by the stove in the back, putting in more wood. When she closed it he saw her hands, how red and tough they were, like a little man's.

"Well, go and sit then," he said. He snapped at her without knowing why. She wasn't anything but dutiful but why did she insist on standing there, dawdling, with all the men looking at her? She never seemed to have any sense of what was going on when it came to men, and it worried him, she was so naive as to seem a little stupid, and he wondered, not for the first time, what he had done to his children by raising them here, so far from anything resembling a town, a school, even a road.

But in the moment it was better to not be seen reprimanding her, and anyway, it was time to begin. He walked to the front and stood there, aware of how the candelabras at the altar framed him on either side. He motioned to Simmon to begin singing, since Simmon always started services this way as he had an aggressively loud voice, but as there was no instrument to help them along the melody wandered everywhere, and by the time the front of the church finished a verse the back was still in the middle, but this, too, didn't matter, he was determined for it to not matter. He looked instead at his wife, his sons and daughters, pressed against each other in the front pew, and the Finns behind them, rows of small somber faces in black wools and gray scarves, a dark foreground for the Sámi behind them in their fur coats, their red scarves, their red and blue woolen caps, their dogs at their feet, even two mothers nursing, the mounds of their breasts exposed.

"Let us gather together," he managed, when the congregation was as close to quiet as they ever came, "let us beg to sup for one more day at our Father's gracious table." He bowed his head.

As he prayed, he did not look up; he heard nothing but himself. He was speaking today on Daniel in the lion's den, and he had come up with a phrase he liked, though he was aware of his own vanity in liking it, and he was repeating this phrase— "and did Daniel, in understanding his own sin, seek to be devoured"—when he sensed rather than saw that everyone was turning to look back at a man who had just entered. Even his own family was turning around, even the black-kerchiefed head of his wife turned around. For a moment it was not clear to him, or to anyone, why they were all staring, since it appeared to just be another reindeer herder, a lone older man, and why should they all stare? Were they staring because someone else had stared, and then someone else had looked to see why they were staring, and so on and so forth, until now they were all making a fuss about something that was utterly ordinary?

The lone man was a reindeer herder, in a thick outer coat of fur and dark pants of reindeer leather, and fur boots turned up at the toes, and on top of this such a firm carapace of ice and snow that you could hardly see the shape of a man inside. Maybe that was why they all stared, or maybe it was the way he walked, down the center aisle, with slow and sure purpose. He drew closer, then stopped when he was standing beside the second pew. This close Lars Levi could make out that it was Biettar Rasti, a man of some significant standing, a man whose grandfather had once had the largest herd east of the Tornio River, but who had drunk his own herd down to nothing, had squandered every bit of the inheritance, but claimed so staunchly it was due to thieves and bad luck that no one dared disagree. Anyway, the Rasti family still retained enough of a kind of stature that no one liked to admit his downfall, either, and after all his wife had died, a long and tragic illness, and now their only son was a drunkard, too, and yet Biettar walked then and now as if he were still king of the Lapps; he stood there like it was Lars Levi who should come bow to him.

Lars Levi could not figure out what to do. Should he approach him, should he wait for Biettar to come all the way up to the altar?

They stared at each other, like two creatures crossing in a field, wary.

Even in the candlelight Lars Levi could see Biettar's eyes were unnervingly blue. He did not blink. It struck Lars Levi that the old rumor was true, that Biettar was some kind of shaman, had some kind of power of prophecy, but as if he'd heard this thought Biettar slowly lowered himself to the church floor. His back was straight, his arms loose at his sides. Lars Levi came closer slowly, like Biettar was a bird. He held out one hand and began to bend a little at the knees.

"What is it, my son?" he whispered, though Biettar was as old as he was, and though his whisper, in the sudden and total silence, surely carried. Biettar bowed his head. He smelled, very much, of his way of living—he smelled of years of smoke from the fire, and beneath that smell, like reindeer fat, and beneath the reindeer fat, he smelled unwashed. "Do you feel the awakening within you?" Lars Levi asked. "Have you come with remorse to the altar of Christ?"

But Biettar did not move. He didn't speak. His eyes were down and he might have been anywhere, been thinking anything. He might have come here entirely by accident, in a drunken stupor, and only just now realized where he was after all, in which case he might very well just stand up and leave, but Lars Levi couldn't allow that to happen. What a coup, if Biettar should be saved, here and now! Usually it was the women who were saved, the women who dragged their husbands or sons to church, desperate to cure them of their drinking, when half the time they were just bringing them closer to the dark house . . . he was in alliance with these poor women, they were fighting together not just for these men's souls but for this very way of life, and it could not be kept up, this drinking, not when the men were supposed to be herding, not when a bottle of brännvin cost more than a pelt . . .

The silence was becoming unbearable—the church itself, its very windows, its pulpit, seemed animate with expectation, and Lars Levi felt it was not his hand but a public hand, a hand on loan, that reached to grasp the head of the not-shaman; his not-hand that felt the shaking of Biettar's shoulders through the shaking of Biettar's head.

Old Sussu, nearby in the front pew, began waving her hands in the air, and Lars Levi was overwhelmed with relief, because the ecstasies were here, the rejoicing was here, and they were all going to be swept into it, even Old Sussu, and what a morning this was, Biettar and Old Sussu, saved on the same day, and he had the same pleasure he had when he shot a bird and it fell perfectly from its roost to the snow—the day was going his way—when he realized dully, slowly, that Old Sussu was not shouting with rejoicing, and Biettar was not rocking back and forth from the sheer force of salvation, but was shaking from an earthquake—they all were—he was, too, he was going to fall, he was stumbling—he waved his arms for balance until his hand landed on the arm of a pew. What a force she was, what a proper dam—her face hardened in resolve, and with her very eyes she urged him upright.

The shaking stopped and the floor stilled but the children screamed, and their mothers tried to still their screaming, and the men alternately laughed and shouted their fear. Lars Levi was filled, mostly, with amazement—hadn't this happened when Christ had died? Hadn't God sent an earthquake to mark the moment of his sacrifice? The force of this realization nearly made Lars Levi fall to his own knees. He looked at his congregants, his parishioners, his reindeer, skittish on the snow, and he saw them multiply before him, ten upon ten, so that the back of the church was not littered with drunks who stank of their drinking, but instead each face shone clean and each body's blood coursed with the mysteries and the magics of Christ . . . he found himself, suddenly, saying this, some form of this—he was talking without hearing himself speak, speaking without feeling himself think—this was what it was to be a mouthpiece for God—this!

But this extemporaneous address was interrupted by another earthquake, smaller, but a quake nonetheless, and this time people cried out with even more noise, and when he looked at his family he saw one of his sons crying, his face red and growing redder, crying so hard he could hardly breathe. It scared him, as any upset in his sons always did, it brought him back to the death of Levi, he saw Levi's face thick with measles and how Levi would not, could not, stop crying. His wife, though, had the baby nearly smothered to her chest, and he looked to Nora as if to ask, would she please take the crying boy outside, but Nora was staring at Biettar with unseeing eyes.

"Nora," he hissed, but it was Willa who heard, and she picked Lorens up and began to carry him, his legs beating against her chest, down the side of the aisle.

He had to put Levi out of his mind.

What was it he'd been saying? What had been the thought? He wiped his brow with his sleeve, but he had done that so many times that morning that he only moved the sweat around on his forehead.

AT THE DOOR, his daughter turned to see why he had stopped speaking— she thought, even from this distance, that he looked sick, though she knew he wasn't; she was familiar with this side of him, his near-hysteric states. Actually, Willa envied him, how he loosed himself on people like that. She herself was nothing beyond or below well behaved, quiet in the evenings, diligent about her chores, always first to offer to go out for wood, or put the cow in the cow-house, or pluck or skin whatever needed to be plucked or skinned, even copying her father's sermons with ink she mixed from blueberries and soot. But her outwardly manners bore little relationship to her insides, she felt if anything she kept herself as contained as she could, making herself smaller, quieter, more palatable, like she couldn't scare any-one with who she really was or what she really thought. She had no rebellion in her, though, or none that she had ever exercised, she was a kettle left at a gentle boil, and with her heat she did nothing more than make coffee or tea.

As ever, then, she did not do what she had been told, but what she knew was wanted, and she opened the door. Outside, the silence was absolute. The snow muffled even the smallest of sounds, so she heard nothing, not the reindeer tied to the posts, not the titmouse in the tree, not the services inside. Right then the wind was blowing the snow so that the scene was almost picturesque: the ten wooden cabins, most chimney-less, with shut-ters for windows, pelts of various kinds nailed to the plank walls (rein-deer, squirrel, fox, even a lynx); storehouses on their stilts, some atilt; the cow-house, with its lonesome inhabitant, pacing in place to keep warm; the frozen well; three small saunas, each a few steps from the river; six woodsheds, two with their doors hanging open; beyond these, the fruitless fields, a wheelbarrow abandoned and now stuck until spring—and along the river the tracks of so much coming and going that the river seemed more road than ice, though following the tracks you reached on all sides only the unceasing tundra; the overwhelming sense was that this was the only habitable place within days and days. They were entrapped by emptiness—it was like being at sea—the snow might as well have been ocean, and they a caravan of small and weary boats, adrift. It was true what the Lapps said, it was always better to move than to stay; staying only fortified your sense of loneliness, that no visitors would ever come, that you were the only human life.

She didn't sense that she was being watched, but she was, for while she looked down from the slope at what had entirely comprised her world for nineteen years, Henrik watched her from his store window, his curtain pushed to the side. From Henrik's vantage point she made an odd shape, as she still had Lorens on her hip, and for a few moments Henrik couldn't make out who she was. He'd hoped, of course, that she was Nora, but as soon as Willa turned to one side he could see it wasn't Nora at all, because Nora didn't hold children on her hip—he didn't strictly know this but sensed it to be true—and because she was much taller than Willa, and she didn't have Willa's slight hunch, which always made her head arrive before her body.

Henrik had rushed to the window with the first quake, thinking the world was at Lars Levi's ever-threatened end, but now Willa stood so stoically that he wondered if he'd imagined it. He thought: it's happened to me, the hysteria, it's here. People had joked about it when he'd moved north, they had said everyone lost their minds up here, but back then, with all the fuss and scandal, the prospect hadn't bothered him, it had seemed like a pleasant thing to lose one's mind, but now he saw the terror of having no control over what one believed, of having lost any fastness to truth. His whole body shuddered.

He shook his head, of his own volition this time, and he closed the curtain that Mad Lasse had told him was a vanity to have put up in the first place, with the same thought he always had, about how it was too cheap to be considered a vanity—he had cut it from a bit of leftover muslin and tacked it up with nails—but as if called up by the sinfulness of this thought the whole cabin began to shake for the third time, worse than before. On the walls and shelves everything was coming down, the spools of thread, the portrait of King Oskar I of Sweden, the fox tails, the candles hung by long waxen threads, and the things on the counter were sliding, glasses, his pen and ink, his accounting book, a ferret's pelt, a sack of goose feathers, the candle in its candlestick, down it all came, like a giant was hoisting up the store on one side, and then, tired, the giant dropped it, and walked away.

Emelie had told him not to move here. She had told him it was a bad idea to deal with the Lapps but he hadn't had much of a choice, and anyway his uncle had promised it would be easy, that there was a fortune to be made off of their drinking. What was needed was someone with gumption, someone to buy the vodka, brännvin, whiskey, whatever, from the merchants in Tornio and then sell it at triple, quadruple the price, and Henrik had thought he could be that person, he had thought by now he would be rich, and instead he was in debt, badly, to his uncle—he was, in fact, nearly bankrupt, and every time he put wood in the stove he thought: what will I get if I try to sell this stove? Who would even buy it? It had cost him a small fortune to have it hauled here, but now he saw the problem was not getting here but leaving here. Once you came here you had sunk in so much you couldn't afford to leave, and you waited for the cold to kill you, your whole life long, that was all.

He had to leave, he had to get out of here, not just the cabin, but the town, not just the town, but the north itself. It was suddenly intolerable to be alone, and he threw his coat on and hurried his way up toward the church, head down, chin down, the wind on his wrists, in the arms of his coat, in his boots, his ankles, the inside of his ears aching with cold, the snow wetting his head and his cheeks and his neck. The hill up to the church seemed steeper, the reindeer more restless, and Willa was gone, and suddenly he was afraid, afraid for Nora—what if something had happened to her, to all of them—and he opened the door with unusual force.

On the floor, lying flat, totally still, possibly dead, was Biettar. Henrik knew that coat, how patchy it was, because Biettar was one of his best customers, or worst, depending on how you looked at it; Biettar owed him a small but significant fortune: he held the record of having drunk the most brännvin of anyone the past winter, unless of course, you included Henrik, which Henrik resolutely did not do. As it was Henrik could not look at Biettar without thinking; there walks the worth of my stove, and now his stove was maybe dead on the floor. Lars Levi was bent over him, and the congregation bent around Lars Levi, but no one moved, as if it were too late to do any good.

"You must be risen, you will be risen! You are not of flesh and blood," Lars Levi was saying, in a coarse whisper. "There is no one more holy than a Sámi, you are pure and good, be awakened! Any sin you have done Christ can take from you!"

To Henrik's relief Biettar's legs, the fur trousers, began to twitch, or rather, seize. Lars Levi bent down and put his hands on Biettar's chest. "Do not forget what Christ said to his disciple, he said that thou art Biettar, thou art Peter, and upon this rock I shall build my church," Lars Levi said, almost with admonition, and Biettar's legs kicked harder. Biettar was saying something in Lappish, or for all Henrik knew, he was speaking in tongues.

"What is it," Henrik asked a man standing near the door, "what's he saying?" But the man ignored him. Henrik looked around for Nora, but she wasn't in her usual pew, nothing was in its usual place.

"Biettar," a woman shouted. It was Old Sussu. Her voice was strained, it might have been a cry of fear or a cry of encouragement, it was impossible to know.

Lars Levi reached down and took Biettar's arm, and pulled him up to sitting, but Biettar's head remained folded into his chest. "Do you believe?" Lars Levi asked. "Are you saved? Have you taken Jesus Christ into your own heart?"

Biettar turned suddenly; he was looking around the room, for someone, for something. "I am not flesh and blood," he said, "I am with God," he said, "I am forgiven," and his eyes watered over into tears, which he did not wipe away.

The church door opened. It was Willa, holding Lorens's hand. She had taken out the braid in her hair, or maybe the wind had, and as she drew near her shoulder brushed Henrik's and he looked at her, but she didn't look back at him, her eyes were fixed on Biettar.

"He's being awakened," she whispered. Henrik thought she was explaining it to him but she was explaining it to herself. She wanted, for some reason, to weep.

"The herd," Biettar said.

"This all," Lars Levi was saying, "this is for you." But Willa wondered if her father had it all wrong, if the earthquake was meant for her, if God had seen into her heart and found her wanting. He had searched her and known her, he had tried her and known her thoughts. He had seen there was a wicked way in her. Yes, it was why Biettar had come. God might as well have sent an angel to fill the church so that its wings singed against the stove, its head lodged sideways against the rafters, demanding, its finger pointed at her, it is not he who should be on his knees but she. Not he but she.

2

WELL EAST OF THE CHURCH, AND NORTH SOME, A SOLID DAY'S TRAVEL BY ski, the snow was coming down with a preposterous beauty, dropping in fat flakes that wafted through the smoke-hole and wended their way to the fire. They are throwing themselves to their deaths, Ivár thought, but they go with such grace. With some difficulty—his fingers had no bend to them, and his shoebands were stuck together with ice—he took off his boots. He poured the shoe-grass out of them and looked at his toes, wrinkled and a little damp, sort of white, but otherwise recognizably his feet. The fire singed his heels and all around him he felt the lavvu settling into being warmed again, the frost steaming off everywhere, so that he was living, briefly, in the clouds. It was so nice, it was so pleasant he could have fallen asleep at that very moment but in the past few days he had lost not one but two calves, clearly to the same wolverine that had been stalking the herd, and the thought of losing more was unbearable—he was already dreading when his father would come back and see the pelts stretched out on the drying rack and know it was Ivár's fault, that Ivár had snuck off again for the sake of a woman.

Part of the difficulty though was that Ivár didn't know when his father would come back; his father was Bietar, and though Ivár did not know his father was then in the throes of awakening on the church floor, he knew his father had not been his usual self, he'd been especially surly lately, and practically silent. They'd slaughtered the eating-reindeer a week ago but not any reindeer for the debt, and in this there was a silent acknowledgment that they weren't going to pay the debt, and when his father had set off for town Ivvár had assumed that he had gone to inform the storekeeper of this fact, and to try to wheedle something to drink out of him anyway. In this case his father would have been gone at least two days, maybe three, and Ivvár had been careful to be off at Risten's only the one day, but he hadn't been prepared for his father to be gone four days, and now five, and still Ivvár was out with the herd alone. In Ivvár's mind the carcasses were becoming, slowly but surely, his father's fault, because it wasn't fair to leave him alone for so long and still expect him to keep the herd together, not when his father could see perfectly well that the wind was blowing up from the south, which meant the reindeer were going to want to wander south, where they'd cross and mix into the Unga herd, and they couldn't have that, they needed the herd to graze this valley and they needed to not lose more time to more herd separations; his father knew that. His father knew that because it was his father who had taught him these things.

But his father had left him, as if it were possible for Ivvár to never sleep, to just sit forever at the southern flank of the herd and keep turning the nose, keep sending the dog off to ring the males back in. And, his father wasn't here to see what Ivvár was seeing, which was that now that they'd slaughtered those old females, the balance of the herd wasn't right, and there were too many males, and they ought to have slaughtered those three-year-old bulls instead of the old females, even if it was unlikely they'd calve again this year. Or castrated the bulls, at least, what with Borga getting old, and there being so little time now to train new draft reindeer to pull the sleds, which, not incidentally, needed repairing—when was any of that going to happen? The more he thought about it, the more he agreed with himself that his father ought not to have left him like this, and the more he resented his father for probably enjoying himself; probably he was passed out on the store's floor right now. And of course Ivvár couldn't say a word of complaint, he'd tried that once and to teach him a lesson his father had left for even longer, and when he'd returned he'd just said how it was the job of a herder to deal with what was, and not waste one's time wishing things to be any different. No one controls nature, he'd said bitterly, and I am part of that nature.

Even though Ivár should have just reused the old shoe-grass drying by the fire, he rewarded himself for his sufferings by reaching up for the fresh bundle, and he let himself have a pinch of salt in his coffee as he stuffed his boots, and then he let himself have a bite of the cheese Risten had given him that he was not going to tell his father about. The cheese was warm from being pressed against his chest, where he kept it, so his father would not accidentally chance on it and stuff it all in his mouth immediately, and while he chewed the sweating cheese he thought of Risten, milking the reindeer on the slopes, then turning the milk to cheese, and he even had the strange and perverse sensation of eating or drinking her milk, and he regretted it was winter, and that when he'd seen her the other day she'd been wearing her heaviest fur coat, the one that made her look twice as wide as she was, and barrel-like, so the only womanly thing about her was her fur cap, with its embroidery running around her face. She'd given him so little time before she'd run off, though she'd teased him by pushing at him hard enough that he fell, and she'd rolled with him a little in the snow, thinking what, he didn't know.

It was all a mistake, of course, a grand mistake, all of it; it had been a mistake this summer to have gone to her family's summer grounds, and it had been a mistake two days ago to go see her, mostly because she was engaged to Mikkol Piltto (who was, he had heard, going to actually come and join her siida instead of the other way around, an emasculation Ivár was proud to pretend he would never have allowed), and because Ivár was aware he did not love Risten and had never really loved her and had been leading her on for years, and so to appear to her now was neither prudent nor purposeful, though he couldn't have said why he had done it. Not that she would ever have been encouraged to marry him, of course. Not even his family's old and good name would have allowed for the shame of her going so far beneath herself, for if her father despised anything, he despised anyone who he didn't see as a serious Sámi, a real herder, and everyone knew that he wouldn't let her have her reindeer if she tried to marry someone who wasn't serious about herding. That was how he always put it, someone serious, and Ivvár was serious, in his own way, mostly about not taking things so seriously, but Nilsa only understood seriousness in terms of reindeer, and a herd like Ivvár's was so far from serious as to be laughable. It was not even a herd, it was a small flock; it was an embarrassment.

He finished his coffee to the last drop, thinking he needed all the luck he could get, and he tightened his shoebands one more time. Outside the wind had relinquished its hold on the valley and the moon was rising over the fell, and the little trees and the little hills and his little reindeer, they threw long and dark shadows on the snow. All around him the herd was gathered. He could see, at its edge, his father's dog, Mirre, resting with one eye open, his tail over his nose, and he turned back to his herd and listened for the big bell reindeer, who was right in the middle of the herd where he belonged, and then he looked for Borga, his favorite, his beautiful all-white Borga that even his father wouldn't dare harness and take to town, and then he listened for the bell on the new mother who never could stay with the herd, and there she was, on the fringe, rooting around, her missing antler giving her the appearance of a joke. His father didn't like to use bells like Ivvár did, and Ivvár only put them on when his father was gone, taking them off when his father returned. A bad crutch, his father said. If the big bell reindeer wandered and the rest followed the bell, like they tended to do, all you'd done was mark what was missing. But Ivvár liked the bells. With his eyes closed he could still watch the reindeer, hear where they went, how they moved, where the wind was sending them, what the birds said, and while he listened the snow became its own weight, took its own shape against his back.

Although he thought at every minute that his father might appear, in fact he was alone with the herd for two more days, sleeping at most six hours in those two days, six hours in which he woke up each time certain the herd had wandered, each time coming outside to see Mirre's watchful eye, and all around him the lumps that the reindeer formed when they slept and it snowed on them. So he was all fog, all delirium when he heard the sound of his father's sledge, and he stood and brushed the snow off and began to move around the herd, closing them in together, tightening their edges. His father's form grew slowly, Mirre barking his happiness and Ivvár's relief until his father raised his arm, elbow bent, and on cue, quiet fell.

Ivvár followed his father into the lávvu, and Mirre followed Ivvár. Inside they all went to their usual places, Ivvár to the right and his father to the left of the fire, Mirre near the door. His father snapped bundles of branches in half and placed them with care inside two half-eaten logs. His father's fires always looked the same, very neat, and the branches always looked too thickly set to light, but it was never the case, and soon the ice on their eyebrows and hats dripped onto their cheeks but neither wiped them off.

We lost two calves, that was what Ivvár should have said, but he was afraid to call it to his father's attention. Clearly his father was avoiding talking about it, because he kept sniffing and resetting his hat on his head like he did when he had something to say but couldn't get the words free of himself.

"You remember your mother?" his father said, finally. Ivvár was so surprised by this he looked straight at his father, and for what felt like much too long they looked at each other. It was always a strange exercise, looking at his father, because he was aware he was looking at himself. Everyone loved to say it, you have the same eyes. What was it that French lady had said? I didn't know natives could have such blue eyes, magnifique, she had said, like he was a particularly nice pair of sealskin mittens.

Ivvár looked around for something for his hands to do, anything, so that he didn't have to look at his father at all. He settled on a piece of wood that was on the edge of the fire but hadn't yet burned. He took out his knife and began to peel the edges of it into long curling strips that bent backward over each other.

His father sighed, expelled a large burst of air that joined the smoke of the fire and went up with it.

"It's nothing," his father said.

Ivvár thought, just be done with it already.

"I—" his father said. Ivvár looked at him again. He couldn't remember his father being like this. He made all of his decisions swiftly, resolutely, and did not bother worrying about them once they were made. Never any going back, not in his mind least of all.

"Did you end up paying Rikki anything?" Ivvár asked. His father didn't like this rude nickname for Henrik, but Ivvár used it anyway, as if to remind his father what side they were both on. It came out of him before he knew he would say it. It was clever of him, almost mean, distracting his father this way from the calves, making explicit what belonged in the realm of the tacit, and his father looked hurt, his tired eyes looked more tired, and this gave Ivvár the sensation of having stepped on a calf's leg, or knocked over a child in the corral.

"No," his father said, and Ivvár felt the bitterness of his win, the coldness of it, because his father got up and went back outside, though he hadn't dried out his shoe-grass and he'd hardly warmed himself. They hadn't even had a cup of coffee. His father's stubbornness was impressive like this, Ivvár had never known anyone to carry a grudge as long as he did. So Ivvár expected his father not to come back for several hours at the very least, but to his surprise his father promptly returned.

"You want something to drink?" Ivvár asked. This was, they both knew, another attack. Of course there was nothing left to drink, there was never anything left. There was no such thing, really, as a bottle half-drunk, not to them. So you went to Rikki's and got drunk, Ivvár saying, plain as could be, and his father shook his head. The pained look again, the calf's bent leg again.

"Let's take some coffee," his father said, and he reached for his rucksack, and took from the frozen leather a sack of coffee beans, and after that a loaf of bread that wasn't made from bark flour, and then a bit of cheese. Ivvár felt guilty, thinking of his own cheese, wrapped in the bit of leather, sweating slightly against his chest.

"Old Sussu?" Ivvár asked. She had a soft spot for them, she was Ivvár's godmother, and though she lived on so little it frightened him she was prone to sending along things anyway, you could not refuse them no matter how much you tried, you would say no and find the new mittens stuffed into the bottom of your rucksack later, even though you couldn't recall a single time she had been anywhere near the bag.

"No," his father said. He seemed about to offer up the answer, he opened his mouth, then closed it.

"Rikki's decided to save us from ourselves, is that it?" Ivvár asked.

"No."

"Well, don't tell me anything then," Ivvár said, knowing how petulant he sounded. "I don't want to know."

His father looked unimpressed by this. "It's from the preacher's daughter," he said.

"The preacher's daughter."

"You know, there's a few of them."

"I know," Ivvár said, but this all seemed to be beside the point, he could not gather why his father had things from Mad Lasse's daughter, he could hardly bring to his mind an image of them at all, they faded into the background of everything to do with the church. They had such serious faces, and they stared too much but without giving him any sense of their admiration for him, and they stared too much but without giving him any sense of their admiration for him, and Ivvár's pride could not account for this. His looks were, he knew, the last real value he had left, and it was why he had gone to see Risten, wasn't it, to be admired, to know she looked and she liked it, she couldn't help herself. She wanted Ivvár to smile at her, she would go back to her stack of soft pelts and she wouldn't think, oh Mikkol, she would think, if only, Ivvár!

"She gave it all to me," his father said.

"Why?"

"She wanted to, I guess." His father looked so guilty saying this that for a moment Ivvár thought, he's lying, and for a second he thought, they pitied him? They thought they were starving? His father had begged? "I was staying with them," his father said. "They put me in, you know, they have that main cabin they mostly live in and then the other little one. It has one of those stoves in it with all the stone."

Ivvár nodded, unsure why he was hearing any of this.

"I slept in there, they gave me a mattress on the floor. They put hay in their mattresses, did you know that? Well, they said the parents, Lars Levi and his wife, they sleep on goose feathers."

Lars Levi, his father had said, not Mad Lasse. No one called Lars Levi

Lars Levi except, Ivvár thought, people who mistook his madness for ministry. It unnerved him.

"So you stayed with Mad Lasse," Ivvár said.

"I didn't know it would be this hard," his father said, as if there was someone else in the lávvu with them.

"What would?"

"You know, for a son, you're not an easy one."

"It's hard to be easy when you haven't slept."

"If you were a reindeer," he said, "I would never try to tame you. You would be terrible as a draft deer. You would never go which way I wanted." It was the closest his father had ever come to a kind of compliment, and it surprised Ivvár, it almost hurt to hear. Or was it not a compliment at all?

"And you would?" Ivvár said lightly.

"Well, that's it, isn't it," his father said, "I've been very wrong," his father said. "About many things."

Somehow it was awful to hear this, it made Ivvár sick to see his father like this. "Don't," he said, "no, you—"

"I have," he said. "I've been, I've been drinking the Devil's piss!"

"Don't say—"

"I've been awakened," he said.

Ivvár stared, he stared at his father's nose, its red and waxen bulb, at his father's lips, cracked, he felt like he was looking at a stranger, he did not know this man who was speaking. It was a joke! His father, one of them! His father wasn't going to drink anymore, he was going to start telling people what was wrong and what was right? He was going to start speaking in Finnish, or in Swedish? Or what, he would learn to read like Smålek had and go around reading the Bible at people whether or not they wanted to hear it—was that who he wanted to be? Most certainly, if he was anything like the rest of them, he would lecture Ivvár if he drank, maybe go so far as to dramatically pour it out, the believers were always doing things like that. But maybe he would go further still, maybe he would scold Ivvár for turning the kettle spout toward the kitchen, for laying the wood so that the root was turned toward the door, even though it was his father who had stopped at the sieidis to give offerings, who had pointed each one out, who had insisted, when they went by one, on complete silence, though he hadn't gone to one in a long time, maybe since his mother had died. Ivár laughed, a rough and fake little spur that neither of them believed in.

"And while we're at it, while I'm saying things . . . I heard Risten's broken off her engagement with that Piltto. What's his name. Sámmol."

"Mikkol," Ivár said. He could not figure out which news was worse. He could not understand what was happening to his world, why everything insisted on looking the same but being quite different, why his father's hand on the fire-stick suddenly seemed old, and why a new dread came through him, like he'd just crested a fell and been met with the reality of the wind beyond it.

This was not good, he thought. This was not good. He almost felt sick.

"Wind's coming up from the south now though," his father said.

"East this morning."

"Maybe we'll have to move in a few days, I was thinking down—"

"To Bálggesgurra."

His father grunted, assented, and Ivár wanted to shout, don't speak of normal things, don't you dare, don't you behave like you haven't done what you've done, but he felt tired, he felt so tired, and he thought, maybe if I sleep I will wake up and things will be different. This was a nice little lie, and if he was good at anything he was good at taking a thought and sticking it in a little hidey-hole, and never digging it up again. What was important was to just keep going, just think of what would be pleasant next, what could be pleasant next, and Ivár lay down, and sure enough, in the sharp heat of the fire Ivár found himself falling asleep, he was pulled down and down into the earth, he was covered with thick pelts by the underlings, and when he awoke his father was gone. They didn't speak of it, and instead the next day his father announced they would move the herd, to get away from the wolverines, so they did, but when they got to Bálggesgurra they found more wolverine tracks, and they moved the herd again, skiing with the herd down along the river, the snowbanks on either side piled high. Each time they moved south Ivár felt more and more aware they were closer and closer to the church-village and thus closer to Risten. He did not want to see her, not now, it seemed impossible to manage that on top of his father. But he was saved that confrontation by his father's announcement they would head east, though the land was so uneven here, punched down in places, and it was hard to see the reindeer all at once, but his father read the snow and said it was all right, the lichen spread thickly over the ground and up the tree trunks, and the snow, though brittle, had no crust on top, nor ice on bottom, and moreover was only a hand deep; they could stay there awhile.

But his father, although he worked as much as ever—setting up new drying racks, finding new branches for the floor, fetching water, fetching wood, fixing the harness strap that had worn down—did not seem like the father who had left for town two weeks ago. First it was his humming, he had never been one for humming, and now he hummed loud melodies that Ivár realized were church hymns, songs that hardly went anywhere at all. Then Ivár realized his father was always quiet now, in a new way. Before he was quiet if he was upset, or sometimes if he was very drunk, but now it was as if something inside him had gone still, and what had been a rolling sea was now a placid pond. It was like the stories of underlings who stole good babies and swapped them for bad ones—his father had been swapped out, but for whom Ivár did not know.

One night when they were lying down and smoking after dinner, his father said, apropos of nothing, "Come to church with me. You know," his father went on, when Ivár gave him no encouragement, "there's something powerful there." Ivár thought he would do anything, give anything, if only his father wouldn't talk about it. "I couldn't see it on my own, but your mother showed me," his father said. Ivár willed his ears to close. "I was going to Rikki's and then . . . remember when you got into the corral when the big bull was in there?"

Ivár said nothing, to punish him more, but of course he remembered, his mother had liked to tell it as a story of luck, a story of Ivár's good instincts, even as a very little boy—you could barely walk, she liked to say, but you could duck. But he wanted now to hear his father tell it, he wanted to hear about how his father had rushed to get him out, while the bull's antlers—wider than this, his mother would say, stretching out her arms—went swaying just over Ivvár's head.

"You remember," his father said dismissively. "Well, it was just like that, I was going to Rikki's and then I heard a noise. Someone shouted out. It was the same shout your mother made that morning in the corral, the same one, and when I stopped the shouting stopped. So I stood there a minute, then I stepped forward again and the shout came. When I stopped moving the shouting stopped. This time to trick it," he said slowly, "I sat down in the snow. And I listened very hard, I could hear the wind, that was all. I had a very bad feeling, and after I had waited I went forward again, but this time when the shout came I knew that if I kept going to Rikki's I would die." He nodded. "So I went to church," he said.

There was a silence that was so long Ivvár came close to falling asleep, his pipe in his hand.

"You don't believe me," his father said sadly.

Ivvár lay down and turned his back to the fire, watching the bottom of the lávvu-cloth get tugged by the wind, watching his pipe smoke up, as if the wind were having a good puff. As the bottom of the cloth blew up he could see the snow outside, he could see the reindeer in the distance, they were exposed to him briefly, then hidden again. He needed to go out and fix the cloth, weigh the edge down with more rocks.

"Ivvár," his father said, "I'll pray for you," and this was so uncomfortable for Ivvár that he got up to go outside. He would go look for some rocks. He would fix one noisome thing.

3

OLD SUSSU DID NOT KNOW WHAT TO DO ABOUT IVVÁR'S FATHER EXCEPT to gossip about it. She was as taken aback by Biettar's conversion as all the other Sámi who did things the old way, that had always been her kind of Sámi; she usually didn't have anything to do with the ones who went to the mines or who shepherded settlers from one town to another with draft reindeer, like Simmon did, it was why she and Simmon barely acknowledged each other, even though they were the only two Sámi to even live inside the bounds of Gárasavvon. Probably, she often thought as she walked by him, he doesn't even call this village Gárasavvon, probably he says Karesuando, like a Swede, or Karesuvanto, like a Finn—both Karesuando and Karesuvanto iterations of nonsense, a simulation of the Sámi name "Gárasavvon," which had come first, the Sámi word the one to bear the meaning, the word that carried, in fact, useful directions—where the river widens, near the hill of Gára.

It disgusted Old Sussu, these kinds of betrayals, small as they were, and thus the largeness of Biettar's betrayal—she couldn't see it as anything else— had shocked her, she told whoever would listen that it had been the kind of shock you get when you're young and you realize how terrible the world really is. Like the first time your favorite reindeer is slaughtered, she said now, to Anna and her daughter Risten anyway, since Nilsa was the sort to hardly ever leave his herd. Old Sussu had traveled for four hours on skis out to their siida just to talk about the Rastis, both Biettar and Ivvár; they were her people, even if Ivvár's mother wasn't alive anymore, and even if Ivvár so unabashedly avoided visiting her in that way of young people, how they were afraid of old people. The fact was that she had been his mother's closest friend, and she was Ivvár's godmother, so in her mind, talking about them wasn't gossiping so much as it was investigating, keeping an eye on them. Besides, she had always suspected Anna and Biettar had been in love once, and she suspected now that Ivvár was behind the end of Risten's engagement with Mikkol Piltto, and though the Tommas weren't ones to say interesting things about themselves—lest, perhaps, anyone notice or resent the disparity in wealth—she was curious to know if Ivvár really was going to end up with the Tomma girl; it was too interesting, the most eligible herding woman in the district, ending things for a derelict's son who, in Old Sussi's view, had both too much pride and too much trouble in his blood to ever marry.

Maybe it was the foolish musings of an old woman, she admitted that, but she was very good about these things, it was hard to keep anything from her. She didn't have her teeth but she had her eyes and they worked wonderfully well. I can see a lie a dog-mile away, that was something she liked to say. As soon as she'd arrived they fussed about how far she had come to see them, but Old Sussu felt strong from the skiing. She was laughing inwardly even now, as she saw how diligently Risten was focused on her sewing. It was impossible to sew when it was this cold out, the second you took your hands out of your mittens they went to wood; it meant that Risten needed some distraction and she didn't want to look at Old Sussu at all. She didn't want Old Sussu to see, but Old Sussu saw.

Risten looked around in her sewing box, found a little purse of leather she'd been working on and abandoned several months ago. She put the purse, with its tongue all hanging out, in her lap, and looked for her thimble, her needle, but of course she had run out of thread and hadn't rolled any more. She wanted to quit, but now that she had made such a show of it, it was impossible.

"I've got some," her mother said, nodding. She went into her own sewing box and took out a loosely wound wreath of flaking, half-frozen sinew. "You want to roll it, Old Sussu?" she asked. In this way she was saying, without saying, how Risten wouldn't roll it very well herself, she would give up halfway through. Her mother's work was so precise, each piece so well ornamented with embroidery, it made Risten want to not bother to do any of her own work at all. It was impossible to live up to, a mother who made handicraft like that—the very cradle she had made for Risten was still taken out on occasion to show to strangers, its birch bark perfectly bent, the white fur still cupped inside, and here was Risten now, with her sad sack of purse, the leather not softened enough and bunching all wrong.

Old Sussu put her hand out and her mother passed the sinew to her, and Old Sussu took off her mitten and took the cords, began rolling a strand of it against her cheek so rapidly and evenly and tightly you would have thought, this is what Old Sussu's cheeks are made for, tightening and smoothing sinew into thread.

"Well," Old Sussu said, "and how is the herd?" She had seen them for herself, of course, the mass of them was impossible to miss, Nilsa must have had well over a thousand head, so many they spread out of this valley and into the next. It was nearly slaughter-time, too, if she'd timed it right, and she knew Nilsa and Anna, they would never let her leave without feeding her well, and would send her off, no doubt, with fresh meat of her own. Probably, she thought, Anna is looking at me right now, amazed that I know exactly what day to come by for the slaughter.

"Well enough," Anna said blandly.

"A terrible winter for wolverines," Old Sussu said. Everyone had been saying it.

"Yes," Anna said, "it's so upsetting for Nilsa."

"She's talking about the other day," Risten interrupted, "a wolverine jumped onto a three-year-old female's back, it just clung there and wouldn't let go."

"She didn't run," Anna said, with a mix of pride and admonishment, "she went and got the dogs, followed behind them with her ski pole raised, like she was going to clobber the wolverine herself."

"I didn't go that near it," Risten said, exasperated. "I'm not stupid."

"It's hardly ever anyone sees a wolverine hunt," Old Sussu observed, "it's a perverse kind of luck."

Risten flushed. She couldn't have explained, then or now, what had led her to do such a stupid thing—when you saw a wolverine, the thing to do was to leave, let it have what it wanted. Her father, who believed above all that she should be safe, who worried that every snowstorm was too thick to be skied in alone, and every boat not seaworthy, and every knife too dull and bound to cause her to push too hard, had been furious when he'd heard, but she hadn't had any way to explain, she'd just seen Ivár, and her heart had already been in her hands and it had seemed to her, when she saw the wolverine, that she had to take her nerves out on something. Anyway it had been a reasonable risk, she'd had the dogs, and she had said this to her father, several times, that she would never have gone after it if she hadn't had the dogs, all three of them, but by then her father was too furious, and now they were back to their usual pattern at home, where her mother was especially nice to try to make up for her father.

"You know what I always think is so interesting," Old Sussu went on, "is how the wolverine is the only animal that kills more than it can eat. Some people are like that, too, don't you think?"

Risten's face, which surely was already red from the heat of the fire—her mother always built it up when someone came by, and in Old Sussu's case especially—went, surely, redder still. How was it, she thought, how did news about her ending things with Mikkol make it all the miles to town? Whose legs had carried it?

"Well," her mother said, "on the other hand some things should be met head-on with a ski pole."

"Yes, yes," Old Sussu said, "no use to being shy about what you want, I suppose."

"I wasn't alone out there anyway," Risten said, having some trouble keeping both conversations in her head at once, the inferred conversation and the active one, and then realized she was close to admitting Ivár had been nearby.

Old Sussu took the sinew from her cheek and inspected it. She had rolled it so tightly Risten could hardly see any fibers breaking off from it at all. In the meantime her mother had put coffee to boil, and was slicing dried meat into thin and perfect strips, even though they both knew her father would be by anytime to say, I'm slaughtering now, and they would go out, and there would be, soon enough, fresh meat.

"So, Anna," Old Sussu said, returning the sinew to her cheek to roll it through again, "what do you make of Biettar?" The way she asked it both-ered Risten, her tone suggested that what she wanted was a conversation in which they all agreed how awful it was, how embarrassing and strange.

"Oh, well," her mother said, "it was a surprise," surely the kind of vague sentiment Old Sussu did not want to hear.

"Did you realize," Sussu said, "it was on the anniversary of the day she died?"

"Was it really?"

"It was," Old Sussu said, "anyway, I was there when it was happening, and," she said, matter-of-factly, "when the shaking came, I heard him say her name."

"We didn't have it out here," her mother said, taking the bowl full of the slices of meat and passing it on to Old Sussu, who set the sinew down and selected the piece with the whitest and widest strip of fat, and then cut the fat free of the meat and put the fat between her cheek and her gums like it was tobacco. "I thought maybe it was something people were saying."

"It was really a sight. Shocking. It was too bad you weren't there to see it," Old Sussu said. She shook her head. "Biettar fell to his knees in front of everyone——"

"To his knees? Really?"

"Yes," Old Sussu said, "I'm quite serious." She was enjoying this now, it was as if she were making it happen again each time she told it. "He was on his knees and that's when the shaking happened. And then he was awakened," she said, "he added, "he was saved." She said "He repented," she added, "he was saved." She said these words in such a way it was clear she found them worrying.

"Did he mean it, though?" Risten said. "Maybe he didn't really mean it. Maybe it was for show." She was aware when she said this that she was defending Biettar, and thus Ivár, and thus furthering the suspicion that she had broken off things with Mikkol for Ivár, and while she did not want people thinking this until she had straightened things out with Ivár, until they had firmed things up, she couldn't bear, not really, to hear Biettar talked about this way. It wasn't kind, she thought, and it wasn't respectful. Wasn't he Biettar Rasti? Her father had always said he had a way with things. He knows things, her father had said, and he had warned her, once, not to cross him. You don't want men like him upset with you, he'd said, you never know what they know about you, and this phrasing she had never forgotten, it had left her with the sense that Biettar did know, so that on the rare occasions she saw him she was nervous, sure that he knew of her infatuation with his son and how futile it all was, and pitied her.

Old Sussu dropped the string of sinew so it lay in her lap, then leaned forward and said, "People are saying it was Mad Lasse who made the earth shake." She nodded firmly. She answered her own question before anyone else could, as if afraid someone would guess it and lessen the blow of it. "I think it was Biettar who did it," she said. "I think he had something to do with it. You know what I mean," she added, quietly, like they did know, and they did, Anna more than Risten, but still, they did. "I saw Biettar," she went on, "afterward. He came to my cabin and he said, 'Sussu, you don't know what I've seen.' He looked drunk."

"I thought that was the whole point of these new believers," Anna said, "that they didn't drink."

"He wasn't drunk for once is what I mean," Sussu said, "he was just so wild-looking I thought he was. And I said to him, so are you done, now you don't do anything like the rest of them, no drinking, no yoiking, and he began to give me his own little sermon. I couldn't believe it, he said all kinds of things, about how I could be saved, too, but I didn't stand for it, I told him I didn't like people saying those kinds of words where I sleep, I didn't need that kind of bad luck, not with the winter we're having, and he said he would pray to Jesus for me, and I said Jesus was like a horse, well enough in its own place but not much use around here, so, well, you can imagine how that went!"

"How upsetting," Anna said, in such a tone that it wasn't clear which party she gave her sympathies to, and Risten wondered what it was her mother thought. It was really a very irritating habit—why couldn't she say her own mind? Why must she always be so polite? Risten liked to think of herself as more like her father, a man known to be uncomfortably direct, though his version of direct would not have struck anyone but a Sámi as such, and Risten's version of directness even less so—she was prone to posing everything as a question, or often made it seem like someone else had said something she actually thought, to distance herself from it—my mother says, she would say, since she herself could not.

"I've been trying to warn people for a long time," Old Sussu went on, not dissuaded in the least by Anna's ambivalence, "but do they listen to me? You saw last year, how many more were coming than before—"

"His sermons changed," Anna agreed, "he didn't used to be so—forceful."

"You know who came last week, the Ungas came, and three families from Soppero, three! They come in the evenings and go to the parsonage and they have more sermons. I can hear them, late into the night, sometimes I think, what are they doing there, it sounds like shrieking, and then I can't sleep." She said all this as if the important part was that she couldn't sleep.

"It'll settle down, though," Anna said, "it always settles down eventually. Remember when Smálek used to go around with that Bible? He even tried coming here once."

"He did try," Risten said dryly. She recalled, herself, her father bodily throwing Smálek out of the lávvu, and, as if afraid to lose his reputation for hospitality, throwing some cheese out the door after him. It would have been funny if Smálek had not looked so pitiful, had not resumed (after picking up the cheese) reciting Bible verses as he'd walked away.

"But he doesn't do any of that anymore," Anna said.

"Yes, he's just a harmless——" Risten said.

"Well," Old Sussu said, "I've not seen him once at Rikki's since. And he'll be back to the Bible reading again soon, you just watch. It's a real preaching sickness, this time."

"Sometimes it's hard to know which is the medicine and which is the disease," Anna said.

"Of course not drinking is better for the herd," Old Sussu said, "and they are doing so terribly, you know. It's really a shame, what it used to be, how it looks now. Simmon said, last he went out to collect on the debt, it was not what it used to be." It took Risten a moment to realize: Old Sussu was talking about Ivvár and Biettar's herd.

"Maybe they were split up, or separated," Anna said.

"Biettar usually herds with his brothers," Risten added.

"Simmon has his faults but not when it comes to counting reindeer," Old Sussu said. "He sees one reindeer and he sees two silver riks-dollars and there's very little that will keep him from his riks-dollars. I've heard he's hidden all the silver away, too," Old Sussu said, "but someone else found it and he won't admit it."

"It's terrible how much some people drink," Anna said. It was surprising to hear the vehemence in her tone. It seemed like she was bitter about Biettar drinking in particular, though why that would be Risten couldn't have said.

"Ivvár and Biettar are the kind who like to have a bit of fun," Risten said, "they're always so lively." For a moment she didn't know what she herself meant, she felt the lie of her implication: of course Ivvár was worse, crazier when he drank—he'd found her at a festival in a lávvu with another herder, and had proceeded to invite himself to join them, becoming awkwardly raucous, laughing too loud, at one point stumbling in and out of the lávvu for no reason she could see. She had been embarrassed for him, had wished, desperately, he wouldn't be like that.

"And it's hard to get ahead when Rikki is making sure you always stay behind," she went on. Risten avoided her mother's look. She was embarrassing herself, she knew it, and she could practically hear Old Sussu already, telling someone else, oh yes, it's a sure thing, Risten broke things off with Mikkol when he's so good and principled and for what? And she isn't getting younger! Of course there's hardly a man that wouldn't marry her but she managed to find the one in Ivvár! Anyway, what was wrong with Mikkol? Not the most handsome, to be sure, but a solid sort. Yes, that was what Old Sussu would say.

That, in these imagined proceedings, Risten assumed all men would want to marry her was not in fact an inflation of her self-worth. She was not the greatest of all beauties but she was pretty, she had dark and thick hair that she combed carefully to keep out the lice every morning and every night, and she had the self-confidence that comes with always having been liked by men—she expected to be liked, and she was, and this made her more attractive still. But even she was not so self-enamored to not realize it was her reindeer that made her so valuable, and, moreover, the fact that her parents had no other children—she was a windfall for someone, she had the power to change some herder's life, so long as her father went along with it. In some ways Mikkol's feigning of disinterest in her herd had been part of what had attracted her to him—he had seemed not to notice the difference in their wealth, and he didn't express any embarrassment at joining her siida. She had told him at the time that it was because she couldn't bear to leave her parents but really it was that she trusted no one but her father with the herd; she was too close to her father, and even in the prospect of marriage had trouble allowing anyone to usurp his role.

But then Ivár had come with his smile, his taunting, as if to tell her, he knew she didn't really love Mikkol, he knew there wasn't real desire there. He had come with his straight white teeth and his surety and his disdain for her, for her wealth, and he had said it, so I heard you're going to marry the Piltto boy, good for you. It's very sensible of you, he had said mockingly. You're making your parents very happy. It's time to settle down, isn't it. No more childish games, he'd said, and she'd pushed him. He'd put snow on her neck, like they were kids, and she'd yelped as if she'd minded, and both of them of course had been thinking about the summer—it had come back to her then and it came back to her now, she was blushing again, worse than before.

She was saved, more or less, by the appearance of her father, who opened the door and put his head in. "I've got them waiting here," he said, a little irritation in his voice, and Risten got up.

"You stay here," she said to her mother, "stay with Old Sussu, I'll help him," and her mother looked doubtful, Risten could see her thinking—she won't be careful enough and she'll spill the blood, she'll cut through the intestines, she'll nick the stomach . . . "I can do it," she said. What did her mother think would happen if she had married Mikkol, and gone to his siida? That she'd be wasting every slaughter? Ruining every pelt?

"I'd better come," her mother said, "there's sure to be a lot to do."

"I'll wait here," Old Sussu said.

"It'll be awhile, of course . . ."

"Oh, I'll nap if I need to," Old Sussu said, and Risten had to admire her for staying. She was sure to get the good marrow bone, and an eyeball, and she was sure to stay the night, sleeping near Risten's feet while she slept on Risten's pelts. But outside brought the relief of activity—there were the reindeer, four calves, on their sides like dogs in sleep, knives still held in their throats to keep the blood in. There was, thankfully, so much to do, and she hurried to fetch everything, the bowls for the blood, for the meat, the knives, and to set up the rack for her father to put the calves on, but even while she was helping her mother, blood warming her fingers and her wrists, the long arm of a tongue in her hand, she found herself thinking again of the warm and sturdy rock, the sun flashing off the sea below them in the fjord, and around them the calves, bawling for their mothers, the seagulls whining and whining around the sides of the sea.

4

THE NEWS OF BIETTAR'S REPENTANCE SPREAD LIKE A HEATHER FIRE, IN part because of the concomitant earthquake, but more likely because it was Biettar who had been awakened. Those who knew Biettar best credited the awakening to either a supreme drunkenness or to something uncanny within Biettar himself; those who knew Lars Levi best gave the glory to God, and spoke of it as a miracle, the miracle of Biettar repenting being greater, in many ways, than the earthquake itself. Almost no one remembered that something similar had already happened: two years before, a young woman had repented, during which a small earthquake had appeared, causing a painting of Jesus Christ in his final agony to fall from its hook, and frightening a bird in the rafters. But a woman repenting was of less significance. Moreover, Lars Levi had actually received his own repentance from a Sámi woman, whom people began to call Lappish Mary (though her name was not Mary), an acknowledgment of the foundational importance of her role, though no one really knew her particular story, how her extraordinary suffering had impressed Lars Levi (she'd been wed off as a girl to an older man who beat her, and yet had run off barefoot in the snow, trying to get to church), and turned his visit to offer Communion in a peasant's home into a greater Communion for himself. And so this line of grace, extending back through the hands of women, was easily eclipsed by the importance of a man having done the same thing.

As such, even though Lappish Mary was very much alive, no one went to see her, though now they came to see Biettar, who was at the parsonage as often as he was able, sometimes two or three days out of the week, a shocking amount, really, for a herder, though those who were not herders did not appreciate the profundity of this absence, and thus did not wonder what it meant. The relationship between the herders and the settlers was one that was managed by the Crown, which tracked each of its citizens via the State Church, which was to say, every church, so that everyone, Sámi and settler alike, was recorded at birth and at death as a parishioner of the Church, and moreover, could not be married outside of the Church. The Church was functionally the Crown, and its pastors not only the arm of God but the arm of the law. The two were even more intertwined in that tax-collecting happened on holy days, times of year when everyone was required to come to church or be fined for absenteeism.

But the whole thing was a muddle, since Sweden and Norway were technically a United Kingdom, ruled by a king of Swedish descent, Oskar I, but they still had separate parliaments, churches, armies, and even constitutions, so who "the Crown" was didn't change when you crossed one border or another, but the entire system of government did, and if this muddle were not muddied enough, there was still Finland to Sweden's east, except it wasn't Finland at all—the Finns were an ethnic peasant group that had never held any power, and were ruled over the centuries by either the Swedes or the Russians in turn; currently, it was a "Grand Duchy" of Russia, though precious few Russians lived there. To make matters worse, the various ethnic groups did not even share languages comprehensible to each other, though they still intermarried to some extent, and most of them solved the problem of belonging to different language groups by learning multiple languages, usually according to hierarchy, so that someone was who Sámi was likely to speak Sámi as well as Finnish as well as Swedish, but someone who was Swedish was not likely to speak Finnish, much less Sámi.

In some ways, Gárasavvon served as a prime example of the slippery nature of geography this far north, and the impracticality, moreover, of official ideas of borders. Technically speaking, Gárasavvon sat on the

Swedish side of the banks of the Tornio River, the path of which demarcated the border between Sweden and Russia; as such, you could stand at the church doors in Sweden and wave to someone in Russia, when in all likelihood that person would not really be Russian, but Finnish, unless, of course, the person was Sámi—which was, then, statistically more likely than an ethnic Finn this far north. As such, if you stood at the church doors in Sweden and waved across the border between Sweden and Russia, you were probably waving at a Sámi; a Sámi, that said, who probably spoke Finnish in addition to Sámi, and attended Gárasavvon Church in Sweden, and moreover probably spoke at least a bit of Swedish, and enough Norwegian to organize the sale of butter and reindeer.

The Sámi, by and large, had survived the centuries of being pushed north by seeming to go along with the rotating powers outwardly while inwardly they did whatever they wanted, even while they relied on the land itself to protect them: this far north, it tended to be too inconvenient if not impossible for others to bother very much with them. To varying degrees this worked—a treaty had been signed between Sweden and Norway a hundred years before, the Lapp Codicil, which granted them the freedom to be essentially neutral citizens, to not fight their wars, for instance, and to move their reindeer through their borders. In essence, then, they paid a tithe to be left alone, and they had even made the matter of attending church worthwhile, by turning the holy days into days of trade, sometimes even festivals, and by and large, they were in town as rarely as was really possible. As such, what was seen of them in town was such a small and insignificant part of their lives—it was like trying to understand Lars Levi himself by meeting him on a street in Stockholm. You would have met the man, but having no context for him besides his shabby clothes and his unkempt hair and his habit of speaking too loudly and intensely, it would not have occurred to you he was a pastor at all, nor that he spoke so many languages, and had once gifted hundreds of pressed flower and fauna to the king of France; most of all, you would not have thought that this was a man leading a spiritual revival, and that he was revered, and adored, by many.

In the same way that Lars Levi was impossible to understand outside of the context of his subarctic parish, the herders were impossible to understand if you only judged them by what they did in town, since it bore so little relation to what they did normally. Which is to say: the settlers in general, and Lars Levi's family in particular, were aware of the basic facts of being a Sámi herder, but they did not appreciate the significance of Biettar's frequent presence at the parsonage. Instead, Biettar appeared to them as someone who was, rightly, very invested in the preservation of his own soul, as well as someone who could prove very useful in the saving of other souls, but more than this he appeared to them as someone who increasingly took up a good deal of Lars Levi's already very limited time. He was talkative to the point of tiring them, especially since he seemed interested in talking, almost exclusively, about points of theology, but always in philosophical ways that they could not meet. He liked to sit in the rocking chair with a pipe that was even longer than Lars Levi's and make conversation by asking questions that in their broadness became impossible to answer satisfactorily. "What is sin?" he asked, one night, to the room, as if expecting the walls, blackened from floor to ceiling with soot in ever darker shades, to respond in kind.

Lars Levi, as was usual, had been reading to himself, a sermon he had written; when he was thinking like this he often did not hear anyone else speak at all.

"Biettar has a question," Willa said, when no one said anything. She was worried Biettar thought it was rude, that her father didn't appear to hear. Her impression of Biettar, gathered more intimately over the past two weeks, was largely one of admiration mixed with unease, and she avoided him out of a kind of respect.

"The turning away of the heart from God," her mother said. She was knitting, a woolen sweater for Lorens, and she managed to do this while rocking the baby's cradle with her foot at the same time.

"Can it be turned toward God and yet be sinful anyway?" Biettar asked. "Therefore to him that knoweth to do good, and doeth it not, to him it is sin."

"So a person knows if what he does is sin? Can a person sin without knowing it is sin?"

"Lars," her mother said, "Lars Levi. Biettar has a question."

"It's a matter of precognition," her father said, "pre-phenomenology. What we know before we know."

"Knowledge," Biettar said, "is a snowflake. You put your hand out and"—he flexed his fingers, opened his palm. He had the thick knuckles of the herders, and the thickened skin, and his hand seemed to open and close reluctantly.

"Yes, but—" her father said.

"Or," Biettar said, "you go to lasso it." He gestured by holding out his right hand, as if he had the lasso at the ready. He stood up, bending his left hand behind his back. He looked around the cabin and they might all have been the very reindeer he was looking for, whose ears he was eyeing. "And you stalk your reindeer, you walk the ground very carefully. You are thinking where it will go and where it will be, not where it is right now."

"You're saying that knowledge doesn't exist," her father persisted, having set the sheaf of papers down on his desk. "I'm saying that knowledge comes from other sources, from within ourselves. Our feelings, our irrationalities, our emotions, are knowledge. And if God—"

"You can throw with speed, but you will never catch it," Biettar said, interrupting, clearly annoying her father. "Knowledge will always be the calf that gets away."

Against this backdrop Willa was sewing. When she wasn't doing some other chore, it was what she was doing, sewing. There were plans in place, lassos to be thrown into the summer, when she would go with Nora south to Uppsala to stay with her mother's cousins. It was understood without ever being said that it would be very useful if they met someone, an educated man especially, since they didn't have many chances to meet men here at all, excepting impoverished Finnish farmers and itinerant Lapp herders, and as to the first, they were simply too poor and uneducated, and as to the second, while her father loved to say that there was no better man than a Lapp, this did not include the possibility of marrying Lapps who did Lapp things; a careful circle had been drawn in which they were to be kind and gracious to her father's parishioners, who after all were so much in need, but this pity did not extend toward joining with them in anything beyond a spiritual alliance—after all, the children of Lars Levi were educated, more or less, in patches, by their father, and he believed they belonged with someone like them, perhaps a verger's wife, or a sexton's, or a school-teacher's, and at all costs they could not, must not, return to the poverty of his own childhood, and anyway, what good was a settler's daughter to a Lapp? What could she do beyond keep a house he did not live in? And what could she do for a farmer, but make him feel badly about who he was—what man wanted a wife who knew more than he did?

Probably, though, Willa mused, she would get to Uppsala and Kare-suando would become a dingy little church-village and the Lapps would become the wild natives of her childhood, and her father the madman missionary, and any skills she had with trapping or with skinning or with milking cows would be useless, and even embarrassing.

So she had settled on making do. She and Nora were sewing new dresses for Uppsala, dresses that were naturally not at all what women there would be wearing, but it was good for her character to not fit in, to not look as if she was aspiring to that kind of vanity. She would not aspire. She would root down low, and she picked up the dress's hem to look at it in the light. The stitches were small and evenly placed. She was the kind of woman who, when she made a mistake, went back for it. "Just keep going," her mother said, but Willa never did. Her mother thought it was vain and even crass to care so much how a dress looked, the dress was an object with a function, and its function was to, as modestly as possible, delineate femininity while providing warmth. Anything beyond that was a sinner's errand.

It took a moment for Willa to understand that something practical was being discussed—Biettar was wondering if they should invite Henrik over for Christmas dinner. He was saying, if Henrik stopped selling liquor to the Lapps, wouldn't that solve most of their problems? Willa could see the discomfort on her mother's face at the very thought of it; to her mother, there was hardly a worse human than Henrik, and she did not feel it was appropriate to even have him in the house, and as such, he had never been. He combined all of her mother's least favorite qualities: he was here by virtue of nepotism as a nephew of the dean, probably installed in part to keep an eye on the goings-on of their father; he had a propensity to drink;

an outward vanity (he was always touching his hair and straightening out his vest); and of course, his greed—he had come to Karesuando and wasted no time raising prices. Then there was how he had never shown the slightest sign of awakening, nor the smallest bit of remorse about selling so much liquor to the Lapps, but most of all, he was from the south, he was not like them. When they saw him, he tended to complain, a southerner's weak habit, and they all expected he would not last very long—another winter here at most.

"I suppose," her mother said, after an extended silence that very effectively indicated her displeasure with the idea, "it would be the Christian thing to do. What do you say, Lars?"

But Lars Levi had already returned to the sermon in his hand. He nodded, but at what, it wasn't clear, and yet the thing was decided. Willa looked at Nora, they looked at each other over the dresses on their laps. Everything is different now, Willa thought, for what must have been the tenth time in two weeks, everything is changed, but she did not stop to think why it was Biettar would have wanted Henrik there at all; it did not occur to her even that they knew each other; it did not occur to her that there was any context to the dinner at all beyond her own.

For his part, Henrik was quite nervous to be invited at all, it seemed so out of the ordinary. Absurd to be nervous, maybe, around people who were otherwise so far below him in the social ladder, but still, Nora had always had a nervous-making effect on him and it was a chance, anyway, to show his refinement, how well he ate, how well he spoke—was he or was he not, after all, the nephew of the dean? The nephew of her father's superior? He sensed Nora liked that. It was how he had made her out to be in his mind, that she cared about these things, about sophistication, that she felt trapped here, among the natives. He dressed much more carefully than he ever did, trying to put on a waistcoat he had worn to a Christmas service just a year ago in Stockholm, but which now, he saw, couldn't be buttoned shut. He fretted, and at last chose a shirt with a starched collar, and on top of this a woolen suit-jacket and fine silk cravat, cranberry red, in the spirit of Christmas. He even shined his shoes with the tin of bear fat.

At their cabin door he knocked and waited. Who knocks, they all thought, why doesn't he just come in? Nora went to get him, feeling nervous herself, aware of the way Henrik looked at her as he passed her his hat and coat, which she hung on a hook cleared for this purpose. She liked that he looked at her like that even as she didn't like it; she wanted the flattery but not the responsibility of having encouraged his flattery. She walked past him, feeling his eyes on her back, but when she turned around he was just standing there, not following, and she watched his eyes move all over, watched his eyes pronounce, you live like rabbits in a hole, and she blushed.

It was difficult for Henrik to find something to say. Normally at this point he would have said something like, what a nice home, but he couldn't bring himself to say it, to have any other feeling besides how small the cabin was. In Uppsala he had always walked into a home with a sense immediately of what everything had cost, how fine of a quality this or that thing was, and here he was struck by the fact there was nothing to examine. There were no extra things. There were no curtains on the windows, no paintings or hangings on the walls, which were merely wooden logs stuffed with tar through which, he could tell, the wind made it through. A large rag rug covered the wooden planks of the floor, but even the rug was grim and darkly colored. The only decoration, if you could call it that, was meat and hardtack hanging from poles along the ceiling, and candles kept in plain wooden candleholders. Otherwise the room's use was confined to benches that were built into the walls, and a desk covered in papers and books, more books stacked on the floor beside the desk—Henrik could make out titles in French and Latin, and even some Greek. The sight of all of this was masked somewhat, though not actually mercifully, by all of the smoke that leaked generously out of the hearth and into his already watering eyes.

"Everyone is in the—this way," Nora said, and she led him from what must have been the living room of sorts to what was a kitchen of sorts, or dining room—here was the table, a large wooden thing built of three thick planks, on which was set three large bowls, presumably of food, though for chairs there were old church pews, pushed up against the table. A small cooking area was behind the table, and there was a large basin that must have served as a sink, and there was another hearth in here from which hung a long iron chain and a thick iron pot. But it was more difficult in this room to see anything, because the room was so full of children, Lars Levi's children, who all stared at him in a way his mother would have despised. There were so many of them, they massed together into a single brown-headed blur. And in the corner, to Henrik's astonishment, was Biettar. My God, the man had nerve. Slaughter-time come and gone and nothing from him to pay his debt, nothing, not even a skinny old doe.

"Hello, then," Henrik said, nodding at Nora's mother. He would have used her name, Mrs. Laestadius, or even Brita Kajsa, or Brita—no one seemed to stand on formality here—except he sensed whatever he chose would be wrong.

"Merry Christmas," Brita said, in a tone that contained politeness and not a whit more. He could feel how much she didn't like him. That's fine, he tried to say in his smile back, I don't like you much, either.

He jumped a little when a door opened from the back, and Lars Levi appeared. So there was the bedroom—he glimpsed a single bed, chests, drawers. Where did everyone else sleep?

"Mr. Lindström," Lars Levi said, almost formally.

"Rikki," one of the little girls tittered.

Their mother looked at her and the laugh went out.

Lars Levi, as if this had been enough fanfare, moved to the head of the table and the children sorted themselves into the pews, Biettar taking the other head of the table as if this were perfectly natural, and no one indicating to Henrik that he should sit anywhere in particular. In another house he might have angled for a seat by Nora, but he went instead for the spot nearest where he already was, which left him wedged on one side by Willa and on the other by the brother who never spoke at all.

Lars Levi said a prayer, it must have gone on for ten or twelve minutes, he barely spoke about Christmas at all; he referred, several times, to those who worshipped the whiskey dragon, and those who drank the Devil's piss, and Henrik began to wonder: had he been invited to be chastised? Was this dinner some kind of Trojan horse, in which he would not be allowed to leave until he threw himself on the floor, crying out to be saved? He looked at Biettar to check this theory but the man's bowed head indicated nothing at all.

THE STEW, TO no one's surprise, was reindeer, but there were carrots in it, and potatoes, and there was bread made from rye, and butter. Henrik was dangerously low on potatoes, given the poor harvest, and not for the first time he wondered, what good was a land that couldn't even grow a potato?

Outside the wind blew so that the shutters, though they were fastened with wooden bolts, seemed in danger of coming off their hinges, and the smoke began to issue more fervently from the hearth, giving the whole dinner the aspect of taking place at least partially outdoors.

"Henrik," Lars Levi said, from across the table, "did I tell you already about my father?" Henrik shook his head, his mouth full of stew. The broth was thick, almost viscous. Clearly the meat had been cooked in butter. It was soft and rich. He could have eaten bowls of it. "He melted reindeer hooves into glue," Lars Levi went on, "and when I was born my mother strapped me to her back and skied forty miles to have me baptized. In a blizzard."

"A horse can barely do forty miles in a day," Henrik said appreciably.

"Oh, it's a common enough feat around here," Lars Levi said lightly, as if Henrik had noticed the wrong part. A silence fell that no one seemed to know how to fix. Henrik watched Biettar, who, he noticed, had combed his hair back and trimmed his beard. He was wearing the blue woolen tunics the Lapps wore, with the embroidery around the edges, and his was particularly fancy, so that the embroidery ran across his shoulders, giving him epaulets of a sort. So, Henrik thought, he has money enough for clothes, but not for me. What was it he had to do, to get Biettar to pay? Did he really have to go out to the herds on his own, like the last storekeeper did?

"Tell us, then, Henrik," Brita said, "what does your father do?"

Henrik paused, caught off guard. Up here, no one ever showed curiosity about him; he hardly ever had a chance to tell anyone about his father, about what it was to be a Lindström.

"Well," Henrik said, grateful and even a little excited, "my father was a shopkeeper, textiles mostly, he died a number of years ago, but it turned out it was my mother who had a real talent for trade, and actually, the business did much better after she took over." He wasn't sure how to indicate how well the business had done, he did not know what markers would mean what to these people, and it seemed like the normal rules of how to indicate one's status in society were utterly absent. He had a feeling he could explain what street the shop was on, and it would mean nothing; he could explain, even, that it was his mother's side of the family that was connected to the seats of power, she had just had the misfortune (as she always put it) to need to be married off quickly so her more beautiful but younger sister could marry much better than she, and while Henrik's father hadn't had any nobility about him he'd had wealth, even if it was new.

"Once we even had the royal governess—Countess Taube—in our shop," he added, but this appeared to also have no effect. Still, he went on, feeling like a soldier in battle, cresting over the next front against any self-interest. "She bought four yards of jacquard silk, had it imported from France," he said lamely, aware that he should stop, but he couldn't. "A sort of paisley design on it," he said. "And velvet. Velvet border."

"I see," Brita said.

"So you must have some appreciation for the gáktis around here, then," Lars Levi said.

Henrik made a noise that expressed how he felt, which was that he did not know what Lars Levi was referring to in the least.

They all looked at him, even the children, like he was quite stupid.

"The gáktis," Lars Levi repeated, as if saying it again would confer a new knowledge via repetition alone. He pointed an elbow toward Biettar.

"You can tell from a gákti," Brita said, "where someone is from. By the style, by how much embroidery is on it, by the coloring. If the embroidery is around the shoulders or not."

"Oh, yes, the tunic things, those costumes," Henrik said, "and sometimes you even wear the funny hat with the pompoms on it, don't you, Biettar?"

Biettar looked at him like he didn't understand, but Henrik knew he understood.

"The word for *costume*," Lars Levi said, when Biettar clearly intended not to answer, "would imply something that is worn in order to pretend to be a thing, no?"

"Well, of——"

"There's a lot to appreciate about the Sámi," Lars Levi said. Henrik glanced at Biettar, to see what he made of this defense, but Biettar appeared to be looking at the shutters, or in any case somewhere behind the children.

"It's a whole new world up here, isn't it," Henrik said blandly. He saw his error now, that the goal was to approach the matter of all things native with reverence, deservedly or not.

"Did you know," Lars Levi went on, "in Sámi, there are over two hundred words for *snow* and *ice*?" He gave no opportunity for anyone to answer. "There's a wonderful word for *snow* in the northern dialect—the moment when the snow falls so hard you can't tell the difference between the sky and the land—at that precise moment, there's a word for that."

"*Borga*," Willa said, using the soft pronunciation of the Lapps. "And when you go outside and the snow is new and is sitting on the fingers of the trees, that's called *ńikvit*."

"And when the snow is crusty and holds your weight——" Lars Levi said.

"And when the snow is crusty and doesn't hold your weight," Willa said. "And even months are named after how the reindeer look," she added. How annoying, Henrik thought, why does Willa have to tell me everything. He resented this information coming from her, she was too pleased with herself for knowing it.

"Well," Lars Levi said, clearly thinking about it, "August, yes, and October."

"And April," Willa said, "which means, when the snow is as hard as a table. That's when they can move north on it, to the sea."

"As I was saying, it's a whole new world up here," Henrik repeated. He tried to say this in a way that conveyed both politeness and mild disinterest.

"What were you expecting?" Biettar asked. The fact of his speaking did not seem to surprise anyone else but it surprised Henrik, perhaps because thus far Biettar had not acknowledged his presence.

"Expecting?"

"When you decided to move here," Biettar said, "from the south, what did you think you would meet?"

"Yes, I've been wondering that, too," Nora said, and Henrik reveled in the warmth of her interest.

"Oh," Henrik said, "you know, that, that the Lapps would be, well, that the Lapps would be heathens. Wild," he said, trying to soften the word in Biettar's presence. "That you would all live in, in, dirty tents, that kind of thing. Also that they would have shamans and beat drums, go into trances. Witchcraft," he went on, "I heard a lot about witchcraft. I was hoping to get some witchcraft myself," he joked, but the joke went utterly flat.

"And I heard that you were a very unusual kind of preacher," he went on. "My uncle's the dean of the diocese, this diocese, you know," he said, "on my mother's side, of course, but anyway," he said, suddenly realizing he was about to say more than he should, or maybe he already had. "But anyway," he repeated, clearing his throat diligently, like something was truly stuck in there, "then I also heard, you know, rumors," he said, "the other day, some Lapp came into the store one night, very drunk. Wasn't my doing," he joked, but again, no one laughed. "He told me, he said, there are still shamans, they're just secret-like, they don't tell anyone, the Lapps keep it all to themselves, and they just say they're Christian but they're nothing like it at all. The shamans still beat their drums." He was describing it all wrong, he wasn't conveying how Simmon had said it. Simmon had said it as if he were trying to scare Henrik, to make Henrik afraid of the troll-drums and the witch doctors and what-have-you, and in fact it had left Henrik feeling spooked, but when Henrik said it now it all sounded childish and stupid.

Across the table, Nora and Willa looked at each other. The children were tittering again, the adults were stone. Biettar had stopped looking at Henrik, he might not even have been listening at all. It bothered Henrik enormously, that Biettar wouldn't pay attention, that he showed no respect for Henrik at all, when Henrik was the one extending him credit. Biettar ought to have been obsequious, doing whatever he could to stay in Henrik's good graces, and, anyway, had they not had many a drink together? Had Henrik not poured him many a glass? Mostly silently, but still.

"How very interesting," Nora said, because it seemed like no one would say anything else.

"Then this Lapp went on and said," Henrik said, remembering Simmon's face when he'd said it, how Simmon had been standing up until this point in the story, and then had turned his face away. At the time he'd thought very little of it, and anyway he'd already heard a number of highly implausible stories from Simmon and this could have been another one, but now, sitting here with Biettar across the table, a little thrill came through him: what if it were true? And what if he, of whom they thought so little, whom they thought knew nothing, was the one to know everything? "He said that you used to be a shaman, Biettar, and you had your own drum. You were a kind of medicine man. But now you would have to burn your drum, now that you were saved."

Henrik was pleased with the effect this had. Biettar turned his head slowly toward him, and Nora and Willa both set down their spoons, they looked at each other and back at him. Brita put on a face that said, well, isn't that amusing.

Lars Levi was chewing, slowly. He wiped his mouth with a yellowing handkerchief and he said evenly, "Well, they used to burn them at the stake, anyone who was said to be a shaman, and they burned their drums, too. Made them recant and swear they were Christian, so the drums started, naturally enough, disappearing, and no one claimed to be a shaman after a while. They put them on trial, too. The last recorded trial of a shaman was in, oh . . . end of the seventeenth century, 1690, I believe, a shaman who claimed to have a few powers but you know, even the records show no one thought he was much of one. An interesting case, you should read it. In fact, he was supposed to be executed but then the morning they went to get him for his execution he had already been murdered. But it's all gone now, that was a long time ago, and even then all that kind of thing was dying out."

"Well," Henrik said, though he found his face was heating from shame, he sensed that everyone at the table knew he had believed it and was now being taken to task, "I didn't imagine any of it to actually be true, of course. It was more, well, what a story, eh," he said weakly. He wanted to move the conversation on, and yet didn't want to look like he was avoiding it. "But what did they do with the drums anyway?"

"What do you mean?"

"I mean, why a drum?"

"Oh, they would beat on them, rhythmically, I think, to induce a kind of trance. They would hit them with a little hammer. If you wanted to know something in particular they had these drawings on them—you can go look at the drums in a museum, you know, in Stockholm, I believe, also in France—and anyway they would paint drawings on the drum, little man figures, or reindeer, the sun, a tree, even a church. So you might bring the shaman some silver, a coin, something like that, and the shaman would place the silver on the drum, and beat the drum, and wherever the coin went, that would tell the shaman something. Of course they also had healers, guvhllárs, they called them. They mostly used knives. Knives to heal, how's that for a paradox."

"I see," Henrik said, "yes, just like some old Gypsy woman reading tea leaves in front of the carriage house in Uppsala, or some old Finnish witch who will heal you with her brews."

"Yes, like that, I suppose," Lars Levi said. "Though here, you know, they also have their sieidis, and they could burn the drums but there isn't a good way to get rid of sieidis. Usually very large rocks that seem out of place somewhere, you've probably passed one without knowing it, or very dramatic land formations of some kind or other, Saana Mountain, actually, you must have passed it on your way here from Tromsø, they say that's one. They went there to make offerings, antlers, reindeer—"

"Humans, I heard," Henrik said.

"Nonsense. Utter rot. That just tells you the perversity of whoever made that one up. But they took the stones very seriously, they prayed there, before they went to the sea, for a safe journey, for good weather, for good luck, and so on. They might have yoiked there, gone into a kind of trance themselves, who knows. You know what yoiking is, I take it."

Again the tone of speaking to an idiot—Henrik nodded. "The kind of shouting they do," he said, "singing,"

"Na na na, nana na," one of the little girls began to sing, in a strained voice, her head thrown back and waving around, eyes roving around in her head.

"It's nothing to joke around about," Brita cut in, so sharply the girl—Lisa, maybe—looked down at her hands at once. "It's calling the Devil," she went on, very seriously. "They still do it, we've all heard it one way or another. Very eerie sound," she said, "gives me the shudders."

"I see," Henrik said. There was the sound of their spoons, scraping on the bowls.

"When you sing, you sing about something," Biettar said gently. He was looking at the little girl who had been pretending to yoik. "Yoiking, you yoik a thing. You yoik a mountain, or a person. Some yoiks have been around for hundreds of years. The same person being yoiked, still alive in the yoik, hundreds of years later."

"Well, no one does it very much anymore, do they," Lars Levi cut in, "but old people like Old Sussu, it comes out sometimes."

"Old Sussu," Willa said. "Remember—"

"We remember," Lars Levi said.

"What was it?" Henrik asked.

"Oh," Lars Levi said. "It's not so interesting as that. Well, once Old Sussu went to see the merchant here, the one here before you, and his two servants threw her out of the house. Well, so the story goes, she yoiked and she threatened the clerks, and she said, the dogs of Karesuando won't bark at you next year. And that same year the two clerks drowned."

"Really," Henrik said. Henrik had heard the servants had drowned, but he'd just been envious of the man having two servants instead of only Simmon, who after all was less of a servant and more of the town drunk. It hadn't occurred to him that Old Sussu had anything to do with his bad luck. Still, it was a good story, he would have to go home and write it down, send it off to his uncle.

"Of course," Lars Levi said, "it's just a story."

"Well, if you ask me—" Henrik started to say.

"There's another story about her," Biettar suddenly interrupted. They all fell silent. He was looking at Willa, across the table from him. The effect was odd, like the rest of them weren't there. "Sussu was out on the migration, and three blackbirds landed on a drying rack and began to eat the meat. Sussu knew it meant three people in the siida would die, and she warned all of them, but when the next day her nephew was kicked in the head by a bull and died, and then her sister, the boy's mother, was found hanging from the drying pole inside the lávvu, and then her husband got caught out in a snowstorm and never came back, no one wanted her there anymore, and that year was the last year she ever went to the sea. People started to feel like it was her fault, for predicting it."

"But despite how interesting this may all sound," Lars Levi said, with a prominent pause, "I have lived here all my life and I have seen very little in the way of magic. Very, very little." It was a declarative sentence; the subject was finished.

"But Henrik," Nora said, looking at him, "I'm sure there's a lot you understand now that you didn't before. When I go south," she said, blushing for some reason he couldn't catch, "I'm sure I'll feel like I don't understand anything at all, even if it's the same country." Was she blushing, he wondered, for maneuvering so agilely to spare his feelings?

"Oh, of course, many things I get now," he said. "When I first got here, I didn't even know what a siida was. Someone would come into the store and say they belonged to such and such siida, but their last name didn't even match the name of the siida, and I never knew what to do. Couldn't figure out how to organize my books for months. Now I know, of course," he said, glad for the opportunity to demonstrate, "that siidas are just loose collections of people who herd together, and they aren't even really named officially, it's all very unofficial, the way everything is around here." He laughed, suddenly nervous, aware as he tried to explain he didn't fully understand it himself at all.

"You know what the ástahat is?" Biettar asked. Henrik shook his head.

"The ástahat is the stick you use to poke the fire. It doesn't mean it's the same stick that you bring everywhere. It's the stick that you tend to use for a given fire, but it can change. The ástahat is a"—he waved a hand—"a thing that exists in the moment of use." He said this like it made a beautiful amount of sense. Henrik nodded and he looked at Nora, hoping she would look at him and say, I don't quite get it, either, but she wasn't looking at him, and he thought, I've done it again. She's embarrassed for me. What he wouldn't give for a little touch of vodka or brännvin, something, to steal the shame from him for a minute. Why did he ever open his mouth? Why did he ever try to speak at all? Better, he thought, to seem wise, by staying silent, like the Finns.

"A thing that exists in the moment of use," Henrik repeated, as if he admired the statement very much, though he hated it. But just then he met Nora's eyes and he stopped minding that he would be there all night, and that the coffee was coffee, and although he was desperately bored when they moved into the front room and Lars Levi began to preach again, he consoled himself with staring at the back of Nora's neck, at her hair, which she had braided and pinned up in a wreath on the back of her head. Several times he coughed, trying to get her attention, but she didn't move, like she was focusing so hard on not giving him any attention that she meant something by the absence of it. In this Henrik was, in fact, right—all night Nora had been keenly aware of Henrik, of his very presence at the table, at how he held his spoon like a delicate object, how his jacket was so finely tailored. She wasn't even sure what material it was—it was fine and gray, and so tightly woven. He had cuff links, even, probably of real silver, and a small ring on his pinkie finger that embarrassed her. He appeared to have tried much too hard to look nice, he had combed his weakly blond and thin hair, he had shined his shoes. All of this she had noticed, but mostly she had noticed him noticing her, it was the double consciousness cursed upon all women, of living in the gaze of the men around her as well as, and before even, her own. The exertion of it enlivened her; she enjoyed the difficulty of preparing to be seen at all times, from any angle.

She was aware, too, of her mother's eyes, which followed her and Henrik both. Even when he said his goodbyes, and left, she looked up for precisely the amount of time that would convey politeness and nothing more. But it was disappointing now that it was all over, she wanted it to last, the excitement of his attention, and afterward she went with Willa to the sauna. Willa sat where she always sat, where the steam would hit last but hottest, and Nora sat where she always sat, in the opposite corner, her knees tucked into her forehead.

"Did you notice anything about Henrik?" Nora asked.

"Notice what," Willa asked, "what an outlander he is?"

Willa threw more water on the rocks, and the rocks seethed with pleasure. When the sauna grew so hot that they felt the heat on their teeth, and their hair hurt their backs, they hurried into the snow. Willa rubbed the snow on her arms and her chest, but Nora stood there, watching her own arms and chest smoke. She looked at the river, she wondered if anyone ever saw them like this, from the other bank.

Inside the sauna they ladled boiling water from the kettles into buckets, mixed it with the cold water. They soaped themselves.

"Do you think there are really still shamans?" Willa asked.

"You would listen to Henrik?" Nora laughed. She was bitter that Willa hadn't said anything about Henrik showing interest in her, and she was worried it seemed, in bringing up Henrik, that it would look like she was interested in him. "He doesn't know anything," Nora said, "he just goes around spreading rumors. He's worse than Old Sussu that way."

"I guess so," Willa said. She seemed disappointed. Nora watched Willa close her eyes as she poured the remains of her bucket over her head. She had a soft wobble of stomach but the rest of her, even her large hips, were muscular and wide. Nora's own body seemed so thin in comparison, skeletal and weak. Willa's leg was lifted and opened in such a way that Nora saw the patch of hair between her legs and could not look away. It seemed almost ugly, her sister's sex. It seemed truthful.

"What?" Willa said, catching her looking. She set her leg on the low bench and picked at a scab.

"Nothing," Nora said. She could feel the wind, coming under the sauna door, reaching its way to her feet. It was so greedy, the wind, there was nothing it did not want for itself.

AS OLD SUSSU HAD PREDICTED, THE WINTER WAS TURNING OUT TO BE A difficult one. It had been a lemming summer, and the dogs had gone wild chasing them, snapping their little bones in one swallow, and now the wolves were here, and wolverines, and lynxes, all of them padding around, leaving carcasses half-chewed on a trail. The herders were half-crazed with not sleeping, and the women were herding now, too, watching along with the men on the slopes, everyone smoking to keep awake and warm, everyone's eyelashes freezing shut and their urine turning to ice before it hit the ground. To Ivár it seemed as if all of his mistakes in life had caught up to him at once, and he was being punished for it in one go—his father came and went, and Ivár had lost two more reindeer, a young doe and her calf. It was a needless loss and a loss they couldn't afford, and he tried desperately to avoid the ruinous calculations while he stood on the slope and squatted, waiting for the blood to run back up to his head.

The calculation was thus: Ivár and his father had between them enough reindeer to stay alive, enough to eat, but not enough to support, say, a wife for Ivár, or to pay another herder to help them with anything. To stay afloat, to keep from starvation, the general allowance was that for every person you needed twenty reindeer per year (some said fifteen)—

that was the barest minimum on which to subsist, it accounted for the herd to keep going from one year to the next while still allowing for the slaughter of the reindeer you ate and the reindeer you sold for supplies, for flour or salt or needles, for a tent-cloth, but even at that number there was no room for anything extra whatsoever, and it was not a number that allowed for the herd to grow, only subsist. Given that reindeer were not merely a measurement of wealth but wealth itself, life itself, the size of the herd was a sensitive topic; it was rude, for instance, to ask someone else how large their herd was, in precisely the same way it was rude to ask someone how much money they had, and as such there were those who did not want others to see their herds—this was, in part, what had led Biettar to want to break off his herd from his brothers'; his own herd had been dwindling too much in comparison, and he could not stop noticing the difference, how few reindeer went by with his own mark on their ears. And so, even though it was wiser and easier to herd them together, he'd insisted on separating his herd out.

At this particular juncture in time, January 1852, the month of bitterest cold and darkness, of course Ivvár knew precisely how many reindeer they had, though he did not say the number aloud. The main point was that it was far too few, especially since, if he was right about how much they owed Rikki (he was wrong, he was well short of Rikki's own inflated number), they owed him the reindeer they ought to have been using for new coats and boots; and, they needed to reserve a male and castrate it to become a draft reindeer, and he guessed they would owe Rikki that reindeer, too. Why didn't Rikki just come for them? How much longer could this game go on? Of course now it wasn't a good time of year to slaughter anymore, the males had lost their antlers and most of their summer weight, and the females were growing thin, and their coats, while thick, were already beginning to go patchy in places.

He was freed from thinking any further on this predicament by the arrival of a visitor, whom he knew to be a visitor from the first, because she arrived of all things in a sledge, a sledge on which she had hung bells as if she were going to church, or as if she were (the irony of this was not lost on him) a man, coming to ask for his hand in marriage, Risten's countenance, though, was very cheerful, almost lighthearted, like there was nothing really of note in her visit, as if she hadn't planned this so as to arrive precisely when his father was away. Of course she had planned this, though she didn't admit to it, and he didn't ask, and instead they both behaved as if it were natural for her to have come by, even though by now he and his father were a good day's ride from her siida, at the very least.

But this awkwardness was dwarfed by his embarrassment of his herd, so that while she chattered the could hardly speak, he could only see her avoiding looking around at his herd, avoiding counting them, as if to say, don't worry, I haven't even noticed how small your herd is, though of course she had. She was too smart a herder to miss it, and anyway it was the kind of thing you could feel, the size of a herd, without looking—the reindeer behaved differently when they were herded in different numbers, and when it was smaller like this they tended to be tamer, less cautious.

Over and over again he thought: I should not have gone to see her. But she was here, and of course he had to invite her inside and make her coffee, he could do nothing else, especially with the herd as calm (and small) as this. So he invited her in, and he regretted everything, regretted how he had not bothered to clean his bowl with boiling water, and how everything was turned out of the rucksacks and chests so that it was difficult to find a spot to sit down, on his father's side of the fire as well as on his own. Oh, it was very embarrassing, and everything being out on display meant that she could see, moreover, how what was spilled out all over was falling apart. The butter box had a crack in it, the top of the wooden chest was bent askew over the bottom, the woolen underclothes hanging to dry had holes in them, and right there in front of her was one of his father's shirts with the hole so large at the armpit you could have put your head through it. Unfortunately, she also looked very beautiful, her cheeks were just the right amount of red, and her sealskin hat ringed with white fox fur made her seem sweeter than he knew her to be, almost soft.

What made her think to come? What made her think this was a good idea?

It was a question that Risten was now posing to herself, too, in part because she did feel taken aback by the state of things in the lávvu, though not so much as Ivvár supposed—they could get a new kettle, a new butter box, all of it. So what that it was all in shambles. Didn't she have enough reindeer for them both?

But she knew better than to say this, letting him make her coffee, and since he seemed shy she talked, but the more she said about how well her mother was doing, and how Old Sussu had come to visit them, and how her uncle had got himself caught out in a storm and didn't make it back for three days, and so on, the quieter Ivvár seemed to get. It was making her nervous. Surely he had heard about Mikkol. If he hadn't, then maybe he didn't know why she was there—was that possible?

"By the time he got back," Risten was saying, "we thought he was gone for good, my father had gone to look for him but couldn't even find tracks, and two days, all right, but three days. And then we come to find out all along he'd been waiting out the storm in some settler's hay shed, by the time he got back he still had hay in his hair. And so while we worried he was sleeping on hay!"

"So there's settlers up there, then?"

"They've been there a few winters now. The Peltonens."

"Hope it wasn't the same Peltonens as brought my father to court," he said.

"Was that them?"

He shrugged. "It doesn't matter."

"I guess you heard the news about me, then?" Risten asked.

Ivvár took out his pipe and his little pouch of tobacco. He took off his mittens and he shook the tobacco into the pipe.

"My father was in town," he said, "so, he heard." He was aware this wasn't kind. She was hurt, though aiming to not show it. This wasn't what she'd been expecting. She had her coffee in her hands, and when she moved it in front of her face the steam shrouded her expression and he wondered if she were hiding tears. He looked away. An anxiety of the purest sort was rising in him. He could only think: this must end.

"I should go out," he said, finally. "Check on the herd," he added. He took a stick burning on one end from the fire and lit his pipe, and then he got up, knowing how rude it was, cruel really, to not even invite her out to the herd with him, and to leave her here, but he could not bear this farce any longer. Stupidly, it had not occurred to him Risten would be so bold as to come outside with him, but she was, she was actually following him, and he realized this was even worse than being inside, because now she could do the count, precisely, she would see the worst of it. Walking up the hill the shame ran in his face and in his ears; he had no sense of it being cold outside at all, the shame was warmth enough.

If I had something to drink, he thought, I could blame it on that, I could shout, go home, and it would be done.

He lay down on his side in the snow and she lay down near him, so that their heads were near each other though their legs pointed in opposite directions, and as he packed the snow in behind him she packed the snow in behind her.

Did she see it as invitational, that he was lying down? Was there something erotic, conscious or not, in what he was doing?

"Your calves have nice, long legs," Risten said.

"Well, I guess they're not all dead yet," he said. He inhaled the smoke from his pipe and he sent it out through his nose and he tried to think of something nicer to say.

"The wolverines are beastly this winter," she said.

He nodded.

"I came across one, actually. Actually, it was just after we'd seen each other."

"Is that so."

"I hit it with my ski pole."

"Well, you're Risten Tomma," he said, glad to not be looking at her as he spoke.

"What does that mean?"

He didn't answer, and he sat up, as if there were something he'd spotted going on in the herd, though there wasn't.

"I don't know."

"You do know."

"It's not a good time, right now," he said, at last.

"For what?"

"I have to go to town," he said.

"Oh," she said. "Who will——" she started to say, and stopped.

"You can stay and warm up," he said. "There's meat in the pot. I won't be back until tomorrow."

"You'll stay in town?"

"With my father," he said, realizing this was possible as he said it.

"Oh," she said, "so you'll——"

But he was walking away, and he thought maybe this time she would be too embarrassed to follow, and he was right, and even though he took his time packing inside the lávvu and then took his time harnessing Borga, she stayed, like hired help.

He wasn't sure if he'd ever been this rude in his life.

But he had to be clear about it. She couldn't do this, she could not think anything was possible between them, because it wasn't, it never had been. She was too good for him. He had nothing to bring to her but bad luck and debt, and the more he thought about it the more he wanted a drink, he wanted to get to town and go straight to Rikki's, and that was what he was going to do. He did not so much as wave goodbye at Risten, though he nodded at her, once, and she nodded back, and he thought: as soon as I'm gone she'll disappear.

He was glad, in a way, for the long ride to town, though he would never have gone tonight otherwise—away from the protection of the hills the wind was high and kept picking the top layer of snow up and throwing it at him. Ivvár was more tired than he'd realized, and it was only the wind and the pull of the rein in his hands that kept him awake, and when the steeple appeared, fatigue came over him like a weight, and by the time they made it up the bank and he saw the other sledges, other reindeer, already tied up to posts and to trees, reindeer grazing out in the field, he was a little delirious—he couldn't figure out why so many people would be there. At last it came to him: it was Sunday. Of all things, he had come on a Sunday morning! What bad luck.

He tried to keep his head down as he tied Borga up and gave him something to eat. Borga was panting audibly, like he was trying to get Ivvár's attention, and when Ivvár looked at him Borga showed him his doleful cow-eyes, and blinked with his thick white eyelashes, and Ivvár had the unsettling feeling Borga knew what he was doing and was worried for him. It was the kind of thought his father would tell him not to have about a reindeer, but Ivvár had it anyway, and before he left he gave him a mushroom from his pocket, saved for such a moment. If he'd been alone he would have patted him on the neck and said, it's all right, Bobo, I'm coming back, but that was the thing about being in town, suddenly you saw yourself how everyone saw you. He felt especially watched right now—Sussu, he thought, I bet it's Old Sussu watching me. Of course Old Sussu would want to talk to him, to tell him he should go fix things up with that Tomma girl. That was the kind she was, always telling other people what to do, as if nervous they would make her mistakes, and then she would say something very indirect about how he spent his time, and in the indirectness her point would be clear: he should be visiting her more. He should go and see a lonely old woman, who after all had promised his mother to watch over him.

He walked to Rikki's with his head down. He would not be waylaid or guilted out of his purpose, and he opened the door with more force than was needed. Inside the counter and the shelves and even the floor were covered in things you could buy, and as always he was overwhelmed by all the things he could not buy, all the things he could not have, red and blue and plaid and silk and woolen shawls hanging from ropes, barrels of syrup and tar, twine, cotton thread, skeins of wool, needles, scissors, coffee beans and even a coffee grinder, goose feathers by the pound, sugar, flour, leather already softened and leather not softened, linen, muslin, stacks of pelts, mittens (sealskin or wool), hats (sealskin, fox fur, wool), everything available in the Sámi style and in the settler style, so that nearly everything appeared twice, knives for slaughtering and knives for eating, a long-gun, a pistol—Ivvár was torn between his desire to stare, to touch everything, and his desire to appear as if he wanted none of it. He stood there, instead, trying to not rove his eyes around, looking steadfastly at Rikki sitting on his stool behind the counter, like he always was, some book or newspaper or sheaf of papers always in front of him.

"Ivvár," Rikki said, in acknowledgment. He looked jumpy, or nervous, and this gave Ivvár some strength. He remembered what his father always said, the less you say, the more they'll say. Henrik bent down below the counter and brought up his record book and opened it. It seemed like a nervous habit of his, since whether or not you asked he would take it out and look at it, and frown.

"One bottle of brännvin," Ivvár said.

"Christmas came and went," Rikki said. It was an accusatory statement but it sounded apologetic in Rikki's tone. He didn't meet Ivvár's eyes. The last storekeeper let you go one month and then if you didn't pay up you got nothing, no supplies, no salt, no flour, not a drop of liquor, he didn't let the debt stack up and up, and if you didn't pay he came by with a Sámi and a lasso and a set of knives. But Rikki waited, he was from the south, why he had come here no one knew. Ivvár's uncle thought it was because he was a criminal and had to hide up here, like the French king had, but Ivvár thought it was just a sign of things to come, more settlers coming north, hearing things about how easy it was to get rich off the Lapps, stories about the mines, that kind of thing. "Not a hide of a hair," Rikki said, "not a hair of a hide," and he cleared his throat, "that I got from you."

Ivvár, feeling like his father, put his hands on the belt around his waist. He tucked his thumb under the belt, as if for strength. "We'll pay up before we go," Ivvár said grudgingly. The Swedish was awkward in Ivvár's mouth, it felt stiff, like something he hadn't worn all year. Why couldn't Rikki learn Finnish like everyone else?

"Before you leave for the sea," Rikki said.

Ivvár nodded.

"But you can't pay in reindeer," Rikki said warningly, "they aren't worth anything then. Silver only." He seemed proud to know this. It was too bad, Ivvár thought, that he had figured that out.

Ivvár nodded again, though to even make this promise made him nervous. It was one thing to not pay and another thing to say directly when and how you would pay when you guessed you would not. Easier if nothing was ever really said, and usually Rikki let things go. At last Rikki sighed and he got up, he went up a set of stairs to the side of the shop that were very steep and for a minute Ivvár heard him rustling around up above, his heavy tread, and when he came back, stooping down the stairs, his hand on the logs of the walls to steady himself, he had a bottle with him.

"You want me to open it now?" Rikki asked.

Ivvár nodded. "Why not," he said, though he'd been planning on this all along. Rikki pulled the cork out with a knife as efficiently as Ivvár would have cut a calf's ear, and poured the brännvin into a glass.

Ivvár drank, nodded. Rikki filled the glass again. It was odd to even hold a glass, in Ivvár's hands glass always felt so weak, and the glass felt cold, the brännvin was cold, nearly frozen feeling, but burned as he drank. Summer and winter in one go, he thought.

He drank it quickly, wanting to hurry to the part where the liquor fixed things, and as always he felt a little sick after the first glass and a little better after the second. He sat down on one of the stools, overcome with fatigue.

"Did my father come in here?" Ivvár asked, as if this were why he was here.

"This morning? No."

"When?"

Rikki looked at his books, like the answer was in there, like all answers were in there, like he had no other way of knowing anything. "He doesn't come in much anymore."

"Not at all?" Ivvár asked. He didn't like to say this, he was revealing how poorly he and his father were getting along, but the first bit of brännvin had entered his very tired brain and he was giving himself permission to make a few useful mistakes.

Rikki looked toward the window as if Ivvár's father were standing right there. "He's been," Rikki said, very carefully, "he's been at the parsonage." Ivvár grabbed the bottle by its sweaty neck and turned to leave, but as he was opening the door he felt very winded, almost dizzy. Everything was very warm inside him, his head, his eyeballs. He left, not hearing the door closing behind him. He was going to make his way up to the church, he was going to find his father, to pull him from his pew, and tie him to the sledge, and Borga was going to pull them all the way home.

WILLA HAD BEEN stuck in the parsonage all morning. She was staying behind to watch Lorens—over the summer he'd seemed better but all week during the prayer meetings he'd been making a hideous hacking noise. But now he was sleeping, snoring so heavily Willa was sure he would wake himself, and as he slept she read from her father's intended text, from the Book of Matthew, and she even had a copy of his sermon she'd written out herself, the parable about the foolish virgins who did not buy enough oil for their lamps. It was the same sermon Nora had been using to teach Biettar how to read with, though as of yet he hadn't gotten very far. But perhaps because she'd already copied it she couldn't pay any attention, and she kept going to the shutters and opening them, looking out, though all morning she had only been rewarded by the sight of the hill, thoroughly slushed by boots and hooves, gone to brown, though at least the reindeer were there, at least they were something to see.

She had just gone for the fourth time that morning when Henrik's door opened and out came a herder—his reindeer leather pants told her that, his coat, his fur boots with their curved tips. Clearly, the man was drunk— she was used to seeing that often enough—and she watched him for a few minutes, making his way unsteadily down the main lane between the cabins toward the hill, stopping once to rest his hand on a reindeer, which quickly stepped aside and made him nearly fall, but he caught himself, and then she recognized his gait.

Her face flushed, even from this distance. Ivvár was one of the herders who smoked after church, leaning against the wall, pipe in mouth and thumbs tucked into his belt. She had never spoken to him at all, not even to say hello, she wouldn't have dared. He was much too good-looking. His hair was a mild brown, and very loosely curled, and cut with some-one's knife just below his chin, and he had the kind of eyes you saw this far north that were so wide-set and hooded they seemed to run into the tops of his cheekbones, and he only ever wore fur coats with hoods that he rarely pulled up over his head, like he didn't need to be any warmer. Everything about him had this same easy aloofness, like the matter of his handsomeness was just a matter of course, but his good looks were so obvious that it made any attempt to speak to him smack of desperation or interest; it was impossible to have a normal interaction with him, even she could see how the girls floated around him, practically preening.

But just then she felt sorry for him. He had reached the hill, but he was sliding around, he couldn't get his footing, and his fur boots were slipping—he fell, a hard fall that would have embarrassed her. She watched him wipe at his knees with his hands and try to stand. How could he be this drunk, she wondered, so early in the morning? He fell again and this time he didn't get up, he just lay there without moving.

Willa listened for Lorens's breathing—yes, she would do it. Grabbing her scarf she ran outside and down the road, trying to not slip herself, hesitating to actually call his name in case someone heard. He was rolling, she couldn't tell if it was intentional or not, down the rest of the hill, and then he lay there quite still, looking up at the sky, which today, he thought, had dressed very well, had put on a light pink shawl, laid loosely about her shoulders. How long he lay there he didn't know. He felt unsure, whether to go in, whether to go home. Maybe he should go back for more brännvin, maybe it made no difference whether he went anywhere or not, his father was going to do what his father was going to do, if his father was awakened it was just a new truth in the world.

He remembered lying in the snow with his mother while they watched the clouds graze. She had said, we're going on a long trip to the sea. We have to go see someone to try to help me.

Don't be scared, she'd said, but he'd been scared, the old man had scared him.

Now there were footsteps, to his left. He could tell someone was hurrying toward him, but he didn't move.

"Ivár," the voice said, but he didn't turn to look at her. She spoke in Sámi that was good but not perfectly easy, somehow. He knew without looking: one of the pastor's daughters, not to be had, always wanted more for the not being able to have.

"Are you all right?" she asked. She appeared over him. Her face held real worry, and her breath came out in front of her in short bursts. She was familiar, the way all of the settlers were familiar by dint of being different. She wore no coat, but she had the shockingly red scarf of all Sámi girls wrapped around her face so that it covered her nose, and all he could make out were her eyes, narrow and dark. Their eyes met, and she crouched down without putting her knees on the snow, looked him over. "You fell hard," she said.

"The church didn't want me to go in," he said, smiling a little. She looked at him, as if startled he could speak, and when she sat back on her heels her scarf came down. He was surprised to find she was interesting to look at. It had never occurred to him before. She wasn't pretty in the usual way, even like Risten was pretty—she had so much sharpness to her, she had a heavy front to her brows, and high and thick cheeks, and eyes that were quick and lively.

"Can you get up?" she asked.

He tried to look bored. "I'm just resting," he said, and as if to prove this, he closed his eyes. It seemed to him a strange amount of time went by, a little too long, and still she didn't say anything. When he opened his eyes she was still crouching, looking at him very closely.

"You've been drinking," she said.

"Why aren't you in there?" he asked.

"Where?"

"The church didn't want you in, either?"

"I'm watching my brother. He's sick," she said. She had a little mouth, thin little lips.

He felt a rush of the brännvin, a thick push of some warm feeling or fluid in his head and in his chest. "I can't get up," he lied.

He could tell she didn't know if she should be concerned or not. "Here," she said briskly. She moved down toward his feet and put her hands out and he took them. She pulled and he resisted her pulling, so that she was tugging against him, so that they felt each other's heft. She huffed, looked amused but not annoyed. "You can get up on your own, then," she said.

"I can't," he said. He held her hands, tight, she was going to either tumble forward or break free, one or the other, but she steadied herself and pulled and he did come up to sit. She dropped his hands.

"Now help me stand," he said. He dropped his head like it was too heavy for him to hold—which, in fact, it was; it felt heavy, weighted.

She took his hands again and this time he helped her, putting some effort into it himself, and when he stood up they were very close to each other, he caught her scent, and then she backed away. The wind was up and it took her hair and the ends of the scarf and blew them toward him. He could have bumped against her with his shoulder, but he restrained himself.

"The sermon will be over soon," she said.

He nodded.

"Your brother's sick?" he asked.

"I just said that," she said, but not unkindly. She took her scarf off, so that he was treated to the shock of her neck. It was always so odd in winter to see anyone's skin. For a moment it seemed like she was flirting, but she was winding the scarf over her head like an old lady and then she was walking away, hunching over into the wind, breaking into a little run. What an odd one. He was miffed, or at least surprised, that she hadn't flirted with him. He felt like a rain had appeared for a minute and then disappeared, so that only the wet ground told you it had been there at all.

6

EVERY MORNING WILLA WOKE AND THOUGHT, SOMETHING GOOD HAS happened, and then for a minute she wouldn't be able to remember what it was, and then it would come to her: Ivvár had slipped and fallen. She went through each part of the encounter, trying to remember any fragment that might have escaped her, but the memory was wearing away, and now there were only the smallest gestures left to pick off like crumbs, and she clung to these as she clung now to Nora, breathing into the pocket of warmth she made between her chest and Nora's back. She always wished her father would come in and build the fire, but he was firm about these things, he said that people sleep better in the cold, he said the best people he knew were poor, he said hardship was edifying, and there was joy in strife.

Lorens coughed. Each refrain of his cough she felt in the back of her neck. It was a sinister noise, aggravating to hear, it spread its sickness in its sound.

Again she slept, again she awoke. She moved her toes in her socks, she hoped for the birds asking each other, is it morning? Is it—is it—is it— morning?

It was the month of light after the month of darkness. There was the relief of the next new bit of sun each day, at first just the top of its head coming up over the river, then its eyes the next day, and its nose a few days later, though the fact of the sun did nothing to weaken the cold itself;

it merely shone on it, and magnified the breath in front of the face. But at least in the cover of daylight Willa could go out, take long walks again without anyone worrying—she was expert in inventing small tasks that would take up time, in finding reasons to be waylaid on the return home. Lately she set traps for ptarmigans that were doomed to fail, claiming she had seen them out there, that kind of little lie. Once she was out of sight of the cabin, she dawdled, stopping to examine anything of interest—the tops of trees sticking out of snowbanks like waving hands, the tracks of a fox dragging a bird. If the tracks interested her for any reason she followed them. She liked to tell herself she was being very Lapp when she did this, letting the natural world dictate her movements. She had heard a lot of talk like this lately, with all the Lapps so often at the parsonage now.

"I was walking to the spring for water," one of them recounted, "and it was very cold, the wind came at me hard and it knocked me onto my back. I'd been drinking the night before and I didn't feel well. I sat up and right there was a bear, not ten steps in front of me. I was going to shout out, I don't know why I didn't. I didn't know why it had come out of hiding in the winter, and it opened its mouth and I said, Holy Father, I won't drink anymore, only close the mouth of the bear, and the bear shut its mouth and went away, and that was when I knew, I must repent, and do you know, later when I went to look, at the same spot, there weren't any tracks at all. Not mine or the bear's . . . but it hadn't snowed."

Otherwise there were stories of sledges that stopped moving, sounds of someone singing a hymn when there was no one there at all, birds with unusual markings. In some ways the stories moved Willa by the power their tellers gave them; on the other hand, they made her feel ashamed, since she hardly thought about faith at all. She ought to have been strengthened by the confessions of others, and she ought to have wept with them, but instead she found herself feeling outside them, and even in the midst of, say, someone weeping and feeling God's forgiveness move through them, she thought instead of Ivvár—the entire moment would be interrupted by how his hands had felt in hers. It was not so much that she had no inkling of the presence of sex in the most innocuous of circumstances, it was more that she had never experienced the desire to think about sex in the most innocuous of circumstances; that had always been the purview of men, men whom she hoped to avoid, and yet, rather than experience horror at her own desire, she experienced only pleasure; miraculously, she had almost no guilt over it at all. It felt light, free, natural, usual—she had a wonderful secret, and she could not bring herself to feel sorry for it, though she tried. When Jussa Jongo began to recant his sins, which included, in addition to infidelity, lust for others, she saw his shame and his sorrow for it, and she thought: that is how I should be. That is how I should suffer.

She enjoyed, in a perverse way, the stories of their sins. Really, Old Mother Unga had marked calves as her own from her mother-in-law's herd? And Rasmus Tornberg had fought so much with his brother over their inheritance that they hadn't spoken for six years? And Elna Spein had tied her father to a sledge to stop him from drinking, but then gone and drunk the brännvin herself? And Oula-Antti Juoso had beat his wife, and she had come at him with a burning log? Many, though not all of the stories, had drinking in them, and she began to wonder—was her father reaching the Lapps at last because he was solving the problem of those who drank too much? Or, was it just that it was popular to recount sins of drinking? Certainly stories of one sin seemed to motivate stories of similar sins. But why did they drink, and then do such frightful things? It made her, still more perversely, want to drink, if only to know what it was that made it so compelling, when it appeared to do so little for you. But she would not have dared, she would never dare—and so as to keep herself from it, she told herself how wrong it was, and how pitiful. The poor Lapps, she told herself, they just can't stop themselves!

She had no sense whatsoever of the actual politics of it, beyond a knowledge that there was a prohibition on the sale of liquor in Lapland as decreed by the United Kingdoms of Sweden and Norway. She knew of course that the law was widely ignored, but she didn't know why the law had been made in the first place, that the thought had been that the Sámi had to be protected from themselves; that is, that the usual assumptions put upon indigenous people everywhere had been put upon the Sámi in this way and in every other way. The Norwegians, and the Swedes, and the Finns, and thus all of Europe, and later all the world, called the Sámi Lapps (*lapp* from an old and half-forgotten word for *path*, a reference to their perceived poverty), and they called Sápmi Lapland, and they pointed to the heavy drinking as proof of their assumptions. Such gross caricatures ignored the fact that the settlers of the region from every parentage and path drank at very similar rates to the Sámi; the great difference was that the Sámi were more likely to be punished for their drinking by the authorities, and, moreover, the consequences of drinking were greater for the Sámi because the demands of their life were greater.

The Sámi could not, like Henrik, merely wake up with a sour stomach and headache and dry mouth and move along with their day, a routine that had become, recently, a fact of life for Henrik. He hardly thought about it himself, how drunk he was, and how often. It was a matter of habit to the point of survival. He drank to put off the cold, he drank in order to be as one with his customers, who always wanted, if they came to drink, to share one with him. He drank because he was a coward, and he couldn't bear to think, he had too many things that were too painful to think about, the affair with Emelie for one, his father for another, his mother for another, the debt, his uncle—he had a letter from his uncle, for instance, that had come the other day that he hadn't even opened. He had left it beside his bed on top of the wooden barrel that served as his nightstand, and he had told himself he would read it, in the morning he would read it, but then he'd woken up feeling foggy-headed and that didn't seem like a good time to read it, and he let another day pass, and now it was the third morning, and before he could let himself do anything he tore it open.

Dear Henrik, the letter read, greetings from your mother, and of course may God's blessings go with you in your endeavors there. I have some concern that it has been eight weeks since we have received word from you, although the post has arrived from Kiruna and Luleå twice now in that period. I was meant to be back in my post at Härnösand much earlier, of course, but the archbishop's business here in the south has kept me; all to the good, and all as God wills. Your mother, as you know, gets so much sustenance from her worry, and she lays at my feet entirely her fears that you are very ill. She herself has been suffering lately from faintness and a weak heart, though she does not let this stop her from the Lord's work and even yesterday was out, handkerchief to her mouth, giving alms in the cold. We have had a difficult time of it this winter, and yesterday the carriages could not make any progress in the snow at all, but were stopped entirely in the streets, and it struck me that reindeer would have been much better suited to our plight. Although what would they make of the noise of Uppsala, if, as you say, they cannot even be tied beside each other in a team of horses, and cannot be controlled? My fear is that the Lapps are entirely like the reindeer, and can't be yoked to anything. I hear from B—that the King has some interest in opening boarding schools for them, but of course the mine at Gällivare has not turned out to be what we had hoped, though I don't think he will close it down as of yet. But in the meantime we await news from you directly. I have heard through a reputable source that Laestadius has told the Lapps that our pastors are not to be trusted (besides him, of course), and even are servants of the Devil, though it's to be hoped this is all rumor and without merit. I tend to not be as worried as this kind of "pietism" moves through the Lapps every so often, but of course it is eminently to be wished that they would find some way of taking Christ into their hearts in a more civilized way for once! I will make a visit there myself soon, perhaps this winter or the next summer at latest, and see for myself, though in my experience when I've been on my inspection tours in the past they have always struck me as hopelessly illiterate and interested in God to the extent that they are interested in being confirmed, which of course is itself dependent on their interest in being married.

I impress this all upon you in hopes you will write back speedily with your news of him directly. I've written to Dean Laestadius myself and I trust the letter will get to him, though I expect he will write back thirty pages that are legible only to Our Heavenly Father. Still, send some of their better jewelry along with the next letter, or anything interesting you may find. I know a merchant here who knows some Frenchmen who say the French go in for these kinds of things and you might do very well by them. Finally I need not impress upon you how essential it is that you make timely remunerations; let us not forget, you have pledged to become responsible, in things both fiduciary and moral, etc., and such further irresponsibility on your part will not be abided. I hope that God has been preserving you as His trusted servant, your Uncle, etc., Frans. P.s. Your mother wants to know if it is true that they castrate reindeer with their teeth. P.p.s. Your mother says to pray, as do we all, for God's mercy, and harder still that we may not require it.

The letter struck dread in Henrik. Clearly Frans knew that Henrik was avoiding all communication as a way of avoiding the matter of the debt. Avoidance was his primary method of defense; even now, he looked at bills and his uncle's letters through squinted eyes, as if only half reading them would lessen something, and as was his habit he threw the letter into the fire directly so he couldn't see it again, and in fact he felt proud for having read it at all.

But even after throwing it in he could not forget the larger point, which was that his uncle had promised, threatened, to come there himself. So he would collect. He would come and see for himself. Henrik had been hoping that maybe his uncle was richer than he'd imagined, or somehow his mother was softening in her old age and would pay Frans off herself, in reality, she'd acted like he owed her for this horrid life, like she had saved him from his own disgrace, and since he had come here she'd had nothing to do with him at all. It struck Henrik she was the real writer of the letter, and she had dictated it, maybe, so as to not communicate directly with Henrik herself.

The question was, of course, how long he could go without writing his uncle back, offering his uncle something. He hadn't written to him with the story about Sussu and how the servants had drowned, he hadn't written to him even about Biettar and how the women screeched in services like cats, he'd said nothing, even while what there was to say was growing increasingly more interesting, would have been met by his uncle with gratitude, if not pleasure—was that why he didn't write? To deprive his uncle of any inside knowledge, anything good at all? After all, though, his uncle would never consider it any kind of payment on the debt, and if Henrik really thought about it—he poured himself a whiskey in reward for thinking this through—did he not write because he knew what would happen next? His uncle would come, on the pretext of investigating what nonsense

Laestadius was preaching, but also to collect on the debt, and then not only would he collect what he could, he would send Henrik off to debtors' prison; he would say, I wash my hands of you, and he would never think of Henrik again. Someone who didn't know better would have said, of course your own uncle wouldn't send you to debtors' prison, but this was said by people who had yet to meet Frans.

Henrik went to the window with his whiskey to continue one of his only hobbies, which was drinking with a stool set just so, so that he could see out onto the main walkway and toward the parsonage, in case Nora came out, but as always it wasn't Nora who appeared but Willa, her scarf pulled up around her like battened hatches. She was on her skis, and she pulled behind her a little sledge. Where was she always going, he wondered. She's going to meet her lover, he decided. The thought was so amusing he choked, slightly, on his drink.

WILLA ALWAYS HOPED she would see Ivvár, she hoped to see him on her outings, she hoped he might come to town, for supplies, for church, for his father. She didn't think he would just show up, looking for her, since this stretched hope too far, but despite her fantasies of running into him she wasn't prepared when he did appear. She was right, he wasn't looking for her, he was trying to avoid his father—his father was back and now Ivvár was the one to disappear, aware he was trying to make his father feel too guilty to leave himself, since his father would only leave if he felt the herd was being watched. Or that was how it had been before, and Ivvár was trying, more or less, to trap his father at the siida, becoming more useless to force his father to be more useful, and as such today he had invented an errand, which was to go see Jáhko-Duoma about a new knife. He did need a knife, of course, but he shouldn't have been spending any money for one, so the enterprise was entirely speculation—a fool's errand issued by himself, the fool, and carried out by himself, the fool.

So he hadn't expected to see Willa any more than she'd expected to see him. He hadn't forgotten about her, though he didn't think of her anywhere near as often as she thought of him, and when he did think of her, it was mostly with embarrassment, remembering how he'd flirted with her when she hadn't flirted back. Thinking of this would make him think of Ris-ten, how he'd flirted with her, too, and then it was all too unbearable to think about, and he'd do whatever he could to direct his mind somewhere else. But now he was standing stock-still on top of a snowy knoll and she had seen him. For a few long moments they observed each other, neither willing to do any more than watch, waiting for the other to move or keep going. Maybe because he'd behaved so badly before, he thought this was a chance to show her he'd meant nothing by it. To say hello, to seem very indifferent. He started to ski toward her, aware he was skiing with unnec-essary bravura, but it was too old a habit to ski like that when someone was watching.

He stopped just short of her with a sudden skid that kicked up snow onto her skis. In the thin sunlight she seemed more fragile and more real than he remembered. Her coat was down past her knees, and made of so many different animal furs he felt sorry for her. He didn't know why but he smiled, his most tactical smile, the same smile he had used on Risten.

"Willa," he said. He was revealing he knew her name, which he'd uncov-ered from his father in a conversation about his father's visits to the par-sonage.

"Ivvár," she said. She raised an eyebrow. Her mouth was serious but her eyes were almost laughing.

"What?" he asked.

"Nothing," she said.

"You're laughing at me."

"I'm not laughing at you."

"You are," he said, aware this was flirting, unable to stop himself.

"Would you like me to laugh at you?" She smiled a little, but it wasn't a shy smile. It wasn't coy. It was like she disdained him for his looks, or didn't need them, didn't have any interest in them.

"I'm going to see Jáhko-Duoma," he said, a little stupidly, suddenly unsure if she knew who that was. "And where are you going?" he said, with the tone of accusation that told him, and surely her, that he was flirting. It was like it fell out of him, the tone, like it was impossible to speak to her any other way.

She looked around her, at the sled, at the tracks she had made behind her, at the snowed-in steps in front of her. "I'm going to go visit the big old nothing in the traps," she said. She seemed embarrassed.

"Why do you visit them if you know there's no one home?"

"I don't want to be home," she said lightly.

"Where do you want to be?" he asked. She looked at him and raised her eyebrows and looked away. "You want to be in heaven," he said, "but aren't we already there?" He realized as he said it that he felt slightly serious about his bad joke, it occurred to him he had said it in part out of a kind of belief in it, it was too beautiful out today, the sun was like the snow, which was like his chest, wide open plains of white light.

"You know," she said, suddenly quite serious, "Jesus always said what heaven was, but only in parables. He never said directly, this is what it is. I always wonder why not, why not tell us what Heaven is? One of the parables, he said, the kingdom of Heaven is like a treasure hidden in a field, and when a man has found it, he hides it," and here she stopped, seeming to think, her eyes rolled up slightly in the way of someone reciting something, "and with joy goes out and sells all that he owns, and buys that field."

"The Sámi often hide treasures," he said. "Once, someone heard from a noaidi that there was a treasure hidden in such and such place, right beneath a stone. When he got near the stone there was a thick fog, and he couldn't see anything, so he had to go back home. So another day he went back, but this time, there was a ptarmigan on the stone, and when he got closer, he saw the ptarmigan was really a human."

"And?"

"When I was little," he said, "we would dare each other to go near the stone. But none of us ever did. We all knew it was the stone from the story. But we didn't go. And then when I was older——"

"What?"

"I never went."

"You just never went to the stone?"

"It would have been bad luck."

She cocked her head, she might have been a bird. "I never know what you are going to say."

"Should I be more predictable?"

"I didn't mean *that*," she said, and to stay unpredictable, he turned and left, waiting to see if she would call after him, if she would say, where are you going, come back, but she didn't, and when he finally turned to look back she was pulling her sad little sled behind her. It bothered him that she was so able to resist him, that even though he flirted, she went into reciting lines from the Bible, and even though that should have have annoyed him, he felt interested in her strangeness. He felt interested not in that she had known the lines but that she had said she didn't understand them. What an odd bird, he thought, wanting to just stare at her, but he made himself go, and he went to Jáhko-Duoma's, which he regretted immediately, having forgotten how much he talked, in such long bouts it became difficult to maintain respect for one's elders, as Ivvár knew he should, and there was a fight within him, to not just seem respectful of Jáhko-Duoma but to feel it, and it took enormous patience to not cut him off, to wait for an appropriate moment not too early in the conversation to say that he couldn't stay very long, actually, his father needed him back at the herd.

"Your father, eh?" Jáhko-Duoma said. He was short, even for a Sámi man, and he had long, curled gray hair that he wore pulled over the same shoulder. His stomach was large, it protruded outward so strongly it gave the unfortunate and obvious comparison to a pregnant woman, and as always Ivvár felt some distance between them, between Ivvár, who herded, and Jáhko-Duoma, who stayed put, always in this same little hut, always alone, but always fat. How did he stay so fat, Ivvár wondered. Even his dog was fat, and hadn't even looked up when Ivvár came in. "How has your father been?" Jáhko-Duoma asked, and the way he said it Ivvár flushed. Even Jáhko-Duoma knew about his father's awakening, which meant everyone knew.

"He's with the herd," Ivvár said, as if that was what Jáhko-Duoma had asked, as if that were the simple truth. So Ivvár just nodded when Jáhko-Duoma said his price for the knife, he didn't counter, in case it seemed like he couldn't pay, but afterward he was embarrassed, that Jáhko-Duoma would look down on him now, and Ivvár found himself in a new game in which he tried to see no one, so there would be no one to look down on him, but it was a game that he was bound to lose, because to be so alone was also to suffer. After two weeks he found himself itching to talk to someone, anyone—when he and his father were around, they did not talk about anything that wasn't necessary—and finally Ivvár, feeling pathetic, feeling as poorly as Jáhko-Duoma must have, as desperate to tell someone all of the stories of his life, sat on the same crest of hill at which he had seen Willa before and he waited. He was good at waiting, and he came at the same time three days in a row, though he would never have admitted that to anyone, and like one of his mother's stories, on the third day she came, with her same sad little sled pulled behind her.

The day was entirely different: there was a thin fog that, combined with a weak sun, gave everything a tenuous feeling, like the whole earth might collapse in at any moment from anything of greater strength, a loud noise or a bright light. He approached her tentatively, expecting he might scare her, but if she was scared she didn't show it, and for a while they did their teasing, or rather, he teased and she appeared to accept his teasing without any particular reaction. He hadn't prepared what he would say or not say, despite all the time he'd had to think about it, but there was no dangerous silence, they fell easily into their surreal and serious talk, and she asked him, as if time had not passed, what it was the Sámi heaven was, and he told her, though he was sure she knew, about sáivu, the lakes thick with fish and the land coated with lichen and the reindeer fat as could be.

"It's so interesting," she said, "that even in Heaven, there are reindeer. What would the Sámi be, do you think," she asked, "without the reindeer?"

"In the old days before there were reindeer," he said, "there was a Sámi man who went wandering around. He mostly lived by snaring ptarmigan," he said. "Like you," he added.

"Ha, ha," she said.

"But one day he had been out getting ptarmigan all day and his traps were empty again——"

"Ha, ha——"

"And he sat down in the forest to rest. A pretty girl appeared in the forest," he said, and he couldn't help but look at her to see if she looked at him, but she avoided his gaze, he thought, quite purposefully. "Actually," he said, "the man knew she was a magical being, and belonged underground, but she was so pretty he wanted to keep her with him. So he took his knife and he"—here Ivár leaned over, and he grabbed her mittened hand, but unlike another girl would, she didn't pull away, so it was a simple thing to take her mitten off and take her hand and pinch the top of her finger when he said—"and he pricked her finger with his knife. And when blood came out she said, oh, that was my heart!" He gave a pause, to see if Willa would say anything, but he was forced to go on. "But just then an old woman appeared, she said to the girl, now that you've shed blood, you have to stay on earth! And the man took his knife and tried to throw it at the old woman but she escaped."

Willa was staring so fixedly ahead of them that Ivár wondered if there was something she saw in the fog. "And?" she said, turning back to him.

"Oh," he said, "I thought you were bored." He hadn't, actually, but he wanted her to say she was interested. She shook her head; she might have been blushing. "Well," he said, "they went to live in a hole in the earth, so that they were neither in the underground nor above it. But they couldn't stay there forever. And the girl said to the man, wait here for three days, and no matter what happens, no matter what kind of strange noises you hear, don't come out. And she disappeared. And for three days he waited, and there were terrible noises, he thought he heard terrible things, cries of death, but she was so beautiful he decided he would do as she said. And on the third day she brought him up to the earth and there was a herd of reindeer, and also a lávvu. And that's how the Sámi came to take care of reindeer. Actually," he said, "there's more to the story, about how they milked the reindeer and why now the herders don't joke or swear around the reindeer, but it's not the good part of the story."

"What was the good part of the story?" Willa asked.

"The part with the pretty girl," he said, but she seemed almost affronted by this, possibly annoyed, and after they'd exchanged a few cursory remarks, how is your brother, how is your father, and so on, he disappeared again, feeling embarrassed that he'd flirted like that, wondering why he'd done it—the loneliness, that was what did it to you. You were alone that long and then anything came out of your mouth. She wasn't even a very pretty girl, that wasn't the thing about her, anyway. But he found himself coming back, the next week, watching for her again, this time sure she was on her guard for him—she was—she could hardly walk, at that point, away from town without feeling slightly sick, it had gotten so that at home, before she went out to the forest, she couldn't eat anything, she was so nervous about the thought of even seeing him, and she would be a little light-headed by the time she made it out to the forest, her eyes aching in their sockets from staring, hoping for the shadow of his figure stretching down the snow toward her, hoping he would come lazily and powerfully down the slope, showing off for her on his skis. She had never been teased like this, it stuck with her so that she could hardly sleep, she treasured each of them, each little joke, each implication that she was beautiful, each flick of his eyes. To be looked at like that!

He told her another story once as the sun was setting, they were both cognizant of it, that the sunset was so grand, such a sickly sweet pink, that it elevated their speech effortlessly, it imbued everything they said in romance to be saying it in front of such a sky. In such a light he told her the story like the one he had told her the other day, this time about a Sámi man who was sent to retrieve a part of the herd that had wandered. He found them easily, they were near the place the siida had just been, but he was tired, so he went to sleep inside his rákkas.

"You know what a rákkas is?" he asked. "Just the little tent-cloth you set up inside the lávvu," he said, "you hang it from the poles. It keeps the mosquitoes away in the summer," he said, "but sometimes it's nice to hang up other times, too, you can have your own little room to do your own things in."

She nodded, she did not admit to either knowing or not knowing this, and he continued on, how this Sámi man kept waking up to some kind of scratching at the cloth of his rákkas, and finally he took a needle for sewing leather out of his needle case, and he stabbed through the rákkas. A girl screamed out, now I can't return to my people because I've seen my own blood!

Against this story the pink of the sky subsided into purple.

"It reminds me," Willa said, "of the story about the man who throws the lasso around the Háldi girl to capture her and her reindeer herd."

"That's another one, yes," Ivár said, though he seemed disturbed. She wondered, was it better to seem as if she didn't know? "You know your Háldi stories then?"

"No, not so much," she lied, "a few that Old Sussu told me." She didn't want to say, I have spent so much time reading them, because my father has been writing them all down, and he is making a big book of them, all of the Lapp mythologies, which I read when I am supposed to be copying down his sermons. Why she didn't want to say this to him she didn't know, and she didn't inquire within herself.

He looked surprised to hear Old Sussu's name.

"What else did Old Sussu tell you?" he asked.

"Mostly sayings," Willa said.

"Like what?"

"Like," Willa said, thinking, "like no one was born with an axe in his hand."

"No one is so short he doesn't need to bend down," he said. At first it was maybe a question, did she know it, or maybe it was a challenge, she wasn't sure.

"Still water is never clean," Willa said, after a pause.

"How can a stranger know what a squirrel eats?" he said. Of course he was fast, faster than her, but it was tricky, actually, to sort out the Swedish ones from the Sámi ones.

"I've made soup out of all kinds of stock," Willa said, at last—even her mother said that one.

"You've never been a pole in my lávvu," he said. Her mind stuck—she couldn't find another. She grimaced. Of course there were more, so many more. "My favorite, though," he went on, "is probably, a log can't burn on its own," and he winked, and the blush she'd already had worsened.

"Well," she said, and then she made herself say it, the worse one, she could think exactly of when she'd heard it, she'd been inside the store and two Sámi men had been in there. One of them had said to the other, you shouldn't lick until it's dripping, and they had laughed, the old storekeeper, too, and she had been aware for the first time of her presence as a woman, of what her body meant to others, she was aware that her presence heightened the laughter, because it made the joke more offensive to have been said, but when she had looked askance one of them had said, oh it's nothing, it's no snoallan, and it had taken everything in her to not leave immediately and to stand there, waiting, to ask for whatever it was she had come for. She shocked herself, repeating it now, saying to him, you shouldn't lick until it's dripping.

Ivár clapped his hands against each other, he laughed and gave to her his strongest smile, deep laugh lines pouring out from his eyes and bending around his cheeks. "I never thought I'd hear you say that," he said. He had to stop and lean over, he laughed so hard. "And here I thought you were a good little báhpa nieida, good little church-girl who has to pretend no one does anything until they are married and then has to pretend they liked it."

"It was just a joke," she said, suddenly defensive, and ashamed—she shouldn't have said it. She shouldn't have said something that made him say something like that. He seemed to see he shouldn't have said what he had said, either, for as he stood back up he looked sheepish, he was fairly red himself, and he might have mumbled an apology, she wasn't sure. "Well," she said, bitterness rising, "isn't this the part where you run away?"

"Run away?" he asked.

"Yes, like you do, how you leave so you don't have to stay."

"Why wouldn't I want to stay?"

"So it's not so—so it's easier."

"Don't we enjoy ourselves, talking like this?"

"Yes," she said, "but don't we also enjoy ourselves because we are good at talking sideways?"

"What are we sideways about?"

"Your father," she said, finally. She looked at him, very directly, and then she said, "He's always at the parsonage."

"I know," he said. He looked uneasy.

"Did you know," she went on, "he's going to be a lay preacher? He's going to do the travel my father can't do anymore, he's going to read his sermons and travel from one siida to another, up in the north, during the summer."

"And?" Ivár said, so evenly he might have known, though she wondered how he would have known; it had just been decided the night before, she had been shocked herself to hear it. She had never heard of a Sámi man leaving his herd to do something like this, even if it were temporary, and it didn't seem, from what Biettar had said, it was going to be temporary at all.

"And, that's all," she said. She began to pull the sledge, which creaked against the snow, the wooden runners whining, loud after the softness of their speech. Slowly she began to walk again, but he didn't walk beside her. She turned to look back at him and he shrugged, as if to say, so I guess that's it, then!

She nodded, and turned back, she was furious, she wanted him to follow her, she regretted they had ended that way and now they were leaving it that way, it made her feel afraid, like they were never going to see each other again. That was all it had been! So little for so little. For a long time she kept thinking, he will appear back at my side, at any moment, he'll show, but of course he didn't, he was already very far away, he was almost as bitter as she was. He wondered if she knew how much it would hurt him, if she knew the shock of it—he would have been less shocked if she had thrown him into an ice-hole in the river.

Suddenly Ivár understood: his father had been practicing, letting Ivár practice being alone with the herd. His father had been preparing him, his father had told everyone but him.

As he skied away he knew already what he would do, he could feel his mistake coming. He wouldn't go back to the herd at all, he would wait until Willa was well on her way home and then he would follow her, he would watch her go into the parsonage and he would go straight to Rikki's. He would get a bottle of brännvin, he would say whatever needed to be said to make Rikki give in, and Rikki would give in, Rikki would write down in his log the next of Ivár's sins, and this new sin would just join the others, what did he care, let it grow longer, let it grow and grow like a weed, like maggots, like the flies that festered in the reindeer's nostrils, the only thing to do was to gain some ground, some foothold, some relief. He could not just sit and think of his father, and Willa, and Risten, he must, must obliterate them, obliterate if he could himself most of all. Obliterate the worst of everything that came crawling back, most of all his father drunk and tottering on his knees, his mother hiding in her rákkas so he wouldn't see how much she suffered.

WHEN RISTEN HAD BEEN A LITTLE GIRL, A TRAGEDY HAD COME TO HER family, one that was common enough and no one's fault in particular, but a tragedy nonetheless. Only Risten had witnessed it—her sister, Elle, drowning. The fact of Risten's presence had effectively doubled the tragedy; it was a tragedy that continued, for Risten, well into her adulthood, mostly in the form of dreams, but also in a persistent guilt. They had cut over a frozen lake in late March, and there was no reason to think the ice wouldn't hold, as a whole sledge had gone over just the day before, and anyway the lake didn't begin to snap and thaw until the end of April at the very earliest. Why that particular spot was so weak, and moreover, weak enough to open beneath the steps of two fairly little girls, no one knew then or now; it was unreasonable to the point of being nonsensical; it was the simple, brutal happenstance of nature.

The reason for the ice's weakness did not really matter, what mattered was that Risten had been hurrying ahead of her sister and she'd heard her little scream, so short, so quick, and of course she turned around and rushed back, she stuck her hand out and tried to reach her sister without falling in herself, but Elle was weighted down by her heavy coat and her scarf, and her boots and her mittens, and the woolen underclothes, and Risten, even with the gift of terror, could not get close enough to get her out. She couldn't get her out and Elle fell under the ice, the lake was large and had its own current, and it took her, and with Elle it took Risten, even now as someone who was about to be married she still felt that hole in the ice, like nothing could really be trusted. She had a fatalistic streak, she expected everything to end. No one would have suspected her of such fear, but she always felt Elle beneath her, like Elle was under every frozen surface, even though she had been pulled out after the ice cracked open in spring, and buried in the churchyard.

Easter had taken on a special importance to Risten, because that was when Elle had been buried, as was usual—if you died during the winter your body was stored until the ground warmed, so that all the winter funerals happened all at once, usually at the same time as the weddings, at Easter, if Easter fell late enough that year. It was efficient; everyone was already in town. But this meant that as Easter loomed so did Risten's old grief and guilt over Elle. With the guilt about Elle came the guilt about Ivvár, and Mikkol, with whom she had promptly become re-engaged: Risten had heard nothing of Ivvár since the great humiliation, and she had only seen Mikkol the once to repair things, a meeting that had both pacified and distressed her. Mikkol, for his own part, had just seemed relieved, easily convinced that it had been a matter of her jitters, and after all, maybe it had been. There had never been anything real, or possible, between her and Ivvár. Better to be with Mikkol, safe and responsible Mikkol. Mikkol had been so clear from the first, he had played no games, he had come as soon as it was possible to visit them, harnessing his best reindeer so beautifully with bells. Her mother had poured him coffee. Mikkol didn't drink, and would never drink. Mikkol didn't say one thing and then do another. Mikkol didn't feign disinterest for years, barely speaking to her, only to appear one summer day, drunk as could be, shouting for no reason, walking her out to the rocks. Soon, she thought, Ivvár will fade, the bruise will lift and lighten, and underneath will just be Mikkol.

There was the possibility, faint, that somehow Mikkol would hear about her and Ivvár, both the encounter from the summer but also that she'd gone to see him while their engagement was off. How he would hear she didn't know, as far as she knew no one had seen them, but that was the trouble, it was only as far as she knew. It was possible, too, that Ivvár would tell someone himself, after all when he was drunk he was liable to do anything, that was what had happened with them, wasn't it?

It was impossible to imagine, actually, what Mikkol would think if he heard. He had the protection of innocence, since it would simply never occur to him, and if he heard it, he was just as likely to not believe it. But she would know it was true. Even then she was sitting out with the herd, watching it for her father, and she hardly saw the reindeer at all. The reindeer were dozing and standing up, the ground everywhere dirtied with pellets, but Risten didn't see any of it, not really—she was trying to see what the herd would be like when Mikkol's reindeer joined theirs. How many he had exactly she wasn't sure, actually; she had the idea that he had at least a hundred or two of his own, but she could have been wrong. Still, her father had said that Risten would get to keep all of her reindeer, the full rádju. Six hundred and seven, that was what she had, and once Mikkol's herd joined hers they would be on their way to her father's thousand.

But was that all it was, then? You said a thing and then it all changed, you lived with another man now, someone else came into your lávvu and slept with you across the fire from your parents. There would be a new dog, and even their dogs would have to learn to get along.

Into this reverie of worries came the sound of her father, skiing in his steady way straight past her. "Where are you off to?" she asked, but he didn't answer, which was its own answer. Probably, she thought, he was going to a sieidi—he was too worried about the wolverines, and he wouldn't feel better until he offered something. The gray tail of winter, always much longer than anyone wished, was moving everyone, human and wolverine, into restlessness. They were in the strange stage now of full sun and full snow, where the sky said summer and the ground said winter, and the backs of everyone's eyes hurt from seeing so much sun coming off of so much snow, and people skied, as much as they could, with their eyes mostly closed. The Sámi were waiting for Easter to leave with the herds, and the settlers were waiting for the Sámi to leave, because it meant the snow would melt, and they would see, briefly, something green again. But in the meantime winter persisted, it was very good at overstaying its welcome, and only Willa did not want it to end, because once it ended her chance of seeing Ivvár was gone; for five, six months, at least, she wouldn't see him, while he was with the herd at the sea.

Idiotic, of course, to still be thinking about him. When Ivvár had said that, about how he'd thought she was a good little church-girl, but even more so, when he'd laughed, she'd felt the first real wave of shame for pining after him, ashamed for the fact of their bodies between them. She'd been betrayed by her own body, and she was being betrayed by it now, she thought about him more than ever. It occurred to her she was being humbled, brought low by him. She could not make it through the Lord's Prayer without landing on the word temptation and thinking what a nice word it was, temptation, and then thinking how nice it would be to be led into temptation, to have temptation take her by the hand, and take her out to the tents, to the siidas. Every day she saw, more and more, that she was unfit and unclean and not Heaven-acceptable.

And then these doubts and failings began to multiply, double in front of her like smallpox. She had been so used to thinking that there was God and there was her father and there was the church and that these would always be uppermost in her mind, but now they were nowhere, they were little nothings—the real miracle of the world was the ability of the body to set aside the soul. Now her father's warnings seemed much more sensible—this was her trial and as he'd warned, she did not have the faith for it, she was happy, eager even, to take up league with anyone or anything if that anyone or anything brought her to Ivvár. Worse, it was just how he'd warned: everything about church, about God, began to bother her, so that even the mention of Jesus Christ irritated her, and her father's followers irritated her, mystified her, even, so that one day she found herself wondering what these people were doing on the cabin floor. The woman with the little boy, why was she here? Why was she crying so hard and saying she was so full of sin? Where was her husband? Why did she grab her little boy and try to make him be awakened, too?

The second time Márjá rolled on the floor she lay there for a long time, very still, and Willa thought, some discomfort roiling up from somewhere: get up. Why did she think that? Because she didn't want her own sins absolved? Everyone must be a sinner, like her?

Her heart was jumpy, all the time. She went out to the field and looked at the frozen ground, kicked the snow away, tugged halfheartedly at the frozen wheelbarrow, but it didn't move. She wouldn't be the one breaking the soil, planting the seeds that would not really grow, that would give up halfway through summer. She would be in Uppsala. When she thought of Uppsala she felt panicky, and she crossed the river into Finland, and she went out to see if any ptarmigan were there; or rather, to see if Ivár was there. She liked to imagine that even though the last conversation had ended so awkwardly he would return to it, that the power of their attraction to each other and the power of an inevitability between them would keep bringing them here. She reached the first trap, and almost didn't look at it, since it was hardly her real purpose at all, when she saw she had caught a ptarmigan. It was a male, and its feathers had not changed into its summer browns yet. Up close she saw it was still alive—it thrashed—she was surprised it had been caught at all.

She leaned in and tried to grab it by the neck, but it was beating its wings, and its feathers were coming off all around her, like the bird was snowing, and she tried again to grab it, and it bit her mitten, pulling off a bit of wool in its mouth. She stood up, and then she knew, she could feel him behind her, and a spot she could not identify, maybe to the right of her heart, coursed and opened. He stopped near her with his soft, expert skidding. She felt her hands tremble, and her skin pricked along her neck and down her back. What absurdity! What an idiot she was!

She felt her smile stuck on her face—she couldn't stop it.

"I thought you were angry at me," he said.

"I am," she lied. "I thought you were angry at me," she added.

He made a noise that said, and maybe so he had been, and then he added, "But I've been practicing."

"Practicing what?"

"Being charming and handsome," he said.

"Really," she said, "what for?"

"So you will think I am charming and handsome."

"Hmm," she said, "I'd rather you be useful."

"What should I do to be useful?"

"You can kill this poor ptarmigan," she said, and he dropped his ski pole and went near the trap. He leaned over and held one hand out, steady, and the ptarmigan fluttered and squalled and he caught its chest in his hand, and then took his other hand, and turned its head on its neck. There was the popping sound of its bones, and then it was quiet. He freed its claws from the snare, and handed it to her. Its eyes were open.

"How do the Finns make ptarmigan soup?" he asked.

"How?" she asked, not understanding the question.

"Well," he said, "first, they get some vodka."

"Okay," she said warily.

"Then they pour in a little vodka, into the pot, and they heat that up. Then they add some more vodka, and taste it, see if it's okay. Then they drink it. And that's how they make ptarmigan soup!"

"That's your joke?" she asked. He was laughing—he even had tears in his eyes, he was laughing so hard. His deep laugh lines emerged again, and she thought: he is the very picture of jollity and happiness.

"Finns," he said, and he wiped his eyes. He shook his head.

"You're a Finn," she said.

"Well, I live in Finland," he said, "in winter. That doesn't make me a Finn, any more than it makes the Finns Russians because their land is called Russia. No?"

"Do you enjoy ptarmigan soup?" she asked.

"It's my favorite," he said solemnly.

"Yes, I was afraid of that. I saw you that way. On the hill."

"Oh," he said, "yes, yes." He didn't look embarrassed at all. "Where are you going?" he asked.

"I was checking the traps."

"Let's go, then," he said, and he started to ski, leading the way, like he was showing her her own route. "Aren't you coming?" he asked, turning back to look at her.

"You're going too fast," she said, which wasn't completely true—she wanted him to slow down, and ski next to her, and as if the day were all dream, he did slow down, and she caught up next to him, and they skied side by side. She looked at him and grinned, and he grinned.

"Tell me a story," she said.

"About what?"

"About the people who live underground."

"You like my strange stories."

"I do."

"How come?"

She hesitated. "Maybe," she said, "because of the Old Testament," which might have been true.

"Well, this story is much, much older than the Old Testament."

"The Older Testament."

"Yes," he said, seeming pleased with this, "the much Older Testament. Well," he said, "once, a man was driving his sledges. He was with his family, his wife and his two daughters. They were traveling, in fact," he said, his eyebrow raising meaningfully, "to go to church. All of a sudden, the reindeer didn't want to go any further. The man pulled and pulled at the reins. Finally he climbed out of the sled to see what was wrong. He went to the front of the string but there wasn't anything wrong. He pulled on the harness of the lead reindeer but the reindeer wouldn't budge, not at all, and the reindeer bucked and kicked at him. The man tried to walk forward. He didn't know why but he felt strange, or sick. I'm being very stupid, the man thought, and he shook his head and moved forward again, a few more steps, but he felt worse." Ivár stopped, clearly for dramatic effect.

"Go on," Willa said. She was so happy to hear his stories, this story especially, a story whose ending she didn't know. The story, like all good Sámi stories, had the element of a sudden misbehavior in nature, something inexplicable—something the world knew that humans did not. She waited. "Go on," she urged again.

"Well," Ivár said, "the man suddenly realizes in front of him is an eahpáraš, an äpäräš. You know what an ihtriekko is?"

"No," Willa lied, because she wondered how he thought of them.

"It's the spirit of a baby that a mother has abandoned. But the problem is that because they die without being named, they come back as eahpáraš, and they are very bad, everyone is very afraid of them. If you have water nearby to cross, it's not so bad, because the eahpáraš can't cross water, but this man was nowhere near any water. So the man shouted to the spirit to go away, that he had not done any harm to it. And suddenly the reindeer were quiet. So the man——"

"That's all he had to do? To tell it to go away?"

"I didn't finish the story."

"Well," she said, "go on."

"Well," he said, "the man, seeing that the reindeer were calm, turned to go back to his sledges. Suddenly, though, he realized that at the back of the sledges the dogs were barking, and his wife was shouting. He went to the back sledge, where his eldest daughter had been sitting and where everyone was now crowding around. And she was dead, a shoeband tight around her neck."

Willa looked at him and waited for him to say something.

"It's an old story," he added, at last. "Next time," he said, "I'll tell you one with a happier ending. The one about the Stállu who eats his grandchild. It's all the same story," he went on, "first we are flowers, and then we die." He laughed but it was not a bitter laugh, it was a laugh that contained death calmly. They were at the next trap, but it was empty; of course it was empty. There was only one more to check—Willa could feel again how short this would be, could already see him hurrying away home, and she felt maddened by it. Why always these brief, too brief, encounters?

"But why was the daughter dead?" she asked.

"You don't see?"

"I just want to understand."

"Yes," he said, "that's the outlander way. Always wanting to understand. Always wanting to know the reason for things."

"Yes, like the French rationalists," she said.

"What?"

"The rationalist philosophers and theologians. They believe that God exists in reason, that you can use rationality to reach God."

"You talk a lot about God," Ivvár said.

"Yes," Willa said, suddenly embarrassed by it. "I guess it's hard not to. What," she asked, "you don't?" She had been joking, but he took it seriously.

"I guess you know about the noaidi," Ivvár said, "the stories of them," he said, "they used to be powerful." I know, she wanted to say. She wanted to say, I have read all these stories. I have read about how they drummed until they fell into a trance from which they could not be wakened, I have read about them using the spirits of animals, of birds, to do what they needed done, I have read about the noaidi who stopped a boat from landing on shore, I have read about the noiadis at war with each other, exchanging curses, and I've read about Ráidenáddja, the god of gods, and Mátaráddja, Mátaráhkká, and their two daughters, Sáráhká and Uksáhká.

"Do you know," she said, "at dinner, Henrik, Rikki, he came to dinner. And he said that he'd heard that your father used to be a noaidi. Well, he didn't use that word. He said shaman. But he said he'd heard it." She was relating the story as an anecdote about Henrik—Henrik as someone to make fun of together—but when she looked at Ivvár, he looked uncomfortable, almost upset.

"A noaidi? What else, and a guvhllár?"

"A guvhllár?"

"A healer," he said, exasperated, maybe. "Some guvhllárs—healers—they are really powerful. They fix things . . . they know things." But he said it like he resented saying it. "My father—what does he know anymore about anything," he said bitterly.

"It was just what Henrik said," Willa said apologetically.

Something had changed in his face. He didn't want to look at her. "Why do you want so much to know?" he asked.

The question surprised her, she wanted to say, of course I want to know, why wouldn't I want to know? She wanted to say, this is more interesting than anything else, more interesting than the awakenings—two thoughts collided in her mind: the awakenings are happening because Biettar is making them happen. He is using his noaidi powers—or guvhllár, was that what he had been?—to make the awakenings happen. The thought was so shocking she paused, it seemed everything must pause while she considered this, this heretical thought that could contain no truth and made no sense and yet made some sense.

"I guess I don't have to know," she said.

"No," he said, "although I guess it depends."

"It depends, it depends," she said, frustrated. She let herself show it.

"Everything always depends," she said, in imitation.

"That's true," he said, "it does."

"What does it depend on?" she asked, no longer sure what the conversation meant, what they were really talking about or not talking about—love or God or a noaidi or a guvhllár or the ptarmigan, dead on the sled.

"The weather," he said, "probably the weather," and he winked at her. When he winked at her she was forced to face, again, his handsomeness. It overwhelmed her, the wedge of his cheeks, the even line of his teeth. She wanted to kiss him. She wanted to bear his children. She wanted to make a mistake, a good and large mistake, she wanted him to be worth a tragedy.

"The next trap is empty," he said.

"Yes," she said, "probably," and then like always, like a spirit in a fairy tale, he was turning around, skiing away, not looking back, and she wanted to shout, goodbye, and I love you, and don't go, and she shouted none of them, and now she was sorry he'd killed the ptarmigan. She should have let it go—though that was nothing so much as a feeling she could not parse—but it was dead, and she took it home, her entire body weary from so much feeling, wanting only to lie down and never move, never think, to sleep off hope until it was gone.

When she pushed in the cabin door, she was overcome by the sameness. No one looked up, as if they had not minded her absence. Through the open bedroom door, she could see her mother, sleeping on the bed with the baby. Her father wasn't home yet from church. The older girls, ever bossy, were directing the little kids in forming small pats of dough. Nora sat on the floor on the straw mattress with Lorens, feeding him oatmeal he did not care to eat.

"Oh good," Nora said, "it's your turn," and rose, and Willa, her heart still fast from the skiing, and hands and feet tingling with the pain of the sudden warmth, took Nora's place by Lorens. He lay back with his eyes very open.

She stuck her tongue out at him, to see if he would smile, but he ignored her.

"Is he even eating this?" she asked Nora, while moving the spoon toward his mouth.

"Not really," she said.

"Open," she cajoled, and he opened his mouth sullenly, but did not close his mouth around the spoon.

She felt frustrated, unbearably and suddenly so. "Close your mouth," she said, and she pushed his jaw closed for him, but he didn't swallow.

"Lorens," she said, "you have to eat."

"You just got home," Nora said, "do you have to be so impatient with him? He's sick." Willa put the spoon back in his mouth and focused on the action of it, tried to see Lorens as pitiable and lovable and in need of her care. But the act of feeding him was so slow, so dull, and she couldn't bear the difference, the feelings she'd had outside and the ones she had here. She wanted to be a child, and throw the spoon and bowl on the floor, but she didn't, and she fed him, and she read to him, and she put him to bed, and she put herself to bed, and the next day she woke and the world of the cabin was dried, devoid of any life, it was so dull to go get water, dragging the sledge down to the hole in the ice, and then dragging the pails back up, and then back down. It was not the labor she minded but the sameness of it, and she found herself wishing for the Sámi to come and do crazy things and have the preaching sickness, just to be distracted, but the next time Biettar appeared, with Márjá again, and some old man, some old herder Willa didn't know, and a handful of children, all of them inside, it was as if the cabin's walls had collapsed around her. The cabin was just a small building, it was a hovel, really, and her father was just a person, and the congregation a lot of worn-down women who were worried about losing their husbands and their livelihoods to drinking and to the loss of their herding lands and to the pressure of taxes and to bad luck and to forces beyond them, and who had every reason, then, to turn to something, anything, and why not her father? He promised them something, safety, answers, abstinence, and he told them they were not below anybody—or rather, that no one was above them, something the Sámi had not heard recently, if ever, from anyone in any position of authority.

In a way the transformation of herself was difficult, almost painful—

she went through the sermons or notes her father left behind, and she saw a man who called women whores, and unbelievers dogs, and anyone not awakened unwashed and filled with the Devil's piss, and she thought, watching him eat at the dinner table, he has no restraint, he really is Mad Lasse. He is never home, he is always up at church or at his desk, writing, writing—there is nothing he doesn't write down, does not record—he saves all of his energy for his preaching or his writing, to his children he says almost nothing. She saw now, too, and newly, that he was patronizing, to everyone, except the Sámi who repented before them: them he loved, and no one else, and he loved them because he was so clearly lord of them. She and her sisters, they were either useful or not, that was all—and still Willa only wanted to make him happy with her, even with all of this new seeing she sat at the table and ate with her elbows in toward her sides and if one of the children dropped a fork or spilled their water she picked it up. It was only in her mind she thought these things; she was like Mary, she decided, like that line in the Christmas gospel—and Mary took these things, and pondered them in her heart.

Now one day passed, and then the next, and she ate the same porridge and the same reindeer stew, and she moved the same wood from the fells to the woodshed, and she moved the same wood from the woodshed to the hearth, and she went out to check the traps, she went out and in the traps and in her trips outside she found only disappointment. It seemed to her she did what she did each day because there was no choice behind it, it was just where she had been born, and why not have been born a reindeer herder? Why not have been born Mary Magdalene, and find herself at the foot of the cross, looking up to see Jesus's dusty feet? She sat, reading again the stories she remembered loving, she might still have loved them, she didn't know, Elijah rising in his chariot of fire up into the sky, Samson pushing down the pillars with his blinded eyes, Jacob wrestling with the angel, Job speaking with the Devil, Laban selling his daughter for seven years of labor, and then seven more.

8

It was Easter morning and in the church-village there was the usual little delay getting out of the sledges and straightening everything—the fringes on Risten's shawl were all tangled, and her mother's braids had come undone, and they went to work on each other while her father shook the wrinkles from his four-cornered hat, and straightened his belt so that it sat at his hips and not above them, and he even took a handkerchief and wiped at his silver belt squares. The perfection of the marriage to come seemed to rely, in the moment, on the perfection of their preparations, or anyway Risten wanted to project such perfection, both now in the church and later in life, especially for Ivár, who was bound to be there—she had to exude the absence of regret, though in focusing on the absence she didn't focus on the presence of welcoming the marriage within herself, but that was impossible to do—she was too aware of the performance of it all, it was too big of a role, the bride.

Was it a mistake, or wasn't it a mistake? Was the mistake that she was not listening to her own worries, or was her mistake that she was expecting Mikkol to be more like Ivár, when in fact to be Ivár was to be utterly unavailable in every way? And after all, didn't you at some point have to pick someone, and live with your choice? There was no such thing as a perfect marriage, there were problems you could live with and problems you couldn't, and you were picking problems you could live with, and wasn't that what Mikkol was? Was he not so mild, so easygoing, as to be eminently amenable to anything?

It wasn't too late to say no. Her mother would say, well, that's all right. Surely Ivvár would be there, watching her walk with Mikkol, and he would be thinking: she's only doing it because she can't marry me. She's doing it so that she continues to do everything when one is supposed to do it, because she is good and wholesome and here is her good and wholesome husband. Ivvár would know, would even dare to think about, how he'd already slept with her.

But where was Mikkol? They were supposed to meet outside the church and when she looked from sledge to sledge, from family to family untangling their own strings and shawls, she didn't see him. It wasn't possible he was not coming—she didn't even worry about that. But it was rude, and it made her anxious; it was not a good sign. It was already not the day she had wanted.

At least her father had worn his bright blue gákti. He looked like a man who was proud, and didn't mind being thought proud, and moreover, she was his pride. Her mother was wearing a red silk shawl patterned with flowers, and though she hadn't had time to make a new gákti for herself, she'd added fresh embroidery to an older one, and, like Risten, had put on silver brooches, and she shook her chest a little so the silver leaves on her silver brooches jangled, and her father shook his hips a little so the silver leaves on his belt jangled back at her, and it occurred to Risten they were happy together, and she was afraid to not have this for herself.

The bell for the start of the service was ringing, again and again, and so as to seem unafraid she walked up the hill with strong steps, the leaves on her five brooches announcing the tinkle of wealth, the lavishness of her protection from bad luck. She had thought she would be feeling secretly proud, delighted to have such an excuse to be so vain, but instead she felt disappointed—there were so many people there, more than she'd ever seen at Easter, and no one seemed to notice her arrival at all. Worse, she still didn't know where Mikkol was, and though she knew no one else from his family would likely make it—they had left for the sea already—she hadn't anticipated that he would make her wait like this. She saw other couples, she saw Matthis and Márjá, of course, and she saw Biera Oula and Liisa, clasping each other's arms, and Risten had to admit, Márjá was someone who, despite being very plain, was winsome in this context, as a bride. She had a very beautiful fur hat on, it must have been fox fur, and she had laboriously detailed embroidery around the bottom of her gákti that made Risten envious to see it, despite her own—she would have preferred the gap between them to be even greater.

In some ways, it seemed like every other Easter. Easter was always the busiest day of the year, the most festive, a day of trade and talk and usually some kind of merriment, and some kind of fight mixed in, and everywhere there were sledges, and reindeer tied to anything that didn't move, and reindeer being watched over in a field for a token price by young people with pimples, and people were selling things from their sledges and from inside little lávvus set up everywhere: butter and cheese, purses, shoe-grass, coffee, bags of sorrel, ptarmigans, knives, wooden cups, pelts, leather straps, sinew, thimbles and needles, kettles, pots, rátnu rugs, wool blankets, wool mittens, wool scarves, leather lávvu-blankets, wool lávvu-cloths, wooden spoons and ladles, butter bowls, packing cases, chests, more sledges, skis, outer fur coats, inner fur coats, reindeer leather trousers, shoebands, fur boots, plain fur hats, fox fur and sealskin hats, women's wool caps, men's hats with pompoms, men's hats with four-corner edges, belts for men, belts for women, silver circles to put on your belts for those who weren't married, square ones for those who were, baby rattles, silver charms hung with silver leaves to keep off the bad luck. Everywhere there was the scent of food—people had set lávvus up all along the edge of the town and along the riverbanks, and it seemed like there was something cooking in all of them, reindeer stews, sorrel soups, fish soups, milk soups—and the steam from the lávvus filtered up into the clouds and they mingled, and the day, which had begun in gray and misted wanness, stayed that way, the two scenes at war with each other, the staidness of the sky above and the gaiety of the festival below.

In the center of this was the church—its steeple, the bell out front still ringing and ringing, the pews inside full enough that everyone's shoulder was pressed against someone else's, and people sat along the floor in the center aisle, and stood along the walls. Someone was smoking inside and then others began to smoke, and a small shouting match broke out—nothing serious, it was all done in a good humor. Everyone was cheerful; it was, in a way, the end of the year, the beginning of the next—once Easter was finished and as soon as the weather was good, they would all go, and this knowledge gave them all a pleasant restlessness, since the trip to the sea was always better than the trip back, and with the warmth of the sea ahead of them they could all bear this dull and cold longer, because there wasn't that much more of it.

But it wasn't like other Easters, not quite, because so many had come to hear the Madman of Lapland speak—he was the centripetal force, a fact of which he was aware; he was happy and proud, and no bride could match him. Maybe they were curious at first, just wanted to know, what was this preaching sickness, and was everyone in Karesuando just crazy, but it didn't matter to him why they were there, they were—it had happened, the kindling was on fire, and now the branch was close to burning, it would maybe, that very day, burn even in the snow. The possibility of it thrilled him, and he was so cheerful he talked as a nervous person does, too much and too loudly. But by the time of the sermon he had calmed, he had collected his powers to himself and he was ready to stride in front of everyone and bring them all to God.

The sermon began and plunged on as sermons do, some of its listeners more or less engrossed but most drifting in and out, catching pockets of phrases, established more firmly in the feeling created by the sermon than its words. Lars Levi had a fancy way of speaking, and he used florid metaphors (liquor was "the syrup of stolen grace," the "whiskey dragon") and he enjoyed embellishments; he was infamous, for instance, for having once referred to "whores whose juices of fornication leak onto the pews." He was less strident this morning, though he leaned most heavily of all, as was his wont, on drinking, and on the need for those listening to come to

God and be saved. The message was not, of course, new, but it was made more effective by the crowd that had come to hear it—maybe there was something to this, maybe he should be listened to, now that so many were so impassioned about it—and look, just like people had said, there was Biettar in the front pew, nodding his head vehemently to almost everything Mad Lasse said.

Not listening, whatsoever, was Willa—she had a sick feeling that had been there all morning. She was sad. It was a sadness rooted in disappointment to come, a preemptive strike against the self—this was the last day she would see Ivvár before she went to Uppsala, and before he went to the sea. She felt old, and sorry for herself, and envious of all of the couples in the pews who were waiting to be married. How beautiful the women were, with all those brooches! Her mother said it was gaudy and embarrassing, and her father said it was vanity at its worst, but Willa would have loved that, to wear the brooches of her mother and grandmother and great-grandmother and so on at the same time, to signal so clearly to everyone: I come from these generations of love, and I am loved by my family, and now I am loved by this man; I am not alone.

The thought made her feel so alone she pitied herself, self-indulgent as that was. She was, in fact, so pathetic that she let herself take a single, lingering look behind her at the masses of people in the pews, knowing she was looking for Ivvár, expecting not to see him at all. How would she find him in this crowd?

To her own shock her eyes locked on him straightaway. He was looking at her, and she flushed so wildly he must have noticed it, even from where he was standing at the back of the church. She turned around quickly, wanting to smile or laugh, wanting to get up, but of course she didn't, she sat still as could be and watched her father talk, his mouth moving and his hands open in front of his chest. He paced the front, his boots noisy on the floor. She imagined she could feel Ivvár looking at her, there was a spot on her neck he was studying, and she felt like her neck was burning, or itching, and she found herself constantly adjusting something, her hair, her white kerchief over her head.

Ivvár was not the only one to spot Willa, and to see her turn around—Risten saw. She was sitting at the far end of a middle pew where her mother had forced them in, and it had been so distinctive, that white kerchief turning, like a flag being waved up front, that it had caught her eye, so that she saw Willa's face go red, and when she followed Willa's gaze it was plain as anything, there was Ivvár. She didn't know who Willa was, only that she was the preacher's daughter, but that was enough to irritate her, since on his face was his impishness, the impishness that had not very long ago been hers, and now it was only jealousy that was hers, and when she looked again at the rows of women in their shawls and kerchiefs, the reds, the yellows, the blues, they didn't feel to her anyway as some flowers in a field, some bouquet for her wedding day, they were a sign of warning.

Mikkol appeared beside her and she shifted over for him, closer to her mother. "Sorry," he breathed in her ear, and she clutched his arm. He hadn't left her, he had come like she knew he would. He looked more frazzled than seemed appropriate for a wedding day—his dark hair, which came down to his chin on either side, was parted unevenly in the middle. He looked like a little boy who had been out in the fells all day, and she held back the desire to fix his hair, the quick rush of disappointment that although he was nice enough to look at, with his straight and serious nose, his dark eyes, he wasn't Ivvár. He didn't hit you with the force of his handsomeness, he didn't make you shake your head with the absurdity of it. But once he was sitting beside her everything calmed, and it was pleasant to have him whisper in her ear, pleasant to feel the press of his leg against her own, and the church transformed yet again, and the bitterness that had been welling was quelled, and he took her hand and that helped, too. His hand was thick with calluses, and so stiff he didn't or couldn't really bend his fingers around her fingers, they couldn't really intertwine, but it was all right. She sighed and the silver leaves on her brooches sighed with her.

They were still holding hands when the ecstasies started. Seven or eight women were standing, waving their arms. They cried out, their voices uncomfortable to hear—they were too vulnerable, too open with their griefs and their penitence. By now Risten's hand had gone sweaty, but she didn't want to let go of Mikkol's, not on a day when she needed comforting, and she kept her hand in his even though she could sense he wanted to free his own. She looked at him, and he smiled at her with his mouth closed. The crease of his eye was wet. He was so moved to be marrying her, she thought, and she was gratified, comforted even more. In her sleeplessness of the days before it had occurred to her he had forgiven her for breaking off the engagement in part because he had never really loved her at all, and the marriage was purely transactional, purely for the reindeer, so the sight of this feeling in him was placating, even heartwarming, or she felt that way until he pulled his hand from hers and clasped his own hands together and bowed his head. His mouth moved. He was praying.

He was praying along with Mad Lasse, who was reciting the Lord's Prayer. The room was reciting it. Risten looked at her mother, whose mouth did not move, who sat there looking like she always did, unflustered, a bird who does nothing while the rain beats down, and does not even bother to clean its feathers.

RISTEN MIGHT HAVE convinced herself it was just the Lord's Prayer, and that Mikkol was just being particularly observant given the importance of the day, particularly well mannered, if she had not heard a small groan come from him. It was so small she was sure no one else heard it, but there it was, the kind of sound that clearly he hadn't meant for anyone to hear. It shocked her, profoundly, that he was moved by the sermon, by Mad Lasse, who was himself so agitated now his hair had gone wet at the roots from his sweat. "Only now does the terrible unbelief which lies hidden at the bottom of the heart reveal itself," he said, and Mikkol's breath came out sharply.

For the rest of the sermon Risten could not so much hear Mad Lasse as Mikkol, and she became so finely attuned to every sound or movement he made as to warrant her own insanity, and by the time the couples began lining up to say their vows her nervousness was blending with bewilderment, her hands shook, her knees wobbled in their sockets. She was officially in a dream of her own making, she walked up the aisle with Mikkol and it made her want to laugh, that she could see Ivvár watching her, and she wanted to turn to him and laugh, laugh wide with her mouth open, like a ptarmigan. It was the same laugh she'd had once at a funeral, the laughter of the wildly inappropriate, the laughter that comes when you most should not laugh. So funny! So funny to be getting married to this man! Ha ha! She heard the ptarmigan laugh with her, hahhh-ha-ha-ha-ha-ha-ha, its chortle.

She stopped laughing when Mad Lasse put their names down in the registry—the solemnity of paper always impressed her—but by the time they were outside the laughter was spilling back up again; people had come to congratulate them, give them little gifts, coins and shawls pressed into their hands. Risten congratulated the other couples with a sense of sur-reality, she floated through the afternoon, and when one of the grooms offered her a sip of his brännvin she took it, she took several long swigs of it, and by the time they made it to their wedding dinner the snow wobbled slightly under her feet. The tipsiness helped, it granted her a retreat from it all, and while they sat in the lávvu and her mother served them the finest meat, all of the delicacies of yesterday's slaughter, Risten looked for more to drink. Sure enough, when she went to look inside the rákkas where her mother had stashed their wedding gifts, there it was, some dear and under-standing one had given them a bottle of brännvin, and while her father didn't really approve of drinking, she was a married woman now and could run her own household, and she poured herself brännvin into the same guksi she had been drinking from all her life, the same guksi from which she had sipped at coffee, and tea, and reindeer milk, but never brännvin.

"What's that?" Mikkol asked. He said it with such surprise she was surprised. She looked at him with an effrontery she didn't actually feel. She felt the same kind of laughter she'd had in the aisle, the chortle was going to come out again, she was going to burst.

"I'm having a drink," she said, "in celebration. Oh," she said, seeing his face, "it's just this once. You never drink?" she asked, teasing. She laughed more, stupidly. Surely she had seen him drink before—at Jokkmokk, defi-nitely, but also—or had she?

"After that sermon?" he asked. His shock was clear.

"Well," she said, "all right, it's not important," and she set it down.

"I thought you were serious!" he said with relief. He laughed, and when she looked back around the lávvu she saw people watching them, so she looked elsewhere, and when it seemed the attention wasn't on her she poured it out, but when she put her coffee in afterward she could still smell it, the sickly wine and whiskey mix, and she was sad to have left it behind, sad when the tipsiness began to go away and then everyone went away, and left her to their lávvu for the night, while her parents went back to the lávvu, and now it was just them, Risten and Mikkol, and somewhere, watching them, laughing from the smoke-hole, Ivvár, winking at her as Mikkol covered her with his body.

WILLA'S DISAPPOINTMENT WAS of a very different sort, and there was nothing to lighten it. After the service was over, and all of the couples had been coupled off forever, and after she had stood mingling with those in the front pews for a polite amount of time, she hurried outside while trying not to look like she was hurrying. It must have been so obvious to anyone what she was doing, how hard she was looking for Ivvár, and twice she pushed past people so roughly they turned to look at her in surprise, as if to say, who pushes on Easter?

Willa pushed on Easter. Outside in the freedom of the cold she looked for him, for his dark and curling hair, his gray gákti with its high collar, and she kept thinking maybe, even, he would appear behind her in his sly way, but he didn't, and even after she had wound around the crowds twice she hadn't spotted him. His father was easy to find, surrounded as he was by a gaggle of gasping women, half of whom appeared to still be in tears, and even once Willa had given up her search she kept her eye on Biettar, wondering if, at least, Ivvár would come to be with his father for Easter dinner, but he didn't appear, and her own dinner, laid out so nicely in front of her by Nora, had very little taste to it. She put more salt on it but it didn't help anything, and nothing helped, not the distraction of all the dishwashing that came after, and not the Sámi that crowded into the cabin, singing, smoking, filled with high spirits, and not the sight of Lorens, well for once, back to his pranks, stealing a man's hat, one of the ones with big pompons on it, and running around with it so that no one could catch him. When Lorens had, not very apologetically, been forced to return the hat, the man put his hat on top of Lorens's head and the hat fell down to his nose. "I'm a reindeer man," Lorens shouted into the hat, and people laughed, but not Willa. Biettar came up to her later that night, wishing her a happy Easter, and when he looked at her, the intensity of his eyes reminded her too much of Ivvár, and depressed her. So this was it, then—so this was Easter, the happiest day of the year, the third day on which He rose again from the dead, and ascended into Heaven, and sitteth at the right hand of God, the Father Almighty, from whence He had come to judge the quick and the dead.

Ivvár, too, had the special bitterness brought about by holidays for those who stand outside them—the sight of his father, his head thrown back toward the rafters, his hands raised above him, his strained keening noise, had been more than Ivvár was prepared to see. It had been too obvious, the comparison, what his father had once done in the lavvu for his mother and what he did now for Jesus—it wasn't the same tree but the roots touched—and it nearly made him sick to see, like something had been bent in a way it couldn't bear, and he was embarrassed for his father, that his father either did not see this or did not care. He couldn't conjure any sympathy for his father, and he wanted nothing to do with it, and this shame had sent him straight outside, where he had been accosted by Old Sussu, who put her hand on his arm. It felt so light, her hand, and yet her grip was so strong, and she said, not facing him, but looking elsewhere, as if wary of someone hearing her, "I've been thinking about you and how you have been living," and he said, vaguely, they were fine, they would both be fine, and she said she needed to talk to him, and then he actually lied to her and said he had to go pay Rikki back for the debt, and he would come to see her straight afterward, and once free of her grasping hand he joined the men at Rikki's, where he lied again to Rikki that they were just waiting for the sale of some reindeer to some Finnish farmers who were going to keep them tame for meat, and then he would have real silver to give Rikki, and of course he would come by before they left for the sea. While he stood there he had seen, through the window, Willa's small form, her white kerchief bobbing through the red shawls around her. He knew she was looking for him, he knew at any moment he could step out and say hello. He felt that possibility, the pull of that current, but he stood where he was. He waited for Easter to end. He wanted, right then, to run with the reindeer, to see their white eyelashes. He wanted to see the skittering legs of the fox, and the ferret fishing along the shallows of the sea. And the oystercatchers, their orange legs, the way they waited for each other, bickering and bowing. He wanted a good smoke and a cup of coffee with no one around, only the silence of a waterfall, or the jibber-jabber of a mountain stream.

9

LORENS WAS COUGHING BLOOD, AND IT WAS LEAKING DOWN HIS CHIN onto the blanket and onto his nightgown and Nora gasped, whispering, "Willa, Willa—Willa—"

Willa moved without thinking, without feeling the cold; she was still in her dream but somehow she was out of bed and somehow she was in the entry room. It was Dream-Willa who opened the door to her parents' bedroom, who in the darkness thought for a moment there was no one in the room, and that her missing parents were part of the dream, but it was only that the room was so dark and so still as to hide their absence. She must wake up, she must wake them up. "It's Lorens," Willa said, trying to fit urgency into a whisper, and she shook the shape of her father's arm beneath the blankets.

Her father sat up so quickly he might not have been asleep. He left the bed by turning the blankets over carefully and softly padding out, but her mother was up now, too, wearing the wide eyes of the rabbit before it runs. Only the baby was unawares, lying on top of the blankets in the middle of the bed, swaddled so soundly he couldn't have twitched a finger. His lower lip trembled ever so slightly, as if he were still suckling in his sleep. If only she could stay here, close the door and get in beside the baby, smell her mother's smell, retreat into the feather mattress and the feather blanket and the heavy wool and the old order that had been so unshakable.

In the hall she could hear her father, putting on his boots, opening the door, and his action roused her to action. I must face the thing, she told the baby. Slowly she walked back through the doorway, feeling as she did that she had made a definitive choice of a kind, and now she would never be able to go back, though back to what, she didn't know. In the bedroom that was also a living room, in the room in which she felt she knew every nail on the wall, the way God knew every hair on her head, her mother was sitting in the rocking chair. Lorens lay in her arms like the pictures of Jesus in the Bible, when Jesus was taken down from the cross, except he was so small. He was only a little boy. His light hair was painted dark with sweat to his forehead and the gruesome blood from his mouth was now on her mother's nightgown so that her breast seemed to leak blood instead of milk.

"Not another one," her mother was whispering, the words falling out of her like they never did, "don't take another one. I can't bear it, not another one." Her voice was agonized and thus agonizing to hear, so that she was hardly recognizable—she who had been their mother was now inscrutable to them, it seemed not that she had become someone else but rather that she was revealing the self it had been necessary to hide all their lives, and the revelation frightened them; she was so fragile and so pitiful they could not look at her any more than they could look at Lorens.

The children were crying. Nora was crying. Willa wanted to cry but couldn't get the tears out.

"No, no, no, no, no," her mother whispered into Lorens's hair.

"Not another one, not another one."

Lorens made a noise that might have been a cough; there was something repulsive, something wet and stringy stuck in his throat.

The door opened and their father came in, and then Old Sussu came in behind him, breathing audibly. She carried with her a large, worn leather rucksack, and she hurried to Lorens and began to touch his forehead, his hands, his neck, looking at the top of his tongue, underneath his tongue. She put her forehead against his forehead. She turned her ear to him and listened.

"Put him down," she said, pointing at one of the mattresses on the floor, and her mother rose with Lorens pressed against her and gently knelt, leaning down with him as she went so that his head never rolled back.

Old Sussu seemed impatient, hovering, nearly elbowing her out of the way, so that her mother was forced to rock back on her heels and just watch. Old Sussu pressed Lorens's ribs and his stomach with the tips of her fingers. Does this hurt, does that hurt, she asked softly. She was in her own nightclothes and there was a surprise to this: that Old Sussu wore long wool tunics and trousers like a man, that she slept with a white fur cap on, that she kept her hair pressed beneath the cap in a braid, a braid that was white like a fox's tail at its sparse tip. On her feet were thick woolen socks, pressed into boots with the turned-up toes, so that she appeared entirely covered in something warm and something soft. The effect was that of someone Willa wished to be comforted by; Willa wanted Sussu to take her into her arms and lie to her, give her some impossible promise, like her mother never did.

"What is it," her mother asked, "do you know? Have you seen it before?"

"My bag," Sussu said, looking at Willa, and Willa saw the bag on the floor and passed it over to her, meaning for her to take the bag, but Old Sussu put her hand in, like the bag was a hole in a tree, and felt around. She pulled out two smaller leather pouches. She opened one and sniffed it, opened the next, sniffed it. She chose one and opened it and took out a pinch of dried leaves, and rubbed them between her fingers, and sniffed the dried leaves again so hard some of them entered her nose, and she sneezed.

"Is this a good idea?" her mother asked, seemingly to no one.

"Let her do it," her father said snappishly. Willa had forgotten he was there. It was rare for him to be anywhere and say nothing, to not make his presence known. Her father looked how he always looked when her mother was in the sauna giving birth, afraid of his own helplessness.

"Someone should go to Muonio," Old Sussu said.

"Now?" her mother asked.

"You asked me to come look. The Finns have a doctor there. Someone should go."

"I'll go," her father said.

"No," her mother said, "no, you can't, what if——"

"I said I'll go," he said.

"That'll take days," she said. Her eyes flew around her face.

"This can look worse than it is," Old Sussu said, but her voice was so grave that no one was very reassured. "I don't know if the blood is coming up from his stomach or from his bowels. It's very red so I would say stomach. But he hasn't lost that much blood yet." She said this apologetically, as if she'd had something to do with it.

Willa felt Nora take her hand and bear down. Her knuckles were being pushed into her palms, and any other time Willa would have complained but she let it hurt.

"What else can you do? Nothing?" her mother asked. There was an unmistakable accusation to her voice.

"Not so much," Old Sussu said. She shook her head. Then she got up and went to the kitchen table. She found herself a bowl and spoon as if she lived there, and no one got up to help her, as if they all agreed she lived there, and they all watched her go to the water pail and, seeing it was frozen, take her knife from her belt and stab the water, where a small pool appeared. She took a ladle from the floor and began spooning water into the bowl. All of her motions were the same motions Willa had seen from Old Sussu her whole life, everything fluid yet sure, unrushed, as if there was nothing that would be fixed by hurrying.

"I'll be back from Muonio soon. I'll switch out the reindeer there," her father said.

"Papa, don't go," Nora begged.

"That's enough," Lars Levi said. The way he said it was cruel, like she was rather stupid, and clearly it made Nora want to cry again.

He hurried out of the room and returned with his big rucksack, the one he used for his trips out to the Lapps, throwing things from the kitchen straight in, tearing a wheel of hardtack from the rafter pole, dried meat, everything going in quickly and carelessly, and then he was hurrying around the room, taking tinder, grabbing the socks dried near the hearth, another hat.

"Brita," he said, "my——"

"In the desk drawer," she said, and he went to his desk in the corner and found something and tucked it into his pocket, shut the drawer with a slam that made them all look up. Now he was off to the bedroom, and Willa could hear him, rustling in the chest, waking the baby.

"Are you going to go wake up Simmon?" her mother called to him. "You think he can take you all the way to Muonio?"

"Biettar can take you," Sussu said, "if you head there first. Their herd must be around, Gelotjávri or maybe a bit south of there, maybe east."

"He's too far," her father said, "too far north. I'll lose too much time."

"But Simmon's reindeer," her mother said, "you think they'll make it?"

"They're old," Old Sussu said practically, "and slow. He doesn't take good care of them."

"I think you should go to Biettar," her mother said. "He can bring you. Better to get there safely than not at all."

Lars Levi went and crouched near Lorens and squeezed his hand. Lorens opened his eyes, partway, like a tired dog, but showed no sign of even recognizing him. "God's peace be with you all," he said, to all of them, like they were his congregation, and he was merely ending a sermon, and then he was gone. How long would it take him? A day, a day and a half, to Muonio. Then back. Maybe faster, if he never stopped, if there were new draft reindeer at the ready, if he didn't sleep.

It occurred to Willa that something might happen to him on the trip, that everyone was in danger, that any sense of safety was naive and imagined. She looked around the cabin, at the little girls, staring in their worried way from the mattress they had never left; at Nora, now patting the baby on his back as she held him on her shoulder; at her mother hunched over Lorens; at Carl sitting uselessly on a pew, swinging his legs. Old Sussu was carrying her concoction in a bowl, walking with it carefully toward Lorens.

"What's it for?" her mother asked.

"Can you——" Old Sussu asked. She gestured for her mother to make room. "Could you fetch me water?" Her mother seemed startled but got up, and as soon as she was at the pail Old Sussu bent over Lorens and lifted his nightgown, exposed the pale moon of his waist, and began to spread her paste on it. Willa came near to ask if she could help but Old Sussu shooed her away; Old Sussu was whispering to the poultice. Her mother was trying to make more room for the ladle and there was the crunch of breaking ice.

"I say to you," Old Sussu was saying, quietly but fervently, as if the poultice in her bowl were a misbehaving child, "you red river, you stay in the skin and the flesh. You will stay and remain as tightly as the biros and riehtis in Hell, I say to you, you will stay . . ."

Old Sussu turned slightly so that their eyes met.

Willa stepped back.

From here Willa could see the blood had been wiped away from Lorens's mouth but it still covered his nightclothes like a bib of blood.

"Our Father," Nora said, from her end of the room, "who art in Heaven," and they joined her, reciting it as one, and Willa said it with them but she couldn't have said where she was in the prayer, which line was next.

Old Sussu rose again and brought the bowl with the poultice in it to Nora. "Put it on," she said, "in another hour or so. Clean the old poultice off, and put this back on. Very thickly. Over his stomach. You know where the stomach is? Right under his left rib. Right there, yes. And don't push when you put it on. Like you're putting egg wash on your bread."

"You're leaving?" Nora asked.

Old Sussu nodded. "I'll come back when it's time," she said, with such firmness it didn't seem any questioning was possible, and she began to leave. Willa felt an urge to follow Old Sussu outside, like an urge to lift the lid of a pot when she knew it wasn't boiling yet. When Nora's back was turned she half ran, half walked to the door, where she grabbed her coat and scarf and slipped out, shutting the door very slowly and thus very quietly, then began to try to catch up, but in the fog Old Sussu seemed to get farther away no matter how Willa hurried.

"Wait," Willa called out, trying to measure her voice so that Old Sussu would hear, but those at home would not.

Old Sussu slowed but did not stop.

"It's so slippery," Willa said stupidly. The snow was so well packed, it was more akin to ice than anything else, and she was having trouble walking—how did Old Sussu do it, in boots made of fur? Willa imagined, briefly, Ivár, rolling down the hill.

"What's wrong with him?" Willa called out, hoping she would stop.

Old Sussu paused. "It's nothing to laugh at," she said, then promptly returned to her task of shuffling impossibly fast over the ice, but the more Old Sussu hurried, the more Willa felt sure of it, that Sussu had left in order to not tell them something, or, maybe, because she was going home to do something she couldn't do in front of them. What was it her father had written down? Why couldn't she remember what it was? She could see in her mind pages of her father's notes on the medicine of the Lapps, reports of how they got rid of warts, and what to do even, about lovesickness, about a boil, about a cyst in the eye. She hadn't read it well, she hadn't taken it seriously at the time, but she was sure there was something, there had been something on a sickness like this.

"I know about Biettar," Willa said, speaking into Sussu's back. Immediately she wished she hadn't said it. It was a mistake.

Old Sussu stopped. Her braid was coming loose, and her face was alight with something, maybe anger, and Willa wondered why they called Sussu Old Sussu at all. "You know what about Biettar?"

"I know what people say," Willa said. "I'm saying," she said nervously, "I wish you would tell me if there's something else wrong with Lorens. If anyone would know something, like Biettar, like who Biettar was said to be," she said, the words weakening as they left her.

"Your brother is very sick. Go see him." Old Sussu began walking even more quickly than before.

"There's nothing Biettar would have done?"

Old Sussu turned around, her brow lowered, and Willa remembered how Sussu had threatened the clerks, and how they had drowned.

"I'm not Biettar," Old Sussu said, "so how can I know what Biettar would do?"

"If he were here. If he hadn't, if my father hadn't . . ." she faltered.

Old Sussu shook her head, almost sadly. "Death is the most important part of life, you have to let it happen. No one gets life without death." Sussu took the last ten steps to her cabin and went inside, leaving the door half-open, and half-shut. Willa began to walk back home, slowly, each step a confession of foolishness. She saw what Sussu said, what she was avoiding, that Lorens was dying, that there was nothing to be done but get a doctor and say the Lord's Prayer or the Benediction or the Creed or any prayer she could think of, and accept that His will would be done—and why had she let herself, even for a moment, think that Biettar was a noaidi or had been one and that if there was one, there were others. That was what she had hoped for, wasn't it, that Sussu knew one, that Sussu would say, for your brother's sake . . .

She was nearly home when she remembered Old Sussu, crouched over her brother—you red river, you stay in the flesh, she had said. Who said that? Who talked like that? Remembering it made her nerves flare again, the entire length and surface of her flesh went cold, the backs of her ears and her knees, the inside of her nose.

She wished she could see Ivvár. She wished she could ask him what it was Sussu had been saying, and then she saw her father's tracks, heading over the bank, not to Simmons's, but to Biettar's after all, and it was so simple. The fresh tracks had been there when she'd stepped outside, only she hadn't noticed them. She wanted to laugh, she wished there were someone around, so she could say to them, pointing at the twin lines left by the skis, Having eyes, see ye not? And having ears, hear ye not? And do ye not remember?

WHAT OLD SUSSU had seen Old Sussu did not reveal, and what Nora saw—Willa, heading out on her skis along their father's path—Nora did not reveal, even though she was bitter about it, about Willa escaping from the waiting, from the confine in which sickness, in being confined, spreads all the more readily. Nora was worried about her mother, and it was easier to keep her mother from noticing Willa was gone than to point out that Willa was gone; it was easier to mother them all, her mother included. It wasn't that Nora wanted to do any of these mothering tasks, it was just that she was good at it because life had forced her to become good at it. At least in the moment the role provided respite. She insisted her mother take Lorens into the bedroom and lie there beside him with the baby, and she insisted she would do everything else, and she did do everything else—she hung sheets out to freeze, and she swept the floors, and she milked the cow of what little milk it had (barely enough to put in Lorens's porridge, but he couldn't eat it, and even this was wasted), and she sent Carl for wood, and she sent the girls for water, and she boiled water to clean the pots, and she scrubbed the last potatoes of dirt, and she set a frozen thigh of calf meat out to thaw over a boiling pot of water, and she went out to the woodshed for more wood when Carl hadn't bothered to bring in enough. When Henrik lingered too long at his window, watching her, she ignored it, for this was a gift of crisis, that the small problems were so clearly small, and Henrik was so clearly a small problem.

The other gift of crisis was the permission it gave to do what one has wanted to do all along—the clarifying burn of crisis gave Lars Levi a reason to flee the cabin and to go out, again, into the wilderness; it gave Brita a day of lying in bed; it gave Willa an excuse to see Ivvár one more time. For the first hour of the trip out to his herd she was sure in her purpose, but when she stopped to rest after the second hour she felt the flimsiness of it: what was she going to say, anyway? She nearly turned around, but the thought of returning to the cabin was too unappealing, and the thought of seeing him was too appealing, and she allowed desire to silence fear.

In fact, though, Willa had never been out to the herds, and though she'd seen them running before on the other side of the river, she didn't really know how herding worked, and what it was the reindeer did all day long, and so when she stood on the top of the foothill and saw, for the first time, the reindeer spread out between the dwarf birch and the pine, the land stippled with the blurred and broad strokes of their shaggy forms, she was surprised to be so moved by the sight. Was it really fatigue from Lorens that brought tears to her eyes? Or was it them, was it the scene itself, the pastoral idyll the sight conjured? The view before her was the envy of any landscape painter, who might have wished to show how many colors there are, really, within snow—its blue and purple veins, and the twilight's orange picked up by the green left in the pines, and the reindeer themselves, shot through with the same orange, and russet browns from their coats, and everything fulsome with color and depth, even if, at first, the sensation was simply one of whiteness. If only, Willa thought, she could just stand there and look! She envied the men herding them, the Lapps themselves, that they had been born into this. They saw this every day, this land, these creatures . . .

In this she revealed how little she knew, since this time of year the reindeer were particularly unattractive, their coats patchy and their hipbones showing and their antlers mostly gone and everything about them tragic enough to be nearing comic. She could not see, moreover, herself, and how she appeared in this landscape, more like the reindeer than she would have thought, the way she was harried and bony. Her coat, too, was horribly patchy, her skis needed waxing, and there was very little about her to suggest to the men who watched her arrival—Ivár's cousins—that she was here, in part, because she was a little in love. Mad Lasse had arrived a few hours earlier, but he was gone already, and in all the excitement they had learned only that he was going for a doctor, and not why, so the presence of Willa gave the impression that everyone was coming running for a doctor, and all of the outlanders were sick.

It was Ánde who approached her to stop her from wandering into the herd. His cousin Niko hung back and watched, amused—Ánde was always the first to approach a stranger, and he was always especially comfortable around women; there was no woman he wouldn't try to win over if he had the chance. The two cousins were not especially handsome men—they didn't have the aggressively good looks of Ivár—but they retained the confidence that ran in the family line, and this had its appeal, though in Ánde it could appear as a kind of brashness, and in Niko it emerged as something soft, almost secretive, and you only saw it when he worked, when he threw a lasso or pulled down a bull. But Ánde was cut off before he could begin by Willa, who asked anxiously, "Is this the Rasti siida? Is Ivár here?"

Ánde turned back to share a look with Niko. This was much better than the preacher who had just showed up. This was interesting, and it involved the possibility of teasing Ivár, who was impossible to tease, since he always tried to rise above it in a way that irritated them, like their jokes didn't apply to him, only his to them.

"I need to see him," Willa said, somewhat nervously, "it's important."

"Oh . . ." The two men looked at each other, again. Niko raised his eyebrows, shrugged.

"You're with the pastor? He left already," Ánde said, clearly prolonging this, and enjoying it. He could sense her agitation, but it didn't strike him as anything serious.

"I'm not traveling with him," she said, reddening, "but I'm in a hurry."

"Luckily Ivvár never takes long," Ánde said, clearly finding his joke very funny.

"But can't I go to him?"

"Oh, the lávvu. Yes, he's there."

"I can go?"

"I can't say what anyone should or shouldn't do," Ánde said.

"Best to let people go their own way," Niko said, but Willa could not parse what he meant by this.

"I guess I'll go see him," she said, though she made it sound like a question. One of their dogs approached and sniffed her, though it didn't bark. Clearly it wanted to bark; the dog opened its mouth nervously, yawned, and stretched.

Ánde shook his head, don't bark, and the dog didn't bark.

Willa started to ski toward the tents, haltingly, as if expecting at any moment for one of them to stop her, but no one stopped her, and instead, the tall one, Ánde, began to follow her. She thought: it was wrong to come. Ánde cried out, with delight, "Oh, I see, you're Mad Lasse's daughter! Niko, the báhpa nieida," he called back.

She would not, did not, rise to this bait. The tents weren't far away, and it annoyed her to feel him following her.

"Not that one," Ánde said, "next one," and she wondered, briefly, if he was lying to her, or playing a joke on her, but what could she do? At the tent she opened the flap, but a large stack of branches and twigs were piled up at the door, and there wasn't a good way to get through.

"Just go in," Ánde said, and she made herself go in anyway, the kindling snapping sharply under her feet.

"Ánde," Ivvár said—and even hearing his voice made her so happy that she forgot what she'd just been afraid of—"you make so much noise, it's like a bear coming through."

"Your girlfriend is here," Ánde said.

Willa could make out his form, a bundle of blankets on the other side of the fire. The blankets moved. Ivvár rolled over and she saw him in the act of opening his eyes, in the act of recognizing her. If he was surprised he didn't show it. He sat up and his fur hat fell back and he pulled it over his brow. His eyes looked tired, slow moving in his head.

"All right, get out," he said.

"I thought I'd take a coffee with you," Ánde said, brightly, jokingly.

"If you don't get out—" Ivvár said.

"All right, all right, stay warm," Ánde said, the laughter clear in his voice, but he left, the smoke of the fire billowing out with him, and then, like that, she was alone, with Ivvár.

Ivvár took some branches from the stack near the door and began to break twigs off of them carefully, laying them down flat on top of the smoke and embers, so that they formed neat little rows, and then on either side of this he laid two logs, again very carefully, like he was building a house that needed to last, and he fished out some birch curl from a small bag and tucked it into the embers, and the birch curl caught, and then, this done, he looked at her.

She felt sick.

"I woke you up," she said.

"We've been moving the herd for four, five days now . . . my father helped me bring our herd, bring my herd . . . we joined it with my uncles' herd two days ago . . . so I've slept so little . . . almost not at all . . . we leave for the sea together soon . . ." He barely sounded like himself and she felt embarrassed to have come and bothered him. His fatigue was so obvious and so great that she thought, he is the sick one who needs to be cared for, and we've taken his father away from him, his father is off to Muonio to help my father, and then his father is going to preach at the sea.

"There's so many of them," she said. "I had no idea. They're all—when I saw them all at once like this I could have cried."

For a long moment he looked at her, his eyes so fully on her eyes that the act of looking revealed itself to be an action and not an accident, it was a thing he was doing, and she wanted him to look at her, she wanted to look at him, even as she was afraid of it; it was too much, it was too hard to be seen.

"So," he said, at last, not taking his eyes from her, "you came all this way to see some reindeer?" But his voice was lighter—he seemed a little friendlier. He fumbled around for his kettle, which he found, but then seemed to realize he had no water to fill it with, so he held it in his hand. His kettle was so entirely black with soot it might have been carved from soot itself.

"My brother," she said.

"Yes, your brother," he repeated.

"We woke up this morning, well it was the middle of the night, because Lorens—he was coughing up blood. My father went for Old Sussu. She came and looked at him. She said to get a doctor from Muonio."

"Yes," Ivár said. "I know." He did know. He knew because Mad Lasse had been in this lávvu not very long ago and had woken him up, and now it was happening again, only this time there was something Willa wanted from him and it made him irritated. There was so much that she didn't understand, and to see her here was proof of how much she didn't under- stand. He had no will to explain it to her, any of it. He was so tired. His eyes hurt in the back of the eyeballs, his legs and his arms were sewn with stones, he wanted to lie down and not get up for many, many days.

"He's going to die," she said, suddenly, very seriously. She said it with assertion, as if she had planned it and was going to make sure it happened. "Lorens is going to die," she repeated, "and——" She stopped.

"Yes," he said flatly.

"Yes what?"

"Yes, he's going to die," he said.

"Why would you say that?"

"You just said it."

"I did, but it's different."

"Why is it different?" He wasn't sure why they were talking like this, with a slight bitterness in both of their tones.

"When you say it, it seems more real."

"I don't have any special power," he said.

"Well, I know that," she said, but he could tell she was disappointed. He had hurt her. He was hurting her. He wished suddenly to hurt her so much it would kill off anything between them, and he couldn't disappoint her anymore, any more than he could disappoint Risten. How exhausting, to always disappoint. He couldn't bear any of it, these women, wanting things from him that could not be given.

She looked at him and she took her hat off. She took her scarf off, and then her mittens. She shook out the scarf and, like she had done it a hundred times before, she tucked her scarf in between the pole and the tent-cloth and then set her mittens on the drying rack above the fire. He had the awareness that they were both watching her set her scarf and her mittens to dry.

She sat there in her coat with her hands and her face and her hair exposed like that, just looking at him. He wanted to laugh, the desire between them was so clear, so obvious as to be preposterous, there was nothing hidden in it, almost no mystery; He could have picked it up with his hand.

His mood had turned—she had taken off her scarf and his mood had turned—he was still very tired, but it was something distant, a memory his body held but not his mind.

How wrong, how crass—to come here for her brother and to have this sit between them like this, and yet, what was there to do about it? If it was true it was true, the fact of Lorens would not change it, nothing would change it, it was another part of the world to which you react but you cannot will away. He smiled at her and she smiled at him; it was the same smile they smiled at each other, with six or seven feelings in it, curiosity and desire, the weight of knowing they were each wanted by the other, the impossibility of anything happening between them looming over it all.

They did not speak for so long that there was something potent now in the silence, and he was afraid to break it, and she was afraid to break it. The fire was noisy enough for both of them, and the herd, too, of course, and somewhere in the distance there was Ánde laughing and Niko encouraging his laughter. She took a breath, but he put his hand up to stop her—he didn't want her to speak, he wanted to stay in the waiting a little longer.

THE SILENCE COULD NOT BE SUSTAINED, AND THE TRANSIENCE OF ALL things—the fire, the snow, their gaze, their lives—was felt when Willa sighed. Willa sighed and the night came down around them, and Lorens was there again, and Ivvár's fatigue, and the fact of her begging here in the lávvu, in the firelight, for what exactly she didn't know. Had she been asked in the moment to articulate what it was precisely she had hoped for, she would have failed; she could not have said, much less admitted to herself, that she had come not only because she wished for there to be some other way to save Lorens but perhaps most of all because she wished for there to be some other way to save herself, because what she wanted was not only a way out of her father's land of church and town but a way into Ivvár's. She sensed that she would have clung to anything if it brought her closer to Ivvár, but what she didn't know she wanted, specifically, was for him to present her with something besides her father's God that would fix things, some proof that if the answer was not her father's Jesus then it could be Ivvár's Raidenáddja; if it was not the Finns' Jumala it was the Sámi's Ipmel; and if Ivvár could save Lorens then she would be free to love him; no, she would be right to love him.

But she could express none of these things, and instead she only knew she wanted something from him, and she wanted him most of all to not disappoint the expectations she could not articulate.

"Do you believe that story I told you? About the eahpárás? The äpárä?" Ivvár asked, and she felt unnerved, like she had been speaking aloud and he had merely continued the conversation.

She nodded.

She could not see it, could not have known or guessed it, where his mind was, but she saw that he wasn't there in the tent with her. He was somewhere else; he was with his mother, in fact, and his mother was in her rákkas and he had climbed in with her, she gathered him against herself and he knew he was beloved, he smelled her warm and human smell, a little like shoe-grass left in the sun. She asked him to help her and he held her up as she hobbled outside, where she turned away from him and he turned away from her while she relieved herself, and afterward he helped her back up, and they were both sorry that he'd had to do it. He had not thought of that moment, those days and weeks of sickness, maybe since it had happened.

Willa sighed again, smaller this time, and he thought of what his mother would say, it was nearly like she spoke: it's kind of Willa to bring me to you.

He looked at her. Behind her the lávvu fluttered, and in front of her the smoke rose.

"You should go home," he said, not knowing, somehow, what else to say—he couldn't sort out his feelings, or his wants, and he didn't like it.

She nodded at him. "We won't see each other again for a long time," she said.

He nodded.

"Not until the snow comes again," she said.

"It all depends," he said.

"On the weather?" she asked, like she was trying to bring the teasing back, restore the lightness that had left them.

"That, too," he said, but without any flippancy, he had none in him; he was suddenly, heavily, sad.

"I'm sorry," she said, and he understood what she meant. She raised herself up to her knees and pulled her scarf down from the tent-pole, and took her mittens, none of which were dry yet, but she put them all on anyway, and he waited for himself to say, no, stay a bit and dry off, warm up, but he didn't say it, and he watched her go but without any pleasure or even relief, because he wanted her to stay, but he couldn't ask her to stay; it could not be done. It wasn't done.

On the fells his eyes stung in the wind, and he wandered from place to place to keep his blood moving, but his mind was running, it seemed to him that his mother had stretched out her hand and pushed Willa toward him, or him toward Willa. People often talked about what they thought the dead would have wanted—she would have wanted you to be happy, that kind of thing—but Ivvár thought that his mother would have wanted him to mourn her, mightily and bitterly, and now he thought she would have wanted him to find a wife, and be in love. She would not have liked this, how alone he was.

What would she have thought of Risten? She would have told him, you're a fool, to let pride win like that, if it's pride that's stopping you. Although she might never have liked Risten, she might have found Risten to be irritatingly wholesome, too above every fray. And Willa? What would she have thought of Willa?

As if he were feeling it all at once, a great tiredness came over him, not a tiredness of sleep but of mind, a fatigue larger than the fells themselves. He watched the herd with half his mind, half his eyes, he thought of the sledge his father had packed to take with him when he left Ivvár to go and preach the name of Jesus. They had said nothing to each other, that was how his father wielded silence, his father had never even said, I'm not going to come back. I'm leaving you with the herd.

While Ivvár walked in his wide circles from one hill to another, in between the small pines and the smaller birch, his form slow and halting, his indecision clear in his itinerant pacing, Nora paced in the cabin, looking for more chores to keep herself busy, and Lars Levi tapped his feet against the front board of the sledge, sure that the doctor wouldn't even be in town, and Brita dreamed of when Levi had died. Only Henrik was at ease, though he could see something was not quite right: he saw Willa's return, and that Lars Levi was gone, and that Old Sussu went in and out of the parsonage, but he ignored these signs and he wondered, only, if Nora was coming outside more often because she wanted him to notice her. So he managed to be surprised two days later when Lars Levi appeared in a sledge, and with him Biettar, and a stranger, the reindeer all looking bedraggled, breathing hard with their tongues out the sides of their mouths like dogs. He was surprised when Brita came running out of the cabin in her night-dress and, as he had never seen her do, threw her arms around Lars Levi, who both tried to hold her and hurry inside at the same time. Everyone, it seemed, was hurrying inside; even Old Sussu came out of her cabin and followed them all into the parsonage as if she'd been welcomed in, and Henrik wondered, should he go in, too?

Outside he halted in front of their cabin, should he or shouldn't he, but once he was inside no one looked at him at all. The door to the bedroom was open, and everyone was crowded around the bed on which Lorens lay, the stranger—a doctor, Henrik was realizing—leaning over Lorens with such reverence it looked like a nativity scene, and the rest of them the wise men, the shepherds, waiting to show obeisance.

It was very quiet. The doctor was touching Lorens's arms, his shoulders, his chest, his stomach—the boy made no sound. He might have already been dead, he was that still. Henrik felt the first pang of real pity he'd ever had for the family, he felt the horror of living up here where you couldn't get help in time for anything, where your children died on you. Hadn't they already lost one of them, to the measles, maybe? Lisa's twin, he'd heard that. It drove Lars Levi mad, Simmon had said, that was when Lars Levi had become Mad Lasse.

"Give me my scalpel," the doctor said, and Brita rooted around in his bag and handed him the small knife.

"And a bowl," the doctor said, and Nora passed him one. The doctor cautiously opened the boy's wrist and let the blood run into the bowl.

The boy groaned.

"What is it?" Willa asked. "What's wrong with him?" When she had come in and gotten behind Henrik he didn't know, but she was standing there, almost pressed against him. He couldn't remember the last time he'd felt pressure of any kind from any human body, and it thrilled him to feel it, even from Willa, and he tried to stop himself from leaning any closer to her.

The doctor used the hand that was not collecting blood to open Lorens's mouth, so they all saw his tidy teeth, which were not white but red from blood, and his tongue, which was not red but white, covered in small pustules. It was the mouth of a ghoul.

Henrik felt his shoulders shudder. The boy's mouth was too compelling, too frightening, he couldn't look away.

When the boy had become whiter still, the doctor began to stanch the blood—he pressed the wound tightly with a cloth.

"Now what?" Willa said. Her voice was high.

"Now we wait," the doctor said.

"And then what else? And then what do you do?"

"Cupping, probably," he said, "though what has he been eating?"

"Almost nothing," Nora said. "Some very soft oatmeal, a spoonful here and there. Old Sussu said to give him reindeer blood—"

"Who is Old Sussu?"

Everyone looked at Old Sussu, who was standing in the back of the room. Her lower jaw twitched back and forth. Probably, Henrik thought, the doctor thought she didn't understand Finnish.

The doctor shook his head. "This is"—he said, reconsidered, and then—"I need to be alone with the patient, please."

The children began to file out past Henrik, and then the doctor said, pointedly, looking at Henrik, "Everyone, please. But the parents,"

They all filed out and stood in the entryway. "All the way out, please," the doctor said, and they started to go into the other room but he said, pointing to the front door, "out," and so they all went outside, milling about, staring at one another. The doctor closed the door behind them, made sure it was shut firmly into place.

"He smells like fish soup," Willa said, her breath puffing out in front of her.

"I gave him a bath yesterday," Nora said, her breath returning the plume.

"No, the doctor," Willa said, stamping her feet.

The children stamped their feet. The little girls were wrapping their arms around each other, maybe in that childlike way of dramatizing their pains, or maybe they really were that cold. Biettar had drifted off outside to the reindeer, taking off their harnesses, freeing them from the sledges.

"Come on, let's everyone go to the store," Henrik said, and began to walk there, regretting this as he said it, remembering that it stank inside, remembering how clean their cabin had been in comparison. He remembered, too late, that he even had a bottle of vodka half-full, stashed somewhere—where—on a shelf? Was it in sight? He walked quickly, to beat them all there, and when he got to the door he scurried—where was it?—behind the kerosene lamp?—he knelt to hide it behind the counter, and when he stood back up Nora was standing there, staring at him, the door open behind her and the sky an even, pleasant blue around her narrow shoulders.

Like she'd seen nothing he went to push aside the curtain windows, letting in light, and then began to clear the counter, stacking the three, four dirty glasses that had gathered there.

She was looking about her as if inspecting the place for her own use.

"Well, come in," Henrik said to the line of children at the door. They looked at him warily; he wondered if they were not actually allowed in the store, if they only came in now because there was nowhere else to go and no one to tell them what not to do.

"No," Nora said, "don't close the door just yet, let's get some fresh air in—" and then she went to the stove, began to fuss with the fire. This was what it would be like, he thought, to have a wife, although a wife would never have allowed the store to become this state. Old Sussu found the stool he kept by the window and sat down heavily on it, but her legs didn't meet the floor and only just touched the first rung. He took out candy for the children and they glowed and they took it to the corner and sat on sacks of flour, the flour puffing up around them like they had thrown themselves into a snowbank. They stared up the stairs at the dark bedroom. Willa refused the candy, stood at the door and watched something—it must have been Biettar, because he appeared then and came in, closing the door. Biettar squinted, as if it were bright inside instead of dark.

Henrik stood behind the counter. Biettar was facing him, so directly that Henrik felt under his inspection, even though Henrik was taller, and Biettar was, ostensibly, his guest, and Biettar had still not paid him—had not paid him at Michaelmas, had not paid him at Christmas-time, had not paid him at Easter-time, and probably the herds were on the move now, and Biettar, if he really was going to be a lay preacher, was a pauper now, a beggar, and yet he stood there like Henrik was in his debt, like Henrik was to blame for something. If Henrik hadn't hated the man so much he would have admired him.

"Coffee?" Nora asked, but gently. He saw she'd already filled the kettle with water from the pail, and he was grateful for the interruption, the little task of looking for the coffee grounds. He found them and passed them and she kept looking at him—oh, she wanted a spoon. She didn't just shake it out into the kettle like he did.

He found a spoon, which he cleaned on his shirt.

Biettar was still standing there, watching this exchange like Henrik was a show put on for his entertainment.

Henrik brought out another stool from behind the counter and offered it to Biettar, who sat on it not in the usual way, slouched over, but used it like a plinth upon which he sat, straight-backed, eyes steady, or, maybe, like an owl on its branch, looking around for its mice. Henrik wanted to say, I've seen you crawling on the floor, don't look at me like that, but of course he didn't, he waited for Nora or someone to say something—what he was going to do with everyone in here, and for how long, he didn't know.

"Let's pray," Biettar said.

Henrik nodded absentmindedly. Praying sounded tiresome to him, but also it would eat up time, and then there wouldn't be a need to talk. Nora and Willa were, oddly enough, cleaning, like he had asked them to do it, or like they simply couldn't stand to be somewhere that dirty for a moment longer. Don't do that, he thought about saying, but it seemed rude to stop them. Willa had found a cloth somewhere and was picking things up off the counter and wiping beneath them, and Nora had poured some of the boiling water into the cast-iron pan, and was scraping at the pan's crusted bottom with a knife. She scraped so hard, her hands so tight around the knife, that her intensity was a little frightening to see.

"Why don't you say it?" Biettar asked.

"Oh," Henrik said. He cleared his throat. "Oh"—he fumbled for something, found nothing there.

"There's no living spirit inside you?"

"Hmm?" he asked, nervously. He was already behind the counter but he felt like it wasn't enough between them, he wished there was something else, a whole wall, maybe, and he looked around for something to do again, and found his record books and took them out. He felt a safety in it, in the book, the book with the list of what Biettar had not paid him, what Ivvár had not paid him, what the Lapps cost him with their dithering and their promises and their half answers.

"There's nothing living inside you," Biettar said, "you're a death-tent." In the corner, Sussu sat in the chair and looked out the window, like she chose to not see what was going on, and the children were oddly adult about it all, expert at sitting in silence and seeming to have no role in what unfolded. Henrik looked at Nora for help, but she was carrying the pan she had scrubbed outside, where she did not even just dump it immediately by the door, like he would've done, but walked a good ways away from the cabin with it. He flipped through more pages in his book—Per-Anders Salmon, he had written, 1 riks-dollar one sack flour, 2 riks-dollars one fox pelt, 4 riks-dollars brännvin, 2 riks-dollars silver brooch, 25 pence salt, 25 pence butter, 1 pence thread, 2 pence needle, 40 pence leather purse, 2 riks-dollars belt, 50 pence knife handle (antler), 3 riks-dollars brännvin—

"I'm a storekeeper," Henrik said, without looking up from his book. He felt the tightness of the debt, the pressure of it, in his voice, his face. "I let God do God's work."

"The truth runs fast," Biettar said, "but a lie runs faster."

Henrik did not look up. Nora had come in and the door was open and a quick breeze came through to him. He could see her feet without looking up, the wet leather of her shoe. Henrik turned the page and saw he had arrived at the Muskoses, who only came to town for meat, of which they bought the cheapest kind. They were desperately poor, he always saw it in their thin faces when they showed up, in the way they looked around his store and envied him even this. "I went so long," Biettar said, "I had eyes but I saw not. I had ears but I heard not."

"And do ye not remember," Willa said, but this made no sense at all.

"And now I see," Biettar said, "you open the door for the Devil." He shook his head. He looked like he didn't know what to do with his hands, and he alternately clasped them and released them, his wide hands with large knuckles, working hands, hands that could strangle or drag or pull.

No one appeared to know what to do or say. Sussu was watching Biettar, Nora was standing with the heavy iron pan in one hand. Willa was the only one moving, still wiping at the counter that was either already clean or could never be made clean, scraping at something with her fingernail.

Henrik turned the page. Marit Unga. Whatever she had bought was illegible to him, a series of scrawls. She had paid in full, now he remembered her, she had brought her husband's reindeer with her, slaughtered it and dragged it here herself on a rickety sledge and she'd fought with Simmon about something, out by the storehouse, he didn't know what.

"The Devil doesn't speak," Biettar said, "he pretends not to know what he does. He sells the Devil's piss and pretends he gives us manna from heaven." It was, almost directly, phrasing of Laestadius's, patched together from various sermons, but in the sermons it had always sounded metaphorical, and made no impression on Henrik besides faint amusement, but Biettar spoke with such plainness that it seemed as if he was not saying alcohol was like the Devil's piss but that it was the Devil's piss, and Henrik was bottling the stuff himself. "You know who he is?" Biettar asked Nora.

Nora just stood there.

"A storekeeper," Henrik said, shame spreading through him. He turned the page, and he turned the page again, licking his thumb, flipping through the thin paper so that a few pages were ripping, something he was usually careful to never let happen, and then he found it, Biettar and Ivár's pages, they faced each other, steady mirrors of each other, so that two riks-dollars brännvin on Biettar's side was met with three riks-dollars on Ivár's, and two riks-dollars on Ivár's was met with four riks-dollars on Biettar's, so that father and son were battling for the most credit owed to Henrik, with Biettar in the lead before the Christmas holiday and Ivvár now well ahead by Easter, since Biettar had stopped drinking. Actually, Henrik saw now he hadn't tabulated it recently—he had put down individual costs but not their total, and he did the math quickly in his head, and another profound shock went through him, that they owed him that much—twenty-three riks-dollars, or ten reindeer or so—he felt his own stupidity, for having lent it, and he felt furious with Biettar, for standing here in his store, scolding him like a child for the mistakes Biettar had made.

He looked up and Biettar was looking at him. He was resting his thumbs on the inside of his belt, like the Lapp men did when they wanted to look a bit more imposing, and Henrik hated that it worked, that Biettar managed to look more relaxed and more defiant at the same time. "That," Biettar said, nodding, "I have already paid for, seventy times seven."

"No," Henrik said, starting to shake his head, faster and faster now. "No, it's written right here, every penny."

"You should ask the Devil to keep you warm at night," Biettar said, as if he was helpless to do anything else. There was blood in Henrik's head, practically swimming in front of his eyes. He thought: Biettar says this in front of them so I can't do anything. So he seems the one who is civil. While next door Lorens has his mouth of blood, and Biettar stands here and says that he will ruin me. Biettar seemed to be looking around like everything was settled, and he went to the window and looked out. "Should we leave this dark house and go up to the church and pray?"

"Twenty-three riks-dollars," Henrik said, "that's what you owe me." It felt like the words cost him to even say them. So Biettar wasn't going to pay. He had God on his side, and God's preacher, and the preacher's children. The whole situation was so absurd Henrik could not believe he was living through it himself.

"I think we should go," Willa said.

He would write, Henrik decided. He would write to his uncle, he would admit to everything. He would leave nothing out. He would catch Biettar by the neck and he would wring him, he would shake every penny from him, he would go to his herd and he would take his gun, he would shoot them, one by one, he would do it by himself if he had to. He looked down and his hands were shaking. On the stove the kettle was boiling, and the store smelled like coffee, and he could feel his pulse in his neck. Nora looked at him. There was something mocking in her eyes but what he didn't know; he only knew she, they, the Northerners, Sámi and Swedes alike, it didn't matter what you called them, they saw him and thought: soft, silly. They knew his own insignificance without it being announced, and they knew, like a wolf studying the herd, that he was secretly the weakest, that he was the mark that would fall first.

II

Every time Ivvár fell asleep, no matter if it was midday or sundown, he awoke the same way, with the same clear thought, so clear someone might have just spoken it into his ear: Willa. It was becoming worse every day, the thinking of her, he would be shouting at the reindeer and waving his arms and she would be there, looking at him from across the fire, and he would think: I want to lick that sweaty neck. It was farcical at this point, the tightness of his trousers, and he kept to the edges of the herd and the men, and when he could he was slow to get up from sleep, and he was mortified, he thought even, she has some witchiness in her, she put something in my coffee, but he wasn't actually angry at her, only impressed by her powers. Usually things would weaken by now, the plain fatigue of the herd would weaken the thought of any person, and he was amazed by her persistence, how sometimes he heard her say his name, not quite like a Sámi said it, but like she loved it, she loved his name, her teeth brushed her bottom lip when she said it and sat there for an extra moment and enjoyed it, enjoyed him.

He was cursed, he thought. Even Ánde and Niko were noticing, and he could tell they knew what was on his mind. Ivvár didn't hear them sometimes when they spoke, another time he simply watched a section of the herd wander west without noticing or doing anything about it until Ánde started shouting at him and the dogs began to lose their minds. Then a few hours later he did the same thing again. He changed his mind twice, three times—first he was going to go, then he wasn't going to go, he packed a rucksack and then unpacked it, and when he finally mentioned to Ánde that he was going back to town Ánde was so irritated he said nothing, just disappeared back outside and Ivvár heard him out there, for a long time, chopping a birch tree down to its bones, so Ivvár just left. He couldn't take any of the driving-reindeer, since they were all with the women, and he had to ski and just hope he crossed into someone going the same way—it wasn't likely, but he hoped for it, and there, hardly two hours into his trip, there was a young couple, with two sledges, traveling down to Hetta for a dying mother, and they offered to bring him most of the way. Their reindeer were old, and the snow was ice, and so they moved slowly, the sledges still sliding wildly about. Soon it would be walking weather only. Walking, and horses. But what did it matter, they had this ride, for now they could make it, and Ivvár felt like the luck of finding the couple had proved it; he was going to get Sussu to help Lorens, and he was going to see Willa, he was going to save Lorens and there was no one who would not say, voiiia, what love, for that love anything is understandable.

The ride must have been very long but it didn't feel very long, perhaps because he was thinking only of Willa, because he felt so good about it, nearly giddy, and the night was hardly night these days at all, and instead they moved under a musky gray twilight that receded to the strength of morning. The sun was warming the side of his neck when he saw the steeple of the church like a pointed cap over the hills. The sun fell flat on the tarred roof of the church, and wavered against its windowpanes, and lit a thousand flames on the surrounding snow.

The reindeer crossed the river and, heaving their way up the bank, slowed. He pointed out Simmon's to the couple, whom he recognized now in their faces were already in grief, but it was a grief that could not, did not, touch him. "Simmon can graze the reindeer," he said, offering them fifty pence but they refused, and he offered it again, and they refused again, and he understood that it was too ugly to gain from their grief, and he wondered if they would stay in town, at Rikki's, at the parsonage, or keep going in their hurry to see death's work.

Was Lorens already dead?

Willa, he thought, Willa, and his heart hopped so that, even though he was thinking of her brother, dying, he found himself smiling, How horrible, how life went on!

The town already had an empty feeling to it, and this was amplified by the brightness of the sun, which took the whiteness of the snow and doubled it. It was this very light that protected him now as he walked down the hill, for no one looking out of a window or across the river could stand to set their eyes on the snow. In the parsonage the sun came in so brightly through the open shutter that Lorens's sickness was too clear, and the sun fell on the sheets and the night-clothes he had sweat through, and all of the sheets and night-clothes that were freezing on the line outside, moving stiffly in the wind like thin slabs of wood.

It seemed at every moment he would stop breathing, but he didn't, and the doctor hovered over him with patience—the doctor felt honored, actually, to have been brought here. His mother was one of the Finns who revered Laestadius; she had heard him preach once and she'd insisted he go to help. So the doctor tended to Lorens with especial tenderness, though in truth he was bewildered by Lorens's illness, it disturbed him profoundly. He had symptoms that made no sense together, the blood coming up with his coughs, a hard and firm ball in his belly, chills, a slow heartbeat. The doctor felt, somehow, that he had been brought here not to save Lorens, who seemed beyond saving, but to serve this preacher, who struck him as so admirable. The man was in the other room, writing sermons, even while his son was dying, he gave his life, Lorens's life, utterly to God. The doctor had never seen such acceptance, such equanimity—it was not indifference, it was a oneness with God, he thought, and as he let out Lorens's blood again he wondered, am I God's will? Is it the angels who steady my hand? He wondered if at this boy's door to death, his own door to life was being opened, and his hands shook with something he didn't understand as the boy's blood pooled into the bowl.

THE DOCTOR'S ARRIVAL had meant that the parsonage was now, in addition to a parsonage, and in addition to an infirmary, an inn—they had given the doctor the only bedroom, which meant that Lars Levi and Brita were sleeping with the children in the main room, so that they all slept with shoulders and feet touching, but no one minded this, really; there was something pleasant to it, a deep security, even as Lorens kept them up and even as Brita worried it wasn't good for them all to be in the same room as Lorens. But where to put him? Better we all go together—that thought had actually crossed her mind, several times. If you take him, Lord, she thought, take me with him. She said it and in the extremity of love that is bestowed upon parents she meant it.

Willa could not join her mother, or the doctor, or her father, in any of these sentiments: she was ruled by fear. She was ruled by what she perceived as a necessity that Lorens not die, and by a habit to approach every hardship with effort of some kind. She was glad she'd gone to Ivvár, even if nothing had come of it, but she looked for more to do, and took over the task of taking care of the doctor, fluffing up his pillows and tidying his bed. She brought him food and coffee, offered to make him a fire in the sauna, and he said yes, he would like a sauna very much, and she went outside to get the sauna ready, glad in some ways for the onerousness of the task.

Willa was just lighting the fire in the sauna's stove when Ivvár's shadow crossed the open door. She looked up and saw, first, only a man, the sun forming broad shoulders and a shock of loosely curled hair. The hair moved, was tossed with impatience to the side, like Nora did when she was getting ready for bed, but it wasn't Nora, it was Ivvár, and Willa's hope rose without her being able to do a thing about it. Swiftly, he shut the door behind him, blocking out all the light so that now there was just the one, two little flames huffing along inside the stove, the flame of the birch curl widening out in a flash—a twig, two, three twigs trapped now.

Ivvár sat down on the bench as if it were perfectly normal for him to be here. He looked at her in the darkness, she could hardly see him but she could see the wet of his eyes, the same way you could see a frozen puddle on the tundra by its shine. Each part of her was alert, sensitive to his nearness—she hadn't worn a coat outside, and she was just in her day dress, and she felt aware of the thinness of the wool. She looked back at him, she felt the phrase in her mouth, I should go, or, you should go. She prepared herself to get up and open the door and leave. It was right there, it didn't lock on either side, the sun was coming in around its edges as if to illuminate its purpose.

She stood up and couldn't figure out where to stand—it was hot near the stove but the sauna was so small there was nowhere to go that wouldn't bring her to him.

"Why are you here?" she asked. In the small wooden space all sounds were tamped down, muted, like they had no real life to them.

"How is your brother?"

She couldn't bring herself to say the answer. If she spoke, she would cry. She cleared her throat, focusing carefully on the words. "The doctor's here," she said. "He's been here for two days now."

"What's he doing?"

"I don't know," she said. "Letting his blood, pouring it into bowls, pouring the blood outside and then the dogs go eat the snow."

"How does he look?"

"He barely moves."

"He eats?"

"Almost nothing."

"Does he say anything?" He had been asking the questions in such quick succession she didn't know what to do besides answer them, but the fire really was too hot at the back of her knees, and she did it, she took two awkward steps and stood practically in front of him, so that the fronts of his knees brushed against the front of her dress. He seemed unfazed by this, and made no effort to either make room for her or make himself smaller; his hands were resting on the bench on either side of him and she had the sensation of standing in front of someone for their appraisal, except that in such darkness it was all suggestion.

"No," she said.

Ivár was nodding, she could tell because the shine in his eye moved up and down.

"What are you doing here?" Willa asked. "Aren't you supposed to be— gone."

"I came back," he said.

"I thought I would go south and get married and never see you again."

There was a pause so long that inside it a thousand futures ran around, raced. "The night is never so long the day never comes," he said, at last. His hand reached out for hers, he touched her hand with warm fingers and she remembered when he had fallen and she had pulled him up, but now the hand in hers had more meaning, now it was a hand she was afraid to touch because it was not a stranger's hand.

"So did you get it?" she asked.

"What?"

"Whatever you came for."

"I don't know yet." The teasing in his voice again, she could hardly bear the implications, it practically hurt to even hear.

"Are you going to tell me what you came for?" she asked, trying to sound teasing, in control of her teasing, but sure everything gave her away, her voice, her knees.

"Why do you ask questions you already know the answer to?"

Her tongue felt large and the roof of her mouth was sticky. Her whole mouth was sticky. For a minute it seemed like they were both listening to the muffled movements of the fire from inside the stove. She wanted him to talk like this and she feared it. Delay, she thought, delay—she was panicking.

"Lorens," she said, calling him back, calling his sickness back between them, hating herself for doing so the moment she'd done it, "did you come because, did you come for Lorens? To help?"

"Once," he said, "I was little. My mother was still alive. That's another story," he said, and sighed. "Anyway, the Tommas came to see us. You know them, the rich herding family, Risten, she used to have a little sister, Elle. It was early spring, she fell into a patch of weak ice and she went under. But then they couldn't find the body. They went to someone and asked where the body would appear when the ice melted. And he told them where she was. It was almost fifteen dog-miles away from where she went in but he knew where it was."

She hid her disappointment that it was not a story about her, but she recognized through the disappointment he was saying something very important, it was a new intimacy, a more frightening one, in a way—it was real. "So they found her?"

"Now she's in the churchyard."

"Where they will bury Lorens." She was surprised by her ability to say the thing evenly, and it seemed then the most true thing she had said, and the truth of it shocked her, like in saying it she was killing him herself. She didn't cry but she felt the pressure of tears behind her eyes, and she was going to turn to leave, to flee, really, she didn't want to cry in front of him, but Ivvár opened his arms, held them out to her. It was an odd gesture, like he was mothering her; she had never been reached for by a man like this and she hesitated, standing there, and he moved a little forward on the bench so that now his knees surrounded her and he put his arms around her waist so that she was inside his knees, so that if she leaned back even a little she felt how firmly he held her. He leaned forward against her chest, and her heart and her stomach and everything inside her failed to be still.

She breathed in a sharp sigh and his arms tightened around her, and she was pressed against him, or he was pressed against her, his head of all things on her embarrassing little breasts, his hair so near to her she could smell him—he smelled wonderfully of reindeer, and somehow something juniper, juniper smoke maybe, and when he began to stroke his thumb against her back, slowly but with intent, she thought, she knew, it was a gesture not of comfort but of want, and it was a question.

When he stood up and faced her it was with the leisurely force she had always seen in the herders, so that she had no thought or time or feeling to resist or not resist, to decide or not decide, the decision was made for her, he pulled her to him, and she felt her teeth bang against the back of her lips as they kissed but it wasn't unpleasant, and better than that was his hands on her, his hands that moved around her and over her.

He stopped and looked at her, grinning.

"What?" she asked, stupidly, not even managing to be coy.

Now, she thought, now is the time to stop. Now is the time for things to end. She should say something, but she couldn't think what that something was, she felt the weird, warm muscle of his tongue, it was alluring and bizarre, and more bizarre for being alluring, and she thought again, now is the time to stop. They were making promises they could not keep, but she wanted, after all, to be a sinner, to be condemned, she wanted to join him in his condemnation, she wanted to eat from the tree of knowledge, and the longer they were kissing the more she was amazed that, after all, her body did know what to do, she was not as childlike as she might have thought at all, she was Delilah and Jezebel and Bathsheba, she was beautiful to behold, a king would see her and send her husband to the front line of war to hide his adultery, that was how beautiful she was, and she felt, briefly, the power of being a woman, a power she had never felt before, had never known existed, the power of desiring him less than he desired her. I am being awakened, she thought, and she wanted to laugh, but his mouth was on hers and his mouth swallowed her laugh.

His fingers were on the buttons at the top of her dress, pushing one button through a buttonhole she had once so carefully sewn, and it seemed to her he would never get the button through, and then there was the next one, and the next, and his fingers were rough and callused and his fingernails were dirty, and this was wonderful to her, and she kissed his neck, and she kissed him right behind his ear and he tasted of salt.

The door to the sauna opened.

Willa felt her breath leave her, her blood leave her. She was going to fall over. She was going to be sick. Ivvár paused, turned his head toward the light.

"Are you two all done in here," her father said. His voice was horrible to hear, she took the step away from Ivvár she should have taken a long time ago. Against the light of the outside world her father was completely in shadow, he was all drooping shoulders, and she could see in the way he stood how angry he was, she could hear his disgust in how he stood there with his hand still on the door handle. He didn't look at her, he didn't look into the sauna at all. Ivvár was trying to look at her but she couldn't look at him, she bowed her head and kept her hand over the gap in her dress and she waited for Ivvár to go.

"Get out," her father said, his voice low and guttural, and she felt the full burden of his revulsion in the two words, revulsion that was meant for her.

He stepped out of the doorjamb and held the door open and Ivvár brushed past him, he didn't turn and say anything to Willa, he didn't take her hand, and just like that it was all dissolving, and he was walking away and she was standing there. Just then, just now, just that minute ago, she had felt an unbearable intimacy, she had been overcome by how close she had felt to Ivvár, how little separated them, and in the rightful place of that intimacy now there was only shame, so powerful, so all-consuming she felt sick, she did not know what penitence was possible, what prostration would serve. She could have pulled out her hair and thrown herself to the ground but it would not have done any good at all, her father would say it was an act, would say her remorse was false, he could not even look at her, he did not wish for her to be his child, he thought she was an adulteress and a whore, and she was an adulteress and a whore, there was no word too strong for her, he didn't even have to say it for her to know it was true.

Her father turned and walked away.

She stood in the sauna, pretending there was something to do. There was nothing to do—the fire was still going, softly, and she smoothed out her dress, though it didn't need to be smoothed, and thought: what if I never go back? That seemed preferable. As she walked to the cabin each step seemed to waver, seemed dreamlike, and she thought how nice it would be to not exist, to remove oneself from the world, to have the power to leave the body to suffer whatever it had to suffer while the mind roamed free. She wondered if Ivvár watched her walking, watched her approach the cabin door, if he pitied her, if he knew what was to come like she did, if he knew the price.

She looked at Nora, sitting on the floor, amusing the baby with the doll Willa had once been amused by, a sad sack of cloth stuffed with feathers. Nora shook it in the baby's face but paid no attention to it herself.

"How is Lorens?" Willa asked, feeling her voice shake.

"He's asleep," Nora said. The way she didn't look at Willa, Willa knew she knew. So they all knew already—she was so hot she couldn't breathe. She would faint.

"Come here," her mother said.

Willa walked toward her mother. Each step seemed to be a year.

When Willa drew close her mother stood, and slapped her face, very hard, so that Willa drew back in shock—held her hand to her cheek. Willa took a few steps backward, and turned to the room. She didn't know where to go, what to do. The cabin was so small. She didn't dare cry—to cry would be to invoke comfort and there wasn't comfort left for her. She looked around the cabin, for the worst chore to do, the one no one ever wanted to do, to begin the punishment that would last as long as she might presume to live.

12

FOR FOUR DAYS AND FIVE NIGHTS IT SEEMED LIKE LORENS WOULD DIE, BUT he didn't die. They were days that passed with unbearable protraction; the doctor was always underfoot, and what little room they'd had before shrunk still more, and Willa's penitence and sourness were unbearable to be around; she was alternately very sorrowful or snappish, so you didn't know which Willa you were going to get, and moreover, Nora wasn't sure what had happened, exactly; she couldn't bring herself to ask. But even if she didn't know what had happened, she sensed the wrongness of something, and afterward she had gone out to the sauna and stood in there, where her sister had stood with Ivvár (she had overheard her father say his name to her mother), and wondered: had Willa now passed her by? Was Willa now a woman in a way she was not? What did Willa know that she didn't? Why should Ivvár have any interest in Willa, and not her?

But it was so painful to see Willa like this that Nora even tried to cheer her up when they were alone. She tried to point out that Lorens seemed a little better, and that people were praying for him, all the time, and Biettar was becoming much better at reading, even if a lot of it was memorization—he was still very good at memorizing, wasn't he? When she said these things Willa was so dour Nora was annoyed that she couldn't bend, at least a little, to Nora's attempts at cheerfulness. Of course it didn't help that their parents didn't speak to Willa at all—she had practically ceased to exist, and the little girls had intuited Willa's shunning, and no longer came to her for anything. Carl's silence to Willa was not a loss, since he rarely spoke, but Nora could see Willa striving to have someone say something to her; she would bring their mother coffee that their mother wouldn't touch at all, would not even look at, much less drink. Only Biettar hadn't changed, he talked to her just the same, probably because no one had told him what happened, because if he knew it was something with his own son, what would he have done? Wouldn't he have avoided her even more than others?

Biettar did know, actually.—Lars Levi had told him, but anyway he had suspected something else was going on with his son for a while, so the news that Willa and Ivvár had been found together in the sauna relieved him a little. He was embarrassed, of course, that it was his son who'd done that, when he wanted so much to be approved of by Lars Levi, and when he wanted to believe more than anything that his son would be all right without him, but in the end it was clear that the incident would be much more costly to Willa than to Ivvár, the way it so often was between men and women. Willa was so confined now to the cabin, to the walk between the privy and the cow-house, she reminded him of a calf he had seen rejected by its mother who wandered around bleating and bleating, only to be kicked by some other calf's mother, until it became clear someone must intervene, and do the mothering, if the calf were to live.

He understood why Ivvár would be interested in her, and he would never have said this to Ivvár, not to anyone, but actually Willa reminded him a little of Ivvár's mother. She was overly sensitive and overly proud at the same time, she felt things strongly even if she didn't act strongly. He could see that. She was wounded now because of her pride, because she had brought herself low like this and didn't know what to do with the feeling, she had never been like that before; Biettar understood this. Of course he understood this. It was a brutal thing that was happening to her, to be brought low in this manner could kill a man. He told her as much, on the fifth day at Lorens's sickbed—when she went out to the river for water he followed her. He watched her ladle water into the pails, carefully, so as not to disturb any silt at the river's bottom, though it wasn't likely, with the river still frozen like this.

She didn't watch him watching her, she knew he was there and she behaved as if she expected him to ignore her, like everyone did now. She was outside with no jacket on, and the sun was out again, mottled by thin clouds that were stretched along the sky like a wet calfskin. He was only five or so feet from her, so that she could hear him clearly, but to someone looking it might not have seemed he was speaking to her at all, because she kept ladling and because he stood so still. I have a story for you, he said. And he looked out at the shore and he began.

FOUR YEARS BEFORE, or was it five now, Biettar and Ivvár and their siida, they had been south of Gilbbesjávri, they were coming up from the sea, like they always had, the same route they had always taken, the same route his grandfather had taken, and his grandfather's grandfather before that, and so on and so forth. They had come down only a few months before in April without any trouble. Anyway, that year they hadn't realized that some Swedes or maybe Finns had moved next to the river and started a farm, started clearing the land and tilling the soil and planting whatever they planted. They were so far north that surely the ground was frozen only a few inches down, but somehow the farmers had managed to grow something, a few acres of patchy, thin wheat, some hay, but Biettar hadn't known that, and anyway this wasn't the important part of the story, the point was that the reindeer herd had found the hay and gotten into it.

It wasn't anyone's fault, in Biettar's view, as there was no way of knowing someone would have put a field there, and anyway whatever they had trampled it clearly wasn't much and was never going to have been a successful harvest in the first place, and anyway why would you put a farm in the middle of a migration route, but the Swedes had felt very differently, they had settled on the land and they had papers to prove it, and if they were able to build a barn and a house and so on within five years, the Crown would grant them the land, and they wouldn't have to pay taxes for fifteen years, Biettar's herd was ruining the greatest chance of their lives; it wasn't just that the reindeer had taken some hay.

At the time, some sum had been agreed on, Biettar no longer remembered what, maybe sixteen or seventeen riks-dollars in compensation, which was far more than Biettar thought it was worth, but he was willing to pay for peace, but then the next year, they realized that the settlers had been burning the fields to make tar, and huge swaths of it were burned, all of the lichen that takes a hundred years to start growing, it was gone, and not even just in the parts the settlers needed, and Biettar had realized, it was retribution for the hay and the field. And so the reindeer had walked many miles looking for grazing again. You might not know this, Biettar added, but reindeer are not like horses. They can't go days and days without food and be all right. They starve very quickly. They get fat quickly. But they starve very quickly.

In any case Biettar had nearly forgotten about this incident when he found himself being dragged away from the herd by a sheriff. This farmer was saying that Biettar had not been responsible again with his herd and more hay had been eaten. Biettar couldn't say if this was true or not, he didn't remember seeing anything but burned fields. But you couldn't blame the reindeer for eating hay if their lichen was all gone!

But now Biettar had to appear in Kiruna in front of a judge who only spoke in Swedish, and spoke very rapidly, and demanded he explain why he had destroyed so much property without offering any compensation. And Biettar had said, he had paid the man, and the judge asked him, did he have proof, and Biettar said, he didn't think he needed any, and so he was fined twenty-five riks-dollars for allowing his reindeer to go near a farm a second time, and then he was fined more for the destruction of two harvests of hay, and then he was forbidden, moreover, to bring the herd through that section of the fells again, although the judge, being Swedish himself, had no understanding that such a demand amounted to more than merely skirting around this one spot; with the mountains in the way, it meant they would have to shift a large section of their route by tens of miles, and, moreover, their siida did not know another way to go; it was the way they had always gone.

And so the next year, despite their best scouting, they misjudged the pitfalls of the new route and had lost a section of the herd, and they'd lost days trying to round them up (crossing, as it were, straight through the Speins' migration route, which had already been grazed over, an annexation of the Speins' route that embarrassed them to take, like taking water from someone else's spring), and they'd all been bitter, seeing these mountains they did not recognize half as well as the others, shamed at their inability to predict the reindeers' movements.

At first it had been very small, they had all split a few bottles of vodka that someone had stolen from a Swedish farmhouse in revenge for having been called thieves and liars in the first place, but Biettar in particular, he'd had a particular taste for it, Biettar would admit it, it had gone straight to his head, and for a few hours he'd felt how he used to, like a man with a large herd, a man who was respected by everyone.

But then they got some more from the market in Ivgobahta, and within a year Biettar could drink a bottle without much noticing and without having any pleasure at all. They were all drinking too much, Biettar said, and he was the worst of them. He had drank and drank whenever he could, which was whenever he was near a town, until one day he had woken up and it was the day he should have slaughtered to pay the debt to Henrik, and he had realized he was about to owe Henrik half his herd, he was in danger of losing the whole herd to drinking, and all because he was a man with too much pride, and instead of accepting this, he had started off to town fully intending on going to try to get more to drink, he had told himself if he had a drink then he could decide what to do next. But when he'd gotten to town he had been called upon to enter the church, there had been a voice in the wilderness that had stopped him, and sent him the right way. Until that very moment he had been sure there was no relief for him, no end to it. He had thought, this is all my life can be. But he had heard the voice, and then the earthquake had happened, and he knew God was telling him, God was using these things to say, Biettar, no more, Biettar, come to me and be saved. Now he saw, all those years, he had just been a coward. He'd just been a servant of his pride. It was too painful to admit he'd been wrong. But all along, it'd been sitting there, waiting for him. All he'd had to do was put his pride away, and listen to the voice crying out loud in the wilderness, and be saved.

AT THIS JUNCTURE Willa turned to look at him, because his voice had gone so quiet she could hardly hear him, and because the pails were full. She didn't know what to say, and she didn't know why Biettar was telling her this story, but she felt such an overwhelming grief for Biettar; she remembered seeing his herd when she'd gone to see Ivár, and she felt in that moment what a loss it would be, to lose your herd like that. If she'd been a different person, and he a different person, she would have gone to him and put her hand on his back. Instead she looked at him and she thought, it's my father who has given him peace, and she was glad, in a way, for anything that gave Biettar peace, but she was also bitter, and she felt his story like another lesson she didn't feel like learning. She understood his message perfectly; he was telling her she must bear this lesson of hers with grace, she must give herself to God and find her peace in Him, that there was nowhere else to go.

She gave him a smile with nothing but politeness in it, and she stooped to pick up the pails and carried them up the bank, her arms shaking from the weight of the water. She didn't feel appreciative of this moral tale, and she didn't feel reassured, only more heavily burdened with guilt. Inside, no one looked at her while she poured water into the pot to boil, and she thought, even if God forgives they will not forgive. Even if God takes my sins away my father will always see me like that, and he will always be disgusted with me. It was futile, all of it, and she was angry, angry at the field outside that her father was always trying to plant, angry at how Biettar talked like her father, how people so willingly imitated her father, like he was some great man when in the very same breath he forbade them from idolizing anything, he wanted to be idolized, when he cultivated their admiration as carefully as any shepherd, any farmer in the field. But for them to idolize him they must first believe he was saving them, and for them to be saved he had to first convince them of their evil; the need for forgiveness, for grace, was predicated on the belief in sin, and her father was a merchant like any other, but his trade was the worse for teaching people to despise themselves. He demanded, first and foremost, that you must hate yourself to be loved, he demanded a life of endless prostration for desire you had always had; you must always apologize at his altar, you must always be saved from whom he had made you.

The stones of the hearth hurt under her knees. Behind her, Biettar had come into the room and her father was talking about getting him copies of the sermons he would need. Nora and Willa would make them, her father said, they would have time now that they weren't going to Uppsala.

"I didn't realize they weren't going," Biettar said mildly, and Willa wanted to say, neither did I.

There was too much going on, her father said, they were expecting so many more people at church this summer, and anyway, they would need to get started now on copying the sermons.

The sermons, Willa thought, the sermons, always a sermon; Christ's Sermon on the Mount, and Biettar's sermon at the river. What had he said? All along, all he'd had to do was put his pride away, and listen to the voice in the wilderness. What pride did she have remaining to her anyway? If she could have gone to anyone, she would have gone, even then, to Ivvár—she would have said, I have no pride anymore, I am holier than no one and nothing. It made her laugh, this perversion of Biettar's advice, it made her giddy. It made her giddy, and then it made her afraid.

Her father was speaking impatiently now, he was telling Biettar not to worry, Nora and Willa would finish the copies well before he left for the sea.

AT THE MENTION of the sea, Biettar winced slightly. He was going to go preach at the summer pastures, it was true, but he had been avoiding thinking about it as much as he could. He was deeply nervous about the idea of going up to the siidas, appearing as this new kind of Biettar to these people he had known his whole life as another kind of Biettar. The burden of his role to come: how would he do it? How would he keep the gospel alive through the summer months, and spread the gospel to places that hadn't even heard of Laestadius yet? And he was so ill-equipped to be even a lay preacher, and there was the uneasiness of trying something so different so late in life—it was too late, he was a fool to think anything else.

It was very difficult, he was realizing, to keep one's faith. It was easier to have flashes of faith than it was to have anything constant, and he wondered—if he traveled up there, if he was away from Lars Levi for so long, would he, too, lose his own? Just then the floorboards began to vibrate, ever so slightly, and for a moment he thought, it's God, it's the earthquake again, but then he realized it was the herds, someone was going to run a herd through town. Always it had gone the other way, always he had been the one to run a herd through town, feeling pride if the herd was running well and staying tight together, or embarrassment if they were all in disarray, but anyway he had been there, one of the men at the back, waving his pole, skiing like mad, shouting at the dogs, shouting, cus, cus, the loose fur flying so thick you had to spit it out of your mouth as you went.

Jealousy filled him like he had never known it. What a mistake, what a mistake, to not be with the herd. And the sound—here it was now, not just the shaking floor but the sound, those thousands and thousands of ankle-bones cracking as they ran, a susurration of snapping that made everyone, Biettar, Willa, Lars Levi, Brita, Nora, Sussu, Simmon, think of the same thing; they all saw reindeer but heard rain. The illusion of rain was especially strong, moreover, because of the size of the herd—it was easily a thousand reindeer that hurtled through town along the frozen river, some of the reindeer pushing up along the banks, a strand of them simply using the main road, passing by the store and the parsonage, the men following them on their skis, careful to not look at anyone as they passed, to make it clear how much of their attention the herd demanded.

It was the Tomma herd, in fact, that was passing through; ten miles and a few hours before Risten had watched them leave, feeling left behind even though she would soon follow. Only Mikkol had stopped at the top of the knoll and lifted his hand in goodbye, and Risten had lifted hers, and just like that, her husband of two weeks was gone and she wouldn't see him for a month, not until they caught up to the herd at Gilbbesjávri.

The two weeks of marriage had, in their own way, felt slow, or maybe full, like time was so saturated that it sank under its own weight, so that she was constantly tired with the newness, the newness of staying in a lávvu with him instead of with her parents, trying to sort out his preferences and realizing how set she was in her own—she had her way of making coffee, which she liked to make straightaway when she woke up, while he was a slow riser and would lie still for some time in thought, which always annoyed her: why not make coffee? He wanted her to make the coffee, that was what she'd landed on, and while in some ways it was natural enough, she wasn't used to it, because her mother had always made the coffee, and it hadn't occurred to her that she was to be her mother now, and always make the coffee, and it was a small thing but an annoying thing, to crack the water in the pail and look for the grounds, and patiently wait for the boil, and only when it was done and she was pouring it in his cup would Mikkol sit up, as if he'd just woken.

Then there was the newness of his body itself; he was so nervous compared to Ivvár, and yet tender, almost boyish. He was shy about touching her. She sensed that he desired her but was embarrassed of his desire, and he didn't want to have to see her in the daylight or in the firelight, and he always started things under the rákkas, and if she tried to start things outside of the rákkas, he moved her into the rákkas, where things were dim and where their breath mixed together and she just wanted cool air, and she found it impossible to not think about the warm rock with Ivvár, all the air she'd had there, and she found it impossible to not think about how Ivvár did things slowly and Mikkol did things hurriedly, like he was just trying to get the thing done with. And he was sweaty, it seemed to her he was always sweating, so that the fur from the pelt stuck to him, coated him, and when he'd finished he would sit up and brush at it frantically, as if he hadn't found a string of fur in his stew every day of his life. And she would lie there and roll her arms on the pelt to gather even more strings of fur on her skin and she would tell herself, I will not compare him to Ivvár, and I will not regret my choice, I do not regret it, but in the end you have to do these things, in the end you want to be a mother and you want to have a husband, and you do not pick someone because he is nice to lie with on a warm rock.

But these thoughts required her to tighten her stomach and her chest, and bite her tongue, so she didn't get tears in her eyes.

Outside of their lavvu Mikkol was nervous being around her father and her uncle, always hurrying to please them. Risten had naively thought all of that would be over now that they were married, but he behaved as if he had even more to prove than before. Possibly worse, Mikkol had taken to reading a copy of the Bible Biettar had given them as a wedding gift, a habit that embarrassed Risten, especially when Mikkol did it when her father was around. It was a habit, moreover, that always felt threatening to her, like he was about to turn to her and read her a passage about adultery and say, so I heard about you and Ivár. But amidst the new realities of her marriage, at least Ivár was being left behind as surely as she was leaving behind the stones from the fire. The uselessness of the fantasy of him was becoming more clear—he could not be had; he could be held, at most, for a moment—he was like the herd itself, he ran by and left you with a mouthful of fur.

Now there was the wait on her own end, though, to get all of the sledges packed, every little spoon and every mitten, a fallen needle found in the pelts, a spool of sinew someone had stuffed in an empty butter box—all of it had to be sorted, and carefully put away to survive the journey, and yet packed in such a way that what they would need as they went was accessible—it was a feat of engineering. No pack could be too heavy for the reindeer it would go on. No pack on one side of one reindeer could be heavier than the other. No sledge could have a harness too weak for the pull of the reindeer. Extra lichen had to be gathered and bundled, in case they came across a place with poor grazing.

In two days they were ready to leave. The draft reindeer were restless from watching other herds go by, and even Muzet was impatient, always facing north, pacing in place, his head held high like he was trying to smell the sea already. His head, without its usual bowl of antlers, lacked some majesty; but he was the kind of reindeer who always looked like he carried a full and regal set even when he had none at all, like it didn't matter that they hadn't come in yet, they were there in his mind. It might have been Muzet that infected her with it, with the giddiness of it, but Risten felt like she could bear anything just then, and she began to feel how she'd always felt all the other years, the eagerness that preceded the journey; she wanted to be skiing, to be moving, to be going north, and it was a relief, even an ecstasy, to put the south behind them, Ivvár behind her, the various shames of the year as the new one cycled in, goodbye, goodbye, she would see them next year but by then the sea would make her a different Risten, like how reindeer grew the same shape of antlers every year, year after year, similar but different. It was rare for her to be this hopeful but she took it, she didn't fight it, and she smiled to herself as she skied, and hardly had they gone one, maybe two dog-miles, when one of the harnesses came loose and they had to stop. At first it seemed it was just a matter of rear-ranging the harness, but then her aunt held up the loose end and they all saw it had snapped. The children groaned. Her mother said they might as well make some coffee if they were stopping.

"Do you have your thimble handy?" her mother asked. Her voice was still chipper. How she did it Risten didn't know, it was not endurable, this stopping and starting.

"No," Risten lied, but she did make a quick fire, and she found the kettle to have coffee, and they all sat with their coffee and watched her mother sew the strap back together. Her mother sewed carefully, evenly, as if there were no hurry at all, and then went on a search for extra bits of leather to sew on for reinforcement. Risten would have accused her of weakening the strap herself so it would break if that were not so entirely unreasonable, even for her mother.

Then, naturally, her mother took her time drinking the coffee, and then she said they might as well have a little something to eat, even though they'd had a large meal just before leaving. Only when everything was packed back in, and they had made it more than a hundred slides of the skis, and then more than two hundred, Risten let relief settle in. She put her eye to the low hills in the distance and yoked, softly, to herself. It was so pleasant to travel in the long dusk, in which there was never any true darkness, in which they were never alone; at its darkest, a burned violet, the quarter moon made its appearance, and the stars showed they had been staked in their watch all along. The familiarity of it all was soothing; it was soothing to ski to the sea; the skis said that strange times came and went but the move to the sea remained.

By morning, though, Risten was tired, and her body was recalling how many days of skiing they would have to do. The old doubt came: it was too far, she couldn't go on, but as always, once they had stopped and had more coffee, and put up the lávvu, and lain down to sleep, she thought: well, and maybe I can. She woke sure she hadn't slept at all. Of course her mother was already up, packing their things, boiling water, shaking out her pelt, and Risten closed her eyes, thinking, this is the last real rest of the day.

"Do you hear that?" her mother asked.

"Hear what?" Risten asked.

Risten listened carefully, but she could only hear her aunt whispering to the children in the rákkas across the fire, and the driving reindeer, outside, nosing around the snow.

"Someone's coming," her mother said. She nodded, her eyes turned up though her head stayed still, as if this someone were going to appear through the smoke-hole. "Yes," she said, nodding. She looked relieved. "Hear it?" she asked, and now Risten heard it, the sound of skis. Someone was skiing fairly slowly, an old woman, maybe. Old Sussu? Could Old Sussu make it out this far?

"You know who it is?" Risten asked.

They waited, the sound of the skiing coming closer, the slow rasps of the wood against the crust of snow growing louder, more quick, as if the visitor were afraid they would disappear. As the sound came closer Risten heard the driving reindeer, edging away, and now the breathing of the visitor, hard, short bursts of breath, and then the sound of skis being pulled off, but it was taking a long time, and it sounded like someone was struggling to breathe.

It was news about Ivár! Something had happened! The thought bubbled up and she shoved it back down. Why should she think that? What was wrong with her that she didn't think of Mikkol first? She was a married woman! How could her mind betray her like that? She was disappointed, bitterly, with herself.

The flap opened partway, and a face banded with scarves and with a fur hat on top appeared. Her face was red, an uncomfortable, berried sheen, slick with snow and sweat. It was the preacher's daughter who had been making eyes at Ivvár. "Hello," she said, trying to sound at ease, but she was breathing hard, and her legs must have been tired, because she could hardly crouch through the flap, and nearly took down the lávvu with her, and then she stumbled in, knocking over the branches in front of the door and sitting across from Risten, by her aunt. It was clear she must have been wearing everything she owned, since she moved with the stiffness of someone in clothes too thick to allow for bending, and when she pushed her hat off her forehead, her hair underneath was frozen into a small nest. It was a misery to even see.

"There's coffee," her mother said, as if this were the most ordinary thing, to be a full day's journey from their winter site, and at least two days from town, and to have this strange woman here in her heap of frozen clothes. The woman's breath came out everywhere, all around her—she smiled weakly at them, and nodded.

"I'm Willa," she said to them, but no one said anything in return. She awkwardly unbuttoned her coat and put her legs out in front of her. She looked like she might pass out. Her hair was melting, and she was blinking hard to keep the water out of her eyes. "Maybe you've seen me, in the village, in town, I mean, I'm the, well, my father is the pastor, I'm so sorry to bother you," she managed to say. Her voice was too loud, and she spoke too quickly.

"Here," her mother said, and found her cheese, and dried meat, so that Willa's frozen lap was full of things. She was still breathing heavily.

"I haven't slept in two days," she said, laughing.

"Risten," her mother said. "Go get snow."

"Where are you heading?" Risten asked, trying to turn toward Willa.

"Risten," her mother said. "Snow."

Risten lifted the cloth of the lávvu behind her, even though it wasn't what her mother had meant, and scooped some snow inside, which she put into a bowl and passed to Willa.

Willa sat there and looked at the snow.

"Rub your hands with it," Risten said, "you can't get too warm too fast."

It was her mother who leaned forward and took Willa's hands. She pulled off the mittens and looked at the fingers, alternately white and red. She shook her head, and took the snow, and began to rub and rub.

"Get her feet," her mother said, "hurry," and Risten began, dutifully, if a little resentfully, to untie Willa's boots, and when she couldn't open the laces she took her knife from her belt and cut the ice from them and pulled, and they came off. She took off three layers of wool socks, each frosted, and to Risten's horror the pinky toe looked gray, and there was no red in it at all. Risten looked at her mother and her mother looked at the toe, but they didn't say anything.

It was so strange to hold Willa's foot in her hand, too intimate.

"I can do that," Willa said, bending forward toward her toe, but failing to reach it, "I can."

"Nonsense," her mother said.

"Ooooh," Willa said, and her breath caught. She breathed in tightly, breathed out tightly. "It hurts," she said, "oooh, that does hurt."

"That's good if it hurts."

"Yes, it's good," Willa said, but her face belied this. Her pain was obvious—as they rubbed her feet and her hands her body spasmed, so one moment her leg kicked out and the next moment she shook all over. "It hurts to cry," she said, "my tears are too warm." She laughed, a kind of grimace with a laugh stuck in it. "Oooh," she said, "it hurts my cheeks, the tears are stinging my cheeks!"

"It's bad now," her mother said, "but in a few hours it will be like it never happened."

"What about my toe?" Willa asked. She was watching Risten's mother's face, to see if a lie was forming. "Oh, it looks gray," she said, "that's bad, isn't it?"

"It isn't black," her mother said. "It hurts?"

"I think so," Willa said, "but I can't really tell where the pain is coming from, the whole foot is burning." The melted water from her hair was running along her neck.

"Where are you going?" Risten asked pointedly, knowing it was rude, but unable to keep herself from the question. "Once you're warm," she added.

"Don't bother her with that," her mother said. "Leave her be."

"I know it was bad to ski with so many things on at once," Willa said, "but I was trying to take everything with me."

"Where are you going?" Risten asked again. Her tone wasn't mean but it wasn't nice, either, and she was aware she spoke like Willa was a child who had to be slowly reasoned with, so they could see the mistake they'd made, and come to an obvious conclusion on their own.

"I thought, if I keep going, I have to run into someone . . . I know where I'm trying to go, that's all."

"You're traveling all on your own?"

"I had to keep moving. That's just how it is."

"There's coffee ready now," her mother said. "I think you should have some." She had poured the coffee into her own guksi and handed it to Willa. Willa cupped her entirely red hands around the wood and sipped with a relief that was awkward to witness. "If I could get, even—if you could point me the way to go," she said.

"Where are you trying to go?" her mother asked.

"Kilpisjärvi, I think," she said. "Yes," she said, nodding, "I think Gilbesjávri." Her eyes looked far off, like she imagined Gilbesjávri to be a wonderful place. It was, in a way—it was situated at a crossroads of sorts for both settlers and Swedes, since from there you could cut through the mountains to get to the sea via a de facto road formed by the valleys of old. It was also prominent, and obvious—the broad and hulking back of Saana Mountain made for a clear place of orientation, and so a little trade had sprung up there; in the summer Finns would stand there at the roadside and try to sell you their grain, and sometimes even Russians made it, and the trading-house became an impromptu tavern. In a way Gilbesjávri was a no-man's-land, because while it was in Finland, Sweden and Norway were to the west and north—it was the kind of place where it was never clear which language you should choose when you approached a stranger.

"You think in Gilbbesjávri there will be, what?" Risten asked. She tried to sound nice about it.

Willa fell over. It was not like anything Risten had ever seen. She had, Risten supposed, technically fainted—the coffee fell out of her cup into her lap, and her head fell to the side like an anchor, landing on her mother's legs. Her mother stared at this stranger and began to pat her head.

"Is she okay?" Risten asked. She thought Willa was going to have a fit—for a moment she had looked like the old women at church, like Biettar at Easter. "Probably pregnant," Risten said, "probably running away."

"Don't be rude."

"I'm saying, why else is she running off like this?"

"What does that have to do with you?"

"I'm not—"

Her mother reached over Willa and lifted up the bottom of the lavvucloth, grabbed some more snow, and began to rub it on Willa's neck and face. Willa opened her eyes but still lay there. She was looking at nothing, at everything.

"I can pay my way," she said, nearly crying, as if they were in the middle of a conversation. "Would you take me, if I paid?"

"Take you what, where?" her mother asked.

"To the sea," she said. "Take me to the sea. I'll help. I won't be in your way. You can give me anything to do, clean or sew, I'll do it. You tell me what to do, I'll do it." Her voice was slurred, slightly. She was so pitiful Risten did feel for her, how wretched this woman's life must be to run away like this.

"Not just to Gilbbesjávri then?" Risten asked.

"You're very tired," her mother said, and she put her arm behind Willa's back and lifted Willa up. Then her mother began to rearrange everything, setting everything up so there was room for Willa—not just to sit down, Risten saw, but to sleep. She even took the wool blanket from her own pelt and put it inside a ráhkas she was hanging up for Willa.

It occurred to Risten her mother simply had to do whatever the right thing was, to the point of exhaustion. Everyone must always see and know what a good and caring woman, and wife, and mother she was—everyone must eat her food and recognize how fatty the meat was, everyone must see her embroidery and admit it was the most evenly lined—she lived in that way entirely for others. It was not in her to say no to anyone, much less Willa, and she would give Willa, moreover, not only refuge, but sanctuary—she would give Willa whatever was needed, boots and food, she would clean Willa's coat of lice, Risten could see it all now, how it would happen.

"As the first day goes—" Risten said, unable to keep bitterness at bay.

"So goes the rest of the journey," her mother said, cheerfully, as if unafraid of this saying, or really, any other.

PART TWO

13

THE FIRST NIGHT OF TRAVEL WAS THE HARDEST, AND THEN THE SECOND night was the hardest—they were all, each, the hardest—Willa's body was a beast of burden, and the burden was herself. She could not go on, but she went on. She could tell no one thought she would make it, that they all watched her, waiting for her to collapse, or need to be put in the sledge, and she waited with them for her body's betrayal. Her legs already spasmed at the knees, and her thighs wobbled with each step, and there was nothing, not even her blood, that had not been slowed by the cold. She was being made into a new body, she was being reshaped; her face had gone hard, and her lips were peeling, and her hands were so stiff she could make no fine movements at all. In a way, the suffering was a mercy; she was only a body, only a collection of flesh; she was given sustenance and she used that sustenance to move her collection of flesh across the whitened earth.

It was necessary to travel at night because the snow's upper crust was more frozen then, and the heavy sledges could glide more smoothly, but it meant that they lived backward, so that evening functioned as morning and morning as evening, and the reindeer took "dawn-rests," and thus, so did they, so the sensation was that you were most alive when the twilight was deepest, and most tired when the sun peaked. If the others were ever cold or tired, they were careful not to show it, nor to speak of it, not even the children, who must have been ten and twelve, Willa thought, although in fact they were eight and nine, only with the severe faces of adults. Still they served as a kind of inspiration to her, and she found herself thinking, if the children can do it . . . she told herself that, and they told themselves if a Swedish settler who was only half-Sámi by blood could do it, they would say nothing, even though the little boy, who was a little lazy, wished they didn't have to go so far every day, and even Risten was relieved when Anna finally grabbed a branch of juniper and threw it on the sledge, since it meant, though Willa didn't realize this yet, they were going to stop soon.

When they did finally stop there was something surreal about setting up the lávvu in the sunrise, dragging the poles together, locking the forked ends of the tent-poles just right, Risten snipping a little at her cousins to hold still, she had it, and then finally the tent-cloth coming out, the ropes of it being pulled this way and that so that the cloth inched up and up along the poles until it was pulled taut, and there it was, a door; there it was, a home. To Willa it was like something magic had been made, something from nothing; she had a childlike wonderment about it that the children themselves did not have, and she hurried to gather firewood, since this was her chore, because collecting firewood required almost no skill. But once she had brought in stack after stack of wood, Anna and Risten had already laid out the pelts and started the fire and there was the smell of meat cooking, and of coffee, Willa permitted herself to think that maybe she wouldn't die after all. They all gave way, when they rested. The children were made into children again, and they became annoying, begging for things, pinching each other, and Risten whispered under her breath to her mother: did she think they were going too fast for Willa? Ought they to slow down?

This was not actually Risten's anxiety but it was a useful cover for her real anxiety, which was her fear of seeing Mikkol again, a fear that had started once she'd realized they were halfway to Gilbbesjávri and seeing him again was no longer an abstraction. She was afraid, on the whole, of feeling disappointed when she saw him, and of realizing what a mistake she had made, and for once it seemed better to simply not get anywhere. She tried remembering that he was very kind, he was very reliable, he was a good man, but she couldn't recall his face for some reason, not as a whole—she could only see him in gestures, how he picked up the kettle's handle with the fire-stick and so cautiously poured the coffee in. What remained, mostly, was a feeling that he wasn't as handsome as she wished, and a mild dread that he would lie around reading the Bible or talking about church things. Then, when they were only a few days from Gilbbesjávri, she realized: what if Ivvár's herd went through Gilbbesjávri at the same time as Mikkol's? What if they talked to each other? She remembered, horribly, a moment Mikkol had been touching her and Ivvár had come to mind; ever so briefly, it had been Ivvár's hand on her breast and then it had transformed back to Mikkol's again, and when she'd looked at Mikkol he'd said, what is it, like she'd been thinking something very sweet, and she'd said, I just like the way you touch me, and kissed him with vigor, to cover her tracks.

FOR A GOOD while they had been in the lower fells, where the land was full of hiccups of hills, valleys like divots in the earth, and there were still trees, albeit small ones, and lakes, still frozen, masquerading as earth, but now the land became tundra, and they began to feel rocks beneath the snow, and the sledges bumped, and if the packs were not strapped tightly to the reindeer and to the sledges they tipped out and over. Willa tried, she really did try, to not fall too far behind. The reindeer pulled slowly, almost carefully, and Willa skied behind the sledges, and if something fell she shouted hoarsely for them to stop, and every once in a while she fell so far behind one of the children came back for her, herding her forward. Aren't you coming with, the little girl would say, skiing backward, smiling at Willa before she turned around again and took off speedily. The girl's coat was thick and looked new, and her little fur boots puffed up over her skis, and Willa would look down at her own boots, thick and clammy leather things, always in a different stage of dampness, and ahead of her she would see Risten, leading one of the strings, not looking even the slightest bit affected, and despair would come, and she wondered how many days she had been with them now—it seemed like thirty, though it was eleven. But each time she thought, I can't go on, I will sit down and never get up, something would appear, a flight of two birds, a white ferret, the tracks of a wolverine, an owl observing their passage, and she went on. Sometimes the world they moved through became too beautiful, the sun stained the snow too richly, and she resented Risten and Anna, and the rest of them, that they had always been able to see these things. It seemed to her they were almost indifferent, since they never pointed or said, oh, look at that—even though, to Risten, every time Willa smacked her mouth in amazement at something, crowed, babbled on, she was annoyed—couldn't Willa appreciate anything in silence? Couldn't she be still? Risten was not, in fact, untouched by the beauty, not in the least—she was sure, even in her own exhaustion, that they were the most fortunate people to live on the earth, but she didn't like to speak of it, only move quietly through it, so as to not profane it with speech.

Often for long stretches of time, none of them would speak, and there would only be Anna, yoiking, her voice mellow and sweet, but unbound, the yoiks nothing like the hymns Willa had grown up with, the way they went where they wanted.

But now they had reached a good place to rest, and they rested.

"How long will we be here?" Willa asked, and the women tried to hide their amusement. How long would they be here! What a question to ask. As if that could be answered! It was as if she expected them to know precisely what the weather would be like today or tomorrow, she did not realize yet they depended on the weather and the weather did not depend on them; she still had the pretense of control over the world. It was almost charming in its stupidity; like a dumb calf that wanders into a thicket and gets its head stuck, and it seemed to Risten at least that it was useful to leave her there for a while, and rather than explain anything Risten shrugged, she said vaguely, waiting for Willa to see for herself, I really can't know.

Anyway, Risten mused, what could she do about it? What could any of them do about Willa? What could Willa do about herself?

And so Willa stopped asking when they would leave, even though, as tired as she was, she wanted to leave again. It was when they sat around the fire and said nothing that her mind let in the dreaded things: Lorens's bloody mouth, Ivvár's knees pressed against her hips, her mother's slap. Was Lorens dead? He had to be dead. She had run, and she had made her parents lose two children at the same time—but these thoughts were so unbearable that if they came she did anything to destroy them, pinching her leg, looking around for something, anything, to do, but the fact was that she was relatively useless. She had never suffered such ongoing uselessness—she had always been useful, it was what she was, who she was, she was capable, she managed things, and now she might as well have been crippled; it might have been better to be crippled so as to have an excuse. She was not Risten, who dragged entire birch trees to the encampment for firewood; she was not Anna, who hoisted the tent-poles up against each other with easy aim; she was not Risten's aunt, who skinned calves that died along the way. Willa was trying to learn, at the least, the household tasks, like how to lay fir branches down beneath the pelts so they formed springs, and how to lay wood so that its roots faced the same way and the right way, but each task had some rule she was bound to guess wrong, and each rule came with its own allotment of luck, and she kept managing the luck wrong, causing Risten to suck in her breath and say, no, no, not like that.

Anna was kinder. "It's just the silent rules, and there's no reason you should know them," Anna always said, when Willa set the kettle's spout down the wrong way and it had to be fixed, and she said it again when they finally packed to leave and Willa, convinced she was being helpful, harnessed the wrong reindeer to the wrong sledge, not realizing they had to be put in any specific order. She had been feeling proud of even figuring out how the harnesses worked, and now Anna had to undo her work, and Risten was standing there, on her skis, looking impatient, and Risten's aunt was sighing loudly. But she would have to make it to the sea. She had started and now there was no way back—she could not have found her way back, not even back to the fell that had looked like the head of a sheep. So she was quiet, and she waited for them to move again, and she stood to the side, out of the way, and she saw Risten's little cousin's shoeband was loose.

"Someone's thinking of you," she said to the girl, pointing, "you must have some boy who's in love with you," and the girl looked surprised.

"How did you know that?" she said, her face a little red.

"I know some things," Willa said, feeling pleased. She saw with this little saying she had stumbled on something, and she smiled and the little girl smiled back.

"What else do you know?" the girl asked.

Willa laughed, she laughed so hard that Risten and Anna stopped to look at her laughing, and she saw she was laughing hard enough that it was making them laugh, too. It hurt to laugh so hard, even though she could hardly recall what it was she was laughing at—at laughter itself—but her mood was light, light enough that for a moment she let herself recall something else, which was that she loved Iváir. She was in love with Iváir. She was pretending, had been pretending all along, that she had run away because she had shamed her family and herself, but that wasn't what had done it, not really—no, for pride or shame she would have stopped skiing long ago. No, she moved with the stupidity and strength that belonged only to the province of love—it was for Iváir, every idiotic step. It was disingenuous to pretend it was anything else. Wasn't even the shame of being caught an excuse she had always wanted? Hadn't she wanted, after all, to be caught? To enter a gate that, once closed, could not be opened again? Did she not walk, even now, in the belief that Iváir was waiting for her, that Iváir knew without knowing she was coming?

SAANA MOUNTAIN was discernible from a distance because, unlike the other mountains nearer the sea, which tended to have rounded or cragged protrusions that formed their tops, it had a nearly flat slope, like a table tilted upward, giving the impression of being man-made, or anyway too particular a shape to be an accident of nature. The peculiarity of this shape was accentuated by the absence of anything around it besides a lake; other than the stippling of short, scrubby trees, there was just the tundra, and the suddenness of the mountain's appearance in the plains added exponentially to its surreality. It often gave people a distinct shudder to even see it; Willa, seeing it for the first time, thought: it looks like

God designed it for Abraham to come and sacrifice Isaac. Even Risten, who had seen Saana so many times before—forty-two times, to be exact, if you counted each migration coming and going—got a familiar chill upon seeing it, a chill made worse this time by the sense that Saana's shadow was darker than it usually was, or perhaps longer, or perhaps the lake at its base was just unnervingly smooth and formed too good a mirror so that Saana seemed to have depth that went down as well as up, powers above and below earth.

Risten skied slowly, trying to assess from a distance how many herds were gathered around the base of the mountain. Ivvár's herd was small, though, and could have mixed in—it would be hard to tell from here. To the reindeer, watching from the sides and heights of Saana, there was nothing threatening about these travelers, so the reindeer ignored them and went back to climbing higher, looking for the good wind, where the snow had been blown off the rocks and the lichen greened and the calves waited to be born. Only the men were unaware of the arrival of the house-strings, of the women and children, because the men were mostly asleep, all except Risten's father, who was pacing from one reindeer to the next, seeing if they were going to give birth, and when he heard the dogs bark he was unsurprised—he'd woken up that morning with the feeling the house-strings would arrive that day, and instead of looking up to see them coming he studied a calf that had just been born probably an hour before. The calf was looking around at the snow, a little bloodied and bewildered, his legs tangled beneath him. The mother grunted at Nilsa, not happy to have him so close.

"It's all right," he murmured to her, "I know, it's your baby." It was the kind of thing he would have never said if someone else was nearby to hear him.

He looked down the slope then and he could see them coming, the form of his own daughter. He'd always wished Risten had been born to them earlier, always wished Anna hadn't had so much bad luck carrying children. She had lost so many—four times Nilsa had dug graves on the valley-road to the sea. And then Elle. And now Risten, and her poor fool of a husband.

Risten's poor fool of a husband, who was not actually a fool, only still too nervous around Nilsa, was in a sleep so heavy he slept through his own dog barking. He hadn't expected Risten to arrive—he'd expected her for days, and in being disappointed each day, no longer expected anything at all. But Risten didn't know this, she only knew once she drew close enough that while to her relief Ivár was not there (and, clearly, neither was his siida), her husband wasn't there to greet her. If her father could be out and about, why couldn't he? She knew this wasn't fair, and that all the men were exceptionally tired, and anyway her father was someone with obnoxious amounts of energy, but she was still bothered by it, and wondered—should she go in and wake him? Probably another herder was there in the lávvu with him, also sleeping. But if she didn't go in it would look like she wasn't much of a new wife, and she wasn't excited to see him, but if she did go in she would have to face who he was.

It took some doing but she put her head in the door and saw two rákkas hanging, one to the left with a man's legs uncovered, and his boots still on—she didn't recognize these boots—and the other with the rákkas neatly tucked beneath the pelt. She crept toward the neat one, and lifted one corner. In his sleeping form he was more attractive than she'd feared, but also smaller, and she wasn't sure what to feel. Mikkol opened an eye and an arm and Risten crawled in, and he pulled the wool blanket up over them and it wasn't a minute before she felt him pressing against her, but her cousin was there, and anyway she wasn't ready for it. She wanted it but not like this, and not now—she couldn't relax at all and she lay there tightly, unable to even close her eyes. He squeezed her arm, hard enough that they both knew she was awake, but she didn't move, and how long they lay there, waiting for the other to fall asleep, she didn't know.

By the third day Mikkol felt normal again to her, and she had accepted him; she even found pleasure in little things he did, in his boyishness, how he got excited by everything; to be fair, it was exciting when the calves were born. Their legs were too long for them, and they looked like spiders without any of the spider's grace, and when they tried to stand their legs crumpled underneath them. Unh-unh-unh, they bleated, unh-unh-uh, so insistent, so needy from the start. Good for you, Risten always thought.

It worried her when the calves were quiet, when they sat there blinking; she couldn't help it, she didn't want them to die. Her father always seemed to take the loss of them in stride, like he expected some of them to die now and all of them to die later, while she had only a partial acceptance that with every reindeer born she was welcoming another death, but nature didn't care what she thought of it, and a hundred deaths were born that week, most of them her father's. Naturally Willa clapped her hands and let the calves smear green stripes of feces all over her arms, holding them like they were infants, kissing their soft foreheads, their mothers bleating until Willa set them back down.

Willa was starting to look very Sámi, now that she wore Risten's clothes and had gotten matching red cheeks from the sun and snow. It was occurring to everyone that Willa's presence there was real. When you were in the in-between places you could pretend more, but now that they'd arrived to the midway point, and she hadn't left yet, or fallen back, it seemed they were stuck with her, and now everyone else who passed near Saana knew, or was going to know, that the Tomma siida was bringing the pastor's daughter along with them. Risten, for instance, went to visit with the Speins in the second week and heard from them that they had heard from the Utsis (of Guovdageaidnu, imagine that, people had heard all the way in Guovdageaidnu) that Willa was running away because she was pregnant, though no one knew who the father was—there was speculation it was the storekeeper, Rikki, but it was such a disgusting prospect that Risten assumed, out of a kind of female kinship, that if it were true it had been forced. It occurred very, very briefly to her that it might have been Ivár— the way they had looked at each other in church had not left her—but it seemed unimaginable, even less imaginable than Rikki. She couldn't see the two of them together, because Ivár was such a Sámi, such a reindeer herder—what would he do with a woman who didn't know anything about reindeer? It wasn't in his family to do that, and she put it straight out of her mind. Maybe more disturbingly, Risten could see that even her father was softening toward Willa. He was curious about her. He asked her what it was like at her cabin, where did they sleep. He asked if they ate reindeer for every meal, and why not. He asked if they had a dog, and why not. He asked why they made boots of leather but took the fur off the outside. So Risten disliked Willa a bit more.

Risten tried to retreat, to avoid Willa—she went and checked her calves, again and again. She went out even when there was no real need to, wandering out to the fringes where dogs slept and the occasional herder lay on his side, smoking his pipe, watching her walk around, probably thinking, go back to the lavvu and do some women's work.

It took some time but she found a little shelf of rock to sit on, where she could sit with Saana Mountain at her back and the sun still on her face, and she could turn her gaze north toward the sea, which could not be seen but which she knew to be there. She had wanted to be alone, so naturally it wasn't long before she heard panting behind her, slow steps on the crusted snow. It was Willa, Risten knew this without turning, so she sat still, as if that might tell Willa something, but instead Willa drew close, breathing hard, her hat long ago abandoned and stuffed in her coat pocket, her face red, her forehead sweaty. She was excited from the morning's walk, from the wind's soft edge of spring, from the calves, from the sleep she'd suddenly been getting, and she felt strong. She wanted to say this to someone, or better yet have someone say this to her; to say, admiringly, you look strong enough to make it to the sea.

"It's so beautiful," Willa said. When Risten said nothing she added, "We're going to go that way?" She pointed, to the line of ridges, their blue backsides shadowed in the morning sun.

Risten nodded and Willa was too encouraged by this. "Your mother was telling me about this place," Willa said, sounding stupid to herself.

"Yes," Risten said, a little dryly, "we come here every year."

"Yes," Willa said, "but I meant . . ." She faltered and quit. Sacred, Anna had said, that had been the word she'd used. A lot of people have come here, she said, but she didn't say for what.

Risten didn't nod; her gaze was kept so carefully vacant you couldn't accuse her of not listening but you didn't feel like she was. Her cap was pulled tight over her forehead, and her dark braid came out beneath it. The cap was red and woolen, lined with yellow stitches, and it gave her already round face the aspect of an infant. For a moment Willa thought of her baby brother, how big he would be by now. She sat down by Risten.

"Ivvár told me," she said, "when you first come to a new place, you should ask the Ulddas if you can stay, for permission to be there. Do you think—should I have, when we first got here?"

Risten was so awash with fear, or maybe that was rage, she could hardly ask, "Ivvár? Ivvár Rasti?" She was glad she had already been looking away from Willa and had no reason now to turn and look back at her.

"Biettar's son," Willa said, "he told me that's what people used to do, and I just had such a strong feeling, that maybe I should do that. Then I thought," she went on, "I might find him here anyway, and maybe I should ask someone . . . this whole trip I've been so tired but I made it up here, I wasn't too tired at all. Look at the lake!"

Risten nodded, unaware of nodding, unaware of anything except envy. "So you know Ivvár?"

A look of shyness came over Willa's face. "You know him?"

"I don't remember not knowing him," Risten said. She pursed her lips. She wanted to shake Willa. She felt no surprise men fought; she felt surprised women did it so rarely. "How do you know him?" Risten asked, too pointedly.

"Well," Willa said, "I suppose we ran into each other, is all."

"So you met him once."

"No, he—we—used to go on walks together. It wasn't anything," she faltered. "I ran into him a few times." Her face, her little snub nose, her ears, her thick neck, were going red, and she had on the most obvious kind of half smile—there was some memory, some joy, that had caught itself up in her. "Do you know where he is?" Willa asked. "Where he goes in the summer?"

Risten kept her eyes on the mountains. They steadied her with their familiarity, the same lumps in the same places every year.

"I'm sure he's somewhere making someone fall in love with him," Risten said, and she bent down and picked up a rock the size of her fist. She tossed it in the air and caught it, dropped it. "It's what he's very good at," she said. She cleared her throat. "Everyone knows," she added, "it's just how he is." She got up and brushed her hands.

Good, she thought, let her suffer, as I have already suffered.

14

Willa had been gone now for an entire month, a fact Henrik noticed but that no one else seemed to; or, if others did, they were treating it with the same silence that had surrounded her disappearance. No one spoke of it, or even referred to her, an erasure made all the more complete by the absence of discussing the act of erasure itself. Henrik had seen her skiing off into the twilight, head down, a satchel tied to her back. She'd been walking neither defiantly nor surreptitiously, with the gait of someone with no choices, like each step was preordained. He'd asked Nora later, where did she go, and she'd said, she's going her own way. The look on her face had made it clear it was not something to be spoken about, so he hadn't, but it was unnerving—even if Willa had run off with, he presumed, Ivvár, it was another thing entirely to behave as if it hadn't happened. With Emelie, it had been bad, of course, for awhile he'd been afraid she would be cut off from society completely, but then again they had managed to keep the affair to a rumor, and of course in the end Emelie had not run away with Henrik, nothing of the sort at all. It made him want to write to her, to say something about how he understood her better now, but it would only make things worse, and he had promised her he wouldn't. But it didn't matter, that belonged to another life, and he was in this life, where they were all in good moods, because Lorens had lived; Willa had been sacrificed and it was an exchange they could bear.

It wasn't that Lorens was now some normal, frolicking boy, running up and down the riverbank, but he was alive. His face had the wizened look of a man returned from war but he went outside sometimes, wearing every winter thing that could be fit over him, and he stood and looked at the river as it cracked open, and he stood there later when the ice had split into shards that tapped against each other, ten, twenty little bells pealing softly into the cold spring air. He had the look on him as he stood there of a person cast by a spell, utterly transfixed in a way that worried Lars Levi, like his body had been returned to them but his mind had not. He was quieter now, almost distant, but no one felt they could complain about it, and, besides, there was the awkwardness of the new attention Lorens's recovery had given to Lars Levi's ministry—he did not say it himself but everyone else said it: Lorens had recovered through a miracle. God had saved Lorens; Lorens's recovery was a fruit of Lars Levi's faith. Lars Levi protested this, insisted of course that they could not know God's mind, they were subject only to His will, but secretly he cherished the thought. He did feel chosen—after all, Levi had died when Lars Levi himself hadn't yet been saved. The problem of Willa was another thing entirely. Apparently, she was yet another trial from God, one that tested him mightily; there were days he could not comprehend that she had come from him at all. She had always been, or seemed, so dutiful—how had the Devil got his hooks in her, and when? How could she do this to them, to her mother? If it hadn't been for Lorens, the news of this might have hurt his ministry . . . who wanted to go to a minister whose own daughter disgraced herself like that? And she had always seemed so much like she cared about people, about the Sámi especially.

Or, maybe, she was meant to be another kind of test, another kind of prodigal son. The prodigal daughter who would return, and he would bring out the fatted calf, and his forgiveness and mercy would return her fully to God's flock. He had told Biettar before he'd left for the sea that if he saw Willa up there (Lars Levi was sure she was alive, under the protection of the Sámi somewhere), he should remind her of God's grace and mercy, and write with news of her, but he wasn't sure what he would do even if they received news. He didn't know, himself, what to do. Certainly she couldn't marry—what respectable man would marry her after this? A farmer, maybe, but nothing much more. Could they bear to have her in the home, helping out? Could Brita bear to see her?

No one knew of these thoughts of Lars Levi's, since he mentioned them to no one, and so it seemed instead that the game was to play as if Willa had never been there at all. It was a game that was slowly crushing Nora. She felt it more than anyone, even her mother, and moreover, she was beginning to feel like her life was shrinking as Willa's was widening. Nora wasn't going to get to go to Uppsala anymore, and she wasn't going to get to run around at the sea—no, her role was to never be a problem, and it was a role she excelled at—even now, with people still coming over for prayer meetings, even though it was summer, she played the role of the devoted daughter. There was a little pleasure in being so good at it, in anticipating what everyone needed, more coffee, porridge, a songbook, more wood on the fire, but she was bitter all the time, and it was wearing on her to hide her bitterness in more and more kindness. She was twenty-two now, which might as well have been thirty, and she ought to have been married years ago, but Willa had ruined it, and now Nora was going to get older out here in the wilderness: she would only have the stare of the occasional herder to remind her she was a woman at all.

She didn't think it through when she first went to Henrik's. Later she might have said, if she were more Sámi in her ways, that it had depended on the weather, but she didn't see that, she only knew it was too warm and too nice of a day—the first day it was pleasant to go outside without a coat—and the mosquitoes hadn't arrived in full force yet, and the river made noise now, a soft but steady tumbling south. Her mood was lighter than it had been in so long, and she wanted to be with someone else in it. Before, of course, she would have just gone for a walk with Willa, but the little girls were homebodies who wanted to sit inside with their sewing and make pretty things, so she thought: I'll just ask Henrik to walk with me. She could, of course, hear ten or twenty reasons in her mind why this was not a good idea, not the least of which they already had one daughter in the family who had disgraced herself with a man, but it was only a walk—and the weather, who could waste this weather?

Once inside the store, in the smell of stale whiskey and smoke and dried meats and something dead, she wished she hadn't come, but by the time they'd returned from their very short and very appropriate walk, always in full sight of the town, she'd been surprised to realize he was the kind of person it was easy to talk to because he would always say what was agreeable in return. He would always say, yes, that's right, or, "very natural," he liked to say, if she ventured to say that it was hard when her mother still worried so much about Lorens, or if she said she wished she had gone to Uppsala after all. He didn't add to the conversation in any kind of intelligent way, but he didn't detract from it, and it surprised her that this felt like enough; it felt, in the moment, like a great deal. Besides, Henrik always looked at her subserviently, as if flabbergasted by her presence alone, and she enjoyed that, the effect she had on him. She had no real interest in him at all, and she would have been appalled to know how he touched himself at night thinking about her, but she wanted attention from someone, and now that her parents were so consumed with their prayer meetings, it was easier to say she was going out for a walk and then disappear to Henrik's store—her parents, she realized, would not check for her there because it was not imaginable to them that she was there, and because they did not shop there, and got all of their supplies now from some Finnish farmers who brought it up from Tornio, rather than support Henrik at all.

Henrik could hardly have been happier. He didn't know what to make of Nora's overtures, especially given that Biettar had said those things in front of Nora, and this had made him expect that she would avoid him even more now, and it didn't seem possible she was actually flirting, but it also didn't seem possible that her sudden visits meant nothing at all. He was confused, and he was also drinking fairly steadily, which wasn't helping his confusion; he had four full casks of brännvin that hadn't sold at Easter as he'd planned, and instead he was drinking his way through them in a perverse challenge he'd given himself, because if he drank it all then he would have to stop drinking, as there would be nothing left. But it was more important to not think about anything, not think about why Nora came to visit, not think about the debt, more important to not do the accounting. It was practically unbearable as it was to have the mail come through and wait to see his uncle's handwriting on a letter—what he would say about the debt, about the news about Laestadius, Henrik couldn't guess—and it was still more unbearable that across the way at the parsonage were Lapps who owed him, who walked around like their debts meant nothing, like they knew Lars Levi would defend them, keep them from the jail, and after all, weren't they right?

A woman came in, bringing a burst of mosquitoes with her. She had blond hair and the long face of a Norwegian but she looked at him beneath weighted lids. He made friendly conversation, selling her coffee and dried reindeer meat, wondering if the way she looked at him meant anything. She seemed to linger, but when they kept talking it turned out she had come all the way up from the coast, from Alta of all places, to be Lars Levi's housekeeper, not as a job, but because she just wanted to offer herself to God, to be of use to him. When she said this her eyes glazed and, though it had been obvious for some time, this was when Henrik experienced it as obvious: they loved him. Mad Lasse was not just a pastor anymore but a leader, he was taking on the stuff of legend, and when the woman had left, he realized it more fully still: it was summer and the Lapps were still coming to church. The year before the summer had been silent—the summer was when settlers came through, beat and wearied by the bugs and the heath, but the Lapps and their herds went to the sea, and stayed there. Henrik had seen it happening but he hadn't seen it, hadn't registered the Lapps in town as more than another oddity of this place, but now it occurred to him: my God, the stuff is spreading. The preaching sickness, it's an epidemic. They're going down like flies.

He was going to go look out the window, but around the curtains' edge was the bright frame of sun, the winter's plague of unending darkness already replaced with a new plague of unending light, a reminder he didn't need that any pleasure could become punishment.

THE SIGHT OF the sea brought the same relief it always had. There was the first relief of having arrived, and then the deep satisfaction of seeing the reindeer swim across the bay to the island, knowing how good it must have felt to them, to let the salted current kill off the flies and midges and pests crawling in their coats, to come out onto the shore and shake and see the greening rocks waiting for them, the snowed heights, the breeze stiff and sure to keep them cold. It made Risten feel good, to see them feel so good, and there was the same surprise as every year upon reaching their island that anything could be so beautiful. The low and snowed mountains hunkered over the bay, the porpoises turned over in the waves, revealing their rounded backs—the land could not stop showing off and she was reminded that seeing could be salvation. It was impossible, even with Willa around, to be unhappy, and for a few days, and even a week, she felt real delight in having arrived, in being on the island with the herd, and with Mikkol, with whom she slept each night in their own lávvu, set apart from the others but not out of sight. He seemed different at the sea, relaxed, and his playfulness, even if it felt juvenile at times, endeared him to her. He did stupid things, he put a live fish in the rákkas while she napped, he dangled sea worms while she was trying to fix the net, he brought sacks of fish and dumped them at her feet as if to say, and I have provided for you. But mostly she was happy because he didn't take the Bible out, and she didn't hear a single word about Jesus or Biettar or Mad Lasse, she only heard about fishing and the doe who refused to feed her calf and how many eagles he'd had to scare away, and the only impingement on this was the sight of the path she'd taken the year before, up and around the cape of the island, where Ivvár had appeared, but there was no real need to go that way, where the small stones of the shore became boulders, green and mossy, dank and slippery, and she managed, most of the time, to not even look that way, and kept her gaze toward the unsinkable sun.

The first time she heard Mikkol mention God she was, of all things, washing herself. She was pouring water over her soaped legs and feet and she was enjoying herself, enjoying, even, being watched by Mikkol, who was pretending to not look at her but was, watching her the way he watched reindeer, with a mix of ownership and admiration and observation.

"I want you to come with me to Ivgobahta," he said suddenly, and at first she'd been surprised. Of course she would go with him to Ivgobahta, she always went to Ivgobahta—it was some of the summer's best days, at the market, seeing everyone, staring at strangers, at the boats, at the Norwegians, and she enjoyed going through the stalls, finding the best wool for the cheapest price, she was good at haggling because she was good at seeming like she was about to walk away.

"Why wouldn't I?" she said then, easily, and even though the back of her knee was clean she soaped it again, for the pleasure of him seeing her do it.

"I heard Biettar is going to be speaking there and I want you to come with me to hear it."

"Oh," she said. She hoped she'd sounded lightly interested, and not disappointed, though the disappointment stung. At least he wasn't saying this in front of her father. There was that mercy. And maybe it was just a little prayer meeting in one of the market-houses, a quiet little reading. She wondered if she should show more interest than she had, put up at least a front of having considered it, be conciliatory. It wasn't good to push against these things; it might just strengthen his interest and resolve.

"Well, why not," she said, "I'm sure that'd be fine," but it didn't feel like it was going to be fine.

Everyone dreamed through the long summer nights, which looked not at all like night, which were, after all, the tails and muzzles of day; from anywhere on Lyngen you could watch the sun come down and, without ever interrupting the fixed line of the sea, rise back up again—this happened against the soft haze of all kinds of sunrises that were simultaneously sunsets, thick orange ones and red striped ones, some with clouds so heavy with pink they fairly drooped, some a little gray and nearly banal, but night after night the sun toyed with the horizon, and with the play of sun was the play of people, it didn't matter really when you slept or didn't, if you went out for a walk at midnight it made no difference, you wouldn't lose your way, and there was a pleasure in not being bound to the delineations of darkness.

This time untouched by darkness gave Ivvár, as it always did, the keenest longings. He craved to be touched, he found himself thinking, with the now-familiar repetition, of Willa; he wandered around like the children without a shirt on, just to feel the sun touch his chest, and he walked on the rocks on the beach just to feel the rocks touch his feet. The trek itself had been grueling, the move down to the sea had been one of the worst in his memory, even in comparison to the first year they had taken the new route east of the rock field instead of west after they had to skirt around the Swedish farmers. It had been worse because they didn't have his father there, and while they were somewhat used to the new route they didn't realize how much they had counted on Biettar to know everything and decide everything until now when he was gone. He was one of those men who were so good with directions, with recognizing every hill, you could have dropped him off blindfolded in a blizzard and he would have found his way home, but maybe because of this Ivvár had never developed the same skill, and he'd found himself looking at an unfamiliar valley with fear. And the fear, the not-knowing, had cost them, the herd had split so badly that it wasn't clear how they would get the herd back together, and it wasn't clear how they should go after the broken-off herd and who should stay with the main herd and try to push on, and finally Ivvár had said he would go get them, and he'd just left. But it'd taken eight days for him and Ánde and Niko to gather the rest of them and get them back on the route, eight days in which Ivvár's stomach was sour from worrying, in which he slept poorly, restlessly, always sure there were more reindeer drifting over the next fell that needed to be collected.

But they had made it to the sea. Three-fourths, maybe four-fifths, of the herd had made it to Gáivuonbahta, though Ivvár was willing to bet Speins had some of their missing ones, a good ten, maybe twenty at least, mixed into their herd; he would go looking later, before the market, so they didn't try to sell any of his—but he was tired. He felt like some noaidi had put him in a great sleep. The first year on your own is always the hardest, everyone said it, it was hard to go from your parents' herd to your own, and now Ivvár was seeing how true it was, each choice seemed wrong, so he changed his mind midway, like now, when he was wandering around, looking at the herd, trying to decide if he should slaughter any—he couldn't make up his mind. It was much later in the year than was usual to be at market, but the winter had run so late—they'd arrived here so late—but it unnerved him, this difference from years before, and made it harder to know now what to do. It could be warm very soon, and the meat wouldn't keep, no one would want it. Every minute he thought something different, he thought, better not risk the bad prices, I'll live on reindeer meat and that's all, I'll patch the coat and the trousers, I really only need a new knife. But then the next minute he thought, well, he did need some new woolen underclothes, they had worn so thin, and he had to have a new hat, and he needed it to be sealskin on top this time, not the fox fur, he had to have it. And he wanted to buy a new harness for the driving-reindeer, the one Borga had was going to snap. So then he would slaughter at least one, he would do a bit of shopping, he would get some extra money on hand—but which one to slaughter?

Walking around he checked each of them, he looked to see, were any limping, were any ill, how bad were their coats? They all looked lean and patchy, except the calves, who looked lean and soft. Out of the corner of his eye he could see Ánde walking up the mountainside with Niko, heading up the slope toward Ivvár. The way they walked meant they had news, because otherwise they would have waited for him to come down, they were lazy like that.

When they got close Ivvár pretended to have made up his mind and held his lasso like he had his eye on the one he would slaughter. For a minute Ánde and Niko stood there, at the edge, so as to not scare any of them. Ivvár looked at them, shrugged a little. "It's okay, I'll grab it right after you go," he said.

"Go on," Ánde said, "we don't mind waiting,"

"No, it's all right," Ivvár said. He knew Ánde knew he hadn't made up his mind, Ánde always complained about it, his indecisiveness.

"We can wait," Ánde said. He looked faintly amused.

"What is it?" Ivvár asked impatiently. "You came up here for something?" Their own carcasses were already down by the shore, stacked in a boat.

"No, not really," Ánde said.

"Just something very interesting," Niko said. The way he was standing there Ivvár could see he was laughing, they had been joking about him all the way up there.

"Well?" Ivvár asked. He dropped the pretense of the lasso and walked nearer to them, reached inside his shirt, felt around for the little pouch of tobacco and put some of it beside his gum and packed it in with his tongue.

"There's news from Lyngen," Ånde said.

Nina was visiting with the Prosts who just saw the Speins," Niko said. "They have our reindeer?"

"Oh, I don't know," Ånde said, "you know we'll have to drag that out of them."

"Well, good news is best spent slowly," Ivvár said, a little sourly.

"It's good news," Ånde said, happily, "depending, of course."

"On what?"

"How tame you like your reindeer."

"My reindeer will let me pet them like a dog," Ivvár said, "I call to them and they come."

"Oh, we know," Ånde said, and he laughed, and Niko laughed. They laughed so heartily Ivvár was flustered.

"Well, just say already."

"It's your white driving-reindeer, you know, the one who is especially tame. A very sweet, very—faithful reindeer."

"Borga?" Ivvár asked.

"No, your other reindeer," Niko said, "she came down to the sea with the Tommas." Ivvár flushed, he knew he did, he felt the blood go up his neck, straight up to his eyes. Willa had come to the sea. Had she come for him? Run away for him? He felt fit to burst, like his body was not his own, it might fall down or break into a run or simply, as it was apparently now, just freeze. Say something normal, he commanded himself, and he opened his mouth and nothing came out.

"Impressive really she made it, your reindeer are very strong," Ånde said.

"Very good driving-reindeer," Niko said.

"I don't know anything about it," Ivvár said, finally, which was not a lie, and perhaps this truth saved him from saying anything more revealing, for when he turned away from them he felt, of all things, a fresh pop of tears in his eyes, almost from surprise. This was madness, he thought, she was mad, what was she doing? What was she thinking? With the Tommas, of all people! And if Mikkol had joined Tomma-village and not the other way around, then Willa would be with Risten. If Willa went anywhere, to market, to church, it was very likely she would be with Risten . . . what had she told Risten? Anything? It occurred to him he didn't know her very well, and he didn't know what she was liable to do or not do, and if she was someone who joined a Sámi move to the sea, what else might she do?

He was much more unnerved than he would have ever thought. His whole chest rattled like someone was stuck in there throwing stones. Willa, here, when he'd been trying——and he had tried, he had really tried——to forget her!

He was doing something, though, what was he doing? He lassoed a doe who hadn't calved, or maybe her calf had died, he couldn't remember, and he pulled, and all the reindeer nearby got up and scurried away. The doe was still strong, and she resisted the lasso, not wanting to be held, but he put the knife to her throat and he plunged it in, keeping the knife still in her neck, holding the blood in. She kicked and she kicked, and he pushed it in further still, it was a bit of a waiting game with this one——he looked up at Ánde and Niko, who watched him without a lot of interest——until at last she grunted and gave way. He put her down in the grass, and he rolled her over onto her back, so that all four of her legs splayed open to the sky, and he leaned over her, and he circled each of her hooves with the knife, and then he began the incisions, down each of the legs, then the cut down the belly, and he looked around for the slaughtering bowls, for the blood-bowl, and he realized he hadn't set them out, and he went to get them, the blood on his hands, his mouth, amazingly, set to laugh, his heart going Willa, Willa.

THE IVGOBAHTA, OR SKIBOTN, MARKET HAD BEEN AROUND FOR SEVERAL hundred years, the progeny of geography and convenience—the harbor, along the Norwegian coast overlooking the inlets toward the Norwegian Sea, was just large and peaceful enough to hold ships from Tromsø, even while the reindeer-roads from the south brought the sledges or carriages from Sweden and Finland to the water's edge. Each of the parties of the Skibotn market—the Swedes, the Kvens, the Finns, the Norwegians, the Russians, the Sámi—had almost entirely different resources and needs for going there—the Kvens had butter, but no meat; the Norwegians had metals and cloth, but no meat; the Sámi had meat, but very little butter; and so on—and as such there had been a habitual agreement three times a year for everyone to meet and barter, and not one but two hotels had even sprung up there for this very purpose, and there were several pebbled streets with cabins and market-houses along them, though there was no church. At least five different languages were spoken at any given time, with most of the men speaking at least two and usually three, and the system of bartering was generally from one good to another, since there was not even a reigning unit of money, and a special dispensation had even been made by the Crown to make the market duty-free, since it wasn't clear who should tax whom or how or for what.

The market was also a dispensation from ordinary life, as it was crowded

15

enough to provide relative anonymity, except, perhaps, for the Sámi, who stood out nearly anywhere they went to the minds and eyes of the not-Sámi, in part because their dress was so different and in part because they came with large sledges of reindeer carcasses, the pelts and flanks of meat stacked as tall as the men, pulled along by still more reindeer. The market was ruled as such by all things reindeer—reindeer hair to be stuffed into pillows and mattresses; pelts for lining sledges; pelts better for coats; leather softened with boiled birch bark; leather yet to be softened; fur from the forelegs for boots; glue, made from hooves; hooks, made from antlers; thread, from their sinews; ropes from leather; needle-holders from the shinbones of calves; piles of woven rátnu rugs from wool. Of course there were also piles of every kind of fish, salted and dried as well as fresh—cod and mackerel, trout, halibut, seals, whale oil, whale meat—and the atmosphere was of nature cut and dried but still stinking of itself. In the background of all of this were the fjords, the mountains more curved than peaked, almost humped, rising up swiftly and immediately from the water's edge, so that even though the mountains were not, in reality, very high, the steepness and immediacy of their slopes gave the sense that they dove straight down into the sea, so that you were surrounded on all sides by grandeur nonetheless. This time of year they were beginning to go green under the snow, and in the bay the sea doubled, tripled the sun's glare, and the wind was cold and clean, and the seagulls croaked with delight at all this chaos.

Willa had not understood what the market would be like. She had agreed to go because she had been invited (Anna had insisted Risten invite her), and because she'd always liked the markets at Easter or Michaelmas, but she had not imagined this ruckus. She had not thought to envision the boats, longboats, boats with masts, boats low and slim and swift, boats heavy in their holds with salt and tar and coffee; she had never seen men drink so openly, one of them crawling on his knees, having pissed himself; she had never seen women in loose dresses smoking at the door of a market-stall that even Willa knew must have been the whorehouse; she had never seen a herder dragging a bleeding carcass by the back leg with one hand while he cupped a smoking pipe with the other.

While Willa stared aimlessly, Risten stared purposefully, searching for Ivár. She had told herself she wouldn't do it but it was all she was doing. It was only a year ago she'd seen him here, only a year ago they had joked about people going off on the lovers' trails up the mountains, and it had been clear that Ivár was suggesting as much, though they hadn't, not then, not yet. The first day of the market passed without her catching any sight of him, and the second day she thought she spotted him twice, only to realize she was just wishing him into being. And still Biettar had not shown up to speak yet. Mikkol had said that Biettar would be at the market "on the third or fourth day," and had given no time or place, so Risten was left, same as anyone else, to wander the streets, taking in everyone her eyes could take in, mostly, in this case, the Kvens and the Norwegians, who occasionally shouted at her or Willa, crassly, invited them inside dark storerooms, offered them sips from their bottles, suggested they give a little spin in their skirts.

"So drunk and so rude," she complained to Willa, but really she was glad to still be shouted at, and thankful they couldn't tell the difference between a square or a circle on her belt, and glad, most of all, that she got more attention than Willa.

Ivár was staring at the drunk Kvens, too, looking at how one of them had his leg crossed over the other man's leg. He was wondering if they had been sleeping there all night like that, when he saw Willa. He knew it was her, even though she was still far off, bent over, talking to a little boy who was trying to sell her something. Immediately he was nervous, and though it would make his nerves worse he put more tobacco in his cheek, and he slunk down against the crates he was leaning against and watched her. The fact of her existence was so surreal he couldn't believe his eyes, he had no idea whatsoever how to behave. She turned to say something to someone—so Risten was with her, they were here together. A rush of headiness came to him, he felt suddenly like he was in trouble but he didn't know for what. He might have run, he was tempted to run, but Ánde appeared with a wheelbarrow, not the cart Ivár had hoped for. Ánde nodded in the direction of Willa and Risten, grinning, not holding back any of it.

"I saw," Ivár said ruefully.

Ánde laughed. "You look like you're going to be sick."

Ivár got up and took one side of the carcass on top of the boat. It was the reindeer that hadn't calved. They loaded another on, and Ivár pushed off with the wheelbarrow before Ánde could offer to help, keeping his head down, avoiding her, aware of her moving through the crowd and keeping himself as best he could out of her sight. He went straight for Anderssen's, and when he got there he kept the conversation very short, very quick, and like usual Anderssen gave him a goodish glass of brännvin, and Ivár got his new kettle and his new set of woolen underclothes and his new leather harness, and even some coins for change. He felt better now after the brännvin, and when he stepped outside the market-house, everything seemed a little more bearable.

The fact of his father came to him with a shock—his father, of all things, was standing on top of a large rock at the end of the street, reading from a set of papers he held with both hands. He wore a simple faded gákti, one that used to be blue and now was gray, and well-oiled leather trousers. He had no hat on, nor a scarf, despite the high wind, but in some ways he looked better than Ivár had seen him look in years; his face was less swollen, like all of the air had been squeezed out of him, and his eyes were sharp and moved rapidly around the crowd.

"Now," his father was half shouting, half speaking, his voice strained, "the—gods are kegs of brännvin, showy clothing, fancy buildings, painted sleighs, cows, horses, and sheep. For Luther says: What a man loves most is his god." He seemed relieved to have arrived at that sentence and repeated it. Ivár wished, desperately, he would stop reading altogether, and come down off the rock—he didn't sound like Mad Lasse at all, like he was using his words to cast a lasso around the listeners, pulling it tauter and tauter as he went. No, he sounded like he didn't know where the lasso was going at all, where the sentence would end, and they were all just guessing together.

Still, there was a small crowd, but a real one, around the rock—they didn't have the fervency of Mad Lasse's followers but they seemed dutiful, or anyway, interested.

"What is your god?" his father shouted toward a Finn who was walking past with the over-deliberated focus of a drunk. The man scarcely looked up at him.

"What is it you love most?" his father shouted again, at another man walking by. "What is it you love most?" "What is your god?" Shame began to creep into Ivár, as if every person who looked at his father with annoyance or with pity looked at him, too. It was worse than Easter, because at least at Karesuando Church people had looked up to his father for his antics, for his performances of piety, but here he might as well have been another drunk, and the more he shouted and the louder he became, the crazier he seemed, and what in the church had been taken for passion and for the power of God was only ill-ness here. Ivár looked at the crowd: he could see it on the Kvens' faces, and the Norwegians', and then he saw Risten, Mikkol standing close beside her in the proprietary way of the newly married, and he looked for Willa and he saw her, but she was turned away from him, and he didn't know what she thought, but probably it was nothing good. Everyone thought he was crazy, he was just a crazy, dirty, poor Lapp, and what was worse was that Ivár, seeing the spittle fly from his father's mouth, he couldn't help it, he agreed.

THE IGNOMINY OF Biettar was like something out of the Bible. From Wil-la's vantage point at the back edge of the crowd she could see him clearly, and for some minutes she stood and watched from the relative safety of the wall of a market-house—beside her was a young mother, nursing while she stood, the baby watching Willa with some skepticism while the mother watched Biettar with mild interest.

More people were noticing Biettar; the crowd was slowly thickening. Someone shouting was, at the very least, something to watch, and everyone was tired of the only other entertainment, a man with a fiddle who played the same Karelian tune over and over again, and that badly. So Biettar was a welcome distraction of a different kind, a different man making a differ-ent kind of fool of himself, and better yet, maybe, a fool to be egged on to more foolishness. But it was one thing to stand and give a sermon to people walking by, and yet another to tell a crowd of drunken men they were drinking the Devil's piss, and once he had started in on this tack it took almost no time at all for someone to begin to shout, "Go home to your herd," and someone else to join in, making the sound, ostensibly, of a reindeer rutting, "Unh-unh-unh."

"But our God is in Heaven," Biettar persisted, "not in the stomach, or liver, or spleen, not in your bile, or your intestines. He is not in your liquor. He is not in the whorehouse. He is not in the barn." Willa found herself unable to watch him. It wasn't so much that she sided with the men shouting at Biettar as she didn't side with any of them, and she couldn't bear either Biettar, or the men, or herself. She turned to look down the street, to see who else was watching, and was surprised to see that more people were coming out of every door, so that some were leaning out of open shutters to watch, and then her eyes met his.

She looked at Ivvár and Ivvár looked at her. He was so handsome, his hair was longer than she remembered and had lightened in the sun, and his face looked browned and strong. She had walked two hundred miles, over two months, and here he was, and here she was, and she was suddenly so embarrassed to have come so far, to have done so much, that she couldn't look at him—she turned around like a fool and stared at the crowd, watching Biettar preaching but not seeing him at all, aware that people were shouting and that Mikkol had begun to turn to people and hush them, but it was a scene that was meaningless, only Ivvár had meaning. What had she done, coming here? Why had she come all this way—how embarrassing—how embarrassing to have suffered so much, and for what?

How impossible, how humiliating, if she should have to go toward him now! A beggar, she was a beggar—she had nothing, not even pride, she had her hardened lips and her sunburnt face and her aching legs, a pop in her hip when she went up or down the mountainside, she had Ristén's old reindeer pants, patched, and Ristén's old summer leather boots. There was not a pretty thing about her, there was not a desirable thing about her, but still she hoped, come to me. Come and stand by me. But she couldn't turn around to look, to see if he was coming toward her or not, she just willed it, calling out to him in her hopes, come here, come here, oh I love you, come here.

Biettar was still talking, on and on, the Devil, the whiskey, who is your god, that which a person loves most is his god. Willa remembered, very dimly, having copied that out, having thought at the time, I will love God and Christ the most, having made that decision, though she had felt like maybe she loved her family most, and it had seemed so trying to imagine a god she had not met and to love him more than those she had, it was the largest demand of them all and even then she couldn't quite meet it.

But she had left that family she'd loved, she had fled them.

She made herself turn around and Ivár hadn't moved. He was still standing outside one of the market-houses the way he used to stand outside church, his thumbs hooked around the front of his belt and one of his shoulders leaning against the wall and his feet crossed. He should have looked like he was trying too hard to look at ease, but he just looked at ease. This time she smiled like an idiot, and even though the crowd was getting louder now she walked toward him. Everyone else walked toward Biettar and she walked away, toward Ivár, saying, excuse me, excuse me, probably uselessly—there was a thick patch of sweaty men to push through, Kvens maybe, she wasn't sure what language to speak, she went with Swedish—and when she got through them she had lost him. He had just been right there, and now he was gone.

She stood there on the main path, people passing by her. No one paid any attention to her, she was neither here nor there, and when she did spot him, he was walking away, his head down, like he didn't want to be seen. He didn't want to be followed, he didn't want anything to do with her, and she might have screamed, chased him, beat on his back, but behind her the shouting was worsening, and by the time she turned around she only just managed to catch the sight of Biettar being pulled down off the rock by a blond man, a tall Norwegian, who was grabbing at Biettar's shins, about to pick Biettar up like he was a child by his legs and swing him over his shoulders and carry him off, but Biettar kicked and freed himself, and fell to the ground. The man seemed satisfied with this, that Biettar was on the ground, and he said, now you stay there, barked it in Norwegian, and he was walking away when Biettar stood up again, and for a moment it seemed like Biettar was going to fight him. Fight him, Biettar, she thought, fight him! She wanted Biettar to take the Norwegian like a reindeer and pull his head to the ground, put his foot on his neck.

But Biettar only stood there, and said nothing.

WITH THE DISSOLUTION of the fight came the dissolution of the crowd—no one wanted to be milling around there anymore; they all felt embarrassed of the scene, almost as one, in part because a group of Sámi women had started to go through the crowd, dispersing them, saying, forcefully, go home, go home, what kind of men are you, and their shame was effective, everyone felt scolded and also resentful for being scolded, couldn't they stand around and watch a fight if they liked? But they didn't have it in them to say anything against the will of these women, and it was easier to just go back to whatever they had been trying to buy or sell or drink.

It was Risten who was left once the crowd had cleared, Risten and Mikkol, trying to look kindly but not with too much pity at Biettar, who held in his hands the sheaf of papers that made up the sermon. One of the pages had fallen and was trampled on, and Biettar tried to wipe the mud off but only smeared the page. He was crestfallen, even humiliated. What he had been expecting he wasn't sure, but he had convinced himself that either God would defend him or that God would allow the men to listen; he had even imagined himself as a new Laestadius, transmuted from herder of the reindeer to herder of the people; he had thought that, last night!

But this was worse, this was much worse—this required him to believe in what he was doing with such clarity that being attacked like this would not change his mind or his purpose, and he didn't know if he had that clarity of faith. It had required so much of him, to go up there and keep reading, and he had kept doing so through stubbornness alone. He was depressed, profoundly, even when Risten and Mikkol invited him to stay with them in their lávvu nearby, even when he got there and sat with Risten's father and smoked with him, and even when Nilsa, to his own surprise, was not rude to him, and did not ignore him. It was only when Biettar saw Willa that he began to feel that there was something special, something larger at work. It was not quite a sign from God but it was something, to see her here, it seemed like Laestadius had been brought before him in this other form, and oddly enough, he felt less alone. He knew, of course, that she didn't want him there; she looked as defeated as he was, he thought, and no surprise, it wasn't easy to walk to the sea if you'd never done it before, if you hadn't had the preparation of your whole life behind you, but as hard as he looked at her he couldn't tell if she was pregnant or not, and he couldn't tell who she was really with—the Tommas? And why should they take her in? But he couldn't ask such a thing.

Of course Willa might have looked at Biettar with pity—she easily could have understood that he had not understood what he was getting himself into—but she had no room for pity for him, she only had pity for herself. The sight of Biettar was a wound, and she could only think of Ivvár, and she could only see in Biettar the little motions and mannerisms that seemed to her to be Ivvár's. She hated him for being there, she resented Nilsa for being so nice to him, and serving him good food like a coward, and she despised Mikkol for looking at Biettar with admiration. When someone finally spoke to her directly, it was Biettar, and she couldn't lift her eyes to look at him when he said, "Willa, have you heard, Lorens is doing well," and even though he said it softly and gently, she didn't look at him, she said, "Yes, I know," although she didn't know. She wanted to cry, or sob, or hit someone, she was all feeling and no sense of what she was feeling, and it took everything she had to just sit there and do nothing with it all, and wait.

When it seemed like an innocuous amount of time had passed, she crawled out of the lávvu and hurried away, hating that it wasn't ever dark this time of year, so there was nowhere to hide, no cover. She went to sit by the sea, waiting for Biettar to leave, but he didn't leave, and finally it occurred to her he wasn't going to, and she would have to go back.

So she stayed out there; she stayed out there all night, listening from the rock as Mikkol cried out to God from somewhere in the lávvu, and Biettar responded. She heard the trance beginning, she heard the cries, and after a very long time, maybe an hour, Nilsa appeared, and he sat down some distance from her and took out his pipe. He looked at her as if to say, what can you do? And for a long time they both sat there, and watched the sea.

16

THE LETTER FROM HIS UNCLE ARRIVED AS JUNE WAS ENDING, NEARLY TWO months after Henrik had sent his own—the post was always slow coming north. Henrik knew before he opened it what he'd done in writing to Frans, but still, to see it laid out so clearly was disconcerting, like he'd cast a line much farther out than he realized and pulled in not a fish but a whale. His uncle was "nearly abject with astonishment," and "gravely aggrieved, lest souls who knew not yet the Lord should be dragged down into this devilry." He cautioned Henrik to "be his eyes and ears," "to continue steadfastly in the service of Our Lord," and so on, the phrases belonging so firmly to the lexicon of the Church and Crown as to hold almost no meaning at all—the exhortations were fervent and yet all the more empty for being so familiar in their phrasing. It was the end of the second page that contained the shock: Frans was going to have Laestadius sent to Pajala, a parish farther south, where his heretical teachings would be "abated, if not abolished," since he would be "amongst a population less susceptible to his sway." Pajala was "still, alas, Lapland," but was comprised mostly of Swedes, and in general the Church had an older, and firmer, grasp on its inhabitants. "I don't expect," Frans wrote dryly, "any of them will take well to being encouraged to stand on pews instead of sit."

Then there was a bit about political news that made Henrik's mind slow . . . it was so dull, it was precisely the kind of thing his uncle loved to talk about in too much detail. It came down to, from what Henrik could gather, talk of Tsar Nicholas I closing the border into Russia, so that no one could pass through, not the Swedes or the Norwegians and certainly not the Lapps, all because the Russians wanted fishing rights on the coast and King Oskar I wouldn't give them any, because King Oskar I was trying to not be like his father, who he thought had given in too much to the tsar. As for him, his uncle went on—the letter was nearly four pages of tightly packed script—he would come through later this summer, at the latest in the fall, on an inspection of all of the parishes, to see that the congregations "grew steadfastly under the merciful watchfulness of Our Lord," and of course, to visit with Henrik himself, and to see that "God had blessed him richly in all things," and to join Henrik in "his newfound prosperity and wealth," which Henrik understood to mean: his uncle was coming for the money Henrik owed him.

It took Henrik the rest of the day to realize the obvious consequence that if Laestadius was being sent south somewhere, Nora would go with him. Somehow, Henrik had thought that any consequence would fall on Laestadius alone, and moreover, it hadn't occurred to him at all that they would send Laestadius anywhere else, because he was so well suited for this particular geographic desolation and deprivation. Henrik seemed to recall his uncle telling him, once, that Laestadius was the only one who had applied for the position here in the first place. Henrik read the relevant parts of the letter again, but it seemed clear: Nora would go south to Pajala, a larger town than this one by far, and Nora would find someone there, while another pastor would be sent here. It was difficult to say if this new pastor would be better for Henrik's interests—it seemed possible, even likely, he would be like other pastors, giving people a glassful of brännvin when they came to visit the parsonage as an inducement to return, but there was never any guarantee of that. The new pastor could be worse. He could have no daughters at all, and he might want to come over every night to talk with Henrik and save his soul. And now his uncle would come, he was going to come collect in every sense of the word, and Henrik felt the temptation to disappear, like Willa, into the tundra.

Nora came in only a day later, looking leprous—the mosquitoes had gotten to her, badly, and she had welts on her neck and one even inside the high flare of her nose, not to mention a line of bites that seemed to extend her eyebrows across her forehead. It was unflattering, especially since she had rubbed mud mixed with tar on her wrists and hands and along her collarbone, so she looked poor and dirty as well as sick. Instantly he felt better about her family being sent to Pajala.

"I was out in the field yesterday," she said, in explanation, and then she hid her hands behind her back.

"I see."

"It's not as bad as it looks."

"I hope so," he said, then realized the implication. "What were you doing out there?"

"Pulling rocks from the soil, mostly," she said. "Every year, no matter what, there's more rocks, it's like they grow there."

"Plenty of stones for soup."

"Exactly."

"They work you too hard," he said, and he leaned against the counter.

"Everyone works hard." She seemed more uncomfortable than usual, and she rocked back and forth slightly on her feet, her hands still behind her back.

"What is it?" he asked. He studied her but he had never been any good at guessing these things. Emelie used to hate that about him, she used to puff up and say, I know you know what I'm thinking, when he didn't at all, he had no idea whatsoever. But Nora just stood there, like she had come there at his bidding and was now just waiting to be told what to do. "Nora," he said at last.

"Yes," she answered. Her voice was dry, and he wished she would drink some water. He looked around for a glass.

"What is it?" he asked. "Is something wrong?"

"You know the story of the prodigal son?" she asked. He nodded and she went to the stool in the corner, and he abandoned the glass of water. She sat down in a proper way, her knees angled to the side while her feet rested on the rung, her hands not folded but laid one over the other. "There are two sons, and one of them asks for his inheritance early and he takes it and he gambles and drinks and whores and has a riotous living, and then he comes home, he says, I have sinned against Heaven and against thee, and his father welcomes him and has dinner for him. His father says to his servants, bring hither the fatted calf. And the other son is angry, and he goes to his father and says, you never killed a fatted calf for me. But the father just repeats what he's said before to the other son, he says, all that I have is thine, and then he says, thy brother was dead, and is alive again, and was lost, and is found."

She stopped speaking, as if her point, in having retold the story, was very clear. Henrik nodded, trying to look pensive.

"But what about the other brother?" she asked, her words overly enunciated, "the father is so glad he's found again, but he's never thought, how does the other brother feel? The other brother did what he was supposed to all along, but gets nothing for it, there is no fatted calf for doing the right thing. Doesn't anyone ever think how much harder it is to be the other brother, the one who didn't run away?" Her voice had cracked but her face was solid. She looked at him steadily and for a second he was afraid of her, without knowing why.

"She'll come back," he said, "and you'll be glad. Probably she's just up the river."

"She's at the sea," Nora said evenly. "I heard them saying it. The Lapps know that she made it to the sea." She shook her head. "Does she write me? Does she tell us she's alive? No, I wait to hear it from some Lapps talking who think I don't understand them. You know what else they said?" she asked.

"What?"

She looked down at her hands, screwing her lips together, but she was smirking at herself. "They say I should just marry you." He nodded, he opened his mouth, but nothing came out. "You know why?"

"I can't say I do." He aimed for levity in his tone, achieved something closer to indifference.

"They said someone in the family should get married, it looked bad that Willa ran away. And then they went on, they said my parents should marry me off before something worse happened and there were two shames on the family, and the reason I hadn't married you yet was just that I thought I was too good for you, and my family has a snobbishness we didn't earn. And I'm not getting any younger," she said bitterly. "What am I waiting for? The king of France?" She was imitating their speech, and it was uncomfortable to hear her like this, both so passionate and so crude.

"Oh," he said. What she wanted in response eluded him—he didn't know if he should seem offended or pleased. In a way, it felt good that someone thought of them being together, and he thought it all sounded not too far from the truth, and her family really was snobbish, amazingly so—their pretensions to a higher class when they were so poor made them even more preposterous and effaced whatever class they did have—but he couldn't say that. He wondered if he should tell her she'd be in Pajala soon anyway. "What do the Lapps know about anything," he said, at last, and he sensed he'd disappointed her, there was something else he was supposed to have said. What? Was it that, secretly, she had wanted him to say, no, you're very beautiful and we're very good for each other, let's get married? And how was he supposed to have said that, when she ducked in here all covered with tar? Or was that the test and he had failed it?

It wasn't until she'd gone that he thought of how he should have said it, how he should have said, I have a confession to make, and then he should have been gallant, and forthcoming, and even proposed. Maybe he should run after her. When would she hear? How long did he have? Time weighed. He must do something. He must work himself up to it. He must get Nora for a wife, and by the time his uncle arrived, it would be settled, and Nora would have cleaned up the store and made everything nicer. Maybe more people would want to come to the store with her there, the daughter of Laestadius. Yes, that was it, that was it—he could get all the crazy believers in here, sell them whatever they wanted; where one went, they all went. That was the secret. He could get his life together, quit drinking, start going for long walks in fresh air. He would become so healthy, so wealthy, that by the time he returned to Uppsala he would dress Nora in the finest jacquard, and they would descend from a carriage he owned himself, and walk up the stone steps to his mother's rowhouse, and she would have no choice but to say, my dear Henrik, look at you and your beautiful wife, how lovely you both are, welcome home.

WILLA HAD TAKEN a milking bowl and was walking up the steep sides of a slope looking for the nursing mothers, not because she expected to be able to get much milk from them—they always edged away from her, and she couldn't get them to hold still even if she managed to lasso them—but because she was determined to try something. She had watched Anna very carefully, and she thought she saw the trick of it, which seemed to be to hold the reindeer from the very back of its jaw, where it didn't have teeth, and she was so focused on this, on trying to move slowly enough to not scare away the reindeer, that it took her a moment to understand that someone was watching her, and that someone was Ivvár.

Ivvár! He was just lying there beside a stream, leaning against the thick peaty moss, with the air of someone who has done something wrong but knows they are not in real trouble, and in fact, knows that the other person likes them for the trouble they cause. What could be better than to meet her here? That was what his smile said.

Willa could see all of this and yet couldn't deny it was true. Where was her anger, her fury at being abandoned—the hurt of seeing him walking away from her, knowing he had seen her, knowing he knew she had come here for him . . . all of that, where was it? How could it leave so swiftly in his smile? She tried to recall the past ten days, when she had waited to be alone somewhere to cry, to relieve the rough saw of sadness—she thought of that and it bore no relationship to this moment, she wanted to be furious but she was relieved, to be bitter and distant, and reject him as he'd rejected her, but she could see she would go where he went; it wasn't about her pride or her sense of self-determination, because he was a part of her pride and her self-determination, and as she stood there and let him smile at her it was all very clear to her: when she was with him she was happy, and she wanted to be happy.

She stood there in the happiness he made for her and the milk bowl hung listlessly at her side. "You are incorrigible," she said, without any scolding in her voice at all. Her heart rose wilder.

"I don't know what that means," he said. He smiled and sprang up so lightly she was startled. "Let's go," he said, as if this were all very obvious, and he didn't hold his hand out to her or look back for her, but began to hurry down the slope, following the side of the stream, stepping over fallen branches laden with so much lichen and moss they were in, surely, a Háldi's forest, though Ivvár went so swiftly there was no time to reflect on this, there was not even time to reflect on the steps she was taking—Ivvár did not so much as step from rock to rock as swing himself lightly from one to the next, with perfect trust in himself, and Willa tried to imitate this trust in herself and her feet, and she moved without thinking about how to move, or where was safe to step, and down they went, down and down the slope with the stream. A stag, all white except for a brown line down his spine, watched them approach from below, his antlers all new velvet, not yet fully grown; the way he stood as he watched them, he might have been deciding whether or not to let them pass. In his left ear was the mark that said he belonged to someone in the Tomma family, and in his right ear was the mark that said he belonged to Risten, but when Willa saw him she thought only, I know that stag, and she was happy to recognize him, and she sensed he recognized her—he did—he stepped aside and ambled away with an indifference that was its own reward. The stag watched them tumble down past him and then returned to the thick plait of lichen on the trunk of a tree, and Willa did not fall, and Ivvár did not fall, and they made it to where the steepness softened and became a mild hill, and the trees made space, and the sunlight that had been there all along came in.

Ivvár slowed and Willa walked next to him. They were still following the stream that went straight to the sea, and as they grew closer the breeze came to their faces, and the pines gave way to brush, and the sponge of moss gave way to the stones of the shore, and then they were at the water, which today was utterly ordinary, mostly calm as the bay tended to be, and mostly gray. There was a boat, old and faded, pulled up on the rocks, and Ivvár grabbed the boat's hull and began to drag it out into the bay.

"Get in," he said, above the scrape of the boat on the rocks. He raised his eyebrows at her and she was so in love with him she would have walked out into the sea if he'd suggested it; she was beaming and she couldn't stop it. What was this, to be in a state of glee, to be suspended in something surely stupid from the outside and yet so profound from within—to look at another and to be entirely and perfectly happy with them, to forgive before a wrong had been done, to have hope so far ahead of fear?

On the boat she watched him row with the pleasure of watching some-one show off for her. She was amused by how he tried to impress her and how he did impress her. It worked, the sight of him and his arms; how swiftly the boat moved over the bay made her feel the things it was sup-posed to make her feel, that he was strong and safe, and that he desired her, and he wanted her to desire him. He was rowing north toward the entrance to the sea, but once they had rounded the island's curve he began to row east, keeping to the shore, and by the time he stopped they had passed two or three other islands, but he didn't seem tired. With her still in it, he pulled the boat up onto shore, and then he held his hand out and she took it, though she didn't need it, and on the rocks he did not let go of her hand, he clutched it as if here, on this other island, she couldn't walk without him.

The former Willa would have asked, where are we? This new Willa didn't ask, only followed him, walking along the shore, following the sun to the island's farthest curve—the fells were not so steep here, and the island was so small as to not be particularly habitable. He knew where to go, and he took her up a ways along the slope, and they climbed the rocks together until they reached a plateau, where a wide rock had been warmed all day in the sun, and where a light breeze came over so the mosquitoes could not make their way to them.

Her face hurt from smiling, the tops of her cheekbones ached. Had she been smiling the entire boat ride? Was life allowed to be this way? Would the visage of her father appear? But even that memory couldn't ruin the rock, and the sun; she could feel how clearly it didn't belong here. She lay back on the rock, the baked heat seeping through her legs and her back, and it was delicious, like a sauna after a day of skiing, a warmth that went inside and stayed. She turned her head. He looked like he was waiting for the right time to do something. Not hesitating but waiting—that distinction felt so clear to her now.

He turned away from her and toward the sea, so she could only see the back of his head. The wind was high and she propped herself up on her elbows so she could hear him. He turned back and looked at her again with too much meaning in his face. He raised his eyebrows. He was trying to suppress something, or to tell her something. "Look at the sea," he said—in the distance the porpoises were gathered together in a bunch, and their fins wheeled up and down in the water, black and glossy tips that came and went without any regularity.

"Listen," he said, and she listened, and she could hear it, soft bursts of aspirations, like they were sipping air.

Why did you leave the market, she wanted to ask. Why did you come for me now? But though she had composed the thoughts she could not say them. I am in love with you. She might have said that, too.

"When we met"—he looked at her—"when we first met, outside the church, we understood each other, in a way we didn't understand." It was so good to hear this it was like feeling the warmed rock all over again, and she wanted to luxuriate in it, and she repeated it to herself, we understood each other in a way we didn't understand.

"It feels good," she said, "to not understand," and she realized this was true. After a long while he lay down on his side with his head propped up on his hand. He was observing her carefully, and she tried to look at him evenly, but a nervous smile kept popping up in her mouth and she pursed her lips together to keep it down. "So you think you understand me now?" she asked. She heard herself, her inability to say anything of any worth and her desire to just have him talk about her.

He poked her solidly on her arm.

"That's how well you understand me?" she asked, but she wanted him to poke her again.

"Fine, I'll be very serious," he said, and he composed his face, pulled it together, bringing his eyebrows down. "I'm a serious person," he said, "I say everything seriously and I mean everything I say. All of my thoughts are very important." It was clear he was someone else—her father, or his father, someone else's father. She laughed, he was good at the imitation, even if it was uncomfortable to see. "Yes," he said, "I know my alphabet very well, and I read in Greek before bed and in Latin before breakfast. I eat my books for lunch. And whenever I have something worth saying, I write it down so no one will forget! And I tell them about it every Sunday, before the plover has sung." He dropped his hand that he'd been gesturing with, but it was clear that in the play of seriousness he'd become serious. A shift had happened, something had turned. Willa wanted to stop it, to catch the other mood back, but he looked bitter.

His real feeling was less bitterness than resentment, and, waiting under the resentment was shame, which just then had emerged too clearly, he was back at the market and his father was standing on the large rock, and his father was shouting at people about their sins. His face flamed with it, he was drawn into the humiliation, and then there was Willa, looking at him, wanting something from him—what—everything—and in that moment he could not give her anything, especially not himself, what was he supposed to do, hand her all that humiliation?

Except now, looking at her, he felt worse than before, because he was remembering how he'd left her. He was aware he'd done this, aware that as always he'd acted without a plan, without thought. He'd known she would be at the market and he hadn't come back for her, he'd let her stay at the market, maybe for days, without returning. He had waited until he'd been able to forget, at least a little, what he had done, but now they were here and she was looking at him and he knew she was in love with him and he had taken her here to forget his father, to forget the market, and instead he was remembering Risten, and it seemed to him it was cursed, they couldn't just be them, there was too much in the way. But even then, while he looked at her with doubt, with worry, she looked at him with plain love. It was both balm and burden to be looked at with love. He desired it, he feared it—I will disappoint her, he thought. She's just like Risten, and she'll expect these things of me, and I'll let her down, I am all charm, I am only charm. I please them, I make promises, I say things I don't mean, or can't mean, and they love me for it, and I do it again, and again. Why am I lying here, on the very same rock, letting the same things be said?

"You're thinking things you aren't telling me," Willa said.

He sighed deeply. Her eyes were too alert, too hopeful. "One can't know everything," he said, at last.

"Can't one know some things?" she asked. She was still trying to be playful.

She looked so sad, suddenly, that it made him want to charm her again, to lift them both out of it—he felt it in him, he could do it, if he liked. He could lean over and kiss her neck, maybe, that was all it would take. He could take her hand and kiss it, the top of it, he could turn her hand over and kiss the sweaty valley of her palm. So he did do it, he did take her hand—it was, he thought, as he kissed her, a little like drinking, a little like entering a place of forgetting. He wanted to forget; he wanted, in fact, to be her, to be where she was, in love, consumed with something that was not himself, away for a minute from the horrors of the world, the dead calf he had found that morning that its mother had kicked to death, its stiff and sleeping form, its tongue caught between its teeth.

17

It was the height of the year—the height of her life—here she was, at the sea at summer's end, in love, the words feeling as grandiose and frightening as the broad, black back of the sea. She'd never had such ease . . . sometimes she wanted to weep from the relief of reprieve from the parsonage, from the mosquitoes, the smoky indoors, the fear that her life was always already known to her. She was here, wasn't she, Wilhemina Laestadius, the preacher's daughter, and she had a Sámi man, a herding man, who came to fetch her in a boat, and to take her places she had never been, a man with whom she was actively sinning all the time, quietly and deliberately, wherever it made sense to and wherever it didn't, it didn't matter, inside a little ràkkas or on a pelt in the grass. There was rarely any softness to it, any sweetness; there were no words of promise. Sometimes they kissed beforehand, and sometimes not, but what she wanted most was the power of being desired and mostly she had this. When they were tired he slept and she listened to him sleeping. She lay in his arms, one of his legs nestled inside hers, her head tucked beneath his neck, and she wanted to stay in there, hibernate for all of life.

But it was not clear if any of this added up to anything besides what it was that day. They did not speak of the future, or what they were doing; they spoke around it, distracting themselves with each other, keeping busy. He took her fishing, he showed her how to catch mackerel, and shad, and even once a halibut, which she had never seen, the halibut's eyes pressed flat into its head, the halibut half as big as she was tall. Together they smoked it for a whole day in a lávvu, to save it for winter, he said. When he said it he looked at her and she wondered, did he mean, for her to take back to Karesuando? Did he mean, they could, or would, eat it together someday, in the dark and the cold?

She couldn't bring herself to ask.

She couldn't bring herself to think about going back to Karesuando, to her father's disgust for her. She couldn't even have said if they would let her come back, or if they would send her off somewhere. What she had done was so unthinkable, so outside prediction, that she couldn't imagine the consequences, so she didn't imagine them.

The mosquitoes bit them and he made little poultices of mud that he put on the welts.

They talked, so much that their mouths went dry, and they made coffee, sipping it slowly while he told her about the time he had gotten lost in the fells in a three-day blizzard, and how his mother had taught him to stuff his boots, and how he only ever wanted to herd, nothing else, he didn't know what he would do if he didn't herd. He told her the story of the first time he'd slaughtered, how his father had been proud because he wasn't afraid, but he'd been afraid then and he was afraid now because Borga was old, and he would have to train another draft deer, but he'd never done that, his father had always done that, and he could tell he was going to be sad when he lost Borga. Who else would he have admitted these things to? He didn't know, he never had. There was something about how she didn't already know everything that meant he could explain things as he wanted—she wasn't a part of anything that shamed a man for being afraid to slaughter. There was a freedom in someone who didn't know any better, and it felt good to tell her what he couldn't tell himself.

In turn she told him about the time Carl had brought home a rabbit and put it loose in the parsonage; how Levi had died of measles but Lisa had lived; how she'd lain awake at night waiting for everyone to sleep so she could read everything on her father's desk, his sermons, his notes on Sámi mythology (she had stopped saying, or even thinking, Lappish), letters from a patron of his Temperance Society, letters from someone wanting to help start a boarding school for the Sámi, letters from a botanist in France, letters from a neighboring parish pastor wanting to know why his pews were empty, letters from settlers complaining about herds on their land, asking if her father would do something. She saw their bills from the Tornio merchant, and she saw how little her father was paid, and how they survived, actually, on her mother's parsimony and on the generosity of their parishioners, mostly Sámi, who gave them meat.

Ivvár nodded like he understood; he found himself still curious about her. He wondered what it was like, to not see land through the eyes of the reindeer, to see the land through what? What did she see? How did she see him? How was it that she loved him? He wanted to see himself like that, and even as he spent less time with the herd, and Ande and Niko grew more fed up with him, he didn't stop seeing her. What was he thinking? Of course he couldn't marry her. In the first place you had to be confirmed to marry and he wasn't confirmed—his only relationship with the State Church was avoiding it, and watching them bury his mother, putting the cross she'd hated so much above her. And who was going to confirm him when he didn't know the Creed or even the order of the Ten Commandments, and what pastor was going to let him marry the daughter of Mad Lasse? Who would want to have anything to do with that scandal? They had their own ways of going about it, what, he didn't know—did she have to be fined for adultery? Would they forbid her to marry him? He didn't know, that was outlander logic, and he had never needed to follow it particularly, the fells had protected him from their formalities.

But even within the fell-logic, or maybe it was illogic, she couldn't be his wife. It wasn't a life you could drop into, and put on like a piece of clothing. She had no conception of its real difficulty, how the difficulty was that it didn't end. She had never tried to live in the depths of January in a lávu, when you couldn't take your hands out of your mittens, when you argued with someone over who got the dog for warmth. He couldn't ask it of her and he wouldn't ask it of her, and anyway, he couldn't afford her; he didn't have enough reindeer for two, especially when she didn't have basic things, like an outer coat, or fur boots. It wasn't possible. It couldn't be done. And so they could only have each other for this little time, this little month—this long day with the sun always hovering over the most final line of the sea.

It would come and it would end.

He didn't speak of it. There would have been, somehow, a cruelty in speaking of it, though it was looming—soon, soon he would earmark, the Tommas would earmark. They would earmark, the good grazing here would run out, and the reindeer would turn their thick coats to the back of the wind, they would want to go up to the tundra again.

And then—what? She would be near Gárasavvon by November, maybe October. And they would take her back, she would do a little scene of sorrow and forgiveness—what did he know. He didn't know, he couldn't guess at the consequences of what they were doing, what they had done, what she had done; he had a vague premonition that it was bad, very bad, for which he was sorry, but only in the vaguest of ways, since the consequence itself belonged to a world he didn't live in, and thus, he couldn't rouse himself to care for in abstraction. One day he looked at Willa and the thought came to him: will people call her a whore? They were up on the mountainside, his mountainside, actually, but Ánde and Niko weren't around. They were watching the reindeer doze and graze in the patches of snow that still remained up this high, and the sun was low on its chain. "I wish Risten liked me," Willa said.

"She doesn't like you?"

"She tolerates me. Sometimes I make her laugh, but I think mostly because I make mistakes that she thinks are funny. But she seems happier now that she's with Mikkol all the time."

"So they're always together, then?" he asked. He tried not to sound too curious.

"Mostly," she said, "except Mikkol, he's always talking about church now, and you know," she said, failing to sound evenhanded. "Mikkol's awakened now."

"I guess that happens," Ivvár said. He shifted, somewhat uncomfortably. He felt like any moment she would mention his father.

"He keeps going on these long trips to prayer meetings, he tries to make Risten come but she usually finds an excuse."

"She loves him?"

"I think so," Willa said, but not with confidence—relief and jealousy fought within him, and jealousy won. Was he going to feel that same way about Willa soon? Was that confusion of wishing well and wishing worse going to be upon her next?

Another time, it was very early August now, she asked him, as they were looking for good shoe-grass, though it was early for it—but better shoe-grass too short than no shoe-grass at all—"How do you get to be a noaidi, I mean, or, say, a guvhllár?"

He'd noticed she never said *shaman* anymore, only *noaidi*, and that she never said *Lapp*, only *Sámi*, and she had fallen out of the habit recently of always asking him about things, as if she had finally caught up to enough understanding.

"Some say you had to be born with three teeth," he said. "Others say that you had to be chosen by someone who was already a noaidi. Sometimes just becoming one could kill you. I don't know, though, how it went," he said. He bent over and grabbed a handful of grass and cut just below his fist, slicing quickly, twisting the swath of grass into a knot with a tail. The sedge grass was thick, and rasped against his hands, and every time he stood up his back felt old, and his feet, submerged in the marsh, complained bitterly to him of their cold, even while the sun roasted his cheeks.

Willa kept tying her knots too loosely and they kept falling out, so she kept having to do them over again, but it was nice to have help, and he felt better about doing women's work with an actual woman around, like he was, ostensibly, just helping her. He twisted the grass and turned the knot, and he scythed, he twisted, he turned the knot. She stopped moving beside him and asked, "Did you ever hear of anyone making their own drum?"

"Well, they had to come from somewhere," he said, a little meanly.

"I guess I was wondering who made them. I read somewhere"—she was always reading something somewhere, he thought, a little bitterly——"that they had to be built with wood that grew on the north side of a tree."

"That sounds right," he said blandly, and he got up and began to walk to a new part of the marsh, and soon enough the conversation had dissolved into something, into the clouds or into the grass, and they could just cut shoe-grass again. She always wanted to talk about things, she always wanted to understand them, pick them up and poke them—she could never be left out of the knowing. On one hand he could sympathize, somewhere in him, and on the other he wanted to say, what does it matter? What will the knowing do?

But he didn't want to fight, he wanted to absorb himself back into the lightness of the loving between them, and when they had filled two rucksacks with knots of shoe-grass, and they could no longer feel anything in their feet, and their hands stung from the lashings of the grass, he made them coffee and took out cheese, and he slivered off long strips of meat for her, strips lined with heavy fat, and he enjoyed himself, he gathered all the joy he could, like sitting in sun that could not be saved for the winter to come.

HENRIK WAS NOT prone to guilt—fear was his motivator of habit—but he was beginning to feel guilty about not telling Nora about her father's transfer to Pajala, and at the same time he couldn't bring himself to hurt his own advantage and tell her, nor could he just propose, because he had no reason to imagine he would be accepted. A letter could come for Laestadius any day, and still he did nothing. She had stopped coming into the store, and she didn't even look his way when she passed by, and once he stepped outside and called her name, but she just turned and nodded, and kept going.

It took him a night of hard drinking to convince himself to just talk to Nora about it, since she wasn't likely to laugh—she would always retreat into politeness—and if he could manage that hurdle, then he could decide what to do about her. That was the secret, to not think about all of it at once, just do the one thing. Perhaps he would mention needing a wife lightly and see what she'd say—maybe that was what she'd been doing, when she brought up "what the Lapps said," maybe they hadn't said anything at all. Was she that wily? That careful, to hide how she felt?

When he finally said something it was so simple he felt stupid for not having done it much earlier. He said, did you ever think the Lapps, what they said, about, about us, was a good idea? Nora asked him to repeat himself, twice.

"You mean," she said, in her forthright yet careful way, like she was extracting a sliver, "that you are wondering whether or not we really should get married?" When she looked at him he couldn't read her face, but she wasn't laughing.

"Yes," he said, and then he was the one laughing, from nervousness.

"Maybe," he said, "maybe. Oh, I don't know."

"You're just thinking this now?" she asked. They were standing in the middle of the main path, so that anyone could have seen them. In some ways it made the thing easier, since it seemed so casual—it looked like they might have been talking about where she'd been to pick cloudberries, and how she'd managed to fill both buckets.

She set the buckets of cloudberries down. She was wearing some kind of bonnet that made her look more juvenile than he cared for, but he wouldn't pay attention to that.

"I've thought of it before," he said.

"Well, don't sound so excited about it," she said. "Are you going to speak to my father?" There was doubt in her voice, or maybe a challenge.

"Yes," he said. "Yes?"

"He doesn't like people who don't know their own minds," she said, "and he doesn't like people without passion."

"For the church?"

"For the church, yes, but for anything," she said, and she picked up the buckets, as if the conversation had ended, and it had; she was walking away and he wasn't sure what any of it meant, but he was so buoyed by their conversation that he decided to go visit Mad Lasse that very night, and in honor of the special night he only had two glasses of whiskey, so as not to smell like it, and he rinsed his mouth with coffee, and he combed his hair and buttoned his vest. He knocked on their door neither too late nor too early, and he asked Lars Levi (and Brita, who sat in her rocking chair, looking sterner than ever, her mouth shut tight), using the most direct language he could but still managing, somehow, to leave them confused—what is it you want? Brita asked—and when they understood they pointed out, hurriedly, there wouldn't be any dowry, and he said he knew, and then they looked at each other. Wherever Nora was he wasn't sure—perhaps she had made sure to not be around, and after all, now that he thought about it—where were the children?

Each of his limbs was cold, though it was warm inside. There was a fire going in the hearth, small but sturdy.

"Henrik," Lars Levi said, at last.

"Yes, sir," Henrik said, though he couldn't recall having ever used this before, this sir. It seemed appropriate, even necessary.

"We've heard the rumors."

"Which ones?" Henrik said, laughing too hard. They didn't laugh.

"Many times I've thought about coming into your store, seeing what's upstairs in your storeroom," Lars Levi said, and Henrik's stomach turned, "or writing to the bailiff in Luleå, but I'd hoped that the rumors weren't true. And to be perfectly fair, you haven't done it in front of me."

"I'm sure I don't know what you're talking about," Henrik lied. It was a peculiar sensation to lie like this, but it felt like a survival instinct of a kind.

"And now, you understand, how it sounds to me, when I've worked so very hard against this precise evil, here you come." Anger flushed through him. As if there were no town in all of Lapland that did not have liquor for sale, as if it were his fault alone, as if he were so terrible a match for their daughter, when trying to keep liquor from selling was like trying to keep it from snowing.

"I didn't come about that," Henrik said, valiantly pushing the thought out of his mouth. He thought of Nora saying he doesn't like people without passion.

"You came about Nora."

"I spoke to her earlier today."

"I'm very aware. But you see, she cannot marry a purveyor," he said, precisely, like he'd planned the line, "of sin. I won't have it, and moreover, she won't have it. It's an insult not to be endured."

"As you say in your sermons, sir," Henrik said, "there's none of us escaping sin." The drinks he'd had earlier felt suddenly futile, too small to have done any good; ironically, he ought to have come here drunk, fully armored—then he would have said what he wanted, which was to let them know what asses they were, self-righteous asses who were not, as much as they might think they were, sent by God to determine anyone's acceptance into heaven. He wanted to say, you're paupers, you have no power, and moreover, I've had my uncle send you away.

"That's so, none of us do," Lars Levi said, "but it's a special sin to lure others into it." He put his hands on his knees, as if he were about to stand up.

"It's every man alone to meet his own end," Henrik said stubbornly. His father had said that, every day, including the day he had died. Behind Lars Levi, Brita looked deeply skeptical. How did all mothers share that look? Did it arrive with the birth of the child?

"You seem well meaning," Lars Levi said, "and Nora is very intelligent, so she sees something in you. But I can't just wave my hands and play along that I see nothing, when you don't attend church regularly, you attend no prayer meetings, you show no signs of the fruits of faith in your body or in your temperament, and very clearly, the Holy Spirit is nowhere near you."

"I believe in Jesus Christ," Henrik said, aware he sounded like a boy, reciting his Catechism.

"Not that I've seen," Lars Levi said, "and if it were true, I doubt that I would be hearing about you selling brännvin to anyone who comes asking."

"I didn't—"

"Let this serve as a warning to you," Lars Levi said. "Let this conversation be a call for you to change your ways."

From that point on Henrik had very little idea of what was or was not said, by Lars Levi or by himself. A numbness came over him, where it began to not matter what Mad Lasse said or didn't say. He nodded. He said, absently, "yes, sir," at awkward intervals. At one point Mad Lasse began to pray for him and he thought he wouldn't survive this. By the time he made it outside he was practically delirious from his face heating and from the feeling of inadequacy that had plagued him his whole life but now had been presented to him in such a formal, and final, capacity, and though it only proved their points he went back to the store and became raucously drunk. Very deliberately, and very quickly, he drank to the point of sickness and then he drank some more, and he had Simmon over, he must have shouted to Simmon in the street to come inside, because at some point he came to and realized that Simmon was inside, and they were laughing. Simmon was very funny; he hardly said anything and yet he was very funny!

Henrik drank so much he took off his vest, and he took off his shirt. He went outside, where it was just twilight enough to see the pale hairs on his hands and his arms, and he went for a swim in the river, utterly nude. Simmon came with him, and they both jumped in and shook the cold from their heads and Henrik thought: this is what it's like to have a friend in this world. He swam frantically, pedaling his arms and legs with gusto, sure that the river was going to drag him in, until he remembered he could touch the bottom, and with relief he stood up and walked up the bank. From here he could see the closed shutters of the store, and of the parsonage, and a little smoke coming up from Sussu's hut. It must have been the middle of the night. He went back to the store and Simmon followed him, and they dripped all over the floor and he didn't care.

In the morning he was violently sick, the worst sickness of his life—he didn't even make it upstairs to bed, he pulled a pelt from the counter onto the floor by the stove, and he curled himself around the water pail covered in a blanket, his hair still wet, trying to gain warmth from the steel of the pail. Of course someone came in, and of course the someone was Nora. If he'd been in any state closer to consciousness he would have had a feeling about it, but luckily he didn't. He felt nothing, only worried she could see parts of his body the blanket didn't cover, his thighs, his legs. She was seeing his gullet, she was seeing everywhere he had hair.

"Henrik," she said, and she knelt down. She looked at him, where he lay. Her eyes were red, puffy, like she'd been crying—over him? "This is what you'll do," she said. "When you are sober enough to stand, you'll go upstairs into your storeroom, and you'll take out every last drop of liquor in this place, and you'll go outside, and in front of everyone, you will burn it, or take an axe to it, I don't care, but you will destroy it, publicly, once and for all. And on Sunday you'll come to church, and at church you'll stand up and you'll say you are a sinner and that you have sinned and that you would like Christ to save you from your sins, and you'll ask the forgiveness of Christ and the congregation. You'll confess to the sin of drunkenness and debauchery and the sin of unbelief. You only need to say it once."

She looked at him and he looked at the water pail. It was dented on one side, how had that happened? When had he dented it?

"Do you understand me?"

He nodded. He was ill, but he understood her. It was the most reasonable thing anyone had ever said. Get rid of the alcohol. It had to be gotten rid of. That was true. He never wanted to see it again, he never wanted to smell it, it repulsed him. Get rid of it and let Lars Levi come in, let them win. What did it matter, he had practically admitted to selling it, and he had made a fool of himself all night, they must have heard him. They would send for the bailiff if he didn't listen to Nora. They would make him close up shop. Thinking about this made him sit up, and sitting up made him want to vomit again. He realized in sitting up that he could smell it, there was vomit somewhere, on his mouth, or on his arm.

"Do you understand me?" she asked again.

"Yes," he said.

"Good," she said, and she stood up, and she left, and as if that was all anything took, as if that was all anything ever required, he did it, he put on clothes, right then, and still drunk, he rolled the casks out—there were only two of them left—and he took the axe to them and then he went for the bottles, forty, fifty glass bottles of the stuff, and he dumped them, one by one, and threw them into a pile, the way the Lapps tossed their antlers, and the dogs came from somewhere and lapped at mush, and Simmon came out of his hut and looked at Henrik like he was going mad, and Sussu came out and looked at him like he'd been mad his whole life, and Nora came outside and nodded, once, and Henrik saw her mother, the shutters open, watching. It was, he knew, maybe the only good thing he ever did in his life, and he thought: I will never be this good of a person again. He watched the brännvin, dark and red and bloody, rise over his feet, turn the dirt to mud. His toes squelched in it. For a second he considered doing what the dogs did, he thought about bending down, cupping his hands together, sucking on the mud, but he remained standing, for a minute more, contemplating his own ruin and the loss of the only thing that had ever made him feel at ease, and then, like a good and miserable boy, he went inside.

18

IT WAS DIFFICULT, THOUGH NOT IMPOSSIBLE, TO BE IN A BAD MOOD DURING earmarking. It was nearly everyone's favorite time of year; if it wasn't it was because, narrowly, you preferred when the calves were born, but on the whole everyone was happiest and brightest during earmarking. This was in part because earmarking was a kind of harvest—you were seeing how your wealth and livelihood had grown—but also because there was too much excitement in being outside in a brisk wind with the sea stretched out behind the herd, lassoing three-month-old calves, pinning them down, putting your own mark on them, a mark that said, this one is mine. The air was festive; earmarking required everyone to be together, and it required the feeling of frenzy. Only those who had no calves could possibly have watched with any bitterness, but Willa was transfixed. Naturally, she made her first mistake early on the first day, chasing along after a calf, roping it around the neck with her arm only to realize there'd been no point in catching it—no one knew whose calf it was yet, so it couldn't be marked, and she had to let it go and, shamefacedly, return to watching at the sides of the corral.

After a long while of watching she began to make sense of the pattern: in the first place, you had to identify which calf followed which mother, and once you knew which calf belonged to which mother (it was rare for reindeer to have twins), you had to be able to read the mark on the mother's ears—the left ear of any reindeer indicated the last name of the family that owned it and the right ear indicated the person within that family that owned it. These marks—two long slits on the top, a small triangle cut from the bottom, say—were distinctive enough that no two marks were technically the same, though as the reindeer grew, the ears folded and bunched, thus hiding the initial slits, so in reality you had to be able to recognize how reindeers' ears folded once cut, a distinction Willa found impossible to make.

But the Sámi could see it—from across a fell they could say, that's so-and-so's reindeer; it amazed her. The children amazed her. She had seen them, in the days leading up to it, practicing their marks on stacks and stacks of leaves, and now here they were, sitting atop their calves, knees skillfully pinning down the reindeer's front legs, someone else holding the reindeer's jaws or back legs steady while the child put their mark on with their own sharp little knife, taking a loose bit of ear out and holding it in their mouths while they finished marking, just like the adults. When they were done, they would take the loose little corners of ear—one per reindeer—and thread them onto a long string, and this was how each person knew precisely how many calves they had every year. The children had each been given a reindeer at their birth, and given their own mark, and by one boy's tenth birthday he had eight calves to mark, and he was so full of pride that when the blood from their ears got all over his hands he made sure to wipe his face, as if to remove sweat, to leave their mark on him.

Of course the adults, Risten's father especially, had many more to mark. Risten was being helped almost entirely by Mikkol; they functioned as a clear unit, identifying each other's and helping each other, so that Mikkol sometimes held down hers while she marked, though he also put her mark on her calves, since she had so many more than he did, and otherwise he would have been standing around haplessly, and it would have been too obvious how few he had to mark in comparison to her.

They were doing the earmarking, as was usual, in rounds, so that the main of the herd was clustered together, kept in place mostly by women and children holding up long swaths of cloth that the reindeer seemed to think were impenetrable walls. Once the reindeer already in the corral were marked, the reindeer were let loose and chased off in another direction, and the next section of the herd was called for, at which point the women and children walked the wall of cloth closer and closer to one end of the herd, sending a small batch of the reindeer running toward the corral, so that the work was done in waves, bit by bit of the herd at a time, and they went until someone—usually Nilsa—said they should rest, at which point they set the dogs to watch the herd, and retreated to their lávvus, and lay in a wonderful exhaustion on pelts while the fire roared at their feet.

Depending on the size of the herd, earmarking could take anywhere from a few days to two weeks, and when many herds were banded together it wasn't uncommon for someone to show up to help, but still, that someone would usually be, say, a cousin or an in-law, someone who could see how well the herd was or wasn't doing without any loss of face to anyone there. As such, Ivár's appearance at the fence on the third day of marking was off-putting to people, particularly to Risten—it wasn't that she was embarrassed by their herd but she was embarrassed for him to have invited himself like that. It annoyed her, since it suggested that he was so taken with Willa he was willing to risk rudeness to her family, especially given that everyone knew that she had once chased him down like a reindeer calf herself.

Ivár stood beside Willa and elbowed her. "Look at them," Risten whispered to Mikkol, "they're children!" She was jealous; her time with Mikkol in the flirting stage had been very brief, and she'd always felt so aware of whether or not Mikkol was herding well that when he was around her family she'd been too anxious to even enjoy his teasing. Stop it, she recalled saying to him, once, when he'd thrown the lasso around her and pulled, so that her arms were really caught, but she'd said it very harshly and he'd dropped it immediately. All right then, he'd said, and she remembered thinking: so this is what he looks like when he's irritated with me.

"They aren't children," Mikkol said now, loud enough that Risten looked around to see if anyone was listening, "they're in love."

"They aren't in love, exactly, they're enjoying the summer."

"No," he said, shaking his head. "See," he said, pointing, and sure enough, right then Willa turned to look up at Ivár and her face shone out with—what—admiration, pride, a preemptive blessing for any mistakes he might make, for his impulsiveness and his jollity, his mischief—and Risten said, "Well, I'm sure she's infatuated with him anyway, that's easy enough."

"I'm worried," he said, "it's not easy to be alone like that all the time . . . . anything could happen between them, they wouldn't be the first." He stopped himself. "I've been thinking I should talk to them."

"I'm sure we're well past things that could happen," Risten said, "and well in the land of things that have happened."

"It isn't right, outside of marriage." He shook his head again. "His father's away now. She's run from hers. There's no one telling them right from wrong," Risten looked away and studied the remaining mothers and calves in the corral for her own, even though she knew there weren't any left. She murmured something unintelligible, and began to walk toward the other end of the corral, as if she'd noticed something.

In fact she also found everything to do with Willa and Ivvár shocking, but not in a way that had anything to do with God. At first she hadn't been able to believe that Willa had gone off with him, when it would just look like she was confirming the rumors of a pregnancy in the first place (although Risten had seen no such signs from Willa herself), and, it would make it more obvious that Willa was angling for Ivvár, when Risten had every confidence that Ivvár would never marry her—the most he would do with any dáčča girl was toy with her, and it showed what a dáčča she was not to realize that. On the other hand, Risten had assumed that Ivvár would have drifted out of Willa's life already: he must have so much to do with his herd, especially with his father gone, but instead Willa was always off somewhere with him, and now there was no one west of Alta who didn't know that Ivvár was in a deeply ill-advised affair with Mad Lasse's daughter, and Risten could not really believe their shamelessness. Were they really worth that, to each other? It hurt her, if she let herself admit it, that he would do that for Willa but he hadn't done that for her; he'd been willing to risk nothing for her.

Mikkol approached her, leaning against her slightly, his hand on her back. The hand was proprietary, the hand said, this woman is mine. Ivvár noticed Mikkol's hand there, in the same way he had noticed how Mikkol followed Risten around. Mikkol's worried about me, Ivvár thought, not without pleasure, and he wants to show her what she's won in him, and what I've lost in her.

He went toward Willa and he let the edge of his arm ever so slightly touch hers as he passed her. He felt her admiration of him as he lassoed and pulled; he was in good form today, and his lasso went where he wanted. With each throw he thought of his father, shouting at him, throw the lasso where they will be, not where they are—and when he stalked around the corral he saw his father, how his father walked with his right hand held out, the lasso coiled and ready, the left hand holding up the end of the rope—and when the back feet of the calf caught and he pulled, tight, and the calf balked, he was happy for those three, four moments, especially with Mikkol watching.

Nilsa saw the catch, too, and nodded begrudgingly. Nilsa had always liked him, in his own way, like he didn't want to like him but he couldn't help it. Probably, Ivvár thought, he's regretting it right now, not pushing Risten toward me. Ivvár was in a fever of showing off—once he threw a lasso for the same calf Mikkol was going for and he took it straight from under him. It was Risten's calf and not really Ivvár's place to take it, but it was too satisfying, he could see it coming too easily and there was something delicious about bringing Risten's calf to her and walking away like he didn't notice Mikkol standing there, pulling his lasso back in empty. By the time they made it to the lávvu to rest he wouldn't have been surprised if Mikkol hated him. He would have hated himself. He could tell he was being loud and brash, even in the lávvu, but it was such a relief to feel above someone, anyone, and he kept thinking, besides, of how many calves they had, this family, and it made him sick with envy.

He wanted a drink, badly, but Nilsa rarely drank, and of course Mikkol would be intolerable about that kind of thing. It might have gone like this, Ivvár being a bit too loud and Mikkol silently but obviously despising him, and Risten and Willa watching the two men perform for them in this veiled way, except that Nilsa and Anna left the lávvu to go see about a weak spot in the corral fence, and suddenly, without this older presence—the mood shifted, with just the four of them. Ivvár had run out of things to say and he sipped his coffee loudly. Risten and Mikkol were lying back on their pelts, beside each other, clearly a couple but not openly affectionate with each other, while Ivvár felt the distance between himself and Willa, how they were very careful to not appear to be coupled; for instance, he and Willa sat cross-legged on opposite sides of the fire while Risten and Mikkol reclined, with their feet ever so lightly touching.

A nice long while went by when no one said anything and they all listened to the children fighting over something outside in the corral. The wind was light today, and the tent-cloth gently rubbed against the poles, and the smoke hovered around Ivvár's nose.

"Is it all right," Mikkol asked, in the manner of someone who has been thinking a question over for a long time, "if I ask about your feelings about God?"

The word *God* seemed to sit on the drying-pole above them with the hook and the chain and the pot.

Ivvár shrugged. "God and I," Ivvár said, as casually as he could, "we don't have very much to say to each other."

"Is that so," Mikkol said, with some clear satisfaction on his face, like he was pleased by Ivvár's rudeness. "I think God has a lot to say to you."

"Talk, talk," Ivvár said, trying to make a joke out of it, "noisier than the wind."

"If I may," Mikkol said.

Ivvár took a very loud sip of his coffee, pulling it through his teeth.

"Do you think," Ivvár said, "the wind is God farting?"

"I'm worried for you two," Mikkol said, turning his head to look at Willa. She looked like she'd been slapped, and Ivvár saw the woman she had been before she'd come to the sea; it was a kind of dark magic, how she'd slipped right back like that. "As the Bible says, it is better for a man to marry than to burn."

"I hope there's a big bonfire nearby," Ivvár said. He laughed too harshly, but he didn't care.

"It is not good for man to be alone," Mikkol said. "That's from the Bible," he added.

"It's not good for a woman to be alone, either," Ivvár said. He grinned and showed his perfect teeth. Risten looked at him sharply. Her head moved the smallest fraction, a shake, no, Ivvár, like she wanted him to be calm, to be reasonable, and he thought: Mikkol doesn't know. She never told him about us. He's been awakened—by my father, he quotes the Bible at me, and he imagines himself to be so far above me. "Or didn't Risten tell you about that."

"Ivvár," Risten said, like the problem was him, "don't be like that."

"Like what?"

"Tell me about what?" Mikkol said.

"He's"—Risten sighed—"it's an old thing."

"What's an old thing?"

Now it was Risten who looked flustered. She sat up so that she was lying on her side and she put her hand on Mikkol's shoulder and patted it too many times.

"I just mean," Ivvár said, "I'm not the only one who's burning."

"Ivvár, stop," Willa said.

"I thought, where there's no wound, there's no bleeding," Ivvár said.

Now the thing sat between all of them.

Ivvár shrugged his shoulders and sucked at his coffee again.

"It isn't right," Mikkol said. He sat up. "This," he said, pointing at Ivvár and Willa, "no one will say it but I will. This isn't right. You aren't any good for each other. You," he said, his finger-pointing growing more rapid and aggressive, "how does she find a husband after you? When everyone knows? How does she go back to her family? Did you think about that? Did you think about what happens to her? No, you don't think, you just do what you like, whatever the Devil tells you, it doesn't matter, you're ruled by yourself and by your own flesh. Your god is your flesh," he said, "you'll do anything for it. And you," he said, looking at Willa, "what do you think, when you know so much better than this? Maybe he doesn't know, he's just a herding man, but you know, I know you know, in your heart and your conscience and in your soul, you are ashamed. Your father is Laestadius! Your father is leading hundreds and thousands to salvation and his own daughter spits on it. You of all people, you know what you've done is a serious sin. And you're hardening your heart to it, your heart is going to stone with all the sin, you're throwing everything away and for what? For a man who won't marry you?"

Even Risten looked accosted by this speech, and abashed. She put her eyes down. Willa's eyes stayed on the fire. Only Ivvár kept looking at Mikkol, straight at him, as if willing him to say another damning thing, as if amused by this, when he was furious; if the fire were not between them, if Risten were not even now lying beside Mikkol, he would have—he would strangle him, kick him, in the ribs, in the throat.

Quietly, carefully, Willa rose from her crossed legs and began to get up, heading for the door with the form of apology in her hunched back. "God will forgive you," Mikkol said, "but you have to ask," but she didn't look back at him, just crawled carefully over the branches and opened the door, so that the sweetness of the falling sun came through in wide and fur-ridden rays, and then they heard her, walking away.

Ivvár looked at Mikkol and he said carefully, "But who will forgive you?" He wasn't sure what he meant by this but it sounded good, maybe cruel, though not cruel enough; he wished he had something more, something worse. He leaned over and took Mikkol's cup and poured the rest of his coffee out on the fire, which spat it back at him in pious bursts, and he followed Willa out into the summer night. Above the sound of the herd he could hear a tern chittering, chit, chit, then faster, chit-chit-chit-chit. He looked for Willa—she was climbing back over the fence into the corral. She stood and waited for someone to need her help—there, Nilsa had seen her, he was waving her over, and she hurried to him, grabbing hold of the calf's jaw, and held her face away as the calf kicked.

THE NEWS THAT NORA AND HENRIK WERE ENGAGED WAS FOLLOWED, three days later, by the news that Lars Levi was being transferred to the parish in Pajala, but the latter was much more sensational than the former, and the only surprise to the engagement for Old Sussu, for Simmon, even for Nora's sisters, was that it had taken so long to come about. Nora herself was surprised, and Henrik was surprised; Nora's parents were, in the end, satisfied enough—they could leave for Pajala with one daughter's future secured (they didn't know about Henrik's debt), and moreover, they could leave Karesuando a dry town. They had converted the infamous drunk of a storekeeper, and they felt now like at least some part of their reputation was recovered after the disgrace of Willa; Brita was almost happy about it. In the light of things with Willa, Henrik did not seem so bad after all; God had given her that perspective. And she, they, were gratified to see how upset people were that they were going to leave; people were coming into town all the time now, to say their goodbyes, to sit another few hours in the parsonage and listen, and some of them begged Lars Levi not to go, and some of them brought children and sick relatives for him to bless, though he had explained many times before, he didn't do that, it didn't work like that, he had no power himself, he was just a servant of God like any other, and what mattered most was one's own conscience. But he was gratified they did it anyway.

19

It was only another week now until the wedding. The Laestadius family would go to Pajala the following week, leaving Nora behind. The wedding itself would be, of course, small and minimal, and the dinner after would be held at the parsonage. The plans for it were so unimportant compared to the packing for Pajala that Henrik wasn't sure if anything was expected of him besides showing up, though he did make an effort—he brought his nice pants and vest and shirt down to the river and rinsed them and scrubbed them, and he laid them out on the grass in the sun to dry, and he swept the store, wiped the dust from the windows, wiped down the counters . . . except now that he had cleaned he could see everything was very run-down, and there were scratch marks everywhere—from knives?—and the shutters opened and closed only with force, and the bed linen had holes, and each step on the stairs felt like the last time the step would hold. This was not to mention he had no dresser, and kept his clothing in empty crates, and there was wax melted on every surface that he had never scraped off, so that there was wax on the floor, and wax on his nightstand-barrel, and the storage room was dusty, full of cobwebs, and in one corner some syrup had leaked onto the floorboards, and there were mouse droppings that he continued to pretend to not see, but he was sure Nora would see them. There was nothing he did not see anew through her eyes and nothing he did not find wanting, and he wondered what she would think if she went through his record books. He would have to make it clear that she shouldn't look through them, but how? And then would she suspect him of hiding something?

Two days, three days passed where he wasn't sure what else to do to prepare for the wedding, but Nora seemed so busy he could hardly speak to her; she barely came outside. The fact of their impending marriage seemed more and more abstract to him now, and he felt almost exactly as he had when his mother had announced she and Frans were sending him off to the "hinterlands" to "bury his disgrace in the boreal wasteland"—how that conversation over morning coffee still lingered—and it had seemed like a joke, and he'd been convinced she would change her mind at any moment, but she hadn't. It had been impossible to imagine then that life would really change, but it had changed, and he wondered if marriage would be like that, a new world order suddenly and perfectly imposed. Already it was a new life just to not be drinking. He felt off-balance come evening, unsteady, and he thought about drinking constantly, and the thought of it alone brought up a tickle in his throat, the first want of desire. Also, he had started sweating through the night; he woke up and his underclothes and his sheets were wet, and everything had to be hung up to dry so he could even sleep in it the next night. But he was sleeping better than ever, and he never woke up in the middle of the night anymore, and he remembered everything with so much clarity that it made him nervous about everything he didn't remember from before—how many nights were lost to a haze? What was it he might have done and not remembered? Not done?

So he was frighteningly sober and of sound and even keen mind when he came inside from the privy one morning to see that his uncle was standing in his store, already behind the counter, going through his record books. He looked no older than when Henrik had seen him in Luleå and his uncle had put him in the carriage, first saying a prayer with Henrik, and then, perhaps because the man seemed to be listening in, asking the driver to join them in prayer.

"Uncle Frans," Henrik said. He tried to say it lightheartedly but he felt the old trepidation take over. He reminded himself, it's just my uncle, he's my uncle. I've seen him my whole life.

"Greetings from your mother," his uncle said, looking up but keeping his finger on his spot. He was taller than Henrik, but not by so much, and he was slimmer, though not muscular. He had a languid air. He was in his early fifties, but could have been mistaken for younger—his hair had only just begun to gray, and retained some of the yellow of his youth; when he looked at Henrik it was with the old discernment and disappointment Henrik had always seen.

"Thank you," Henrik said awkwardly, already unsure what to say.

"I haven't been up this way in two or three years now," Frans said. He looked around the store, examining everything, tilting his head up toward the rafters and down to the floor. He sniffed the air.

"Is it any different?"

"Oh, it used to not be a real town and now it's still not a real town,"

Frans said. He had strong eyebrows, darker than his hair, and when you looked at him face-on, as Henrik was now, you couldn't help but think about how they angled down toward his nose so severely that it gave him a permanent expression of scrutiny, or irritation, so that even humor had a faint irony to it. His eyes were blue, and rather buggy—Henrik had always felt that they came too far out of Frans's face, but he was considered to be a good-looking man; certainly his wife was very beautiful. "You look tired," Frans said, "and you got a bit fat. I didn't know you could get fat on reindeer, but you managed it. Good for you." He smiled, as if to soften this, and Henrik smiled back, laughed lightly. "Our cook, she can never cook the reindeer very soft, it's always tough, I chew and chew and chew."

"I cook for myself," Henrik said, aware he was speaking too softly. His uncle hated how softly Henrik spoke.

"You'd think you could afford some help out here, the Lapps can't ask for very much, can they?"

"I don't know," Henrik said.

"I don't know, I don't know," his uncle repeated, in a slight mimic. He smiled as if to say, this is an old and friendly joke, how I tease you for not knowing things, but this kind of teasing had never felt friendly to Henrik, it put him on edge, it was sure to be followed by something more cutting, and the something more cutting was sure to be followed, eventually, by something much worse.

"Who is this," Frans said, peering down at the page, "Anders Anderssen Utsi? And Inger Nilsdatter Palopää? Per Anders Unga . . . well, anyway, they all owe you money?"

"I guess maybe a few."

"This doesn't look like a few to me."

"Well, it's usual to give credit up here . . ."

"You don't ask for it back?" Frans said. He turned his eyebrows up toward Henrik, and then he reached into his pocket and took out his glasses. It took him a moment to place the hooks around his ears and settle the wired frames on his nose. Actually, it looked comical, with how big his nose was, but Henrik would never, ever have laughed at it, though it was something he would have imitated, once, for Emilie.

"I did—I asked, it's quite clear that—"

"They think it's all on permanent loan, interest-free?" His uncle's tone remained light, curious, but Henrik could see the effort in his face to stay that way.

"No—"

"So they think this is a charity? This is run by the church?"

"It's not as easy, it's not simple—"

His uncle leaned back down to look at the book. Henrik began to speak but his uncle raised his hand, and Henrik went quiet. "Bring me a chair," his uncle said, and Henrik brought him a stool, and his uncle sat down on it and kept looking through the book, his eyebrows raised and his forehead wrinkled. Every so often he turned the page, so that the crinkling paper was the only sound except, in the distance, a cuckoo, or Henrik thought that was a cuckoo. It must have been, it was saying, wasn't it, coo-coo, coo-coo?

"Nasty stuff, slaughtering. Makes such a stink. When I was assistant vicar at Ytterlängäs one of them brought me a reindeer and he slaughtered it outside the parsonage. It was absolutely sulfurous. I could hardly breathe around there for days."

That's what happens if they clip the bowels, Henrik wanted to say, but it was never worthwhile to know more than his uncle.

"Well, you made it here all right," Henrik said lamely. A wave of childishness came over him. He was a child, that was all, and he was watching his uncle laugh with his mother, the two of them laughing at someone else's expense, maybe Henrik's. At some point it had become clear to him—and when was that—that he was another version of his father to them, as easily cast away; he could be spoken to in whatever tone of voice, told to do whatever task, sent off to the hinterlands or to the summer cabin or wherever his mother needed him to be. All of this came back to him looking at his uncle, because looking at his uncle was too much like looking at his mother, not because they looked alike but because they were always in alliance; to speak to his uncle was to speak to his mother, and vice versa. His mother always said it was because Frans had raised her when their parents had died but even that didn't seem exactly right. To Henrik it had always seemed like they were in league with each other against the world, especially in their shared ambition to rise above their birth; their father had been a small town's sexton and bailiff, and it had always been his hope to be more, but he'd died of pleurisy when they were children, and their mother had died of smallpox not long after—the way they told it they were miracles, the both of them, for having lived, and they liked to say they were very lucky and very blessed by God but it was always clear they meant that they were special, set not just apart but above. Henrik's father had just put up with them, their planning, gone along with them up until the day he had died, and Henrik could feel he would do the same; he could feel it coming, how he would keep playing along.

"I made it here through sheer determination, I tell you what," his uncle said, as if Henrik were an imbecile. "I would say better late than never, but it would have been better to come here much earlier. But you haven't even been here a year, have you?"

"Almost a year."

"Almost a year," his uncle said. He looked up from the book. "Who is this? This man, Nils Nilsson Siebainen? They have such funny names sometimes, don't they."

"He's not from around here," Henrik said, "he came for Easter—"

"A lot of them came for Easter, is that right?"

"Yes."

"They wanted to hear Laestadius."

"I guess so," Henrik said. He felt tentative about mentioning Laestadius now that his uncle had appeared; he sensed Laestadius threatened his uncle not just with his preachings but with his popularity, and he held over Frans the power of being revered, not just obeyed. Of course Laestadius was just one of his uncle's pastors, and he owed allegiance to Frans, but from what Henrik could see the chance of Laestadius playing the role of sycophant to his uncle was quite small. It made Henrik, actually, a little fond of Laestadius.

"Well," his uncle said. He closed the book. He looked at the counter beneath the book with some displeasure, and he grabbed its edge with both hands and shook it. "It's practically falling off," his uncle said, "you can't fix this yourself? Don't have anyone around to fix it?"

"I'll talk to Simmon," Henrik said mildly, searching for an excuse, but he didn't know how to explain that Simmon did what he pleased, how you could ask him to do something and he would do it in his own time, when he thought it made sense to do it, and anyway the counter only shook if you grabbed it like that.

With a violent dread Henrik realized he was going to have to tell Frans he had axed the casks and was going to marry Nora.

Somehow this had not really occurred to him. It had started to seem impossible that his uncle would ever arrive and more impossible that his uncle and his mother still existed, but now that Frans was here it was the opposite that was true: it was life in the south that was the real world, and this one here in the north that was the imaginary. And yet he had said he would marry the preacher's daughter. He wanted a drink. If he had a drink, two drinks, he would not mind any of this so much, he could find in himself the disdain for his uncle that his uncle had for him, he could work his way up to it. "Well," Frans said, looking at Henrik expectantly, and as if he already knew what Henrik was thinking about, "are you going to offer me some refreshment?" He smiled and for a moment looked friendly, even as if he might have liked Henrik. It was Frans's way of trying to be nice. "I heard everyone is coming into town for Mad Lasse's last sermon."

"Ah, maybe, yes, that sounds right," Henrik said vaguely, though he'd heard no such thing, he never heard anything until it happened. He found the kettle behind the stove, and he put water in it from the pail.

"He's very popular."

"Oh, very," Henrik said agreeably, though cautiously, careful to not say it with too much enthusiasm. "Everyone loves him. He has a maid now, who came from the coast, just to be his maid. Just offered her services."

"What for?"

"She wanted to," Henrik said. He needed to get the coffee grounds from behind the counter, but his uncle was still standing there, and he wanted to avoid, as long as possible, a conversation about the goods that were left, and a conversation about coffee in general, because coffee might remind his uncle about other beverages, about drinking, and then his uncle would have to be told about the casks.

"And people still come to hear him speak? Even through the rest of the summer?"

"It's crazy," Henrik said, "sometimes you can hardly get in the door. I don't know where they come from, I thought they were all supposed to be at the sea."

"They don't all herd," Frans said, in the tone of a schoolteacher, "don't forget there's the Sea-Lapps, and the Mountain-Lapps, and the—I forget—anyway, and more and more of them are farming, or working in the mines. What's interesting to me, though," he went on, "is that the Lapps always say they can't make it to church, they have to tend to the herds or the farms, or whatever the new thing is, and it was like that for years, but lately when it's Laestadius preaching they can make it after all."

"There're so many in church he didn't even notice if I wasn't there," Henrik said, but as soon as he said this he regretted it. He crossed behind the counter but Frans was still blocking his way to the coffee grounds.

"I'm curious to hear all the noises in person," Frans said, "Qvale said he has some shriekers in his church, too, though it sounds like his church has mostly emptied out."

"Sometimes they're very loud."

"Qvale says up there they call it the preaching sickness."

"Here, too," Henrik said. "Excuse me," Henrik said nervously, and he reached in front of his uncle. He got the sack of grounds. Frans shifted away but he put his hand on Henrik's back in such a way that Henrik felt an old memory, how Frans patted him on the back after he used the birch switch. Henrik could practically hear him, I'm your uncle and God says I must love you, but you make it very difficult. With relief Henrik backed away and the counter was between them again, but now his uncle was looking at the shelf Henrik had just taken the coffee from, studying the sack of sugar behind the coffee, and the rye flour beside it, and beside that some wheat flour. He picked up a sack of oats, hefted them in his hand, put them back. He knelt and began to look at the smaller and more valuable things, the silver thimble, needles, brooches, belt hooks, grommets. He picked up a silk shawl and rubbed it against his cheek, as if trying it out for his own use. Henrik was gratified to see, when Frans knelt again, that his hair was thinning on the top, and that he could just make out a faint patch of bare land.

Frans picked up some soap, sniffed it. "What's that smell?"

"Tar," Henrik said. "The Finns like it," he said. He shrugged.

"Put a splash of something in that coffee, would you?" Frans asked.

"Well," Henrik said. He coughed. When he looked up he could see out the window that Nora was walking somewhere. She was the kind of person who was never in a hurry, even if hurry was warranted. "So," Henrik tried again.

"What is it?"

"What is what?"

"What is it?"

"Nothing."

"You started to say something."

"Well, just, there aren't any, there isn't any, I don't have anything else to put in the coffee. Not even milk," he added, as if that were the crucial point.

"Why not?"

"Well, reindeer don't give very much milk, and the only cow here——"

"You know what I mean."

"Oh, well, it's gone."

"Ah, so that's good, then."

"Not so much."

"Why not?"

Henrik felt how this was the critical thing, the critical point. This was the time to say it and to be done with it. "I sold it all," he lied.

"Well, that's what I meant, that it was good."

"Well, now I'm out, so it isn't good."

"I see," Frans said. "Don't you usually get it from——where?"

"Tornio."

"It comes through the border okay?"

"Oh yes, no one there," Henrik said. He pointed toward the river. "You can go look yourself, nothing to it. No one hardly knows which country they're in on which side of the river, everyone speaks Swedish and Finnish both or sometimes some strange mix."

"Do you speak Finnish?" Frans asked, in Finnish. It was one of the only sentences Henrik knew.

"I speak a little," he said, poorly, in Finnish.

Frans took his glasses off and folded them. He took out a handkerchief and wrapped it around his glasses, then put his glasses back in the pocket of his vest.

"But there's coffee, isn't there?" Frans asked.

"Oh, yes," Henrik said, realizing he hadn't even made the fire. He took the flint and began to scratch it, trying to get off a spark. For a minute the scratching was the only sound. It seemed though that the more he scratched the less the flint wanted to spark, and he was making it seem like he didn't know how to make a fire at all, he was back to where he'd been when he first came here, when it had taken him thirty, forty minutes, sometimes two hours, to get a fire going. He scratched and he scratched at the flint, it was agonizing, he was doing something wrong, he was staring at the birch curls and the little twigs he had laid in there earlier this morning but no spark would come, he was blowing slightly, gently, but there was nothing to catch.

"I don't know if you heard," Henrik said, into the stove, into the twigs, "but I'm engaged. Very recently. To the—pastor's daughter."

"You mean Laestadius—Mad Lasse's daughter?"

"Yes, his eldest. Nora. Eleonora." To his relief, the flint finally sparked, a little flicker of fire landed in the birch curls, and he blew, carefully.

"Engaged?"

"It's not a joke," Henrik said. He blew on the fire some more, and the birch curl flared. "Why would I joke about that?" he said lightly, but he said it more to the fire than to his uncle.

"Do they even go to school out here?"

"She speaks three or four languages, and she writes in all of them, all of his daughters do. They copy his sermons out for him and even translate them."

"When did this come about?"

"A few days ago."

There was a long silence, in which Henrik heard what he thought was the cuckoo again, and in which his uncle seemed to be studying him carefully.

"Well, aren't you going to congratulate me?" Henrik asked. He was surprised at himself for saying this, for getting it out at all.

"No," Frans said, "I think it's a mistake, and I think you should end it now."

"I can't, I've promised, and besides——"

"They found you at it again."

"No, no, not that——"

"Well, that's a relief, anyway."

Another silence, more terrible than the first.

"I promised to marry her," Henrik said.

"You haven't even met her."

"I'm sure she's very nice. But Henrik, her father—he might as well be an apostate. I'm here in part not just to censure him, though I'll do that, too, and not just to make sure he leaves, but to clear my own name. He's a dean in my diocese, and I'm responsible for him, and everyone from here to Uppsala knows that Laestadius is out here stirring up trouble——" He sighed loudly; He put his thumb and his forefinger on his eyelids, "And now you're associating us even more with him? This looks, don't you see, like I condone what he says and does. Don't you see?"

"I guess——"

"You don't think, Henrik. You don't think about other people, your mother, how your mother feels about anything, what she needs, what the family needs."

His uncle took something else out of his pocket, a leather book, a small Bible. A thin red ribbon hung from it. It looked well worn, well used. "I don't know what to say, Henrik. I truly don't. I don't know what to tell you."

"I'm here for the family——"

"You're here," Frans said, blustering, suddenly quite loud, his face rather red, "because we told you to be, because we can't bring you around into polite society. Your one job was to come here and not make any more trouble, and to not ruin my chances as a bishop, and not send your poor mother to an early grave from the anxiety over you, and to try, if it wouldn't be the death of you, to keep some measure of respectability in the family."

"I tried," Henrik said, softly.

"Not very hard," Frans said, bitterly.

A silence fell that stuck, even once Henrik had started the fire and even once there was coffee made, and he had poured it out for both of them. Henrik tried several times to start a conversation but only lowered his jaw and then closed it again. They said only what was necessary over dinner—this time of year, fish, always fish—and that night Henrik gave his uncle his own narrow bed upstairs, which his uncle did not fit on, and he put a pelt down on the floor near the stove, and actually slept much better than he thought he would have, with the stove still warm like that, so that when he got cold he opened the stove's door and put another piece of wood on the embers and just waited for it to catch. How long his uncle would stay, though, he didn't know, and his uncle didn't say, he just disappeared the next day, presumably to meet with Laestadius and to say whatever a dean said to one of his pastors when that pastor was leading his parishioners into heresy.

Ostensibly, his uncle was also conducting a survey, an examination, of the parishioners, but since he had come when none of the parishioners were around, this examination was brief, and only involved him asking Sussu and Simmon and the Mággás and the Larssons to come up to the church, as well as whoever happened to be at the parsonage—Laestadius's maid—but it was difficult for Frans to find fault with them. They mostly read a little better than many people in the south, and even Simmon, who did not read (and claimed his eyesight was too poor to ever be able to learn), revealed himself to be uncannily knowing, so that his answers, while not strictly doctrinal, were not wrong, either. What is the fifth commandment, Frans had asked him, and Simmon had said, quite simply, "Don't put a knife in your neighbor's throat." The way he had said it had made Frans slightly conscious of his own throat.

What is sin, he had asked Sussu, and she had said, I guess we are born with it, and it grows in us like a tumor until we kill it, and if we don't kill it the wages of sin is death. Do you admit you have sinned? he asked her. Oh yes, she said. Oh yes. And do you believe you are saved by Jesus Christ? he asked her. Jesus saves everyone who asks, she said, if you ask you will receive.

And do you ask to be saved?

She looked at him and said, I don't wish to have sinned.

And you ask Jesus to save you from your sins? Yes or no, it's very simple, he had said, frustrated. It was like talking with a child, he tried to steer the conversation one way and they resisted, they pushed it off to their own imaginary place.

If I believe I have sinned, she said, then I believe Jesus can save me from them. And that was the most he could get out of her, and he could not exactly say she hadn't understood, he couldn't exactly say she didn't believe, and after all she was very old, and he had trouble understanding her through her missing teeth, and so finally he had noted her in his examinations as someone who had an adequate comprehension of the fundamentals of Christianity, if not a full one.

IT DIDN'T TAKE Frans long to discover that the liquor had not been sold so much as destroyed, though he found out in the strangest of ways: a stray parishioner of some sort had wandered through town, and once hearing that the dean was there, had demanded to see him right away, and then confessed, in a frighteningly tearful litany, all of his sins, and asked forgiveness for them, one of the sins being that when Henrik "had put his axe to the cask so as to get permission to marry," the penitent in question had been very annoyed, because he didn't know where to go get anything to drink anymore, but actually now he "could see it was all as God decides," because now while he was of sober mind he could see how wretched he had been, and he had met some followers of Laestadius, and they had made him a believer.

"A believer of what?" Frans had asked.

"A believer," the man had insisted, "I have the Holy Ghost in me."

"How do you know?" Frans had asked.

"Of course I know," the man had said, "I can feel it, and I was awakened, and I was saved, it all happened to me just like everyone said, and my soul was full of joy, I had never been so happy in my life." The man, to Frans's horror, had begun to weep slightly as he said this. He was a rather rotund man, with a head of thick gray hair that Frans envied. Frans tried as much as he could to explain that one didn't, in fact, discover one was saved simply by deciding one had felt it, one had to live a Christian life, and pray appropriately to God for forgiveness, which required an understanding of one's sins, but the more Frans talked the more the man seemed confused, or maybe upset, it was hard to tell, and Frans had been too tired to deal with it, especially when, in the back of his head, he kept hearing what the man had said about Henrik: he had destroyed the liquor himself?

Henrik confessed to it quickly, without any dignity at all, blushing, his eyes big and wet. Frans closed his eyes briefly and imagined his wife, setting a china cup full of coffee (with whiskey) in front of him. He had to solve this, he had to get their money back, that was all, it was too much money to lose. Two full casks had been destroyed, and in addition to what else was owed to Henrik and never collected, and against the cost of buying the store and starting it, building the inventory, transporting Henrik and his things here, not to mention all of the things Henrik had discovered he needed once he was here——for a while it had seemed there was always a letter with some list of things he "unfortunately required to prevent freezing"——it was getting so that not only had Frans and his sister lost the initial investment, they were actually further in debt than when they had started. And all this, when he had borrowed the money from Karlsson——he never should have done that. He never should have listened to anyone about borrowing that money. And now when he had three daughters to marry off, and two boys to send to school, and Elisabet was always needing something——it had seemed like a sure thing, then. There was a fortune to be made up north from liquor, everyone knew it——everyone else could get rich doing it. Why not Henrik?

He would never get to be bishop of Härnösand, not once people heard about how he didn't pay his debts. It didn't look good. He must be completely reputable . . .

Although he resented how he had to make Henrik do it, Frans sat down with him at the counter and made Henrik make an inventory of everything on the shelves, everything in the storeroom, everything in the storehouse outside, and then, like a schoolboy, made him add up the numbers, made him make a list of who owed him the most, and how much, encouraging him here and there to round up—after all, what about interest? Henrik did everything so passively it was maddening to watch; he even pressed the ink lightly onto the page.

Afterward Frans went up to the church, up to those cold wooden walls. He sat in the pew in the front row, the weak sun from the windows failing to warm anything on him or in him, and he closed his eyes. He wanted to be reassured by God, as he had when he was a boy, he wanted to come into the sanctuary and feel that someone was on his side, but instead there were mosquitoes, whining around his neck—one went into his ear, one bit his ankle, and he couldn't think, much less sit still.

The only thing to do was to face it all, look it in the eye. No more shilly-shallying. Set thine house in order, for thou shalt die and not live. He had let himself believe that the Lapps were under control, even while Laestadius had been letting the Devil in the front door. And now the Lapps were shrieking again . . . he had to do what was best for them, even if it made them hate him. It had happened before. And so? Better to be hated, and do the right thing; better that they had a chance at salvation, than none at all. He would not be like Mad Lasse, willing to say anything so long as people liked him, willing to give way to any of their foolishness. They could be compelling in their own way, the Lapps, he knew it, he'd seen it. They were insidious in their subtlety, they came across as innocent and simple, practically primitive, but when you got down to it they were very crafty. The mistake was to underestimate them, to think they would just pay their debts, just come to church and pray like normal people. They lived in the wilderness and the wilderness lived in them, and just because you put them in a room with four walls for a few hours a few times a year did not mean you had any lasting effect on them.

Thank God Henrik had done one good thing, and written him; thank God Laestadius would be kept away from the Lapps; Frans did not really think Laestadius would have the same effect, anyway, on the Swedish people farther south. If he thought about it, it was like the crazed drunk had said, this was all part of God's plan: Henrik had had to disgrace himself, had to commit adultery with the wife of a viscount, a rather skinny one with hair on her lip, only Henrik would be so selfish and naive to do such a thing, and only Henrik would have had the stupidity to get caught. But the whole melodrama had to happen, and Henrik had to be sent to the north, so that he could let Frans know about Laestadius, even if it meant Henrik, and with him, Frans, were in debt. Maybe there was some luck on his side—after all, things hadn't gotten so out of hand they couldn't be stopped. Everything could be set right. You could make them pay, you just had to meet their slyness with severity. And wasn't this an opportunity? Frans would get the credit for calming them down. The bishop would hear about it, and when the bishop got the better post in the south— sure to happen—he would think of Frans. He would say, didn't Frans manage that mess with Mad Lasse? And, wasn't the sun even shining a bit warmer, as Frans realized this? Wasn't that a patch of warmth on his scalp? It was—he felt it, the hand of God on the back of his neck. He felt it with relief: it was all as God willed it.

PART THREE

20

WHAT ELSE HAD GOD WILLED? THAT NORA SHOULD BECOME, IN THE SPAN of a week, a wife; that Lars Levi and Brita should take their seven children and say goodbye, their goods being pulled for the first time not by reindeer, but by horse; that Frans should decide that he himself would take over in Lars Levi's stead until a new pastor was secured (he had to ensure the debt was recovered; he had to ensure whoever took over could regain and keep control of the Lapps); that Frans should reinstate the sale of liquor and the practice of parishioners sharing a drink with the pastor when they came to visit the parsonage; that Frans should begin to box the ears of anyone who made the faintest noise during any church service, including, more than once, small children; that Simmon should be sent off to Tornio, for more casks of brännvin and whiskey to sell at the store; that Mikkol should now stay up late reading sermons to Risten, and Risten's aunt, and the children, and anyone who was about; that Willa should, in shame, have gone off hiding on the island only to be found by Ivvár, and be brought by Ivvár to his siida, and introduced to Ánde and Niko and his uncles and his aunts, his assorted little cousins, not as his wife or as his fiancée or as his girlfriend but as, only, Willa; that Ivvár's family, after meeting Willa, acted as if she were not there; that Ivvár, furious and insulted at his family's behavior toward her, wild with irritation, should carve his own mark into one of his uncle's calves; that his uncle should see his theft and, furious, threaten to separate their herds; and Ivvár should stop speaking to him, and amidst all of this, that Willa should realize, one morning, fruitlessly attempting to milk one of Ivvár's reindeer, that there was no one around at all, and that the women had disappeared somewhere, and the men. Where they had gone she didn't know, she was sure she had seen them all just that morning, watching her with probably pity and possibly admiration as she managed to just wet the bottom of her bowl with milk. Was that the last she'd seen anyone?

Was it this that worried her—the quiet? Something was, definitively, very wrong, she was sure of it, though she couldn't say what—the reindeer seemed not to know it. Certainly the sun did not know it, giving out the last of its real summer dawns, as if proud to show itself in all its finery for one last go before taking its leave for good. Even the breeze was cooling and calm, but Willa was all worry—she thought; they've decided to get rid of me by disappearing, everyone altogether, all at once. This made no sense but it had its own logic to her, it would have been perfectly reasonable of a thing to happen, in its own way.

She began to hurry even more, her eyes straining for the sight of some-one, anyone, but when she rounded the hillside and saw the lávvus again, it was eerily empty, and except for a good deal of smoke issuing from the top of the largest lávvu, Ivvár's uncle's, there was really no proof of life. When she drew closer, to her relief she began to hear people, the faint commotion of many people talking at once, and when she opened the door she saw the lávvu could hardly have held another stick much less another person; the whole siida was there. Children were squished into any available lap, and even the dogs were trying to find a place for themselves in between knees and buttocks and elbows. At least six conversations were happen-ing at once, some between two people seated beside each other and some across the fire, and for a second Willa was tempted to turn, and leave, but she caught Ivvár's eye, and he nodded at her firmly, as if to seat her with his chin. At least, then, he was talking to people again; at least, anyway, he thought she should stay, even if no one else did.

She knelt near the stack of branches at the door, crushing some with her knee. Beside her Niko hesitated, and then asked—it was the first he'd spoken to her since she'd joined the siida—"You heard?"

"Heard what?"

"She didn't hear," Niko said, turning to Ánde.

"Well, what does she know about it," Ánde said.

"About what?" Willa asked. She wished, desperately, Ivár were not so far away, on the other side of the lávvu.

Then she heard Ánde say the word, dáčča—outsider, not-Sámi, Swede. She blushed, madly. That was it, she was going to just leave when Ivár's voice, loud and insistent and unsteady—was he drinking?—began to take over, and others were quieting down to listen. "So we're supposed to decide, really, which way to starve our reindeer, then?" Ivár was asking the group. "We're supposed to decide if we prefer for them to starve in the summer, or in the winter? That's our choice?" He said it jokingly, but no one laughed.

Willa's mind turned, and turned—she was trying to reason it through, her mind was useless, she was only thinking about herself, could only consider if people had noticed her, if they were bothered that she was there.

"As long as we disappear what do they care?" someone said.

To Willa's left was one of Ivár's aunts, someone who avoided Willa, normally, with precision, and who now kept her eyes turned to the front so fixedly Willa understood the message, but she couldn't help herself, she bowed her own head down and asked, "What's going on?"

Ivár's aunt turned to look at her, as if to say, you should know I don't like you and I don't like telling you this, but because I am so polite, I will give you this: "The border's closed."

"I see," Willa said as calmly as she could, but in fact she was stunned. Her hand was over her mouth without her realizing it, and she sat back on her feet. "My God," she said, not to anyone in particular. Again she couldn't help it—she leaned toward Niko this time. "Russia is shutting their borders? That's the border that's closed?"

Niko nodded. "Closed especially to reindeer," he said. "The old deal's done."

"So either the reindeer have to stay in Norway all year, or Russia?"

Niko nodded. "And," he said, "we're supposed to choose which one to be citizens of."

"But that's not possible," she said stupidly. "The reindeer will starve, there isn't enough food in either place to last the year, they can't make—" She faltered. She hadn't been sure if she should say, they can't make you do that, or if she should say, they can't make us do that.

Willa was not the only one striving to believe it. The borders had always been porous, ill guarded if at all, demarcations of name only; the river Tornio, for instance, serving as a useful line between Sweden and Russia, but not a well-kept one, since it was easily traversed by boat or by ice, but the border between Norway and Russia was even less defined—the curving and wandering lines of the first mountains of the north served as a border of sorts, but not a firm one, and certainly not one anyone this far north had ever bothered to really notice.

"They can't keep us out anyway," someone was saying. "What are they going to do? Line up in fur hats with guns, ready to shoot every reindeer that comes across?" Clearly the man had meant it as a joke, but again, no one laughed.

"I say we just keep going," Ande shouted out. "It's probably just something to scare us." He was trying, Willa saw, to come across as the bold one, courageous where the others were afraid, but it sounded like the bluster it was.

"The Russians probably don't even know where we cross, or when," Niko added.

"You don't know anything about the Russians," one of Ivvár's uncles said, the one who looked like Biettar but, when he spoke, destroyed the illusion completely. His tone of voice was utterly different from Biettar's—not rough so much as strained, like he wasn't used to speaking at all. "If this is the order of the tsar there's no reason to think he won't be tsarist about it," the uncle went on. He spoke in such a way as if to make clear that Ande and Niko were young and stupid.

"Well, I thought we had rights to it anyway," Ande said.

"We did," Ivar said.

"The Lapp Codicil," Willa said, speaking, accidentally, into the quiet.

Ivvár looked up at her again but she couldn't read his face, she couldn't see if he was saying, be quiet, it wasn't her business, or if he was glad she'd spoken. She looked down, wishing she'd said nothing, it would have been better to say nothing.

"Well, go on," his aunt said. Willa turned to look at her. "The Lapp Codicil," she said, "and?"

"Oh," Willa said, "I didn't, it's nothing you don't know."

"None of us has time to pay attention to these things," his aunt said briskly, waving her hand, "just say what you came to say."

I didn't come to say anything, Willa thought.

"Biettar would know," Niko offered.

"Biettar isn't here," the aunt said. What she thought of this was very plain: she hated it. So that's how it is, Willa thought.

"Well," Willa said. Nervousness ran through her, she was embarrassed to speak, and yet felt stuck in it. She looked again at Ivvár, who still watched her, and this time he nodded at her, as if to say, go on, and so she said, almost apologetically, "Well," she said stupidly, "well," and then she got it out. "Sweden and Norway signed the Lapp Codicil, and they said in it that the Sámi could cross wherever they liked between their borders, bring whatever reindeer they liked, have citizenship in both places, all these things. But when they signed it Finland was part of Sweden, and now Finland is part of Russia, so maybe the Lapp Codicil doesn't mean anything anymore there. There's no agreement between Russia and the Sámi at all. Just an old agreement based on that land when it was ruled by someone else."

"Yes, that's it," his aunt said, nodding vigorously, "that's the problem."

"So maybe, also in question," Willa went on, "is whether or not— whether or not—the Sámi—will lose rights to the other parts of the Lapp Codicil, water and grazing rights, citizenship. The right to not be a part of their wars." She touched the edge of her tunic and folded it over nervously. "In some ways, it's a question of whether or not the countries recognize that they once recognized that the Sámi had rights to this land, or whether they now pretend like it doesn't matter, when, of course, it does, and they should. They should keep the old agreement, I mean. I might be getting it wrong, of course . . . the history, I mean . . ."

"Well, the Russians and the Swedes and the Norwegians left any kind of *should* behind so long ago they wouldn't recognize it if it kicked them headfirst into the fire," his aunt said.

"But why would they close the border now," someone asked, "why can't they leave us out of it?"

"The Russians want fishing rights on the coast," Willa said. She'd heard her father say it fifty times. "And the king won't give in to the tsar. So, they retaliate."

"At Varangerfjord?"

"They want to come to the markets and sell our own fish to us," Ande said, "they've always wanted to do that. So do the Norwegians, for that matter." He shrugged.

"They're fighting over who gets to rob us," Ivár said, "and along the way they rob us more."

"Well, it's probably not really about fishing," his uncle said, cutting in suddenly. "They want more of the coast. They want more coastline. They want ships they can keep up there."

"For war," Willa agreed.

"Does it matter?" Ivár asked, too loudly. "Does it matter, I mean, what the why is? The point is not the why, the point is that now they say we can't run the reindeer through, and that we have to choose a side, below the mountains, or above the mountains. That's the reality. Does it matter if it's fish or ships?" Everyone was watching him but they looked, he thought, uncomfortable; he was practically shouting but he was having trouble restraining himself, it was all coming out, little flecks of spittle were coming out, too, that he didn't wipe away. "Anyway," he went on, "it probably isn't either of those. It's probably something like, Oskar hates his father, who was very weak, and couldn't stand up to the Russians, and he doesn't want to be like his father, so now he fights with them when he doesn't need to, and Nicholas, he probably embarrassed himself with his wife in bed, he's in a bad mood one day, and he says, that Oskar, how can he be so rude to me, how dare he, and then he says, what can I do to annoy him? And we are nothing in their way, we are little—we are pellets of reindeer shit, we are just in the way of their lives." He let the full sourness of everything he felt come out. "It's either we run the reindeer below the mountains, or above the mountains, either way. Choose a side to die in. Either way we are reindeer pellets," he repeated.

"It'll take them several years, at least, to work out the rules, though," Willa said, so gently that he was aware she was trying to calm him, she was saying, there, there, and it annoyed him, "the border won't be enforced right away. It can't happen right away. Can it?"

For a moment, two moments, only the breeze blew, and the sides of the lávvu-cloth took breath, expelled it, sucked it in again.

"Never, ever bet on what a Russian won't do," his uncle said darkly. The way he said it made Ivvár think, everyone think, there was something else there, some other story, but he didn't tell it.

"Let's go in a bigger group then," Ivvár said. Everyone looked at him.

"Let's find another siida," he said, "put together a giant herd, the largest anyone's ever seen, and when we get to the border"—he made a whooshing sound, he ran his hands up and over—"what can they do, when thousands of reindeer come rushing in? What are they going to do, drag cannons to the top of Saana Mountain?"

When he said this someone laughed, it was Ánde, who stood up partway, hunched over, and began to squint, and make as if he were pulling a cannon up the mountain, but as he did it he looked, also, like he was painfully constipated, and someone began to laugh, and then they were all laughing, because Ánde was so good at imitating a Russian, he squished his forehead together and looked very serious, and he said, in a bad Russian accent, "Da, da, we stop this reindeer from running," and then he pretended to be so drunk he couldn't walk, and stumbled up the hill, and Ánde kept it going, he glowered and said, "What, what you think is so funny, this?" and then fell in a good imitation of a drunk into someone's lap.

It was good to laugh, a relief—and it seemed like after the laugh the good luck came, because even though no one decided anything in the moment, it felt like something had been accomplished since the weather wasn't right to begin heading south yet anyway, and then, sure enough, the next day Nilsa Tomma showed up. He'd heard the news, and he'd been wondering what they would decide to do, and he'd come over to see, wondering if they wanted to just join up their herds, and so it was decided and done, they would run the herds together, and there was a real excitement to this, even if it was a little risky, and unusual. It might make for a real mess later, separating the herds, and it could cost them weeks, and some of the bulls were likely to fight with the other herd's bulls, but it would be dealt with later, the point now was that there was a plan, they were going to run the herds together, and with this early snow the women might even be able to keep up, and Ivvár would not have to leave Willa behind so much, maybe. And maybe the women would like Willa now! Anyway the women would all be together in a larger group, with Anna and Risten, and Willa got along with them, even if the earmarking had ended a little strained, it was better, she could stay in their lávvu, he was sure of it.

He let himself be hopeful, for a day, for two days, he let hope be, and he even grabbed Willa's hand before people fell asleep and took her behind the small copse of trees left in this windswept plateau and they made love that came not from fear but from hope, they laughed a little as they did it, he felt good, he felt all right, and he would have slept there, right there, on top of her, except she pushed at him and made him go back with her to his spot in his lávvu, where they lay in a rákkas together, very quietly, so as not to wake Ánde or Niko, and he only pinched her, once, for which she took his finger and bit it, which turned into her sucking on it in a way that was too arousing, and he turned over, so she didn't win, and he fell asleep, waking still in his good mood.

They were going to run the herds together—they all felt it. Everyone did their part quickly, carefully, hopefully—the men took their rucksacks and Ivvár took Borga, who was too old now, really, to pull a heavy sledge, and gave him the lightest packs. A frenzied happiness came over him as they pulled the cloths from the fence posts, and lined the dogs up at the back, and the herds were thrilled, and he was just as thrilled as them. They were going to run straight into Tomma-siida's herd, they were going to run them together, straight to the border, Russian or no Russian line, they were going to get to Gilbbesj́ávri and they were going to keep going.

His peppiness, for the most part, cheered others, but when Risten saw him again when the herds got run together she felt worse than ever. Soon

Mikkol would leave with the herd, and soon they would face the border crossing, and they were hardly speaking to each other, or they were speaking in painful little dry bursts about such everyday things that it depressed her; theirs was a marriage of practicality only, because her husband would not touch her anymore, because she had been revealed to be a whore, but she couldn't tell anyone this, and instead she made every effort around her mother or her aunt or her cousins to seem peaceful enough with Mikkol. She let them think that when they left her alone with him in the lávvu that she and Mikkol were making love, when really Mikkol was reading his sermons, and she didn't dare say that Mikkol's devotion to faith frightened her, because it consumed him so entirely, and in consuming him it had begun to consume her, because she couldn't help but see him, every night, even while there was so much to do with the herds, and he ought only to be sleeping, making more coffee, trying to read the Bible, his eyes so tired they shut while he read and he lay there, his hand frozen up above him, until the book fell onto his chest and he would startle awake and keep going. He always left the Bible and the sermons where she would see them, and he even went so far as to sometimes put the Bible in between her and him when they slept, and she felt the insult with precision.

When she finally read the sermon, it was because she knew she had, at most, another night before he left with the herd, and she felt desperate to fix something before he left, and it seemed like understanding the sermon was the only way to understand Mikkol at all. The sermon said, in several different but similar ways that greater than any sin was the sin of doubting, of not believing in Jesus Christ at all, and when she read this she thought: I am on trial, he has put me on trial, and already found me guilty. She read the sermon twice, to make sure she understood it; she was preparing herself for something, a fight, maybe, but when Mikkol returned at daybreak and sat there, eating, not worrying whether or not the noise he made disturbed her sleep, she said to his back: "I read the sermon."

He looked at her, a little surprised. His face was wild with fatigue and she felt bad for saying anything, for bothering him at all.

"Really?" he said, seeming surprised but at least a little glad, and she couldn't help but feel good, it was so nice to be looked at with approval by him, and for a moment she thought, maybe he'll touch me now, maybe he's not as angry with me as I've been imagining him to be.

"And what did you think?" he asked. He put a bit of dried reindeer meat into his mouth with the lip of his knife.

She hadn't prepared what to say about it, she had only thought as far as to say she had read it; she'd hoped that would be enough, to show she was trying for him. "It was nice," she said lamely. "It was interesting," she said, "that doubting in God is the worst sin."

"Yes," Mikkol said solemnly, in a way that annoyed her, like he was the expert on the subject. "There are other serious sins, too, though," he said, and she flushed, unsure if he was referring to anything in particular, to her, to what Ivvár had said, how could he have said anything, how dare he. He was about to say something else, some new serious thing, she could see it, to stop it she put her arm out, she rubbed her hand on his arm.

"Don't do that."

"Do what?"

"I'm trying to talk to you about something important."

"We're talking."

"You always do that when you're trying to change the subject."

"I'm not trying to change the subject," she said. She looked down at the pelt, she plucked up loose hairs in her fingers, she made a nervous stack of them.

"You don't even try. I wait and wait. You have to let Ivvár tell me, in front of us both?"

"Tell you what?" she said, everything so heated in her as to be nearly unbearable. In her ribs her heart was going too fast. She looked at him with all the equanimity she could summon, which was not very much.

"I'd never thought of you as a coward," he said sadly.

"Mikkol," she said, she put all of her begging and pleading into his name. "Mikkol," she repeated, but he was getting up, he was leaving, "don't go," she said, "you're tired, come sleep, I won't say anything," but he was gone, and she thought, that's it, now I've done it, and she hated him, and she hated herself, and she saw it sitting there, the Bible, and she held it up to the edge of the flames. Oh, she would have liked to burn it, watch how fast each page went up, the quick heat of it, the crumpling, and the sermon too, let it all burn, but she thought, then he really will never forgive me, and she thought of what people would say, if they knew, that already she couldn't hold her man, and instead she opened the Bible, and looked at the first page, she wondered, was this what love was, to persist when you didn't want to, to try for patience another time, when as you read your eyes watered over with fury and with scorn.

21

EVEN HENRIK HEARD THE NEWS. HE HEARD ABOUT IT FIRST FROM SIM-mon, but when he went to tell Nora she had just heard about it from Old Sussu, and feeling almost panicked—they lived off reindeer, they lived off the Lapps, what were the Lapps going to do—he went to find Frans, knocking on Frans's door at the parsonage, having a feeling that it was Nora who was going to open the door, or her mother, and that inside there would be ten, fifteen herders and their women, their children, the smoke from their pipes coming out to greet him, the sound inside of a room stuffed with people, but no, of course it was just Frans. Frans hadn't torn down the pews built into the walls, but otherwise any suggestion the Laestadius family had been there was gone. Now inside there was a large desk, and a little table. It was bare, and dark, especially since Frans kept the shutters closed. Right now it smelled good, though, like coffee, but when Henrik looked at Frans it was clear he'd been drinking the night before.

"What is it?" Frans asked.

"The border," Henrik said, "it's closing." He felt slightly out of breath from having hurried from the store to here, and out of breath from the worry that had just overcome him. He pointed to the portrait of King Oskar I that Frans had hung on the wall in the entryway, noticing it for the first time, disliking King Oskar I for the first time, but he couldn't figure out what to say. He wasn't sure if it was the Crown's fault or not. He had no idea why anyone would bother to close the border at all.

"Yes, I know," Frans said easily, "is that it?"

"You know?"

"You knew," Frans said, "I told you about it several letters ago."

Actually, Henrik had no memory of this at all—could he have been told? It was possible, of course it was possible. There were many things Henrik read that later he had no memory of at all, Nora was telling him that all the time now—I told you that yesterday, she would say, and he would stare at her, completely unsure if she meant it, but of course she meant it, she had so little humor to her, and no guile. "But—" Henrik said. He was wishing that Frans would ask him inside, so he didn't have to wait to be let in like a beggar.

"It was a long time coming," Frans said, and he looked outside over Henrik's shoulder, at the evenly gray day, the tone of the world without any variation, so that the same gray color extended to the buildings and the yellowed trees and the pitchfork leaning against the cow-house. "You know those Lapps up at Varangerfjord, they were always fighting about the fishing—"

"Can I come in?" Henrik asked, and Frans stepped aside, and Henrik went in, and he sat down at the table, waiting for Frans to offer him some of the coffee. In the corner Henrik could see wine bottles, empty, lined up in tidy rows. He had brought wine here with him; he didn't even like the brännvin he was making Henrik sell.

"Well," Frans said, "I don't think there's that much to say about it."

"You aren't worried?"

"About what?"

"Business. The Lapps, the Lapps' business. They have to move the reindeer."

"Do they, though?"

"The reindeer are wild. They aren't—they aren't cows, or horses. Nora's always saying that to me," he added, as if Nora were the authority he needed in the moment. "And if the herds don't do well," he went on, "we don't do well."

"They're very adaptable. They'll figure something out. It'll take time to sort itself out, of course, but they will, and anyway, won't it be better for them to keep them all in the same place? Who wants to do all that running back and forth? To the sea, back here—lots of things will be easier," Frans said. He put his hand on his hair and patted it down, but it was already well combed. "Taxes, for one. They can just pay taxes to one country. And then," he said, "they can come to church regularly like regular people."

"I suppose," Henrik said, but he doubted it, even while he couldn't explain why this wasn't true. He was seeing at last the contours of everything he didn't understand, and he saw it through his uncle, through his uncle's own misplaced confidence.

Frans was still standing; he went to the fire and poked at it, and when it didn't pick up he put more wood on it. His stack of firewood was low.

"Did you write to your mother?" Frans asked, as if there were nothing more to say about the border. "You should write to her soon, you'll have to tell her about Nora."

"She knows about Nora," Henrik lied.

"And she's happy with it?"

"Well, I didn't hear back from her yet."

"Anyway," Frans said, clearly impatient, still not offering Henrik anything, "soon they'll be back, and first thing we hear the news, we'll go collect."

"Collect what?"

Frans shook his head, it reminded Henrik of a cow, whisking flies off with its tail.

"You mean going out to the herds," Henrik said, "the debt."

"And we account for interest, too. They were supposed to pay a year ago. Twenty percent on their tallies, thirty if it's been more than a year." He was speaking in such a matter-of-fact way it all had a reasonable sound to it; there was no vehemence in his voice, no anger. This is the way of the world, his voice said, there isn't any use fighting it, it's how things are done.

"I guess that's right," Henrik said slowly. He liked the thought of more money, in an immediate and abstract sense, it sounded good; he had a vision of building an extra room onto the back of the store, where they would put a real bed or a real table. Maybe two rooms, one for a table and one for a bed. Maybe it would only take a year or two to pay off the debt to Frans this way, and almost better yet, if Frans got his money, he would leave, and then Henrik would be alone here—then what, he didn't know. He couldn't ever think past any then what, it was too difficult, there was always just the problem in front of him, and now there was Nora, too, she had to be accounted for— "Thirty percent, then," Henrik said.

"I know many who would charge them worse," Frans said, in the tone of one who has seen it all. "And in the end it helps them, then they learn the cost of not doing things straightaway. And don't forget," he said, "that I'll be collecting my fee, too."

"What fee?"

"Well, I'm your debt collector, aren't I? I'm here, to make sure they collect? And you wouldn't want me to work for nothing."

When it was clear they had nothing else to say to each other, nothing that wouldn't lead to a greater awkwardness between them, Henrik went back out, back to Nora, feeling embarrassed for having thought the matter of the border was something of real importance, and when Nora asked what Frans said, he said it wasn't anything worth repeating, and she looked a little hurt. In the meantime the snow had finally come, it was the middle of October and at church now there were maybe ten, fifteen people, depending, most of whom showed up afterward at the store because they had heard Henrik was selling liquor again, and with Laestadius gone, there wasn't even any danger to it, and they would buy a bottle or two for the week, but Henrik could see that the believers, the Laestadians, they weren't there at all, either at church or in town, and he finally asked Simmon about it, where were they, and Simmon said, as if he were joking, "Well, they all go to Biettar's on Sundays, of course," and when Henrik repeated this to Frans, Frans seemed to realize this was the same Biettar from Henrik's first letter, he seemed at last to see this was something people did with or without Mad Lasse around, and he showed his first signs of agitation. Everything else, even hitting Márjá and Biret-Elle, he had done with control, but now he paced a little, he took his glasses and tapped them on the counter.

He wanted Simmon to take him to Biettar, but Simmon didn't know where Biettar was, and so Frans went on his own to Sussu's, and burst in on her "sucking salmon off its spine" and Sussu had said she didn't know a thing about it. Henrik thought, now he understands! He understands how hard it is here. You want to find something out, something very basic, and you can't, no matter how hard you try. It made him feel good, to see Frans get impatient, and for once Henrik was calmer, and every time Frans snapped at some woman in church for shrieking or crying too hard Henrik was gratified, not because the woman had been stopped (he thought it was a bit unfortunate, church was much more boring without it) but because Frans was coming up against the inscrutability and unmanageability of the Lapps, and he was losing.

"Don't look so amused," Nora said to him after church.

"About what?"

"You know," she said, and she was right; when Frans came for Sunday supper he was in a mood, a barely hidden surliness, and when Henrik tried to suggest, very gently, that Frans stop using a Bible to box people's ears, the Lapps told each other everything, and moreover, he should really leave Márjá alone, she was very beloved by people in general (she had cried out again in church, quite softly, and afterward hastily covered her mouth, but Frans had still descended on her, and with the air of a disappointed father had hit her soundly on the ears again). Frans went quiet. For a long time he didn't say anything, and they could only hear him cutting his meat, and then he said evenly, "You think it's easy? You think I want to be here, calming people?" His knife scraped the bottom of the plate as he held the meat still with the fork in his left hand. "Are you a pastor? Did you go to seminary school? Did you get ordained?"

"No," Henrik said. Nora looked at her own plate, cut her small pieces of meat into smaller pieces.

"Did you accept it as your personal mission from God to save their souls?"

Henrik shook his head.

"Then, please refrain from telling me how to do my job," Frans said. It seemed he would stop there, and they would just eat the rest of the dinner in silence, but then he burst out, with real bitterness, "Everyone thinks because they've heard sermons their whole life they can give one."

"I didn't—"

"If you're going to be on their side," Frans said, "why don't you go live out there? Go live out there, no more bathing, get your head all full of lice, go beat a drum and call up the Devil, go on, then. Get out. This isn't even your store, is it? It's my store."

"I didn't—"

"It's my money," he said, and Henrik thought, he's going to box my ears, he's going to get the birch switch. He's going to throw something at me.

"I didn't—"

"Henrik, quiet," Nora said softly.

"She has more sense than you," Frans said, "and that's saying something." And then he was silent, they were all silent, the only sound was Nora picking up the bones from the plates, going to the door and throwing them out so that the Mággás' dogs came running, and began, immediately, to fight over them. Frans shook his head, disgusted, but Nora didn't see, only Henrik saw, and he braced himself for Frans to say something, to tell Nora how uncivilized they were, but he said nothing, he seemed to disappear for several days, he came out of the parsonage almost not at all. Even from a distance Henrik felt his uncle's disgust for him, that was what it was, he did not even get the respect of hatred, but when he asked Nora if she thought his uncle was upset with him again she said, we can't afford to upset Frans, she said it with real worry in her voice, and he thought, not for the first time, that she was afraid of Frans, actually afraid, and he realized she'd never really said anything when they'd brought all the whiskey and brännvin back into the storeroom, she'd never complained, and he'd always thought it was because she didn't care now that her father was gone, it had been her father's rules, but he asked, suddenly, was she afraid of him, too, of him, Henrik, and she laughed a little, and said she had so much work to do before winter, and she had to make use of the light.

* * *

It took less than two weeks to get the herd from the sea to just north of Gilbbesjávri, quicker than they might have thought, what with so many animals to move, but the herd had seemed to urge itself on; there were so many reindeer in the middle, and none of them could stop with so many still coming behind them, and they moved with terrific speed, flattening whatever grass or brush had been there, leaving behind wide swaths of changed earth. As usual it was the men who traveled with the herd, and the women who followed behind with the sledges and the packs, but because the men had left so late, and because the snow had come so early, there was less distance between the men and the women than was normal, and so Willa didn't have to wait long to see Ivvár again; she had prepared herself for a month, at least, of separation, and instead she felt rewarded by life, by her perseverance—for here he was, was he not? Were they not here, their feet still in Norway but their minds in the south, the reindeer poised a mere mile from the invisible line?

Like the reindeer, Willa felt the anxiety of everyone around her, of the men. They wouldn't rest, Ivvár wouldn't feel easy until Saana Mountain was safely at their backs, and even then, it wasn't as if things would be resolved; the period of not knowing would merely be extended into the winter, and she lay with him one morning, her head on his chest, her leg over his legs, his chin on the top of her head, his arm around her shoulder, the sun out but giving no warmth. Across the dead fire Ánde and Niko slept, they hadn't bothered to put up a rákkas, there weren't mosquitoes anymore, and they were used to sleeping with just Ivvár around. Although she had come down from the sea with Risten's siida, staying with Anna and Risten in their lávu, she had started creeping into Ivvár's lávu while the men slept, Ivvár rolling over and opening his arm, tucking her in around him, but she couldn't tell, really, how welcome she was, how normal this was or wasn't, but no one said anything, and maybe it was best to take the silence as permission, though she suspected it was really just fatigue; they were too tired for her to become something else for them to manage.

But Ivvár, despite it all, couldn't sleep; he slept poorly, fitfully. He turned toward Willa, he turned away from Willa. The back of his eyeballs ached with fatigue but he couldn't sleep. "Is it a bad dream?" Willa whispered.

She was annoyed to be kept from sleeping. She was so tired from all of the change, from all of the newness of being with this other siida, all of these people who would hardly look at her, much less talk to her, but when she saw Ivvár's face she was afraid for him; he looked sick. "What is it?" she whispered.

A very long time went by, so long that Willa began to think, something's wrong, why can't he speak?

"Do you know," he said, his eyes looking up and away, his hands folded on his stomach, "that we have a word for when the Christians came to Sápmi. When they first started coming, I mean, and they took the noaidis and burned the drums, or brought them to their homes and put them on their walls, I don't know. The time before this, we call it drum-time. The time after this we call, when one had to hide the drums. The end of drum-time. But actually it is always ending," he said, "it ends in all these little ways. Not even a big, satisfying crash." He opened his hands and folded them again. "But that's how it is." He sounded calm but there was something ugly in his voice.

"The end of drum-time," she repeated softly, and she turned over onto her back and realized she could see the moon, perfectly outlined by the rim of the smoke-hole. She thought: soon this will be the brightest light we have, all day or all night. Soon only the moon will give shadow, soon we will live in twilight. The people that walked in darkness, she thought, the verse coming to her, have seen a great light: they that dwell in the land of the shadow of death, upon them hath the light shined. But the verse struck her as wrong, it should have been, maybe, the people that walked in twilight, and there should have been something in there about living also in great light, and how it was the land of the shadows of life; the whole verse, which had once struck her as so beautiful, was all wrong, and there was no fixing it, and she wanted to express something like this to Ivvár, but he had his verse, his saying, the end of drum-time, and she had hers, the people who walked in twilight, and she was too afraid they had nothing to say to each other, and she lay there and joined him in not-sleeping, unable to sleep and unable to leave.

During the day she crept back to Risten and Anna; it was easier to spend the day with them there, though she kept wanting them to bring up Ivvár; she wanted someone to say, so, you've been sleeping with Ivvár, she wanted to make it real, for it to be acknowledged and thus confirmed by them and with everyone, made into existence, that she was Ivvár's, and he was hers, but she didn't know how to broach this, because she sensed in their silence on the subject it was something to be ashamed of, and so she felt shame. She was learning, moreover, mostly from Risten's little cousin, that Sámi men, when they wanted to marry you, came to your parents' home with another man to help, their reindeer harnessed beautifully, maybe tasseled in bells, and they were welcomed inside, and the parents indicated their pleasure or displeasure by making the men coffee, and the woman indicated her pleasure or displeasure by drinking the coffee herself, and the suitor would offer gifts that the woman traditionally refused once, but then the man would offer again, and if the woman accepted, then the proposal moved forward, and if the woman refused, the man could offer a third time, but not a fourth—and at some point the men would step outside and talk with the father, and they would decide how many reindeer would be given along with the daughter, what the rádju would be, usually all of the reindeer the woman had accumulated since birth, though not necessarily, and it occurred to Willa for the first time that in marrying Risten Mikkol had become very wealthy—presumably, anyway, Nilsa had given Risten her full rádju—whereas Ivvár, in aligning himself with her, had confirmed his poverty, had decided, in essence, to forgo any rádju at all, since, of course, neither she nor her family had ever owned any reindeer at all.

She was a costly woman, and a burden, and she was a greater idiot for not seeing it sooner.

When she saw Ivvár she couldn't bring herself to say anything, not even indirectly, she kept from anything to do with the future or with marriage or with any ideas of togetherness with great care. She modeled herself after him, and she only talked about the herd, she kept it all safe—she talked about the reindeer with the bad limp and about the two calves who looked so much like each other and always kept together even though they weren't twins. In front of them she could see Saana Mountain's back, the slow curve of its spine, like someone rising up from the ground on their hands, but what appeared the next day was not Saana Mountain but a person, a Sámi man she didn't know in a faded blue gákti, but whom Ivvár knew. She watched Ivvár greet him warmly, give him the one-armed embrace she'd grown used to seeing all summer. She nodded hello at the man, but Ivvár didn't introduce her, and the man looked at her but said nothing. The two of them talked, and the man said he'd heard the news about the border, and he'd decided to stay in Norway himself, since he'd had enough of mosquitoes in the summer, and he'd rather deal with the mountains.

But he didn't have any reindeer, Ivvár pointed out, and he didn't have to worry about winter grazing.

But now he'd have a Norwegian liver! the man joked. Anyway, the man said, the reindeer will cross through just fine, he was sure of it. So far the law was just on paper.

So far, Ivvár said, but so far always comes with an end.

"Knives come with an end," the man offered to Willa. She couldn't figure out if she'd seen him before, possibly at church. "I sell knives," he said, "you need a new knife?" He winked, and she could not discern what this meant, who he thought she was.

She shook her head. Her own knife was safe on its belt, a small but sturdy thing she'd bought at the Iygobahta market that she'd already used for everything from cleaning tar off the bottom of her boot to cutting birch branches for bedding.

"I think a lot of people are going to pick the Norwegian side," he said, "that's my guess. Why stay in the swamp? And too many farmers there now, anyway. It's time to go down to the coast," he said. He shrugged.

"There's not that much more down to go," Ivvár said.

"Is your father still at the sea?" the man asked, and Willa could see Ivvár redden, and she stepped away, seemingly to lessen the embarrassment for Ivvár but mostly because she was too embarrassed herself. Ivvár wouldn't introduce her, even to a little fat man who sold knives. He was afraid the man would figure out who she was. She was a secret to be kept, a shame to be left for the dark mornings and dark evenings, for the seaside. He would probably, she thought, have an easier time with her in front of settlers, who wouldn't know what his relationship with her signified, than with the Sámi—the settlers would care about the fact of the marriage license, but the Sámi would know she didn't have any reindeer, and she didn't know how to herd what reindeer Ivvár did have: that was the difference, and that was the difference that mattered.

She tried to avoid the visitor passing through—Jáhko-Duoma—but it turned out it wasn't possible. He was lonely, he'd been alone all summer, it seemed, and after he had chatted with Ivvár he was chatting with Nilsa, and then he was chatting with Anna, and Willa kept away. She took Anna's lasso out toward some calves in a corral and she practiced, she threw and threw, she missed, she always missed. The children laughed, the children threw with her, their lassos rose—how did they do that—and then their lassos fell, not always where they wanted, but still, they rose and fell, and Willa's just fell. She had only one small mercy—a calf, running away from her—she had asked the nearest boy, was that calf Ivvár's? She thought it was, she thought she could see his mark in its ear.

Yes, the boy had said, like she had asked if it were daylight outside while she stood in the sun.

She was briefly happy, almost giddy, to have read an ear, and when she returned to Anna's, she had thought not being introduced to the man was the worst of it, but it was not—he'd brought the news from town that her father, her entire family, was gone, moved south, and if that wasn't enough, the new pastor was Rikki's uncle, a pastor who made everyone be silent in church and hit you if you weren't. He'd boxed Márjá's ears with the Bible. He was going to start fining people for not coming to church. Nothing like Mad Lasse. Scolded, shouted even, if you made any noise at all in church. Like we were children, Jáhko-Duoma had said, and Frans had taken a ski pole to his back, he'd added.

"Why would he do that?" Willa had asked Anna, her voice raised. "Jáhko-Duoma, he looks so gentle—it's like kicking a calf?"

"He didn't know his Catechism," Anna said. She shrugged. "And Jáhko-Duoma said something to the pastor, that he'd never needed to know these things before, and that Mad"—she stopped herself—"your father—had said being awakened was enough to start."

"I see," Willa said, but she didn't see. She felt uneasy, like in leaving she had left the place to fall apart. She had left, and then her family had left. They were in the south, where they were safe from her.

"But," Anna said, slowly, almost gently, "not your whole family went to Pajala. Your sister stayed, he said. The oldest, he wasn't sure of her name."

"Nora," Willa said.

"Yes," Anna said, as if relieved to have heard the name, "she stayed. She married Henrik."

"Nora married who?"

"The one who stayed, Nora, Nora married Rikki. The storekeeper." If it hadn't been Anna who had said it, Anna who didn't lie, not even in joking, she might have said, that's a good one, and walked away.

Nora was married to Henrik! She'd thought only about Lorens, if Lorens were well; she had imagined, at most, that maybe her mother was pregnant again, and Nora had hardly occurred to her except as someone she wanted to talk to about Ivár. She kept smiling and nodding and talking with Anna, as if the news was of mild interest, but she didn't understand how the day could have brought so much shock with it; the difficulty now was supposed to be the border, supposed to be Ivár, and she wanted to put her hands to her ears and say, no more, no more. Nora was supposed to wait and marry someone respectable, someone with an education, maybe a sexton, or a bailiff. Nora would have liked that, some-one in an official position, she liked that kind of thing, it made her feel safe. But Rikki! They had laughed at him once, when he'd first arrived and he'd asked what his nickname meant, why everyone was calling him Rikki. Don't tell him, Nora had squealed, don't tell him, and Willa wondered now if anyone ever had, if he'd ever learned that *rikki* meant *broken* in Finnish.

Willa thought: I can never go back to Karesuando at all. Gárasavvon. I can never go back to Gárasavvon at all. Was that the question? Was the question, was it Karesuando or was it Gárasavvon—which was it, after all, that she would return to? Both or neither? It didn't matter, maybe, what it was called; if they made it across the border the herds would be separated at some point in the south, and the Speins would run their herd east, and the Tommas would run their herd west, and the Rastis would keep going south, and a choice would have to be made, something had to be done with her—the Rastis had to accept her, she had to make them accept her, and the thought came to her: if only Nora could have married Ande or Niko! Then they could have herded together. But now she couldn't even go back home; there was no home to return to.

In a way this relieved her. If there was no home then didn't that mean Ivvár would have to keep her? She would have to keep him?

So she let herself hope that there was a way to make this life work, where she didn't ever need to go into town, ever again, and other people could go for her. If someone came for church inspections, any such thing, she would disappear, that was all—she would cease to exist, they could write down what they liked in the church record, that she had died frozen in a fell, she didn't mind, so long as she was Ivvár's, and he was hers. That night and the next night, and the next, she pressed up against him, and they could hear the herd, grunting, shuffling, and she could smell Ivvár, his good and salty smell, and she could be a mouse, a rabbit, in its den. Later it would seem she had done everything for these nights—later it would seem that had been the great bargain—all that for this. But she didn't know that yet, and in the moment, had someone asked her, what is this worth, she might even have said, Oh, maybe everything.

22

BIETTAR HAD AGED MANY YEARS IN NOT SO MANY MONTHS. HE COULD feel it, for the first time, his age, as if age had been brought on not by years of living in the fells, but by this easier life, as if it were all catching up to him now that he was in so much relative stillness. Of course, in some ways it wasn't easier to appear in the homes of strangers, introducing himself, making himself unwanted. He'd been spit on. He'd had a man throw his drink at him, down his coat, and laugh, so that he'd smelled it on himself for days, the desirable stink of vodka. He'd been given food, and smiled at benevolently, and sent on his way. He'd been listened to in silence. He'd been propositioned, by an older woman living alone who was, herself, probably drunk, or possibly deranged. He'd slept in cow-houses, and in sheds, and on thin patchy pelts, and near fires, and without fires, and on stones besides hearths, and twice on a boat. In doing all of this he had lived an enormous amount, a tiring amount; he'd spoken more words in one year than the rest of his life combined, but he had not learned, after all that, how to accept that everything was in God's hands, it was a kind of phrase that he said but he couldn't quite believe. It was the most difficult part of faith for him, and when he'd heard about the border closing, he'd felt almost personally betrayed by God—that God would do this to his son, to the herders—and the news gave him a premonition that ached like his knee in the rain.

He stopped in the snow, he knelt, and he prayed, but when he rose again the fear was still there. It woke him in the middle of the night—he had found a storehouse to sleep in—and he realized he wouldn't rest until he saw Ivvár and he knew Ivvár was safe, and the herd was safe. Even though it was the middle of the night he left, he began skiing, and when he heard the church bells ringing in the distance he remembered the old saying, that if you heard church bells while you were in the wilderness, it meant someone was about to die. Of course, it was just an old saying, like so many old sayings, but he hated that the thought had come into his mind. Once upon a time he had believed those things, even that it was bad luck to make the sign of the cross, to even have two pieces of wood cross each other like that by accident, and he was determined to not believe them anymore.

But why was it that the church bells seemed to be calling him? He hadn't been planning on going to church, in part because he had no need to hear any false preacher—he had no intention, either, of paying any fines for absenteeism like the new preacher was alleged to be issuing—but his skis wanted to go there, the tracks wending toward town were smoother, maybe that was all, but this small thing made the thing final. He would go to town, all right, he would go to show his face, and then he could see about this new pastor for himself . . . this was what Biettar told himself, but in fact he went in the hopes there was news of Ivvár or of the siida. Biettar had been on the Swedish side of the river all fall, and the news from Finland and from the east hadn't crossed—maybe someone at church would know. Maybe Old Sussu would know, maybe Simmon would have heard something.

But when he reached town, quite late for the service, in all likelihood, he was surprised to see that there were only seven or eight sledges tied up outside, and one of the sledges was his—or Ivvár's, rather—and one of the reindeer was Borga. He hurried up to the church without thinking, and it was only when he reached the door, and had already opened it, that he thought: why would Ivvár come to church? Ivvár would never come to church, when it wasn't even a holiday. Please, he prayed, let him not be getting something to drink, and when he got inside Henrik was there, in the front pew, and Nora beside him, where Lars Levi and Brita had always sat. Nora seemed small to Biettar, or different, but that happened to women sometimes, where they got married and they seemed different, or maybe you saw them differently, and now he saw Nora's mother in her; it was like Brita had been put back in her place, only in a blue kerchief instead of a black. But where was Ivvár?

Risten was there, and Mikkol, and Ánde, and Niko. All four of them spotted Biettar entering the church, and going to his seat in the pew, but only Mikkol admitted it, nodding at Biettar. So Mikkol was still awakened, then, and Risten was still not. Funny how quickly you could know these things, how much could be learned in a look. Interesting that Ánde and Niko should be sitting alongside Risten and Mikkol, not that it was impossible for those of the Tomma siida to sit near the Rasti siida, but it wasn't the usual way. It would have made more sense if Ivvár had been there, or if Ivvár and Risten had married, as Biettar had once thought they might (and thank God, Biettar thought, they had not; the Tommas would have brought out the worst in Ivvár, with their need for wealth and their need to be above everyone else). But should he go over to the Tomma siida after? Should he read them a sermon? Risten would hate that; she had been so surly in Ivgobahta, she didn't yet see that she was lucky God had given her Mikkol, but she would. It would come. But where was Ivvár?

Risten didn't know where Ivvár was, either, though she assumed he was off somewhere drinking. She was surprised he'd agreed to come into town at all, instead of staying back with Willa, who was growing more recalcitrant and agitated the farther they went. Her habit of staying on the edges of everything had intensified, so that she seemed to hardly be around at all—like everyone, maybe, she had been disappointed there hadn't been anyone at the border. They had all wanted a fight, Risten especially; they had wanted to see the soldiers' faces as the herd ran through them, but on the other hand, afterward a relief had settled in. The settlers, as always, had said one thing and meant another. Maybe Willa was like that, too, maybe she was trying to control something that could not be controlled, probably Ivvár, and Ivvár certainly could not be controlled—lately Risten felt herself in sympathy with Willa more than she had ever been, she saw them now as two women with two men who were, in very different ways, difficult, and she'd begun to see, on the way up to the tundra, that Willa's happiness was too dependent on Ivvár, and in that she saw herself, too dependent on Mikkol, and while they weren't exactly good friends something had softened between them, and they were kind to each other in little ways, remembering how the other liked their coffee, which bit of meat they liked best, that kind of thing. And Willa's uncertain status, her liminality, made Risten sympathetic, and maybe even feel superior—Mikkol could not let go of his Jesus, but at least she was married to him, at least they had a herd—at least she was here, sitting beside him, instead of hiding away at the herd while Ivvár ran off and drank them into more debt.

But Ivvár had been working so hard—maybe now he felt he deserved to drink again. It wouldn't have surprised her. In a way she envied how he had the courage to keep making the same mistake, to come to town when everyone knew he had left last Easter without paying his debt. She would never have done it; it had pained her just to come to town this morning, when they needed supplies, and she had been dreading it, Mikkol meeting the new pastor, whom he already disparaged based on rumor alone, not to mention Mikkol back again around more of the believers, and near Biettar, going to prayer meetings again. But better to be here than to be at home, worrying and wondering; it was inaction, in the end, that was the most unbearable for her.

There was the sound of someone walking slowly. It was the new pastor, and Risten turned with everyone to look at him. Funny how he came in like that, like he was expecting them to stand and greet him. He was handsome to some, she supposed, though she felt repelled by him; he had the face of an eagle or an osprey, with his eyebrows hooked down like that, and his nose so distinctively straight. At the front of the church he announced the hymn and sank down beside Rikki—and Willa's sister, Risten noted—and he began to sing, and about half of the congregants sang with him, in rather weak and wandering tones. Risten didn't know the song or the words, and she didn't have a songbook, but Mikkol sang. Though devils all the world should fill, Mikkol sang, all watching to devour us. Biettar was singing, too. Niko mouthed some of the words. Her mother and father were silent. Her father had put on his face of patience. He would leave as soon as this was over, get his supplies, go.

Risten was relieved when it seemed like the sermon was going to be dull, nothing like one of Mad Lasse's. The pastor had the Bible open on a stand of some kind and he leaned on this stand, reading with the familiar rhythm of someone reading something they have read many times. She didn't listen. She looked around, surprised to see there were some new faces—they looked like Finns, the poor ones with their potato fields, whose clothes were always so patched over, those kind of Finns, and there was Simmon, head sunk so completely to his chest he might have been asleep, and the Mággás were there like always, and that Swedish family, they were still there. Otherwise as ever the women, Márjá was here, and the Ungas were all here. So their herd had made it. No Speins, though. No Piltros, though that was to be expected; they were usually only in the area around Christmas.

Her eyes drifted back to the new pastor, who seemed to be rambling, or maybe he wasn't reading from something he'd written, like Mad Lasse did, maybe he was just making it all up as he went along. "The wages of sin is death," he kept saying, like he couldn't think of anything else to say. "Believing in a false god is a sin. And will lead to death. Calling upon the tongue, calling upon the Devil. Calling upon the Devil with tongues is a sin and will lead to death. God must be listened to—quietly. Respectfully. God doesn't need loud noises to hear you. He already knows what you think and what you say, he knows if you are stealing, or whoring, he already knows. So you listen, quietly. It's how we show respect. Do you shout at your mother and father, or do you listen to them quietly? You listen to them—quietly.

"What else—how else do good Christians behave? How else do we show respect to God? Do we need to go shouting out our sins to each other? No, we can ask God for forgiveness. Do we need to go weeping and screaming? No. In the same way you don't use drums anymore to call the Devil, or go bowing to big stones, or sacrifice animals, you don't do that anymore. Now we know that's foolishness, and devilry. Devilment. Bedevilment. That was what the Lapps used to do before they were saved by our preacher brothers, before they knew any better. But no more excuses, now we can listen quietly, we don't shout. We don't froth at the mouth. We don't see Jesus frothing at the mouth, do we? Did the apostles throw their hands in the air and cry out like wild dogs? No, they listened and they said, Lord, teach us."

It was difficult to listen to, she was vacillating between shame and fury—it sounded ridiculous, infantile, to go to sieidis, the way he talked about it. Sickeningly she feared he was right—they were too loud, too uncontrolled. Wasn't it better to be respectful? Were they not respectful? It was strange, it could be strange, how people were awakened, she could hear when he spoke how Mikkol had sounded in the lávvu. Was it really the Devil?

"Dean Frans," someone interrupted loudly, standing up, "what does God's Word say about preaching when you still have the taste of the Devil's piss in your mouth?" It was Biettar. His voice was calm, but with a lecturing edge to it. "Can you even stand up there much longer? Or do you need to go back for more?"

It was so shocking, they were all so surprised, that no one knew what to do, no one even whispered about it. Frans stepped back, slightly, standing taller. "Don't interrupt," Frans said, "this is the Lord's service." He seemed to expect this to have an immediate effect, and he began reading again, but Biettar didn't sit down.

"I'm asking why you are drinking," Biettar said again plainly, "when it's against the law, and when we all know your nephew sells it." He was speaking so steadily it amazed Risten, she didn't know how he did it, and when she dared look at Frans he was flushed, and his scalp shone red through his hair like a sunset through branches.

"You're interrupting the reading of the Word of God," Frans said. He hadn't raised his voice, like he was following his own admonition to be calm no matter what, but he was straining to stay calm; his affect was of a man whose entire energy is devoted to not doing something he wishes very much to do.

"It's the Devil who makes people drink, and the Devil who sells people something to drink, and you who are supposed to be leading us in the way of righteousness are drinking the Devil's piss yourself." There were some murmurs of appreciation, or agreement. People shifted in their seats.

It was clear Frans didn't know what to do. "The Devil," said Frans, in the same lecturing tone, "is the one who dares to interrupt God's service, who speaks this way in a house of God, to a servant of God. I will ask you, just once, to leave."

"Do you deny that you are drunk?" Biettar asked. He was still standing. He hadn't turned his eyes away from Frans.

"Simmon," Frans said, nodding toward Biettar. Simmon nodded and stood up, but didn't appear to have any idea what to do next. "Usher him out."

Simmon walked down the aisle, padded almost softly, apologetically, toward Biettar's pew. "Biettar," he said gently, "let's go." His long hair, combed but oily, fell in front of his face and he pushed one side of it back behind his ear.

"It's not right," Biettar said, "that this pretender continues to speak for God. He hasn't been awakened, he doesn't have the Holy Spirit in him. He doesn't believe we are already saved. We're the ones who should pass judgment on him." There were loud noises of agreement, murmurs, Niko was nodding vigorously, and her mother shouted, yes, yes, it's so, it's so, though in Sámi, so maybe Frans didn't understand.

"Biettar," Simmon said, over the clamor. "Let's go," he said, but without any real force behind it.

"Go where?" Biettar asked. "Wherever we go, God is there." Yes, yes, people said, it's so.

"You have to leave," Simmon repeated, almost hopefully. He looked at Biettar as if to say, don't do this to me.

"We won't go," Mikkol shouted out.

Risten grabbed Mikkol's hand and clenched it. Don't, she said with her hand, don't, but Mikkol was nodding, and he shouted again, "We won't go. You go! We won't go," and he stood and shook his hand free of hers.

"You have to go," Simmon said, his voice worried.

"You're disturbing a service of God," Frans said, above this, "and I'm trying to preach to those who are willing to listen."

"We won't go," Mikkol said.

Yes, yes, everyone said, yes, yes, Jesus, Márjá was crying out, be with us!

"In the name of Our Lord and Savior Jesus Christ," Frans said, shouting, "be quiet!"

"Thou shalt not take the name of the Lord thy God in vain," Biettar said.

"It's the Second Commandment," Mikkol said.

Someone cried out, a woman, it might have been Márjá again, it sounded like wailing. "For the Lord will not hold him guiltless who taketh His name in vain!"

As if this, the accusation of the profaning of God's name, was what had finally done it, Rikki stood up in the front pew. Beside him Nora kept her head down.

"Biettar, leave," Rikki said. His voice was loud, but cracked in its call.

"I can't go on," Frans said. He shook his head and closed the Bible on its stand. "This is no way to have a church service."

Go, go, people shouted. Get out, get out. Risten's father, her father of all people, he stood. "What kind of preacher hits people?" he asked. "What kind of preacher uses the Bible to box someone's ears? Isn't that the work of the Devil?"

"Unfortunately, then," Frans said, "we can't have a service. We can't listen or hear the Word of God, not when we have this kind of behavior." The murmurs swelled, get out, leave us be.

"Devil-preacher," someone wailed.

"It's true," her father said, "Devil-preacher."

"I'm afraid I'll have to end it here, and I'll resume the service once you all learn to be calm," Frans said. He began to walk down the aisle, not so slowly this time, and he did seem drunk, Risten thought, he walked like someone who was trying very hard to not seem drunk.

"You should pray," Biettar said, as Frans approached his row, "you should pray your Devil-god takes pity on you," this last shouted at Frans as he passed him, going down the aisle. As he went by his coat fluttered, and Risten saw the flare of his green shirt beneath, its silky sheen.

The door closed behind him, but without any satisfactory sound.

Now they were all sitting there in the new silence, Biettar and Ánde nodding, her father with his eyes still watching the door, like Frans might appear again.

"The poor man," Mikkol said, "the Devil owns him," and Biettar nodded.

But Frans didn't return. Simmon sat back down, Rikki sat back down. They all waited, warily, the sound of their waiting almost comically quiet. What to do or say, no one knew. The candles smoked slightly. Winter went on beyond the windows. Mikkol shook his hand free of Risten's, and she realized she had still been clenching it. He smiled at her with a smile that said, everything's fine, don't you see, but she wanted to shout at him, how stupid, how stupid to say anything! How childish! You think that was worth anything, she wanted to shout, you think he'll let that go? The only thing a settler prizes more than money is his pride, her mother always said. I always let them think they have it, she would say, shrugging, it doesn't cost me anything. No, Risten thought, she could feel it, this was not going to be forgotten, and she put her hands to her shawl over her head, and as if it would do anything, she tied it a little tighter.

Ivvár did not hear Frans leave the church; did not, in fact, have any semblance of what was happening inside the church at all. He had come to town with the others in a state of high nerves, not anxiety so much as excitement, as if the confrontation with the settlers at the border had been only delayed, and soldiers might appear at any minute, and he had to be ready. It had seemed possible before something else would happen, something else would resolve all of his various messes; he'd thought his father might leave behind the preaching sickness, he'd thought lots of things, none of which had remotely come to be. Instead, Mad Lasse was gone, and Rikki sold liquor out in the open, and this news had been too tempting—Ivvár had started thinking about it, how tired he was, how nice it would be to have a drink—and he packed nice furs in the sledge, even some sealskin he'd gotten over the summer, he would bring it to Rikki in a sign of good faith. He would say, December, when we slaughter, I'll bring it all, and December was practically here, and he would do it, he was sick of this debt, it would bring a reality to things, to see how few reindeer he really had. He would show Willa, he would say, look, look how little I have.

What that would do he didn't know.

Most likely nothing. He was seeing now she had nowhere else to go, and that, moreover, something had been decided without him noticing. He wanted her, he wanted her sweetness and her adoration, her happiness to see him, like a faithful dog, but he could give her nothing she wanted, or he didn't want to give it. They'd been at their best when everything had seemed impossible, when it had seemed like she would just come back here, or somehow stay forever with the Tommas; he'd felt at ease when she'd been there but not there, but it was a woman's way to want and to need, was that it? And what he needed was to not be needed.

What he needed was a drink. He'd waited, not even slyly, for everyone else to make their way inside the church. Risten watched him, to see if he would come in, then she closed the door, and he was about to turn and make his way to the store but Old Sussu was waving at him from her hut with her bright red scarf like a flag. At first he thought, something's wrong, but then he saw, no, she wanted him to come to her, and though he did want the drink, and though he wanted to go to Rikki's before the service started, he walked toward Old Sussu. In the end I am dutiful, he thought, a little bitterly, but to be so rude to Old Sussu was inexcusable, and impossible. She looked relieved that he was coming toward her, but she remained outside while he approached, as if afraid he wouldn't make it all the way there, and at the door she stood to the side while he crossed inside in front of her.

"You don't make yourself a bigger fire?" he asked. He was teasing; the heat inside was staggering. She had one of those hearths without any chimney, and this contributed to the sensation of extraordinary heat, almost suffocation; moreover, there was a second, lower ceiling amassed by the smoke, though Old Sussu was so short it was possible she suffered much less from this than she might have otherwise.

"If it's too warm you never have the heart to leave," she said. She might have been serious. "Sit," she said, "sit, sit," but there wasn't anywhere to sit besides her bed, and a low stool. He took the stool, which clearly was usually kept by the hearth; he could see there were three grooves from the stool legs worn into the wood floor, and he imagined Old Sussu, sitting here sewing or knitting, whiling away the last days of her life. Her hands shook, but he pretended not to notice, he pretended to notice nothing, not how crammed her little cabin was with every sort of thing, bits of embroidery started and abandoned, pinned to the wall, long strings of sinew hanging from a rafter here and a ski pole there, socks in various states of darning and drying, a little table on which there were so many things, needles and leather thimbles, broken knives, wooden spoons, a swan's throat rattle, that there was no sight of the table itself beneath. It was pleasant in its own way, if cramped, like all of these things meant she wasn't really alone here after all.

Ivvár felt her eyes on him, but when he looked he couldn't see anything in them. He thought, she's about to lecture me about drinking.

She poured water from a pail into a pot hanging over the fire.

She sat on her bed, one of those very narrow ones that is essentially a bench, on which she had stacked pelts until the bed came up to the height of her hip. She put her hands on her knees, and then looked around for something to do, fingering a bit of embroidery, then abandoning it back to the table and clasping her hands back together. "You made it across the border," she said.

"This year."

"One year is not the brother of another."

"That's what I said," he said, "but people think it'll be fine, and they won't really shut the border."

"They will."

He nodded.

"The herd will suffer," she said.

"Yes," he said.

"The herd will have to learn, through its own generations, to stay inside the border, whichever way you go, and a lot of herders will come west into Sweden, to avoid the trouble, to keep crossing north, but then too many people will come this way, and the land will be overgrazed and overcrowded."

"Maybe," he said.

"It isn't a prophecy, it's reality. Everyone crosses where the fence is lowest. What will you do?"

"I don't know," he said. It was true, he didn't know, he hadn't thought about it, he had thought only of getting across the border, only of this winter.

"I told your mother I would watch you."

"I know," he said, embarrassed. Old Sussu often repeated this, as if, somehow, he might have forgotten his mother's extracted promise.

"But what can I really do, this woman who can't go with the herds anymore. And now it hurts to go on the sledges, too much bumping around," she said, smiling, trying to make light of it. Guilt came in from all quarters—he should have come to see her before; he should have come every time he was in town. He should have offered to bring her wood, he should have asked how she was doing. For the first time it occurred to him his mother would have wanted him to watch Old Sussu even more than she would have wanted Old Sussu to watch him.

Old Sussu seemed to be thinking about something. "Do you remember going to see Aslak?" she asked. He was so taken aback by this that he had to readjust his seat on the stool; to be fair, the smoke was coming in his eyes. "You were little when you saw him last. You went to see him, when your mother first got sick," she prodded.

He nodded, but the question made him anxious, though he didn't know why.

"She was quite the woman. Very strong, and very short. Plump. It was strange when she got sick. She seemed like someone who would live forever."

"People liked her," Ivvár said, matter-of-factly, but really he wanted to hear this; he craved to hear his mother praised, talked about in any way.

"I suppose because she liked them," Old Sussu said. "She liked people, she liked being around them. She didn't want your father always going off on his own, even then sometimes he was separating the herd from his brothers, and she wanted to be with the siida. "For some reason this hurt to hear, and his whole chest twinged with it. "Your father…" Old Sussu said. She stopped. "He had his own difficulties. He always wanted more. More wealth, more reindeer. His eyes were always on someone else's pot. He was always sure someone would steal his reindeer. Your mother didn't like it, but she loved him anyway, and she understood the herd was the important thing. But she went to see Aslak up at the sea, you went with her, you were just a little boy——"

"I remember," he said, annoyed, somehow, for her to tell him his own story. He remembered Aslak perfectly well, the knives, how cold the hut was, the briny breeze of sea, the sealskin drying by his fire, his mother on her side, knees up to her chest, Aslak's yoik in his own chest.

"He healed her, for a while anyway, you remember," Old Sussu said, as if he did not, "for a whole year her trouble went away and she could walk without pain, and her stomach didn't hurt her. But then she got worse than ever, and think how hard that was, she couldn't travel, but your father couldn't stay with her and abandon the herd, either, and the herd kept getting farther and farther away from her, and he kept having to travel farther and farther every day to come back and forth."

"He was gone all the time," Ivár said. "We were alone all the time."

"Don't be so hard on him. He tried."

Ivár was finding himself being pulled in a way he didn't like into that past—Old Sussu's directness was dragging it all back, or maybe it was the suffocating room. He wanted to be somewhere else, back in the sledge, or back anyway in the present, where his mother was safely dead.

"Maybe he tried, but it didn't work."

"You mean what?" Old Sussu said. She frowned.

"He tried some things," Ivár said insistently, "he tried everything he knew, but she died."

"Your father is, was—a guvhllár of his own kind," Old Sussu said.

"Nothing worked," Ivár repeated stoutly.

"Sometimes," Old Sussu said, "I wonder what it is you remember."

"I was five, six. Who knows what's real from then."

"These kinds of things tend to be awfully real." When Ivár said nothing her brows went up, and she went on, "Oh, once your father told me how it had happened for him. It always stayed with me. Actually, it seemed like he wasn't sure what was real about any of it, either."

"What did he say?"

"Oh," she said, "well, I meant the night that everything happened. He said he was out with the herds, but I have to tell you, I won't lie to you, I think he was with another woman. I don't say that with any blame, myself, even though your mother was the one I had loyalty to, because it was really so difficult to see her. You would think someone who was around so much death would just be able to see it as another moment of it, but it never felt like that. It was just such a shame, there was just no reason for it, for her to be so sick and so suddenly. So I think the other women, they were actually a part of how much he loved her. He couldn't bear to see her suffering and he was never as strong as her in his own way. Anyway," she said, clearly very chatty, and he could feel the loneliness in her, in how she talked in such long and unbroken streams, without any encouragement, "he told me he was out with the herd and he heard someone calling for him, a voice. But there wasn't anyone around, he said. And he had been gone from you and your mother for four or five days, maybe it was a week, a little while, anyway, but right then he knew, he had to hurry back to her, and even though the weather was bad he began to make his way, and he left the herd. And when he got there you were asleep, in your mother's arms, and she was sleeping. He said it was the most peaceful he had seen her look in several months. He lay down to sleep and at some point she woke up and began coughing again, but you didn't wake. He began to yoik, very softly, to not wake you, but at some point he passed out, he'd been drinking, he admitted. Anyway, when he woke up, your mother was gone."

"Oh," Ivár said. He did not want to hear it, or even be near the story, or near its teller. He sensed something insidious in it, something to put together, Old Sussu was telling him what his father had done but he didn't want to see it, he didn't want to think more about his mother, sick, how she had coughed like a dog with no bark anymore, all rasp and no pitch.

"Do you know what I always thought, though?" Old Sussu said.

"What?"

"I always thought, who called your father home? And I wondered if it was you. And I wondered, even, how you did that." She let it sit there, and

Ivár did not let himself think through what this meant, he felt himself pressing back against everything she was pushing on him, they were in a struggle, he and Sussu, and she was very strong, he was brush giving way to wind.

"When the little Laestadius boy was sick, you remember that?"

"Lorens," he said. The name came to him without thinking; he saw Old Sussu's eyebrows go up. He could hear the water in the kettle, the beginning of its boil.

"There's coffee——," Old Sussu said. "There," she said, "no, to your left. There. Yes, just shake some in. Anyway, that morning—well, maybe I did some things, it wasn't with this in mind, but anyway, I thought to try to help the boy somehow, but it turned out, while I was doing it, Willa disappeared." A long pause, like she was waiting for some reaction to these twin revelations, the name, Willa, like she knew its weight, and the unsaid, what it was she had done. "Then," she said, very softly, so quietly his ears ached to hear her, "I did it again when the new pastor came and when Mad Lasse left. Frans hit Márjá with his Bible—you heard about that? And a little boy. And Old Man Mahtte. Too many things were out of place. I felt something, something bad was going to happen. And for the first time in my life, I got too scared to look. I started sleeping badly."

"My mother used to be afraid to sleep," he said, feeling his mother press back in on him again, and why was that, why was Sussu not even talking right now about his mother but she was here again. "She was afraid to dream," he said.

"Yes," Sussu said, "that's part of it. She knew, maybe, what was coming. Sometimes it's easier to not look. I guess you know about that," she said.

"I don't know what you mean," he said, and he thought, I'm lying, but he couldn't place the lie. It was the heat, the smoke. He was tired. It was all getting to him.

"You left her," Sussu said.

"Who?" he asked, playing dumb.

"You don't think of her," she said, "you don't remember what she taught you." And like that, while she looked at him, she began to yoik, and his neck stiffened, his throat went dry. She was yoiking his mother. It was a slower yoik, a wide river that hid one bend from another, and while Sussu yoiked she was there, he had her, they both had her, she blinked, she laughed with only one side of her mouth, there was a bit of tar under her eye . . . He had never brought himself to yoik her—and why not? Was he so afraid of her? Was he so afraid of this, or was it that he was afraid of when the yoik ended, as it had to end—Old Sussu's voice was giving way—it was a yoik that required some real exertion—and then there they were, in the time after she had yoiked his mother.

The entirety of Ivvár's right arm, but not his left, had gone very cold, and the cold spread, it walked across the front of his chest.

"I have something from her for you," Sussu said, then. And she rustled around on the table and opened a small leather purse, and she took out a silver brooch. It was her brooch, he remembered it perfectly, he could see it holding the two ends of her shawl together, and he knew if he turned it over what he would see inside were her initials, carved next to the pin. It was tarnished now, but no matter, you could fix that. "You have someone to give that to?" Sussu asked.

Ivvár looked at her. So she did know about Willa. Of course she knew.

"Or," Sussu said, "well. She said to give it to you. I thought it was that time, that's all."

For a long time now they said nothing. He poured them coffee, as carefully as he could out of a very heavy pot. He was relieved that even though she had two china cups she didn't use them, and passed him her guksi and assumed he would use his. "Frans knows about your father's prayer meetings," she said.

"I know," Ivvár said, though he didn't know.

"He knows," Old Sussu repeated, "and who knows what else he knows. I can't wait until I die, and someone comes looking for me and finds out someone's already sold everything to a Frenchman for a bottle of whiskey." She laughed, showing her gums. He could count four, five teeth. He felt unaccountably nervous. He kept his eyes on the fire. The desire to drink came back, worse than before. "You have to start doing things, you know," she said.

"I don't know what you mean."

"You haven't been really looking at things," she said, "you know already what you should do and what you want to do, and you don't do it."

He turned away from the fire and toward her. To his surprise, she looked sad.

"What is it?" he asked.

"Oh well," she said, "you're still young."

"You're still old," he said, and she looked amused by this.

"Listen," she said, and he was quiet, thinking she was about to say something, but then he heard it. The church bell, the biggest bell reindeer of them all, its heavy, iron call.

NORA WAS MAKING SUPPER, BUT HER HANDS WERE STILL SHAKING EVER SO slightly, and she cut the meat unevenly, and she let the butter brown too long, and she forgot to add the onion. The scene at the church had left her unsettled, even though Henrik and Frans were behaving like everything was fine; they were drinking, sitting upstairs on the bed, clearly imagining they were whispering even while she could hear Henrik telling Frans ending the service had been the right thing to do, Frans had handled it perfectly, there was nothing really to be done when they got it in their minds to be crazy like that.

"What did Mad Lasse use to do?" Frans asked, as if he didn't remember she was Laestadius's daughter and downstairs making his meal.

"Practically joined them," Henrik said, which was not really true, none of it was true, and she wanted to shout up something, but it was better to maintain the pretense she couldn't hear them at all, and when she had set out the stew in bowls on the counter they came down, and she sat on a stool Simmon had made for her, and Frans sat in the one real chair, and Henrik stood while he ate.

Frans took a handkerchief from his pocket and wiped his mouth. "It's a little chewy today," he said.

"It was an old reindeer," Nora said, blushing.

23

"There'll be fresh meat soon," Henrik said, "the main slaughter's in December."

"We'll have all your debts paid then," Frans said pointedly. He emptied his glass and set it down as if he expected it to be refilled. Nora looked at Henrik, and Henrik poured more brännvin into Frans's glass.

"Let's not talk about it right this minute," Henrik said, and the two men looked at each other. What did that mean, Nora wondered, what was it she couldn't know? She knew about Henrik's debts, it was impossible not to. Did they see her as being on the side of the Lapps? Because her father had been? Was she on their side? She had never had to ask herself the question. She hadn't needed to, because the sides had always seemed like the same one, even if they weren't. But she didn't pry, and she listened to them talk again about the insolence of the men at the service, and then Frans asked her to name everyone who had spoken up against him, or been especially loud, and though she wasn't completely sure of all of them she did the best she could, and he wrote them all down very carefully, asking for correct spellings, and she had a sense that she'd finally pleased Frans, because he had finally found her useful, and when Henrik went upstairs to get another bottle of brännvin from the storeroom, Frans reached his hand out toward her leg and set it gently but heavily on her thigh, like he was comforting her with this gesture. Nora went stiff, feeling welded to the stool. He left his hand there until Henrik's footsteps sounded above them, and even when he took his hand off his fingers dragged a little over her thigh, moving some of the muslin of her skirt. For the entire meal she didn't look at him, and when he was done eating she took the bones from his plate and she stood outside and she threw the bones as far as she could, and the dogs came running, snapping at each other.

She thought, any minute now, he'll leave, like he always did after dinner, but he didn't—instead, he and Henrik went back upstairs, and they were dragging things out of the storeroom, barrels of tar, casks of brännvin, sacks of sugar, sacks of coffee. They were putting it all on a sledge outside the door and then dragging the supplies to the woodshed at the parsonage.

"What's going on?" Nora tried to ask Henrik, when Frans wasn't around, but he just shook his head and said, "I just do what he says," clearly irritated, so she sat with her knitting in the chair in the corner, watching them fill the woodshed with things, wondering if they had a lock for it—it wasn't usual for anything around here to be protected from anything. But what did it matter? Who was there to go rooting through the woodshed? The town was too empty; it had been too empty ever since her family had left. Just then Frans came back and she was alone again with him in the store. She kept her knitting on her lap, the needles pointing outward, purling one, knitting two, purling one, knitting two.

"You don't drink, do you, Nora?" Frans said. He was pouring himself some more.

"No," she said.

"Your father was quite the ascetic." He was, ever so slightly, slurring his words again, like he had at church. It was faint but undeniable.

"I suppose you could call him that."

He turned to look at her and she wished Henrik would come back, she listened hard for the sound of his feet.

"Why don't you try it?" Frans asked. "Have you ever?"

"No," Nora said, "no, thank you."

"You look nice, nice color on your cheeks, like you've been getting a lot of fresh air."

"The same as usual," she said.

"Where I come from, we say thank you when we get a compliment." His tone was light, like he was enjoying himself. It was clear he was in a good mood, though why, she didn't know; it didn't seem to make any sense when the morning had been so agonizing to get through.

"Oh, of course," she said, but couldn't manage anything more.

"I suppose you're not used to getting compliments up here. No one to get compliments from," he said, with the air of joking.

"I suppose that's true."

"Though it's too bad you don't have a barber up here."

"My hair does look like shoe-grass," Nora conceded. She tried to laugh, to show it was a joke.

"What's shoe-grass?"

"They collect it, dry it, then beat it to soften it, then you stuff it in your boots. The Lapps don't even wear socks in winter, just their fur boots and the shoe-grass. Henrik sells it at the store," she said, "look," and she took her hand off her needle and pointed at the rafters where there were a few bundles of shoe-grass hanging. You could tell they were bundles Old Sussu had made, because they were so large and so beautifully woven; other people's were smaller, and their shoe-grass all sprung loose from its binds.

"No socks, eh," he said, "quite amazing when you think about it, going outside in the freezing cold without socks. Makes them seem like, who could do that? It's not natural."

"How is your wife doing without you?" Nora asked. "They must miss you at home."

"It's hard to be away," he said, "but it's as God willed it. There's too much work to do here. Elisabet—my wife—she would come up here if I allowed it, but I won't. Can you imagine it, a real lady here? Anyway, with any luck we'll settle things down very soon now and I can go back. She's very beautiful, did I ever show you her portrait?"

"How nice, I'd like to see her," Nora said, though she'd already seen it before. He had a pocket-watch that opened like a locket, and on the side opposite the watch a small painting had been done of a pink-faced woman with yellow hair pinned up very high. She might have been beautiful, but it was hard to tell as the picture was so small; the main impression was that she had a lot of hair. "Very nice," Nora said. She was tempted to say, but did not say, my father thought such things were vanities, both the hair and the painting.

Frans closed his pocket-watch but he lingered over her. He put his hand on her shoulder and squeezed, and even when he took it off her shoulder he remained standing there, quite close.

"The thing with the Lapps," Frans said, "the thing with the Lapps that surprises me . . ." He wanted encouragement from her to go on but she gave him none. "On one hand, sometimes, they seem perfectly ordinary, just people like you and me. But then other times it's clear there's something—wild, animal, about them, not always in a bad way. They're very primal. Do you ever feel primal up here?"

"I don't know what you mean by that," Nora said. She had finished another row and turned the scarf around. It was lying on her lap, and she was glad she could feel its heaviness, the length she had already made.

"Being up here in the wild, too, it brings it out," he said. "The wind going so fast, the northern lights out, I feel very alive here. I guess it's good you're not like that. You're a good wife to Henrik, at first I thought he could do better but you're good for him, because you're a bit boring, I don't mean that in a bad way, it's good for him. He needs that, he's a grown man but he's a little boy, he needs you to nurse him." Frans leaned back against the counter, and she was relieved to get a little more distance, except that in leaning back he was now pressing his legs against hers. She tried to adjust very slightly, so as to reduce the pressure of his leg on hers (and never had she been so grateful for her thick woolen tights, for her long muslin dress) but he shifted his weight forward more.

"I don't nurse him," she said, though actually she had felt that way many times, how clearly the real role of the wife was to be the next mother for the husband since they were somehow utterly incapable of mothering themselves.

"The thing is that Henrik," he said, "even though he came here in a bit of disgrace, he's trying to make more of himself. He put his life into a disaster, I mean. He might have had everything and he threw it away for that woman, he got caught, you know. It was a terrible scandal," he said. "Another man might have weathered it fine but he insisted on telling the husband he was in love with her, and it came to blows, and Henrik didn't come out the winner, let's say that. And the husband was a viscount, so Henrik was effectively banished. But to be fair, it wasn't just his fault, the woman was known to be like that, a bit of a—seductress, shall we say. But some women are just like that." Against her leg his leg was warm and heavy. It was hard to say what was worse, hearing this story, or feeling his leg—they were each, in their own way, disgusting and threatening.

"Surely God looks with mercy upon whatever Henrik has done," she said, with a blandness she did not feel.

"Yes, God, God is good," he said, almost absently, and as if the words alone had done it, Nora could hear it, Henrik's feet coming along the hardened snow. Tears almost sprang to her eyes. She kept thinking, Frans will step away now, but he didn't—when Henrik opened the door Frans kept standing there without budging at all. "That took you long enough," Frans said to Henrik, as if there was nothing to be ashamed of, and as if he'd been hoping Henrik would appear.

Henrik looked at them with a surprised but vacant look; it wasn't clear what he saw or didn't see.

Frans leaned over and put his hand on Nora's shoulder.

"We were just having a nice talk," he said, and when he took his hand away, she felt his hand still on her, like he'd touched her with tar, and she wanted someone to listen, someone to tell, and she wished bitterly, and sincerely, and hopelessly, for Willa.

It was the noon of the night, and the northern lights were out—they shone through the smoke-hole, and from the smoke-hole they shone through the linen of Willa's rákkas, and through the rákkas they shone through her eyelids. Willa awoke and moved the rákkas, and peered out and up through the curtain of her breath. For what felt like a long time, but was perhaps only a quarter of an hour, Willa lay there, watching. The smoke-hole made a frame for the light, and she had the feeling she had been woken up to see this wobbling globe of green.

And the glory of the Lord shone round about them, Willa thought, and they were sore afraid. It was her father's voice that said it, it was his cadence she heard it in.

She was unnervingly awake. It was impossible to go back to sleep, and she began to pack her boots—they were Risten's old ones, and too large, and they took forever to stuff thickly enough with shoe-grass—and she kept listening, kept thinking, any moment now, he'll come back. Everyone else was already back from town, only he hadn't returned, and Risten had said, it's fine, he's fine, but Willa was sure he would return drunk. At last she went outside to wait, and she walked out to where Ánde was, and he didn't say, why are you up, or, what do you want. The green light walked all over the snow around him. It walked over his hat, and in his eyes, and he nodded. It was too beautiful to speak, or, anyway, there was nothing to say.

After a while Ánde walked off, and she realized he had gone back into the lávvu, and left her alone with the herd. Did Ánde think she could be trusted, then? Was she useful? Did he mean for her to take the watch? She stood out there with the herd, and waited. She looked at the northern lights, unaware she was looking at the same lights that Ivvár was looking at, though he had no real ability to appreciate them, he was just grateful for them, to see more clearly where he was going. The lights were perfectly aligned with his mood, in almost an uncanny way; tonight they were swift, dashing from one edge of the earth to the other, but with the pleasure of someone who knows they can't be caught, and though they seemed to be too sprightly to last, they kept it up all night, so that he reached the siida while the lights were still out, and this gave him the sense of good luck. When he unharnessed Borga he saw Willa was out keeping watch, and he felt her watch him, and for a moment he felt the strangeness of her being outside in the night while he was inside sleeping, but everything was wrong-side-up now, or rather, what had been wrong-side-up was now right-side-up—was that it? He felt the weight of what Sussu had given him in his pocket, the brooch, and he tried to hang on to what he had thought on the sledge here, what it was he should do with it—you already know, she had said, what you should do, and you don't do it.

When Willa got in beside him he was sleeping heavily; she was very tired now, and though partly she wished Ivvár had stayed up to tell her where he'd been, she was too tired to hear anything anyway, and now that the lights had gone out everything in her had gone out, and she fell asleep. When she awoke he was gone, and the lávvu was empty, though someone had left her some stew in the pot. She didn't know, she couldn't have known, where Ivvár went that morning, how he walked and walked, out to the siedi. It did not strike him as odd that he even knew where a siedi was—he knew where many sieidis were, he could have said exactly which ones his father had stopped at, he could have said, and this is where my father left such-and-such offering, he remembered perfectly. And he nearly always felt them, he nearly always saw the large boulder or the hanging rock and knew what it was. He was nervous, of course, going to the sieidi, and he couldn't quite shake the feeling of being an idiot. In the first place, he kept chiding himself, he wouldn't know what to do, in the second place, nothing would happen, and in the third place, he ought to have been helping with the herd, but he had almost a childlike curiosity about it, and he couldn't resist finding out what would happen if he went there, if he—not prayed, that wasn't the word—if he made an offering, and if he were going to be disappointed he wanted it over with; better to know now.

He was so afraid of being disappointed that he had convinced himself, by the time he reached the sieidi that being there would have no effect at all, and that it would mean very little to him, he would get there and it would be another big rock that didn't seem to belong in that spot of the world, an oddity, the shock of something massive in a space of spareness, without any feeling to it at all but stone, ungiving and silent and uninterested. He prepared himself for the disappointment, but in this he was disappointed, because he was greatly moved when he saw it; he was greatly moved to be where he was, on his knees in the snow at the foot of the sieidi, and he was greatly moved to lay the brooch at its feet, at the sieidi that cannot be described because to describe it is to make it a sieidi no longer, and the feeling he had there cannot be known because it belonged in that moment only to Ivvár and to the sieidi; the sieidi protected anyone from knowing or seeing, because the sieidi knew there lies a boundary to all knowledge, even from what we know of ourselves, which is why afterward Ivvár could not have said, to anyone, much less to himself, what had happened, and he could not have described it, nor did he wish to, he wished only to preserve it and keep it for himself to remember at some unknown moment when the memory would overtake him, and he could return again, briefly, to its bounds.

What he did retain, what did appear to him as real, even obvious, was a new fear about what had happened in town. He'd left town well after the others, hearing only briefly from a passerby that Frans had left in the middle of the sermon, but he hadn't thought about it very much—he'd only wanted to do this—but now he was sure, more sure of than anything, that they weren't safe. No one was safe, the herd was not safe. It was possible, even probable, he had gone, offered, asked, too late, and it was possible, even probable, that Frans would have his revenge, and the danger was nearly here. He'd been so insistent on doing it all alone, so insistent on no one knowing what he was doing that he'd lost time he'd had no idea was so precious; he'd even walked out to the sieidi instead of skiing, wanting the experience of getting to the sieidi to be more of a trial, but now he regretted this—the snow was not deep but it was still tiring to walk through. He was strong, of course, but his power was all in endurance, he wasn't built for bursts of speed, so he ran slowly, steadily, his eyes constantly on the sky, on the trees, on the birds—what if they told him something? What if they said, you're too late? But they told him nothing, or what they told him he couldn't read, the world was closed to him, as if he had just been told too much.

He went to the closest lávvu first, not caring whose it was. It happened to be Anna and Nilsa's, but he didn't think what time it was, he didn't care. Inside Nilsa was gone, and it was just Anna and Risten sitting up, while Mikkol was sleeping. "We have to move the herd," Ivvár said, "we have to go, now."

"What is it?" Risten asked. She reached over and shook Mikkol's shoulder, though he continued to sleep.

"Something else happened in town?" Anna asked.

"No," Ivvár said. He stopped himself. Mikkol was slowly sitting up now, he was looking at Ivvár with that doubt he always wore. "Nothing happened yet," Ivvár said, "but we need to move the herd. I'm sure of it."

"Still a few days' good grazing around here," Mikkol said.

"I know," Ivvár said, very irritated, "that isn't what I'm saying, it isn't safe here——"

"Are you drunk?" Risten asked.

"Why do you look—strange," Mikkol said.

"It's nothing," Ivvár said.

"You went to Rikki's," Mikkol said, "you got something to drink."

"How would you know?"

"You look crazy," Mikkol said. "You look like——"

"I think Frans is coming," Ivvár said, "he is, he's coming here."

"Coming here?"

"Yes," Ivár said, "Frans, and Rikki. Maybe others, I don't know."

"For your debt?" Mikkol asked.

"Won't you listen to me," Ivár said, "have I ever asked anything? Have I ever—" But he couldn't stand this, how they looked at him, how they looked, of all things, disappointed in him. Risten's look of pity, like he was some beggar, crawling around, pissing himself, on his knees, slurring his words.

He was so furious, so anxious, he couldn't think what to do next, he had counted on Risten and Anna believing him, and telling Nilsa. Nilsa would listen. He would find Nilsa. But no, there was Willa, looking out through their door, watching him, and feeling a little irked he went into the lávvu, thinking at least Ánde and Niko would be in there. They were, they were sleeping, and he poked them awake with a stick, and they sat up unhappily.

"What is it?" Willa asked. "What happened?"

"We have to move the herd," Ivár repeated. He sounded more and more strange, even to himself, like his voice was leaving him. "We have to move the herd," he said, "they're coming."

"Who's coming?"

"Frans, Henrik." He was sure of it now.

"For the debt?"

He was surprised. He wasn't sure how she knew about that. Had they talked about it? He couldn't remember, he couldn't remember anything, he had to focus, focus on the herd. "I don't know," he said, "but Ánde, Niko, get up."

"We're up," Ánde said.

"If you're going to get drunk in the morning," Niko said, "you should share with us."

"What's going on?" Willa asked.

"We have to go get Nilsa," Ivár said, "try my uncles, even. I think we could get them east, south—over past Buollánvárri—"

"No one's moving the herd right now," Ánde said, "we just made it here."

Ivár shook his head. His right knee was bobbing, and Willa put her hand on it but it kept on bobbing.

"Not in a few days," Ivvár said, "now. If we go now, if we split the herd, if we go separate ways, we have a chance they won't find us, or it'll take too long, anyway."

"Who will find us?" asked Ánde.

"Frans and Henrik," Ivvár said. "They're going to come for us, it's going to be bad, I think."

"How do you know?"

"I know," Ivvár said, then it came out of him again, this time, a bellow, "I know because I know!"

"Maybe," Willa said, "even if we didn't separate the herds—"

"You don't know anything about it," Ánde snapped. Willa was as hurt as Ánde had intended her to be, Ivvár could see the color rise up her neck and suffuse her face.

"We have to go," Ivvár said, "you have to believe me. I—" Was it not clear, was it not seen on his face, that he had gone to the sieidi, and yoiked?

"We believe you," Willa said, but she felt the condescension in it. She was pretending to believe him, to calm him, they were all looking at him—he was crazy.

"No, you don't," Ivvár said, "you think I'm drunk. You think I'm too loud, you want me to be quiet and still."

"That's not true—"

"Today no one can lie to me, today I see all the lies," Ivvár said. He nodded. "Today I can pronounce the perfect truth about things as they are. I can. You can ask me anything," he said, "but the thing you don't want to ask is, what will happen to us, to the herds, if we don't do something now. Instead everyone wants to be quiet, and wait, and wait. Always the waiting," he said, nearly spitting as he said it. "Don't you see," he said, "they're coming for us. Finding my father will be easy, he will go with them like a little lamb—"

"Why would they find your father?" Willa asked. "Ivvár, what is it? What's really wrong?"

"It's amazing," Ivvár said, "it's really something. It doesn't matter if you know anything if no one believes you, you can't do anything with it on your own. I'm very well, I'm very sound of mind," Ivár said, and he laughed. "Ask me."

"You keep wanting me to ask something but I don't know what it is," Willa said. She was trying to laugh herself, to make light of things. "What is it you want me to ask?"

"You want to know if I'm drunk."

"Well—"

"I'm not," he said, "smell my breath, go on." He leaned forward.

"I'm not going to——"

"Go on."

"You think it, everyone thinks it."

"I believe you," Willa said.

He sat back on his heels, almost triumphantly. "We'll move our own herd," he said, looking at Willa. "They won't move theirs, we'll move ours."

"You can't separate them on your own," Ande said.

"I have Willa," he said. Willa nodded eagerly. "And Mirre," he said awkwardly. "I'll get help, we'll do our own herd. We can hurry. We can be out by morning."

"You can't, not now, the herd's only just back together——" But it was too infuriating to be there any longer. He couldn't look at them, with their cow faces. Outside, he went outside, where he felt the wind on his cheek, coming from the west and the north. His nerves flew in him so wildly he was going to be sick. He slapped his cheeks. He could see his uncles watching him.

"We have to move," he shouted at them. He sounded crazy. He felt crazy. "We have to move the herd," he repeated, "don't you see?" he asked, but they only looked at him, and turned back to their watching.

24

HENRIK HAD BEEN IN A SLEDGE BEFORE, JUST A FEW TIMES, BUT NEVER very far, and certainly not in a string of sledges—each sledge was tied to a reindeer, which was also tied to another sledge ahead of it, forming a slack and uneven train. Henrik had been put in a middle sledge, but the sledge was too small for him, and his knees were folded in even while his shins pressed against the edges, like he was a giant who didn't fit into his own coffin. It seemed to him, not that he was any expert, a bad day for such a journey—there was a squealing, high wind that Simmon explained was making the reindeer more skittish than usual, and though it wasn't snowing, the wind was picking up the old snow and throwing it around so badly it might as well have been snowing. Oh God, Henrik thought, as they rattled along, why am I here? He gripped the single rein with both fists, trying to keep himself balanced as the sledge went around and over hillocks, but the sledge bounced, hard, and the reindeer's hooves kicked more snow into his face, and he was terrified of spilling out of the sledge and down a hill, or smashing his head on a rock, or having a low-hanging branch or bush scratch out an eye as they passed, and even when they reached a frozen lake and the ride smoothed, the empty expanse made the wind pick up still more, and now he had to ride with his face tucked down to his chest; it was one tribulation or another, and the only mercy was the variation in suffering.

He wanted to get to the tents; he didn't want to get to the tents. He kept seeing Nora's face, how she had been pleading in a way that was embarrassing to see. He'd never seen her like that; it was entirely unlike her to whine in any way. "Don't go," she'd said, "please, Henrik, please," and for a terrible moment he'd seen Emelie, she'd said something very similar, though in a coy way. Both times he hadn't wanted to go; if he could have stayed, he would have, but neither woman had understood that there wasn't really a choice in it, things had already left his hands, and now he was here with the sledge bumping along a field of boulders, and now past the thin scrubby trees, and now the stunted birch trees, and another frozen lake, on and on it went. The bones all along his legs and his buttocks and his back ached with every slam of the sledge, though the cold was helping; the cold made him numb, and wasn't that numbness useful for something?

When he spotted the first reindeer in the distance, he was so grateful he thought, this is why the Lapps are cheerful when they get to town, they're just glad to have made it alive, but then they were drawing up on them, closer and closer, and then all about him, as far as the gray of the falling day let him see, were reindeer. He was surrounded by reindeer. They were all surrounded by reindeer; there was nothing between this valley and the next that was not being trampled on, shit on, slept on, pissed on, by reindeer. There was hardly the length of a reindeer between one and the next, and half of them were pushing away the snow with their hooves, and half of them were lying down, watching him like wary dogs, and they made far more noise than he would have ever thought, a collective low thrum of grunting and clicking. In the very midst of this mayhem were the tents, six, seven of them, all twenty or fifty or so steps from each other, but it was difficult to pay any attention to them, what with the reindeer all about.

His sledge drifted, roughly, into the back of the draft reindeer's legs, and the reindeer snorted and stepped aside. Simmon had already hopped out of his sledge, but Frans hadn't moved; maybe he felt like Henrik, and his forearms were so tired from clenching the rein he couldn't lift his hands. The Lapps near the tents were looking at them with the same wariness as their reindeer, but in their maddening way they did nothing, they waited and watched, making Henrik feel like he was not predator but prey, like in coming here he had trespassed, when he was here to get what was rightfully his. He had to pay off Frans, so he could get Frans to leave, but there was no way to explain that to them, they wouldn't understand, and he thought, Frans is right, you can't wait for them to do anything, because you'll die waiting—putting things off, avoiding, running away, it's what they do best, and you have to break them of the habit. Frans had said that right before they left and he repeated it to himself for strength.

He made himself get out of the sledge, though he regretted, instantly, the loss of the pelt. The wind was worse once he stood up, and it was blowing so hard that his coat slapped his legs, and he had to keep reaching up to affix his hat more firmly past his ears. He walked as best he could into the stiffness of the wind, though his legs, like his hands, were shaking from the exertion of the ride, and he felt more aware than ever that he was not tough enough, or man enough, and he was giving them more reason to laugh at him. Walk, he commanded himself. With uneven steps he walked toward the tents, toward a man with a lasso slung over one shoulder across his chest, and his knives hanging from his belt, his mouth swathed by a scarf, his cheeks waxed to a high red from the wind. Henrik recognized him, he had just been in his store after all, with Risten, buying supplies, but he couldn't remember his name. Mahtte, maybe; no, Mikkol. Henrik could feel Frans looking at him, waiting for him to do or say something, but more Lapps were appearing—there was Risten, there was her father—and why were the Tommas here? Wasn't this supposed to be just the Rastis' herd?

He looked back at Frans but he realized Frans would understand none of this. It would mean nothing to him, any of these distinctions. He was aware he should speak, or do something; Frans had said it was Henrik's reindeer they were going to get and Henrik would have to lead the way, and he would just be there to make sure it happened, but Henrik's mouth and mind were frozen along with everything else. He felt, actually, a little queasy. If only someone would offer him coffee, or tea, something warm, preferably with whiskey. Ivvár, that was who he needed, and he looked around, and to his relief he saw Ivvár off in the distance, though Ivvár looked in no particular hurry to get to him. Hurry up, it's cold, he almost said, except that would have been stupid to say.

Run, Risten thought, looking at Ivvár, without knowing why, but of course he didn't run. She was alarmed; after all, it had been only a few hours ago that Ivvár had said they had to move the reindeer, and now the Swedes were here, he was right, it was happening. How had he known? Rikki had said something to him in town? She understood, Ivvár's debt had to be paid, but it was clear with Frans there, the timing was no accident; it was retaliation for what had happened at church, and she was on edge, they were all on edge, even the reindeer; they were always on edge anyway on windy days like this. A high wind, especially one that kept moving its front, was one of the most dangerous for herding, and though bigger herds like this tended to stay together more easily, it was also nearing dusk. She wasn't the only one to feel uneasy about this; she could tell her father didn't like it, either—he kept looking toward the southeast, feeling for the wind's changes with his cheek.

She tried to make Simmon look at her, but he kept his eyes averted, the coward, and she looked toward Mikkol but he seemed intent on staring at the Swedes down as they drew nearer. Frans seemed so tall like this, so close to Mikkol. She felt her own smallness, and found herself glad to be covered in her coats of fur.

The men drew close enough that she could see the crust of ice on their eyebrows that the wind hadn't picked off. "Got an awful lot of them together," Simmon said, nodding appreciatively, as if this implied only that he was impressed with the size of the herd and nothing more.

"We'll separate soon," Mikkol said, his tone flat, neither unfriendly nor friendly. Where were her parents? Where was Willa? Of course Willa would hide, she thought, but it bothered her, Willa should be there, to manage these men. They were her kind of men, after all, she would know what to do.

Frans raised his eyebrows. "Quite a sight," he said, nodding toward the herd. "It always amazes me, how you all live like this. Truly a miracle of God." Mikkol raised his own eyebrows and looked down at the ground. He clasped his hands behind his back, like he did when he was waiting to throw the lasso. "I'm just here accompanying my nephew, it seems that he's had some trouble, a lot of you owe him a lot of reindeer," Frans said. His breath came out of his mouth in clouds that the wind quickly took away from him.

"Biettar isn't here," Risten said, "if you're here for him."

"We know where Biettar is," Frans said. His voice was loud, possibly because he thought he couldn't hear him over the wind, possibly because he thought they were stupid. "We're here to settle two matters at once. Efficiency, you see."

Simmon whispered something in Frans's ear, pointing to Ivvár, who had reached the group. Ivvár's eyes were wide, and they looked wet; he was suffused with color, possibly rage, and Risten could see his hands, almost twitching, looking for somewhere to go. The wind had taken off his hat but he hadn't bothered to put it back on, and his hair, almost to his shoulders these days, blew behind him and showed his high cheeks, as if he were trying to force Frans to admit, at the very least, that Ivvár was better looking.

"What do you want?" Ivvár said.

"In your case, thirteen reindeer," Frans said, "six for your debt, six for your father's, and one for having to come here to collect it ourselves."

Risten couldn't help it, she laughed. "That can't be," Risten said, "that's not even possible. They would've had to buy out half the store."

"It's not only possible," Frans said, "but true."

"From what?"

"This doesn't have anything to do with you, now, does it," Frans said.

"Ivvár?" Risten asked, waiting for him to say something, to deny it. To point out they must be cheating him. Thirteen reindeer!

"Six," Ivvár said, "is that so. For me alone."

"It's right here," Frans said. "Henrik, you brought the book?" Rikki nodded. He took out a rucksack and removed the book they all knew so well, with its thin, crispy pages.

"I don't want to see it," Ivvár said, "there isn't any way the list is right. Six, seven reindeer..." He scoffed. "I don't need to see a list of lies."

"Henrik has his faults," Frans said, "as do we all, but I'm afraid he isn't a very good liar."

"Thirteen?" Risten whispered to Mikkol. Ivvár's herd, even with the addition of his father's, was not very large, not what it used to be at all;

it was, in fact, just like Old Sussu had said, and at first Risten had been embarrassed for him, but at least with everyone's reindeer mixed together, it was easier to pretend you didn't notice. Thirteen, though. Ivvár might have had fifty or sixty when they left the sea, at most, and ten, twelve of those were calves.

Rikki took off his mittens and stuffed them into his pocket with clear regret, then opened the book. He was trying to thumb through it, except the wind was going so hard he was having trouble keeping a page down, and he turned his back to the wind, and hunched over, and held the book at its edges with his red hands. "On October fifteenth," Rikki said, "Biettar Isaksen Rasti purchased four pounds of flour, one pound of salt, a new kettle——"

"We never had a new kettle——" Ivvár interrupted.

"——Two bottles brännvin, one bottle brännvin. On October twenty-second, one bottle brännvin. On October twenty-ninth, one——"

Ivvár shook his head. "He didn't go to town that much."

"On January seventh, one bottle brännvin——"

"Stop," Ivvár said.

"Did you mark, Henrik, if it was Ivvár or Biettar?" Frans asked. "You did, I see, yes, so the January seventh, that was Ivvár——"

Risten could not bring herself to look at Ivvár. Mikkol was looking at his feet.

"Where's my father?" Ivvár asked.

"I told you they would have heard," Simmon said.

"Heard what?" Risten asked.

"Biettar has been taken into custody," Frans said. "He's being housed at Henrik's for the time being, until we can get the proper authorities down to conduct him to Luleå."

"Conduct him to Luleå? For what?" Risten asked.

"Ah, yes, so this is a good time for the second matter," Frans said, and he reached into the pocket of his coat, from which he took out two pieces of paper, folded. He opened them as best he could, clearly struggling to keep the wind from taking them, then reached around in his pocket again and took out a pair of glasses, which he set carefully on his nose. In the cold they fogged instantly from the heat of his face, and he took them off and wiped them, but they fogged again, and he gave up and put them back in his pocket. "Is everyone here who needs to be here?" he asked Simmon.

"I think so," Simmon said. "No, wait, we're missing Nilsa and Anna."

"My parents?" Risten asked. She turned around, and she saw the door now they came out, her mother first, her father just behind.

"And Ánde and Niko," Simmon said.

"They're out at Biellovárri," Ivvár said. He nodded, and they all turned to look—Risten could just make out two dark forms on the hill, though they might have been reindeer, it was hard to tell.

"You'll have to give them the news," Frans said, and then he began to read, so loudly that the reindeer nearest him edged away; "I hereby declare Henrik Larsson Lindström to serve in the capacity of Interim Bailiff, to oversee the following: I subpoena all the following defendants, under the compulsion of law, to meet Frans Henriksson Nyberg, in Karesuando Thursday the thirteenth of December at ten o'clock in the forenoon. There the defendants—on account of the indicted crimes and what is therewith connected—will see documents and evidence and hear subpoe-naed and un-subpoenaed witnesses. Examination and cross-examination will be subject to procedure and defendants will be confronted with claims and allegations as well as, in the event of a guilty verdict, receive the suffer-ing of punishment and an explanation of the costs of the trial.

"To the same extra-ordinary court I subpoena as witnesses and defen-dants under penalty to meet: Kristina Nilsdatter Piltto, Anna Persdat-ter Tomma, Anders Einarsson Rasti, and Niklas Johansson Rasti, all of whom will stand trial for having interrupted or disturbed the general wor-ship service in Karesuando or other public religious acts on Sunday the twenty-fifth.

"To be held in confinement until the trial I summon the defendants: Mikael Nilsson Piltto, and Nils Eriksson Tomma. They will be impris-oned on the premises of the bailiff, the aforementioned Henrik Larsson Lindström, and given bread and water until the trial.

"The crimes of Mikael Nilsson Piltto are alleged as follows: having scolded or mocked a state official in the performance of his office, having interrupted or disturbed the general worship service in Karesuando on the same day of Sunday the twenty-fifth, having sworn at the pastor with curses, and having blasphemed God's Holy Word.

"The crimes of Nils Eriksson Tomma are alleged as follows: having scolded or mocked a state official in the performance of his office, having interrupted or disturbed the general worship service in Karesuando on the same day of Sunday the twenty-fifth, having blasphemed God's Holy Word."

He folded the paper up and put it back inside his pocket. Risten's heart was going so hard and fast she had almost no other sensation, and even the wind on her cheeks felt like nothing at all.

"Blasphemed," Mikkol said, "you say I have blasphemed."

"I'll ask just this once," Frans said, "that Mikael and Nils, you come with me now, peaceably, please, we don't want to have to do it any other way."

"What other way is there?" her father asked. It was unclear if he was skeptical of the threat, or curious.

"The Devil will take us along with him, that's his other way," Mikkol said.

"We've had quite enough of that at church, thank you," Frans said, "and I don't think you want to add evidence to your case with more insults and blasphemy."

"We've been saved," Mikkol said, with quiet firmness, "you can't do anything to us. You can imprison us but we will be saved."

"How will we watch the herd," Risten said, tears stuck somewhere behind her eyes, though she didn't let them out, "if you have our men?"

"You have other men," Frans said, "and it isn't my concern."

"We don't have enough," Risten said, "don't you see—you can see for yourself."

"He isn't going to listen to reason," Mikkol said, "or to mercy, the Devil has him in his hold."

"Stop," Risten said, and she turned to Mikkol. "No more," she said, "please, no more."

"So you come for my reindeer and you already have my father?" Ivvár asked.

"He's being confined, yes," Frans said.

"Imprisoned," Ivár said.

"He's a danger to society," Frans said simply. "I can't hold services with him around, I can't meet with my parishioners, I can't conduct daily business—and he's liable, I understand, to go off on his own, preaching his own heresies to whomever he runs into. It simply isn't safe."

"What if," Anna said, "what if we promise, we'll bring Mikkol—Mikael, and Nils to the trial—whenever it is, we'll bring them. We will swear to it. Only leave us our men."

"That's not possible."

"We can't watch the herd—"

"Henrik," Frans said, "why don't you get your reindeer, then, and Simmon, if you can lead the men to the sledges, and let's not stay longer than we have to."

"You're going to take thirteen reindeer carcasses with you," Ivár said. His tone was mocking, his eyes were still bright, and he looked, Risten thought, like he might jump on Frans like a wolverine on a reindeer's back, sink his claws and teeth in and hang on.

"We'll take half for a start," Frans said. "The rest we expect by the trial, or else we'll simply hold a trial for your debt, since the commissioner and the bailiff from Luleå will be in town as is, and we can take care of it all at once. Efficiency!" Frans looked at Rikki. "Well," he said, "go on."

Henrik put the book back in his rucksack. Clearly Frans was impatient, but trying to hide it; it was obvious to everyone he found Rikki slow and maddening. "We're not leaving," Frans said, like he was the forbearing father, "until you get the reindeer." There was something so horrible about watching one grown man talk to another this way, Risten almost pitied Rikki for it.

"Yes, go on, Rikki," Ivár said, "take the reindeer, why don't you go grab one." Ivár was laughing like a nervous little boy. "Just ask one to come nicely with you."

Henrik was standing again now. He was flushed.

"Mikkol," Risten said, and she reached for his hand, but Mikkol shook her hand free. He was going to be a martyr, and play their game; he was walking to the sledges, slowly, while Simmon followed. Simmon was going to tie Mikkol into the sledge, Risten saw, he had brought ropes and everything. She looked toward her father. He was whispering something to her mother, very low and serious.

"Go on," Frans said.

"You have to pick six reindeer," Henrik said, to Ivár.

"It isn't my fault if you can't tell one reindeer from another," Ivár said.

"Enough already," Frans said, but he was talking to Henrik. He nudged Henrik, hard. "If you don't," Frans went on warningly, and Henrik reached into his coat, black like his uncle's, snowed over on the shoulders like his uncle's, and from its depths he took out a gun, a pistol as long as Risten's forearm. Its mouth was a dull silver and had she not seen one of them used before she might have laughed, how Henrik looked like the gun might bite him.

Rikki turned, so that he faced the herd. His back was to them. In front of him the reindeer were, at most, thirty paces away, the draft reindeer, as usual, closer than the others. Rikki held his arm out.

"I want my reindeer," Rikki said. He sounded like a little boy, and he looked like one, with his shaking hands.

"All right, then," Ivár said, "I'll pick," and he meant it, Risten could hear it, but then there was a hideous crack.

In the LÁVVU, Willa heard the gun go off. It was like the river thawing in spring but worse—the sound ricocheted, and she threw the pelts off of her and sat up. What had she been doing, hiding here, when Ivár was out there, when they had come for Ivár's reindeer and she'd known it. Why had she hidden, so afraid of Henrik seeing her, so worried Nora would be there? How slow she was, how stupid, oh, her stupidity was too much for her.

Oh God, oh Heavenly Father, she prayed, almost by accident, and she scrambled over the loose firewood and she went through the door; she saw a big male reindeer had been hit low in his neck, and he was running, careening wildly into the center of the herd. "Borga," Ivár was shouting, running after him, and Willa could see it all unfold the second before each little disaster happened, the reindeer sidestepping quickly away from Borga, their nervous heads darting back and forth, eyes pressed forward out of their heads, and then there was another hideous crack, and a reindeer fell. Ánde and Niko, in the distance, standing up with their ski poles, were shouting to keep the herd in, and the dogs were barking, trying madly to restrain the madness, but Willa could see it now, like she wouldn't have seen it a year ago—the reindeer were too nervous, and the wind was too strong, and the noise of the gun too unfamiliar, and she could see what was going to happen—the herd was going to split, a whole section was going to spill out into the valley in the east, even if Ánde and Niko held the south . . . normally someone would have been in the east, what bad luck, that Ivvár's uncles had gone out yesterday and not come back, what bad luck, all of it . . .

"Henrik," Willa screamed, "stop," and he heard her, he saw her, she knew it. He recognized her and she screamed again, "stop, stop," and for a second she thought, he's going to shoot me, but no, he was just watching the dispersing herd, like he was just wondering what effect the gun would have on the reindeer, if he could make more of them run, and which way, and his uncle was standing there like an absolute idiot, shaking his head like this was just some silly little thing his nephew was doing.

Risten was running. Anna was running. Nilsa behind her. Mikkol for some reason was stuck inside a sledge, trying to free himself. Even Simmon was running to help, but Henrik shot off the gun again and this seemed to do it; the herd as a whole began to look for somewhere to run, but Niko and Ánde could not hold them, not even with the dogs, they were finding holes in the line and slipping through, and now there was another group of them, one with a big bell reindeer, that began to cut west. Willa began to run herself, not sure of where to go, or how to be of use—she should find the wall-cloth. Where was the cloth? She went to do what she always did, which was to just go where others were, to try to help, but Henrik still had the pistol in his hands, like a child determined to behave badly, and it was pointed at the herd—oh God, Willa thought, oh God, and the gun went off again. The cloth, if she could only find it, and just then she heard Anna shouting her name. Anna had the cloth, and Nilsa was holding on to the other side of it, and they were running, she could see they were trying to make it up the far side of the hill, to cut the reindeer off at the top.

Willa ran, as hard as she could, feeling the strength of the summer in her legs, but it was so far to go, and the reindeer were so much faster, and it seemed like in running she was only encouraging them to run, they were all getting too excited. Skis, she should have put on her skis! She was going too slowly, she was getting afraid to be near the herd when they were all riled up like this, there were too many of them, they were going to stampede. Haiii, she shouted at them, haiii, so hard she heard her own hoarseness, and she waved her arms frantically, but they were too scared to care about her, they behaved like she wasn't there at all. Ahead of her she could see Nilsa and Anna, they were trying to keep the reindeer in with the wall of cloth, raising it high, shaking it, running it hard toward them, but the reindeer didn't turn around like they should have, but fled to the side, and the cloth wasn't long enough, and they were splitting, going both ways, right and left around the wall of cloth, west and east; from all sides they were tearing into twos and threes, and the dogs were barking, they were going mad, they bit every reindeer ankle and heel they could, but it was like stones tossed in the lake, the circles only circled out, there was no going in, and every time Willa looked the herd was spreading out, and out, and in the middle the stones laid there, the three dead reindeer, and in the distance there was Ivár, who had caught Borga at last, holding on while Borga thrashed, pushing his knife in, and she watched Borga kick and twitch, and then his head came down, and Ivár's came down with him.

THE REINDEER RAN, SOME OF THEM SOUTH TOWARD LAMMASOAIVI, AND some of them east toward Buollánvárri, but most of them took the easiest way out, which was to flee west toward the river, and when they reached the river, to cross into Sweden, where they stopped to graze. They were, as nature would have it, on a farm seven years in the making, a farm that had so far had four harvests in seven years, mostly rye, but this year had given way to an early frost and snow and rendered the harvest fruitless. Still, the sight of the reindeer enraged the settlers, striking them as another injustice of this impossible place, and they came out with ski poles and pitchforks and shouted, shooing them, and their dog, which looked like a wolf, which might have been part-wolf, barked haplessly, not having any idea of where to send them except away, and the herd continued to split, fragmenting into smaller groups, two here, four here, ten there.

The siida, too, had been split. Frans and Henrik and Simmon had taken Mikkol and Nilsa into the sledges, to take them back to town to be held for the trial—Nilsa had to be forced into the sledge at gunpoint— and Frans, upon leaving, had pulled a bottle of bränmin from the sledge and tossed it at them. It was the old way of trading, sealing the deal with a drink, but no one touched it, and the bottle remained there, among the trampled field of snow, a flag or a marker of some kind: here is where they shot our reindeer and split the herd, here is where they took our men. There was no time to reflect on what had happened—the attempt to round the reindeer up had to be made, and everyone who could be spared was sent out searching, a task that did not become easier overnight or the next day as the wind continued its wailing and a new snow, though scant, fell, and the reindeer, presumably, continued to wander on their own.

Willa was put to work, putting up a makeshift corral, so that the reindeer that were rounded up could be kept somewhere while the rest were gathered, but by the third day it was clear that a good portion of the herd might be lost for good; they had simply gone in too many directions and too many places, and the time it took to track each clump of them would give them more time to get lost—some of them might have already been slaughtered by someone else, or taken by the wolves. The loss of Mikkol and Nilsa in this roundup was especially palpable, as Nilsa had been particularly good at guessing where reindeer would go, and Mikkol had been particularly good at reading tracks, and Ivvár's uncles, upon returning, had not been happy to see what'd happened, or to learn they had to go back out to find more. The search was going to take weeks, unless, at some point, they accepted the loss, and kept to what they had. Even then it wasn't clear if they could keep what remained of the herd, with Mikkol and Nilsa gone. No one'd had a real night's sleep, not the children, even, since the herd had been broken, and they all mirrored each other's faces, eyes barely forced open, so fatigued it felt like work to eat. No one spoke, though, of Mikkol and Nilsa, or wondered aloud what had happened to them, where they were being kept in town, if they were being given enough food—there was no time to think of them, and only Anna and Risten whispered of it to themselves, in passing, as if afraid to remind anyone else of how bad it might be.

No one, when Sunday arrived, went to church. The idea of that was laughable, paradoxical, like asking them to saw off an arm in order to better hold a knife. They might have wished for prayers, for intervention or aid of any kind, had there been time for a wish for such a thing, but they expected nothing, and none of them had anything left over to spend on anything besides the herd. When Willa tried to recall something to comfort herself, she could only imagine her father, reciting as he presided over Communion, "Have mercy upon us, O Lord, and look upon us with the eyes of Thine compassion, as thou looked upon Peter when he denied Thee, and as Thou looked upon the sinful woman in the house of the Pharisees"—but she couldn't finish the sentence. She was losing them, the words, the incantations, she was looking at the herd and she was afraid; they were without stars and without shepherd, there were no angels, there was no Gabriel and no Nilsa, and when Ivár was there she tried to find comfort in him but he ate or slept, that was all; he was a body unaware of her body. She wished she could talk to him. She wanted, most of all, for him to bring up where he'd gone, what had happened when he went to town.

She wanted to say, I know you did something, I know that's how you knew, I believe you. But it didn't matter, no one could speak to him, because Ivár had ascended into anger. No one could speak to him without him snapping, or without him going silent, and when Willa asked him anything—did he want something to eat—he turned and left. Nothing soothed him, and the act of someone trying to soothe him angered him more. He found himself thinking of Borga dying, how Henrik had shot him low in the neck—had Ivár not gone after him, it would have taken hours for the blood to drain from him, and he would have died slowly and painfully, maybe over the course of days. He dreamed at night of Rikki, obvious dreams where he punched Rikki and threw him out windows, bit off his nose and spit it out. He was certain that Rikki had inflated their debts, and worse, that Rikki had intentionally been shooting so as to make the herd break up, he had chosen the precise places to split it, but Ivár couldn't stand to talk to anyone about any of it, and every time someone tried to comfort him, or say that the herd would get back together, or he could start training a new draft deer now, and at least Borga had been old, he became more furious than before, and he took it out on his consoler; any consolation was presumptuous and belittled what had happened.

Ivár was in precisely this mood, one of a hardly hidden rage, when he decided to do two things: he would go get the bottle of bränvin, and he would yoik again. He'd been proud of himself for making it this long without drinking the bränvin—eight or nine days it had been sitting there, something like that—and there was nothing in particular that made that day the right day or a reasonable day to do this, there was no sign from a bird or from himself, there was no excuse he could make up, and maybe it was this nothingness that made him drink. In the end it didn't matter that he had no good reason to do or not to do it, because he did do it, he did drink it, and he was determined to justify nothing, not to himself or to anyone—and was that it? His exhaustion with justifying himself to some-one, that made him do it in the first place?—and he took the brännvin into his own lávvu and he began to drink, and as he drank he became drunk much more quickly than he would have expected. He'd forgotten that it'd been a long time since he'd had a drink, and that he'd had very little to eat the past week, and the headiness the brännvin gave him shocked him and pleased him, and he forced himself to down the whole bottle in the course of an hour, and then he began to yoik.

At first he felt idiotic, yoiking. He was aware everyone could hear him, and he couldn't hear himself yoiking, only them listening, and there was no purity or goodness in the sound, since it was designed for their benefit, in order to prove something to them. To go anywhere, he had to forget they could hear, and he had to hear only with his own ears, but it was difficult to do, and it took a long time to lose his self-consciousness, and he was able only when he thought to yoik Borga, and he realized when he began he had been wanting to yoik Borga, to remember him, and once he had started there it was like sleep, in that you couldn't say when it arrived or how, for in the same way sleep came the yoiking came for him, and when he had returned—it might have been, as with most heavy of sleeps, twenty min-utes or ten hours, he didn't know—he discovered he was still drunk. He opened his eyes and saw he was still alone in the lávvu, but the dark waters of daylight had gone to the darker waters of night. He sat up and felt sick.

He went outside, aware they pretended not to watch him. The women were at the corral; Risten and Anna were trying to shove another rein-deer in even while Willa was trying to keep others from getting out. They glanced his way. His uncles were building more fencing for a new corral, to separate the herds for slaughtering, and they, too, saw him. The children saw him. They'd all been hearing him, whatever he'd sounded like they had heard, and he looked at the children, and he wondered suddenly about the length of their lives, if they would lose their reindeer, if they would go on to live in homes with walls that didn't move, if they would tell their grandchildren, yes, people used to go to sieidis, people used to yoik, I heard it once. The thought made him inexpressibly sad.

He walked, slowly, over toward the corral, where everyone looked at him very casually. He found himself leaning against the fence so that his chin fell on top of the post. He put his arms out akimbo onto the fence's railings.

"We should go to town," he said. He would have said, if it mattered, "it's urgent," but he could feel already it didn't matter.

IN THE DISTANCE there came the undeniable sound of someone approaching on a sledge.

"You see," he said, almost sadly.

"Who is it now?" Risten asked.

"Simmon," Ivvár said. His hair was damp from some sweating he must have done while yoiking, and the curls were icing over.

Risten squinted. It was Simmon, but there was something wrong with him—he was tilting oddly to one side in the sledge, and she began to climb over the fence, past Ivvár's drooped form. Simmon was a fool but he was still one of them. He had his leg outside the sledge and was slowing it down but it wasn't clear if he was extremely drunk, or if he was having some trouble with the reindeer; the sledge wasn't slowing enough and Risten stepped to the side, feeling sure he was going to hit her, or the corral, and she shouted at the reindeer, holding her hand out to try to grab it, only just got hold of the rein—she was being dragged with them—and Ivvár caught the reindeer's antler, which broke off in his hand, and the reindeer stopped suddenly, and the sledge slid forward, banged against the reindeer's back legs, and Simmon fell out at Ivvár's feet. He'd been bleeding and the blood had frozen and left a thick and crusted trail from his forehead down his cheek.

"I'm fine," Simmon said. He was, probably, almost definitely, drunk again, and he was having trouble sitting up.

"What happened?" Risten asked. She wasn't sure if she should help him. It seemed strange to offer, men never wanted to be helped, and anyway she couldn't forget him whispering in Frans's ear, how he had stood there while the herd had broken all around them, and her pity for him in this moment fought with her anger at him in the other.

"The reindeer," he said. He nodded deeply, like his head was loose on his neck. "They wouldn't run," he said. "We got to Biellovárri"—she nodded—"and they wouldn't go any farther. They just stopped. So I said I wouldn't go." If Simmon had not been an older man, and someone she had known her whole life, she would have accused him of dramatics, especially now, when he flipped over onto his back onto the snow, his head up to the sky but his legs twisted and still in the sledge, which was turned on its side.

"Who were you with?" Risten asked. She had her patient voice on.

The reindeer panted, picked up its feet, its eyes huge and unhappy. Ivvár was talking to it, calming it, oddly enough, by scratching it between the eyes with its own loosed antler.

"Frans made me, he wanted me to take him here again, he's coming to arrest Ivvár after all. Maybe you, too, I'm not sure. But we only had one extra sledge so I think just Ivvár."

"Arrest me for what?" Risten asked.

"The reindeer wouldn't go, though," Simmon said. "They just stopped. So I got out of the sledge to see if there was something but I couldn't find anything. I tried to tell Frans, they didn't want to go, and Frans got out and shouted at them and he beat one of them with the rein, he beat it hard, and of course he didn't move, the reindeer I mean, and I said you can't make reindeer do things just like that, it's not a horse, and he said you can make anything do anything if you show them you mean it. Anyway the sledges had been all tied up together, an empty one to collect Ivvár in, sorry Ivvár, and when Frans wasn't looking I cut one of the reindeer and its sledges loose, and just left Frans with the two reindeer and the two sledges, though I don't know at all if he knows what to do with them or where to go. I took off around the other way, and came through Biellovággi on the east side and the reindeer was happy to go without any trouble, but I don't know what the other reindeer will do."

"But he could follow the trail," Risten said.

"Sure he can," Simmon said, "if the reindeer go."

"They might go," Risten said.

"They might."

"So we have to move," Risten said. She kept thinking, would they arrest her and Mikkol both? And if her father was gone, what about her mother? What about the herd?

"I imagine I'm going to be arrested, now, too," Simmon said.

"And then what?" Ivár broke in. Simmon turned to look at him. "So, arrested," Ivár said impatiently, "and then what?"

"And then they're, we're, we get held at Rikki's or at the parsonage. Rikki has a storeroom, they put Biettar in it," he said. "It's upstairs. They put your father in the storeroom and they put Mikkol and Nilsa in the bedroom in the parsonage. Then they wait for the bailiff to come from Luleå to get the prisoners. But it could be a long time. I heard Rikki talking about it with Nora. Once the prisoners get to Luleå it could be a long time until the trial, too. Maybe months. And then if they, if we, if they are convicted, who knows?"

"From Luleå?" Risten asked. "I thought the trial was in Karesuando, in two weeks."

"Well, it seems now those are the initial proceedings, where a judge will decide if they can be held or not and brought to Luleå for trial," Simmon said, "or I think it'll happen like that. And—"

"There's more?" Willa asked. At some point she must have climbed the fence and stood there; Risten hadn't noticed her coming.

"I heard more about the court fees," Simmon said. "The judge has to be paid, and the lawyer, and the bailiff, all of that must be paid. It could be fifty, seventy-five, a hundred riks-dollars—"

"We'll lose the herd," Ivár said, as if this hadn't occurred to every one of them there. "My father and I, we could hardly pay the fine four years ago," Ivár said. "Was that four years ago? Five? That nearly ended us then."

"Would they really keep us," Risten asked, "for months, just waiting for a trial?"

There was an anguished silence, where they all stood there and breathed their warmth out into the air. Around them the herd knew nothing, worried about nothing but how too much snow was covering the lichen.

"I'm going to town," Ivvár said, and his eyes were wide. "We're going to town," he said. It was unclear who the *we* he referred to was. Beside him Willa looked patient, like she did when Ivvár was especially moody. She loves him, Risten thought, she loves him the way we all would be loved in a perfect world. It was beautiful, and yet depressing.

"What are you going to do, then," Simmon asked darkly, "you going to bash in Frans's face?" It was hard to tell if he thought this would be a good idea or a bad idea.

"What I'm not going to do," Ivvár said, "is sit here and wait for them to come for Risten, while they lock up my father for nothing at all," he said evenly, "I'll go to them."

"I'll go with you," Risten said.

Ivvár shrugged. "Everyone is free to do what they like," he said, to everyone, but clearly to Willa. "I'm going to town."

"We'll go," Risten said.

"Ánde and Niko have two more reindeer to put in the corral, and then let's go," Ivvár said, as if it were all very simple, and in a way, it was, it was easily arranged that Simmon would stay at the siida, since he couldn't walk very well, and that Risten and Anna would go, and Willa and Ivvár would go, and Ánde and Niko would go. Ivvár's uncles would stay, and Risten's uncle would stay. The children, with the weird premonitory air children sometimes have, did not, for once, beg to go along to town, or maybe they sensed they wouldn't be allowed and there wasn't any point in asking. Make sure you help with the herd, Ivvár said to them, though he never spoke to them—normally, he never noticed them—and maybe because Ivvár said it they understood their own importance, and they nodded solemnly. While the sledges were being harnessed Risten watched them spreading out around the herd, serious little herders, excited to have so much depend upon them at last.

THE TRAVELERS RODE in a long string of sledges, and other than shouting at the reindeer, they made no noise. They were yoked together by the reindeer and they moved toward the same place, though the six sledges contained six purposes, six sets of passions—Ivvár was alive and alert, even impatient, but Risten was so full of rage she couldn't think, she could only see Mikkol, locked up at the parsonage, and Simmon, the frozen blood on his face, and these two things bled into each other, so that it was Mikkol with the blood on his face, and every time she thought of it she shouted at the reindeer to go faster. Ánde and Niko, for their part, felt dragged along; they would rather have stayed back. They were there to be young and male, they felt, and they resented this, even while they agreed with it, and Ánde wanted to see what losing a herd looked like on someone else's face, and Niko wanted to give someone a good punch—he'd been wanting to give someone a good punch for a long time now, ever since the border. Anna wanted, almost purely, to see Nilsa again, and Willa wanted to not be there at all—she was terrified to see Nora again, even as she knew she had to be there, it was wrong to stay behind, and there was a must-ness to it—she must be there. She must see it all through. She couldn't say she was one of them and stay behind. But feelings of every kind were lessening somewhat as the drive went on; the travel was tiring them out, softening anger into various forebodings, and if they shared a feeling it was a desire for it to all be over already.

The ride was long, several hours. Above them was the usual order of stars, and the moon had come up, brighter than the sun ever was this time of year, and this, their night-sun, it showed whoever had the time to look the old snow, marked by the feet of the wolf and the flailing of its prey; by the slicked-down tracks of sledges and skies; by the hands of herders, brushing the snow away to look at the lichen; by ptarmigans, walking around their nest—but the travelers saw none of these, only the feet of the reindeer ahead of them, the rein in their hand, the branches of the dwarf birch just before they threatened to swat their face, and they did not hear the owl, or the jay, just the wood of the sledge sticking and unsticking to the bottom of the trail, their own breath against the wool scarves pulled up over their noses.

Gárasavvon itself was quiet. In the bedroom of the parsonage, locked in, Nilsa and Mikkol were sleeping on the floor; in the main room, on a mattress of shoe-grass, Frans could not get warm; across the street at Rikki's, Biettar slept quite soundly in the upstairs storeroom, on a pelt Nora had left for him, and on the other side of the locked door Nora was dreaming; in her dream she kept going to the river for water but the pail never filled. Only Henrik was awake, feeling very tired but unable to sleep. The awareness of Biettar behind the wall bothered him so much that sleep was impossible, even though he'd drunk just as much as usual, and even though he was particularly tired from the strain of keeping a prisoner, and then the strain of Frans returning from the fells, alone, the sledges gone, Simmon missing, the reindeer missing, and Frans so close to frozen he could hardly walk. He'd refused their help, insisted on going into the parsonage alone, but it was clear a fiasco of some sort had happened, though Frans wouldn't say what. Later they had seen smoke leaking out from his open door, and saw him emerge with a pot of something very burnt, but when Nora went to drop off a half loaf of bread he refused it. Henrik had been secretly pleased to see Frans defeated, to have him return with these losses, but Nora had been unable to stop worrying—she worried he was frostbitten, and too proud to ask for help, and on and on.

If only Henrik weren't so thirsty, so wretchedly thirsty. His tongue felt too large and everything felt dry, like his throat and the palate of his mouth were coated with velvet. He wanted to get up and go downstairs for water but it felt odd that Biettar would be able to hear him. Why did that bother him so much? As slowly as he was able, bit by little bit, he lifted the edge of the blanket and moved one leg off the side of the bed, his breath held in, listening intensely to the thick woolen sound of nothing. It was very dark but the light from the moon downstairs meant that, for once, he could see Nora's outline, very faintly, her braid coming out from beneath her wool cap. It took him nearly five minutes to leave the bed, and another five to make his way down the stairs, where he relieved himself into the chamber pot as quietly as he was able, aiming the stream of urine against the side of the pot, and then he drank water, lifting the pail to his mouth.

The water was very cold, nearly frozen, and it made his head sting as the cold moved through it. He was shaking so badly that he spilled some of the water all down his leggings and now he was even colder.

He put one foot on the bottom stair, and he had just put his foot on the second stair when he heard a sound like a whistle or a scream, something in between, maybe an owl, sometimes they sounded crazy, the owls. Or maybe a wolf. The window was just below him and to his left, and he bent down to look out, but it was so frosted over he could see nothing, and when he breathed on the window his breath clouded it over more.

He listened to hear if Nora stirred, if Biettar stirred, and he put his foot on the next stair again, and he made it to the fourth step before the shrieking sound came again. "What is it?" Nora asked. The clarity of her tone made him realize she'd been awake the entire time.

"I don't know," he said. He began to walk up the stairs normally, relieved to allow himself to tread heavily, and when he got into bed he shivered and turned on his side, so his chest was to her back, and he curled his hands up against his chest, and she said, "Something's wet." He was embarrassed, to think Biettar heard this, but then there was the shriek again, it was louder this time.

"Do you think it's a wolf?" he whispered.
She shook her head.

"It's a person," she said, softly, so that he thought she was also worried about Biettar hearing. "Someone's coming," she said, "listen, it's sledges." He couldn't hear anything of the sort, and he was going to say something like, you're imagining things, but she was getting out of bed with such speed he would have thought it was perfectly warm outside the bed. She changed, she took off her night-dress and he saw his wife's body, her hipbones and the bottoms of her ribs; she was thin and wide at the same time, especially in the hips, and he wondered, what if Biettar looked at her now, through the keyhole, would he think she was a beautiful woman? Would he desire her? Her nipples were cold and hard, raised of her little breasts like little pegs, but then her wool dress was pulled over all of this, and her wool leggings were pulled on, and her wool sweater went over her dress, and then her fur coat went over the sweater, and she was transformed into something shapeless and armored, and when her socks and boots were on she went downstairs. He heard the stove door open, and then a new, small light came from downstairs—she'd lit the candle from the embers.

"Henrik," she called from downstairs.

He was very awake but his head hurt, and whatever the noise was, he wanted to stay in bed. "Henrik," she said again, her voice more strained than before. "Come down," she said, like she was holding in a scream.

For the second time he got out of bed, this time placing the covers back to keep the warmth in, if he could. Maybe, he thought, they could at least heat the bricks again for the foot of the bed, if they were going to get up like this. This comforted him somewhat, but he didn't see the point in dressing, and he just put his coat on, and he pulled his loosest pants on over his wool leggings, and he looked for his boots but remembered he'd left them by the stove. Down he padded, now he could hear them, someone was coming, shouting at the reindeer.

"Henrik," Nora whispered, "hurry."

"All right," he said, but he didn't hurry, he came down the stairs slowly and then stood there listlessly.

"Go get Frans," she hissed, like this was obvious. He supposed it was. He sat down on the stairs like he always did to put on his boots——"They're almost here," she said, "there's no time," and she shook her head, and opened the door, and began to run, not even bothering to close it behind her. With the door open he could hear several people shrieking. The gun! He'd had it last. No, Frans had it. Surely he had something else, knives? He sold knives, of course he had knives. What else? But hardly had he begun to look around when he heard the sledges arriving, skidding on the packed snow, and his heart jumped, he was jumpy, he couldn't think what it was he was trying to do.

"Come out," someone was shouting, "Rikki, Franski, come out, we want to talk to you." A man's voice.

Henrik looked at the door, wondering if he should go close it, or if that would get their attention. He could bolt it from the inside. But Nora was outside; Nora was at Frans's. Would she have the sense to stay there? She was sensible, wasn't she? He tried to stay focused, he was going to find a knife, a weapon. The cast-iron pan? The cold was coming in through the door, and he could just make out one of the reindeer, shaking itself off. Breathing out plumes as long and wide as its antlers. Someone was coming, someone was walking toward the store.

"Rikki," the man was shouting, "Rikki!" The voice did not plead, but demanded. It's Ivvár, Henrik thought. He wants to talk to his father, that's all. He wants to talk about the debt again. He picked up the cast-iron pan and set it down again. There was a butter knife Nora had washed on top of the counter, and stupidly he picked that up, just as Ivvár came through the door. Henrik's eyes were wide, his heart was beating drunkenly in his chest. He felt so stupid holding the little knife, which wasn't even as long as his hand, he set it down, as if he'd picked it up by mistake.

"Ivvár," Henrik said, in almost a friendly fashion.

"Rikki," Ivvár said, though rather coolly.

"Did you come to drop off the rest of the—" Henrik said, but couldn't manage to get the rest of it out. It was the wrong tack to take, he could feel it immediately.

"No," Ivvár said. "The door to the storeroom, where my father is, it's locked," he said. Henrik's bewilderment mixed with his headache—he could not even begin to reason how Ivvár knew these things, if he had told Simmon and when.

"Of course, he's a prisoner, though."

"I need the key."

"We all want things, but that's no reason—"

"What was it your uncle said, we can do this peaceably or we can do this the other way."

Henrik actually tittered. He amazed himself. His nervousness was so wild in him now it could only come out in weird laughs, he heard how bizarre he sounded but couldn't stop it. "Hehehe," he said, and he could see that this infuriated Ivvár.

"Just get out," Ivvár said, and he flung his arm and pointed out the door. "Get out," he repeated, all the nastiness in his tone, his fury pure and simple and directed at Henrik.

"It's my store," Henrik said, wanting to say, oddly, I can't go outside, I don't even have a real shirt on, and my boots aren't tied, and I haven't got my hat, but how could you say that. He tittered again, and like that Ivvár was behind the counter beside him and taking him by the back of his coat and heaving him forward. His strength was surprising—Henrik was at least a head taller than him but Ivvár moved him easily, and Henrik tried to make it seem as if he were walking himself out the door instead of being shoved, but at the door Ivvár gave him a push that sent him stumbling out.

"The key," Ivvár said, and held out his hand.

"What key?" Henrik said stupidly. What kind of thing was that to say, what key? As if the question didn't matter, he looked toward the parsonage to see what was going on with Frans, with Nora, but there was no one there except Willa, though it wasn't odd at all somehow to see her now like this, dressed like that, standing with reindeer. Had Nora seen her yet? Where were the others? Were they at Frans's?

"Where is it?"

Ivvár's shove hit him before he had composed the answer, before he could say, Nora has it, and he fell to the ground and Ivvár kicked him, and Henrik did the only thing he could think of, which was to reach out and bite Ivvár, bite his leg, but Ivvár jumped on him, he actually jumped on him so that he was sitting on Henrik's chest.

"Help," Henrik shouted, not sure why this word hadn't come to him before, "help," but Ivvár punched him, and there was a terrific crack of pain that seemed to wake him up, even as his head got swung to the side, and his mind blurred. The snow in his mouth was cold. His blood was hot and fell on the snow from his nose, it dripped down the side of his face. He felt himself blinking awake.

"Where's the key?" Ivvár asked again, and then, like Henrik was some reindeer, Henrik's arms pinned under Ivvár's knees, Ivvár took his knife out from his sheath. "Check his pockets," Ivvár said, and Henrik could feel Willa, trying to find his pockets, but they all heard a scream from somewhere—it was Nora, it was Nora's scream, absolutely it was, and while the scream went on Ivvár grabbed at Henrik with his free hand and put the knife at Henrik's throat.

"I can't find the key," Willa said. Henrik was wrestling with Ivvár now, with them both, he was kicking, he was going to get free, and suddenly Ivár let him go. Ivár let him go and Willa stepped back, and Henrik stood up. He wiped at his face and saw the blood on his hands. Henrik looked around, and for a second he thought, there, that's it, it's over—Ivár was panting, standing there, looking at him as if uncertain what to do with him—but there were more men coming toward the store, and he ran for the door, just barely making it inside, but when he went to close the door they were already pushing on it, and he couldn't wedge the bolt in to close it—he put his fat weight against it, he leaned with his back on it, but it did nothing, the men must have been pushing against it from the other side because suddenly the door gave way with a burst and his stomach was slammed, hard, into the counter.

26

When Frans heard Nora at the door, he was still shivering beneath the blankets. He would have told her to come in, but he'd bolted the door, and whatever was going on she wasn't letting up on the pounding, and he set his mind to it, he would get up, he would make it to the door, but it was difficult, he felt slightly delusional, like he either was still asleep or very drunk, but he hadn't been drinking, and it took all of his effort to set one foot in front of the other and make it from the mattress across the room to the entryway—at the door he had to pause before he worked the latch up and open.

"The Lapps are coming," Nora said, her breath and his breath making such large clouds they couldn't see through to each other.

"The Lapps are here," Frans said, confused. He pointed at his bedroom door, where he ought to have been sleeping, but where Nilsa and Mikkol had been put since there was nowhere else in this town with a door that could be locked. Even then he'd had to reinforce the door handle with a chair pressed against it.

"No," she said, "more of them are coming, can't you hear?" She bustled past him and he followed her more slowly, staying focused. He must rise to the occasion, whatever it was, even if it was just Nora having some hysterics about something. He did try to listen, but he could only hear Mikkol and Nilsa locked in the bedroom, they were awake and listening, he was sure of it, he could hear them rustling and talking to each other, and he tried telling her it was very easy to imagine things in the middle of the night here—he had done it himself—once, he had stayed up all night convinced there was a woman, in the distance, who laughed every time he was about to fall asleep; another time, he was sure he could hear someone digging, though the ground was far too frozen to give way to a shovel.

Nora was sobbing.

He couldn't recall what you said to comfort women. "It's just a bad dream," he said, and he put his hand on her shoulder, but it was the wrong thing, she became more agitated.

"Never mind," she said, "I shouldn't have come, what was I thinking—"

"Nonsense, you were right to come," he said. She was turning to go, but he led her by the arm to a chair. "I'll make coffee," he said, and he began to pad toward the pail, this still requiring a focus he hardly had. Who knew that being so cold could take everything out of you! His hands still ached, his feet—the third toe on his left foot looked faintly gray—and he could only think how much he wanted to be warm again. Maybe he could ask Nora to warm the sauna for him, he hadn't had the energy to even walk to the sauna last night.

"They're very upset," Nora went on, "we have their men—what happened last night? Where's Simmon?"

"Oh, I'm sure he's fine," Frans said, but just thinking of how Simmon had abandoned him like that, in the wilderness, with reindeer that he couldn't control, made him even more tired. It was practically manslaughter, was what it was, and Simmon knew it, and Frans had gotten back through sheer perseverance, that was what had led him step by awful step through the snowdrifts, praying all the way. God had saved him, led him here, and Frans felt closer to God than ever before, there was that. What was it he had been doing? Making coffee for Nora?

"Where's your gun?" Nora asked.

"Oh," he said, and he started to walk back toward the mattress when Nora rushed to help him, put her shoulder under his arm. At the mattress his knees collapsed in and he lay down. "Just a bit tired," he said.

"Of course," she said, but he could see on her face she was worried.

"Where's the gun?" she asked again.

He patted the bed. "Sleep with it," he said, "loaded," he said, and since he was already on the bed he swung his legs under the blankets again and luxuriated, briefly, in the sensation of the pelts beneath him.

"Oh!" Nora gasped, and then he did hear it, there was something going on that he couldn't make out, someone was coming, and he knew he should sit up, but the blankets were so heavy, and he was so tired. He turned his head to the side and watched the door, which he hadn't bolted shut again, open.

"I told you," Nora said, and she stood there, in her nightclothes, and he lay there, and he thought, they will slit our throats if they like.

"Mikkol?" a woman called out.

"In here," the men shouted from the bedroom. The men banged on the door, turning the doorknob so violently Frans could hear it shaking. Even from here Frans could see the knives hanging from the woman's belt. She stood there, framed in the front door; it was a small door but the fact that she practically filled it made her stance a little more frightening, and then another woman appeared behind her. They were the women from the tents, from the church, Risten and Anna. The wives of the men in the bedroom. So he understood, and it calmed him down some.

"We're here for our men," Risten said, and in a way, he had to admire her, her directness. They were brave little women.

"Your men," he said, and he sighed as if impatient, though actually he felt out of breath, "are perfectly safe, they'll have their trial soon, and then things will be decided. I thought this was explained already," he said, "and if there's some need to talk about it more, we can do it at a more normal time. You're upsetting this poor woman," he said, nodding toward Nora, "and I'm trying to sleep," he said pointedly. He felt nervous but clever. This was good, he was saying the right things, and he was comforted by this and by the thought of the pistol, which lay beside him, and he reached his hand out, but to his horror he couldn't find it—he stretched his fingers as far as they could go but they didn't touch anything, only more pelt, more blankets.

"We need our men," Risten said.

Behind her her mother nodded, though you could tell she was not the instigator, she was going to stand there silently in a show of force that would never come to fruition. "We don't want trouble," Risten said, "we just want our men," and she put her hand on the doorknob and turned it, but naturally it didn't open, it was like she didn't see the bolt Frans had put on the door, and the lock around the bolt.

"I'm going to ask you to leave," Frans said, as tiredly as he felt. What a nightmare this place was. It was good he hadn't brought Elisabet; this scene alone would have made her faint.

"We won't leave without our men," Risten said stubbornly, but he could see she was afraid; she was in a tough place. Was she going to come and threaten him, a pastor, with a knife, while he lay in bed? Surely even the Lapps had their pride. Surely they could be reasoned with.

"And what do you propose to do?" he asked. "I can't give you the key, I'm afraid."

"You can," she said, her tone light, like she was encouraging a small child up a hill. To his surprise, she pulled her knife out of its sheath and held it out in front of her. It was a small knife, the blade as long as his palm, though he was sure it was sharp, and sure she knew how to use it.

"What's happening?" the men shouted.

"As you can see, I'm not feeling well," Frans said, "and you need to leave at once."

"Where's the key?" Risten asked, stepping forward into the room. She looked at him in bed, then at Nora in the corner. "Do you know where it is?" she asked Nora. Nora shook her head almost madly.

"She doesn't know anything," Frans said. "Please put that thing down," he added, "you're going to hurt yourself."

This made Risten lunge forward toward him, toward the bedside, which was just, after all, a mattress, so she was kneeling over him, squatting right in front of him. He had never been so close to one of them like this, and now he could see the snow dripping off her fur. She smelled like reindeer. She still had the knife in her hand but held it casually, and he turned to look at it. "I know you are Christian enough," he said, "to not harm anyone with that."

She closed her eyes, as if she were focusing carefully on something, she might have been praying.

"Let's pray together," he said, and he began, "Our Father, who art in Heaven——"

"Give us this day our daily bread," Anna said sarcastically, and the women laughed a little, but he kept going, he was determined, he had no sense of the words of the prayer as he said them but that was the nice thing about a prayer like that, you didn't need to think at all, it just came from you, he was just going and going, and then Risten knelt even closer, and he couldn't help but draw his head back away from her.

"You know what I'm going to do," she said, "I'm going to mark you like a calf. I'll start with one ear and I will go to the next," she said, leaning forward so that he could smell her breath, the smell of coffee, and then she reached for one ear and he couldn't believe it, even though he was squirming she began to cut into the lobe, it shocked him that she was doing it, he screamed, and Nora screamed, high and sharp, and he reached out again for the gun next to him but he couldn't reach it, there was no gun, the gun had disappeared, and maybe it was this thought that brought the warm wash of black, the most sudden sleep of his life, thick and dreamless.

"He fainted," Risten said, matter-of-factly.

"I'll get water," her mother said, and she began to look around while Risten picked up one limp arm and then the other. He'd been reaching for something——a gun, there it was. The fact of its nearness frightened her, she leaned over and took it but felt sick holding it, she felt sick from everything, she wanted this all to be over, she wanted Mikkol back, and her father back, this nightmare finished. Nora was sobbing, like she was doing all of the crying no one else could manage to do.

Risten patted Frans's damp cheek. "He was out in the cold too long," she said. She felt his pulse, too fast, an infant's heartbeat in the body of a man, and for a moment she pitied him, but he stirred slightly and the hatred was as vigorous as ever, and she wanted to take out another piece of his ear.

"He'll be fine," her mother said, "we've seen much worse," and she got a cloth and got it wet in a pail of water and lay it on his head.

"I can't bring myself to check him for the key," Risten said, standing up.

"I'll do it," her mother said, and Risten was overcome with gratitude for her mother when the door opened again and it was Willa. She's seen a ghost, Risten thought, she's actually seen one, or she's seeing one right now, she was standing so still.

WILLA KNEW THAT it was Frans who lay in the bed, sick, and that it was Anna who knelt over him, dabbing blood from his ear, but she couldn't shake the feeling that what she was actually seeing was Lorens, all grown up, and her mother, still caring for him. She put her hand over her mouth without knowing why, and her eyes went around the room and this time met Nora's gaze, Nora just standing there in the same old coat, streaks of tears drying on her face. In another life, another body, Willa ran to her, and they held each other, but in this life, this body, Willa didn't move, she had no idea how to behave or what to do with any part of her body, I'm a coward, she thought.

"Where's Mikkol? And Nilsa?" Willa asked, even though she already knew, and even though it was all obvious, with the new bolt someone had hastily put up on the bedroom door.

"In the bedroom," Nora said evenly.

"We need the key," Risten said, "they're locked in." She was at the desk in the corner and she began picking up papers, lifting things.

"Biettar is locked in, too," Willa said, "in the store."

"Ivár was right," Anna said.

"What are you going to do with them?" Nora asked. "Willa," she said, "answer me."

"Do you have the keys?" Willa asked.

"They're not here," Risten announced, from the desk.

"To the storeroom," Willa said, "to the bedroom. We need the keys. Does he have them on him? Frans?"

"You can't let them out," Nora said, "it'll make everything worse." She shook her head frantically, and backed up toward the old pews on the wall and sat down. Willa crossed, finally, into the main room, feeling like she didn't want to do it but she did do it, in the same leather boots she had worn last winter, of all things—she had put them on before they left, and why? For this moment? To seem like the same old Willa? But this winter had no relation to last winter at all, and it seemed as if the boots, and Nora's coat, only those things were the same, otherwise it was all made new, and Willa was the newest of them all, she hardly recognized herself. She sat down by Nora on the pew. Don't be so afraid, she wanted to say, sit up. She looked at Nora and for a long moment Nora looked at her. It seemed strange they didn't touch, didn't embrace at all, but it was as if there were new rules in place that neither of them understood, and she could only think, I've ruined it, it's all ruined, everything's ruined.

"Can you give me the keys," Willa said, "or tell me where they are?" She was suddenly very tired. "You don't have to do anything,"

"They'll just come after you, you'll just make everything worse," Nora said. She was talking with her voice low, and for a moment Willa thought, we're just in bed, and Nora is rubbing her feet together nervously; she's telling me a secret and she's afraid I'll tell someone else.

"Just give them to me," Willa said, "before anything else happens."

"To me?" Nora asked. "To Henrik?" Her voice rose a little.

"No one is going to do anything——"

"Go on," Nora said, suddenly sitting up, unwinding her legs, "go on, do what you like. You always do. Run away, get out."

"No one——"

"I've been so alone," Nora said, so bitterly it shocked Willa. She was going to cry again, Willa could see it.

"You have Henrik," Willa said.

"Don't mock me like that, it's so mean——"

Willa came closer to Nora, they were nearly, but not, touching. For a long time they looked at each other. Willa could not think of what to say. She leaned her head back on the wall. How many times had she sat in this very spot? Her mother could have, should have, been there in front of the hearth in her rocking chair, where Anna was watching Frans, who was moving ever so slightly.

"You're wearing a knife," Nora said.

"Oh," Willa said. She looked down at the knife, hanging from her belt. "Yes, it's very normal." She realized she had heard Risten say that a dozen times, it's very normal.

"I went one way, and you went the other," Nora said.

"That's not true," Willa said, without thinking, but it was true.

"Are you happy?"

"Sometimes," Willa said, and she was going to say something, like, I miss you, but she couldn't say it.

"Do you remember when—" Nora said.

"They just need their men back," Willa cut in, "for the herd, that's the whole thing. You aren't just punishing the men, everyone is getting punished, and they'll lose everything. We'll lose everything, too," she said. She couldn't find the right phrasing. "I heard they want to arrest Ivár, too, anyway," she said, "and he didn't even do anything. He didn't even go to church." She had never said his name aloud to Nora, and she wondered what Nora knew about him; in the moment, she felt proud to say his name, to associate herself with him in this way.

"Yes," Nora said sadly, "he'll go to trial, too."

"It's a lie, he didn't even do anything."

"Vengeance is mine; I will repay, saith the Lord," Nora said, almost sadly.

"I never understood why God does the avenging we aren't supposed to do," Willa said. She stood up, in front of Nora, and she held out her hand. "Tell them I put a knife to your throat," she said.

Nora reached around her neck and took off a long string with a key hanging from it. "It's for the storeroom," Nora said, "the bolt on the bedroom there doesn't work." She seemed embarrassed to say it. Nora's hand touching Willa's was cold, but the key was warm. Willa closed her fist around the key, and Nora got up and began to leave.

"Stay here," Willa said, but Nora was walking toward the door. Willa brought the key to Risten. She kept hearing her mother, don't take another one, her mother said. Lorens was dying and her mother kept saying it, and as if it were still happening, Willa pressed her fingers against her ears to keep out the sound.

27

As soon as Willa had disappeared from the store, a new mood fell over Ivár and Ánde and Niko, in part because Henrik was now quiet and passed out on the floor, and in part because now there was no one to watch them, and the same idea occurred to Ánde and Niko at the same time, which was to loot the store's shelves, and they began to do this rather efficiently, Ánde throwing Niko bags of flour that Niko then threw outside, even while Ivár ransacked the store looking for the keys, or an axe—how did the man not have an axe? Finally he remembered that Simmon chopped Henrik's wood outside—hadn't he seen a stack of wood out there before? He ran past Niko, who was tossing out bags of sugar, and he made his way outside——the axe was right there, out by the woodpile in back, stuck into a stump, and he grabbed it, it was a nice axe, it had a smooth groove in its handle from use, and he hurried with it into the store and up the steep and noisy stairs, but when he got to the door he paused, listened, suddenly shy. His father was in there. "Father?" he called out. His voice sounded weak.

"What are you doing out there anyway?" his father asked.

"I'm going to axe the door open," Ivár said.

"Why bother? I'm not going to come out."

"Of course you're going to come out."

"I'm not. They arrested me. I'm under arrest. Where am I going to go?"

"Come home."

There was a long pause. "We're all going over the mountains, anyway," his father said.

"Father," Ivvár said, and then he put the first heave of the axe into the door. The door was surprisingly thick, surprisingly heavy, almost the same width as the front door, though unlike the door downstairs, instead of a bolt it had a key. Only settlers used keys, Ivvár thought, only settlers had something to put under lock and key. This thought angered him, and he heaved at the door again, feeling it was going to take a while to get through—the blade of the axe went into the wood but didn't want to come out, and he pulled the axe out again. He could imagine his father's face, his mild irritation. Probably he was sitting there, praying—Ivvár didn't care. He would drag his father out by his feet if he had to, he would get his father out and they would take the herd, they would separate it out, they would go away from here, somewhere, anywhere, farther east, farther west, farther north, they would disappear, protect themselves with whatever they could—a thick and heavy weight hit his shoulder, and he fell against the door, his hand got tucked under his shoulder in a gross and unnatural way, and then the thick and heavy weight hit him again, on his head, and he reached for the axe, still in the door, but his hand hurt, he couldn't move it, and he was unsteady, he fell to the ground, the side of his face dragged against the door.

He turned halfway around and Henrik was standing there, panting and afraid, looking surprised at what he'd done. A thick black pan hung from his hand, he looked sorry to have used it and he set it down on the bed.

Ivvár's left hand ached; there was a searing pain running from his hand up to his shoulder. He tested it, lifted it, he saw Henrik looking at him, too, at his hand.

"I need that hand," Ivvár said, "I can hardly move it, look," and when they were both looking Ivvár kicked him in his shins, hard, so hard that Henrik fell forward instead of back, collapsing on top of Ivvár, so that Ivvár could feel the fat of his belly through Henrik's coat. "Get off," Ivvár said. Henrik was trying to pin down Ivvár's good hand and he had it, he had Ivvár's good wrist in his hand so Ivvár elbowed him with his other arm, straight into his neck.

Henrik yelped and Ivvár kneed him, and Henrik rolled over onto his back, grabbing at his shoulder with surprise, and Ivvár jumped up to his feet and threw himself on top of Henrik, he tried to get him pinned down again, but Henrik was so large it was hard for Ivvár to do anything, especially with his bad hand, and Henrik got a hand free and grabbed Ivvár's hair and was pulling it, hard, and Ivvár punched him, he punched Henrik's face so that he could feel Henrik's nose snap under his fist, and he punched it again, but he was surprised, Henrik hung on to his hair and Henrik was nearly managing to sit back up with Ivvár astride him.

Ivvár reached for his knife, he took it out of its sheath and he told himself, it's just a reindeer, and the thought brought Borga to him, Borga's bleeding neck, and he grabbed his knife and before Henrik could do anything, before Henrik could even realize what was happening, Ivvár was knifing him, it was nothing like killing a reindeer, the knife went into Henrik's skin in the same little socket between the top of the sternum and the bottom of the throat, but Henrik didn't gurgle and fall softly to the ground, he was already on the ground, and Ivvár wasn't trying to save his blood for anything, and it was occurring to him while he was doing it what it was he was doing, it seemed hysterical and surreal, he was stabbing a man, and the thought of this made everything worse, and he kept doing it, there seemed to be nothing else to do. Henrik said nothing, he couldn't say anything, he wrapped his hands around Ivvár's wrist, he was choking, he was kicking, thrashing, he was looking straight at Ivvár while he was choking on his own blood, and Ivvár did what he always did when this happened, he pushed the knife further in and jabbed down. It took so long, this went on and on, and finally he took the knife out and stabbed Henrik in the ribs, over the heart, just wanting it to be over. He just wanted Henrik to be quiet.

"Ivvár?" he heard his father asking, through the door.

Ivvár couldn't say anything, he felt sick. Henrik kept kicking, and kicking, and Ivvár couldn't believe he had to stab him again, but he did. Then he stood up, he left the knife in Henrik's ribs. Henrik was hardly moving. On his hands and along his wrists Henrik's blood felt the same as a reindeer's, warm and slick until it became tacky.

* * *

THE FACT THAT Henrik had set the store on fire was not appreciated by anyone for several minutes, in part because he'd set the fire by accident, by knocking over Nora's candle onto its side, though this did not put the candle out; instead, the candle flickered there, dripping wax, until the burlap of a sack of rye nearby began to heat, slowly, slowly, and then it began to smoke, and had Ánde and Niko not been working so hard to fit a barrel of syrup sideways into a sledge they might have noticed; they might have come in and seen that Henrik was gone, they might have stopped Ivár, but this was not what happened, what happened was that Ivár, upstairs, was axing through the door again, this time with bloody hands, while below him he could hear someone shouting, fire, fire, there's a fire. He looked down and realized there was smoke, coming up from the stairwell, but this only increased his desperation and his need to get through, and he kept hacking at the door, more fitfully now, in greater, grander gestures, even though Ánde and Niko, downstairs in the thick of the smoke, were shouting together now, asking, Ivár, are you up there? Did you get him? Come down, quick!

Ivár ignored them, the axe had gone through now and he could see, through a slat he had made, his father, sitting on a pelt in the corner, watching him balefully. "Go away," his father was motioning.

"There's a fire," Ivár shouted, through the door.

"I know."

The smoke was thick in Ivár's eyes now, and he pulled his scarf up around his nose, and he whacked at the door with his eyes closed and then, sensing a weakness in the door, he began to kick it, and he did it, he broke through, so that there was now a hole large enough to pull a smaller man like his father through. The relief was immediate and immense. "Papa," he shouted. "Father, come on."

His father sat there and looked at him, shook his head.

"Don't be stupid," Ivár said.

"And be smart like you?" He motioned to the body through the hole. "The store is going to burn." The smoke was fully in Ivár's eyes, he talked with his eyes closed.

"Then I'll burn with it."

The sieidi appeared in Ivvár's mind, waiting in the fells. Why now, Ivvár wondered, why did the sieidi appear to him now? Why did he want to tell his father about it, about the brooch, about his mother's yoik, like it would change anything?

"Go," his father shouted, "get out."

"Just come," Ivvár said, "let's argue about this later."

"Get out," his father said. He coughed, almost delicately.

"He was going to kill you," Ivvár said, "they were going to take you to Luleå, they'll hang you here or they'll hang you there."

"Get out," his father bellowed, "go," with such cruelty that Ivvár listened. He threw the axe down, stepping over Henrik's large leg, and he hurried down the stairs, where there were flames now, real flames; it was amazing the second floor wasn't completely on fire yet, it was going to be any moment, and he realized his feet were hot, in fact had been hot for a long time, and his skin was hot, his hair was hot, and when he got outside and Risten ran to him and threw herself at him he realized his gákti was on fire, because Risten was beating at him with her hands. "Where's Biettar?" she was asking, repeating herself madly.

"They're inside."

He didn't know where to look or what to do. It was the smoke, he told himself, he couldn't think with the smoke. He wanted a drink, he wanted ten drinks. Ánde and Niko were watching him, standing at the sledges and staring somewhat dumbly at him like all of this had nothing to do with them whatsoever. Only when he stumbled to his knees did they come running, like they finally realized something was wrong, but he hated their faces, their looks of worry.

"Don't look at me," Ivvár shouted. He felt like a child, he was a child, but it seemed necessary, he couldn't stand it, everyone looking at him. "Don't look at me," he shouted again, and it hurt to shout, the smoke was still in his throat and everything was scratchy, itchy. He began to cough.

There was the sound of the two windows bursting open, the glass shattering, and suddenly the flames were tripling. He'd never known a fire could be loud like this, a roar, and he had never known a fire would stink like this, he could smell it, not just wood, but something else, and for a sickening second he thought, it's my father. Everything was going up, and he couldn't look, he turned away and sat down with his back to the store, and he stared at the river, at the birch tree. He didn't look at his hands.

"Look," someone was shouting now, "look," and he could sense Risten running after him but he didn't turn around, he didn't need to see the next thing, whatever it was, and he stood up, thinking, I'll just walk and walk. "Look," someone shouted, maybe Ánde, maybe Niko, "Ivár, it's your father," someone shouted, and he turned around, he saw his father was backing up out of the door dragging something, his coat or his trousers aflame, everything so smoky around the door it was hard to see. It was Henrik, his father was dragging Henrik through the door and out into the snowy street. A woman was screaming, the grating wail of a tern. Ivár realized, in a distant way, it was Willa's sister, but her name wouldn't come to his mind, and he couldn't think through the screaming. The sister was running to Henrik, she got to him and threw herself down to the ground beside him even while his father was also on the ground, rolling around his back on the snow, putting the flames out, and amidst this Risten appeared outside the parsonage door, and Ivár couldn't bear to watch anymore.

He turned back toward the river.

It seemed sensible. It seemed like the only sensible thing to do, to walk, and he walked across the slippery packed snow to the bank, sliding a bit, and stumbled back up. And then he began to walk across the river, he slipped again, but he got up again. He would just walk, he didn't think, nothing to think about, nothing to plan, nothing to decide, go back to the sieidi, that was all. Why and what for, he didn't know; it was the last command. The snow here was thinner than it was at the herd. Icier, crustier. Older snow. Across the bank, though the snow was less packed and it didn't hold his weight, he stepped on it and he fell in, but that was fine, too. It would be slow going but he wasn't in a hurry.

He got up to the top of the bank and he could still hear people screaming. It had the faint sound almost of a festival, if you didn't know better, and if you turned around—he turned around, squinting—he could imagine the store was a very large bonfire, albeit a very smoky one, and people were drinking, and enjoying themselves. Someone would yoik soon.

Someone would tell a story, a good story about dead people, about the Háldis, about the Ulddas. He had a story for them, he had a good one. It was about a son who tried to save his father, and he killed a settler, and his father blamed him for it, for the rest of his life, and the dead Swede came back as a spirit, and he followed the son wherever he went, across the old and weighted snow, snow that was strong, that held up their feet as they went.

WILLA WATCHED IVVÁR WALK AWAY. HE WAS A LITTLE FORM IN THE DIStance, and his mottled coat was already blending into the trees and the snow. He was becoming harder and harder to see, but she didn't look anywhere else, even though her sister was crying, and Henrik was dead, and the store was burning, all of this was happening and Willa had always thought of herself as someone who did something, but her own bitterness held her captive. Why was she never the more important thing? She commanded him, silently, to turn around and face her, but he didn't, and then he might as well have been a reindeer far off on a fell, and then he slipped beyond a hill and she might have imagined him entirely.

I love you, she thought, and she turned away.

Nora was sitting on her heels by Henrik, not touching him, crying in a weird and silent way, her body rocking back and forth, her eyes fixed on some point beyond, maybe the hill, maybe the church, maybe nothing. It occurred to her that Old Sussu had never come out to see what was going on—Old Sussu, who appeared for everything. There wasn't time to think about that. Slowly, she went back to the parsonage, where Anna must have found the other key; she'd let Mikkol and Nilsa out, and put Frans into the bedroom. Willa found a wool blanket atop Frans's mattress, and she brought it back outside and she put it over Henrik's body. Nora was still rocking back and forth, saying over and over, I don't know what to do, over

28

and over again, I don't know what to do, and Willa nodded, I know, she said, I know, because she couldn't think what to say, what was there to say? She was emptied of words. Risten was kneeling near them, watching them, and Biettar had gone limping off to the parsonage, and Ánde and Niko were smoking by the sledges, and the store was still on fire; the second floor had caved, and all around it the snow was melting, the snow and the store were steaming.

It burns even in the snow. Her father had written that, in a letter, he had been talking about the awakenings, he had been so overjoyed, and proud—he had been saving the Sámi, they were spreading the real and living Word of God.

What am I going to do? Nora repeated. Her head fell toward her knees. "You can stay with Frans," Willa guessed, "or with Old Sussu." She wished she could say, you can come back with me, but she didn't really know what she had to offer, what would be there when she got back, if she would stay with Ivvár, if Ivvár would stay there, if he would run into the fells and hide for the rest of his life. Of course Anna and Nilsa would never refuse anyone somewhere to stay, they were incapable of that kind of rudeness, she saw that now—they would harbor anyone if they could, and them taking her in had never had much to do with who she was at all—but it wasn't possible, it was winter and they couldn't keep Nora there, Nora wouldn't know anything, she would get in the way, she would be miserable, even for a day, two days, and everyone's life would be consumed with trying to keep Nora from too much suffering.

"I can't stay with Frans," Nora wailed, "I can't be with him alone, you don't know what it's like."

"What if you went back home," Willa said, "to Pajala, I mean."

"How am I supposed to get there? Am I supposed to crawl on my hands and knees?"

Willa thought, did not say, I could take you. And she could, they could, it would be easy going south compared to north. It could be done. But she couldn't say it.

The fire had become so large it stung at her cheeks and her thighs, and she made Nora get up and move back, and she got Risten to help her drag

Henrik's body away—the blanket had frozen to the ground and caught, and came off of him, and Willa was forced to look at his throat, its hardening hollow of blood, and his chest, his torn nightclothes. One of his eyes was half-open. Some of his hair had been singed off his scalp. He looked cold, and she felt like she ought to give him a hat and scarf, or something else to keep him warm.

When she had covered him with the blanket again she took Nora back to the parsonage, where she found Mikkol and Biettar sitting inside, praying, their hands folded and heads bent, on their knees. Nilsa and Anna were sitting on the floor, their faces absent of any expression at all. They were holding hands.

Nora went and knelt beside Mikkol and Biettar. They were facing the hearth the way the door of the tent faced the rising sun, and Mikkol prayed. Dear Heavenly Father, he prayed, most merciful God Almighty, and he asked for God's protection and for God's grace, he asked for God to take Henrik into Heaven, he asked for God to watch over Ivvár, to comfort Nora, to heal Frans, to watch over the herds. Willa went back outside and stood on the bank of the river and looked at where Ivvár had crossed over, where she'd last seen him, and she sank to her knees and watched all the nothing that was there, the lone dwarf birches, the snowed shrubs, the tracks, and out of the corner of her right eye she could see the steeple of the church, and she remembered when she'd found him, flat on his back, staring up at the sky.

For a long time she kneeled, as if willing him to appear again. Her legs went stiff, and cold, her face and hands were starting to feel less and less.

It was Risten who came to get her, Risten who came and said, Willa, we're going. Go say goodbye to Nora, Risten said, and Willa went to the parsonage—one last time, she told herself, one last time—where inside Nora was lying on one of the pews, a pelt under her and a pelt over her. Biettar alone remained on the floor, praying; Frans, Willa presumed, was still locked in the bedroom. Nora was shaking; her teeth were actually chattering. Her eyes met Willa's, and her eyes said, don't leave me. Willa felt it, clearly, that she should stay put right here and watch Nora, that was her duty; she had left but duty had stayed, and the burden of duty overwhelmed her. She couldn't leave Nora and love herself, it wasn't possible. But if she stayed, what of Ivvár? If she went, what of Nora? Maybe it didn't matter, of course—she knew Ivvár, it was as if she could already feel him, going, and going, and she wondered, was this what he had always wanted? A reason to leave and never come back? He was going to walk away and he would not come walking back for her; he would keep walking until they found him, and they would find him. Frans would send an army after him; she was not so naive now, not so hopeful now, as to think anything else.

She took Nora's hand, and Nora squeezed it. Already she dreaded this, Nora's need of her, this weight she couldn't shake off. She thought, is this how Ivvár felt about me?

I'll be right back, Willa lied, and she went back outside. Inside, and outside, she thought, inside, and outside. Henrik was hidden now—someone had put a fine, white pelt over him, so he blended in with the snow around him, except for his bloodied face, which was turned toward the side so that it was looking toward the hill and the church. Risten and Ánde and Niko and Mikkol were already getting in the sledges; the reindeer were tired but they were going to make them run anyway, Willa could see that, and she could see, moreover, that they had filled the sledge Ivvár had come in on with things, with flour and sugar and coffee and salt. Well, why not. She looked at the sledge she had ridden here and it seemed like a different sledge now, empty and waiting for her. Risten was watching her; she hadn't gotten in her own sledge yet, she was standing there to one side, holding the reindeer's harness.

"Are you coming with?" Risten shouted.

Willa stood still. Behind her was Nora, in front of her was Risten, and Ivvár was not here. She wished to be transfixed, to stay in that paralysis, to wait for something else to decide for her; maybe Risten would get impatient and come get her, maybe Nora would shout again, maybe—how could this maybe still come to her—Ivvár would appear like he used to, and she would say, what are you doing here, and he would say, why do you always ask questions you know the answer to?

For a long moment, she felt Risten look at her, like she were a reindeer, and Risten was wondering if it made the most sense to lasso her or send a dog for her or let her wander back on her own. Willa wanted in that moment to see everything the way Risten saw it, through the eyes of the reindeer; it seemed like it would be a relief, to just be thinking about getting back to the herd. Wiser, simpler. If she'd had her own reindeer, she would have done it, she would have said, I have to get back to the herd, too. She understood why they were all leaving now. They did have to get back to the herd, even if they were going to lose them all, every last one; they would hang on to them as long as they could. She would have done the same. She was doing the same.

Willa nodded at Risten. "Go," she shouted, "go without me."

Risten still hesitated, and for a second Willa thought, she still knows some great secret that will save us, Risten seemed capable of it, but she was getting back in the sledge, and Mikkol and Nilsa and Ánde and Niko didn't even look back at her, they were just going to go, and only Anna looked back, once. It was clear that Willa was going to be stuck here again; she was going to live in the same cabin again with her sister, only this time with two strange men, one the father of the man who had left her, one the enemy of all she held dear, and she was going to be interrogated, maybe imprisoned herself, what did she know, or maybe Frans would think she'd had no part of it, or maybe he would delight in making her part of it, the daughter of Laestadius, the mad daughter of Mad Lasse, Mad Willa.

Mad Willa. That was who she was now, that was who she'd been becoming all along.

It was Mad Willa who nodded at Risten, and it was Risten who saw, before she turned to leave, Willa's back, the red of her scarf.

There was nothing to think about anymore. Risten had no thinking left. She sat down in the sledge, she pulled her legs inside, and pulled the pelt up over her lap. She took the rein in her hand. Cus, cus, Risten shouted, cus, cus, and the reindeer, the reindeer did what reindeer do, the reindeer ran.

Acknowledgments

I AM INDEBTED IN THE WRITING OF THIS TO THE PERPETUAL HOSPITALITY, generosity, and knowledge of many people in Sápmi, especially Nils-Aslak Labba, Marielle Labba, Morten Labba, Niklas T. Labba, and—above all—the inimitable Anne-Maret Labba, who alone taught me nearly everything and took me nearly everywhere. My gratitude to her, and them, is boundless.

I am indebted as well to Oula A. Valkeapää, whose philosophies and phrases ("first we are flowers, and then we die") appear in the novel with his permission, and who, together with Leena Valkeapää, shared with me their home, their art, and pivotal conversations. Additional thanks go to Hannu Valle, Antti Nuorgam, Leena-Maaret Niittyvuopio-Jämsä, Juha Vuolab, and Kerttu Vuolab for their hospitality, and their stories. Thank you to everyone at the corrals, and in the fells—giitu.

Dr. Ellen Marie Jensen was the translator for several foundational texts used in my research; she was assisted in her translations by Harald H. Jensen. Their translations, "Contribution to the Church History of Finnmark; Recollections 1825–1849," by Anders Persen Bær, and "Contribution to the Church History of Finnmark: An Account of the Religious and Moral Conditions before the Laestadius Awakening," by Lars Jakobsen Hætta, were critical to my understanding of Laestadius's followers during this time period. Their translation of subpoenas from

Kautokeino-dokumentene (as collected by Magnar Mikkelsen and Kari Pålsrud) appears here with their permission. Dr. Jensen also provided crucial assistance on the manuscript as a Sámi cultural consultant, and I am particularly grateful for her counsel on naming and North Sámi orthography.

The novel takes its title from *The End of Drum-Time: Religious Change Among the Lule Saami, 1670s–1740s*, the seminal scholarly work by Håkan Rydving, with his kind blessing. Other works of importance to me were *People of Eight Seasons* by Ernst Manker; *An Account of the Sámi* by Johan Turi; the novels of Matti Aikio, especially *In Reindeer Hide*; the novels of Ailo Gaup, especially *In Search of the Drum*; *With the Lapps in the High Mountains* by Emilie Demant Hatt; *The Voice of One Crying in the Wilderness, Fragments of a Lappish Mythology*; and *The Lunatic: An Insight Into the Order of Grace* by Lars Levi Laestadius, as well as his sermons; the journal of Petrus Laestadius; *Notes about the Congregations in Kemi Lapland* by Anders Johan Sjögren; "Constructing Laestadianism: A Case for Sámi Survival?" by Henry Minde; *Studies in Lapp Shamanism* by Louise Bäckman and Åke Hultkranz; *Antiphony* by Laila Stien; *The Kautokeino Rebellion*, a film by Nils Gaup and Nils Isak Eira; the Instagram accounts of Carl Johan Utsi (@cjutsi) and Per Ivar Somby (@colourmypast); the jewelry of Erica Huuva; the music and joiks of Mari Boine, Jon-Henrik Fjällgren, Maisan Thaw, Sancuari, and Sofia Jannok; the art of Reidar Särestöniemi and Máret Ánne Sara; and the work of Nils-Aslak Valkeapää, especially his poems from *Trekways of the Wind and The Sun, My Father*, and his joiks from *Sápmi Lottážan* and *Alit Idja Lahkona*.

Playing in the Dark: Whiteness and the Literary Imagination by Toni Morrison and *The Racial Imaginary*, edited by Beth Loffreda and Claudia Rankine, helped inform my thinking on representation in art, along with *The American Indian and the Problem of History*, edited by Calvin Martin; *Decolonizing Methodologies: Research and Indigenous Peoples* by Linda Tuwihai Smith; and *Fiction Across Borders* by Shameem Black.

Additional thanks goes to Kosti Joensuu, for discussions on his book, *The Physical, Moral and Spiritual: A Study on Vitalist Psychology and the Philosophy of Religion of Lars Levi Laestadius*. Solveig Braastad graciously gave me access to the Storfjord Nord-Troms Museum and shared research on the market in Ivgobahta.

Research funding and time to write were provided by the Fine Arts Work Center in Provincetown, the Lewis Center for the Arts at Princeton University, the Mount Holyoke College Alumnae Association, the English Department and the Center for Humanities at Virginia Commonwealth University, the Lower Manhattan Cultural Council, the Scandinavian-American Foundation, the Whiting Foundation, MacDowell, Yaddo, the Dorothy and Lewis B. Cullman Center for Scholars and Writers at the New York Public Library, and the Lásságámmi Foundation.

I am grateful for support, both moral and temporal, from many: Ingrid Pylvainen, Sonja Pylvainen, Zara Pylvainen, Jaclyn Pylvainen, Karamia Gutierrez, Nathan Heiges, Alexis Knowlton, Mary Johnson, Charlene van Dijk, Hilary Collado, Jenny Warne, Nora Reynolds, Laura Meyers, Chris Rogerson, Kacey Wochna, Anjuli Gunaratne, and Esther Lin.

To my readers, my abiding thanks: Salvatore Scibona, Stephanie Grant, Xuan Juliana Wang, Gretchen Comba, Ilana Sichel, Sammy Sater, Helena Pylvainen, Ian Pylvainen, Sarah Payne, Marisa Silver, Elliott Holt, and Kevin Fitchett. Thank you to Janet Silver, and Caroline Zancan, for editing, and advocating, Thank you to Katie Vida, for travels within Sápmi and without, for her readership, and most of all, for sustaining hope. Thank you to Paul Rusconi, most generous of readers, whose counsel and friendship has been indispensable.

My love to Dan, and to Karl.

About the Author

Hanna Pylväinen is the author of the novel *We Sinners*, which received the Whiting Award and the Balcones Fiction Prize. Her work has appeared in *Harper's*, *The New York Times*, *The New York Times Magazine*, the *Chicago Tribune*, and *The Wall Street Journal*; she is the recipient of fellowships from the Fine Arts Work Center in Provincetown, Princeton University's Lewis Center for the Arts, the Lower Manhattan Cultural Council, the American-Scandinavian Foundation, and the Dorothy and Lewis B. Cullman Center for Scholars and Writers at the New York Public Library, as well as residencies from MacDowell, Yaddo, and the Lásságámmi Foundation. She has taught at the University of Michigan, Princeton University, and Virginia Commonwealth University; currently, she is on the faculty at the Warren Wilson College MFA Program for Writers. She lives in Philadelphia.